Andy

As my official critic I hope you enjoy "Part Two"

Liz
x

Elizabeth Slater

Sky

An Adult Novel

Elizabeth Slater

Bloomington, IN
authorHOUSE®
Milton Keynes, UK

AuthorHouse™
1663 Liberty Drive, Suite 200
Bloomington, IN 47403
www.authorhouse.com
Phone: 1-800-839-8640

AuthorHouse™ UK Ltd.
500 Avebury Boulevard
Central Milton Keynes, MK9 2BE
www.authorhouse.co.uk
Phone: 08001974150

All characters in this publication are fictitious and any resemblance to real persons, living or dead is purely coincidental.

© 2007 Elizabeth Slater. All rights reserved.

No part of this book may be reproduced, stored in a retrieval system, or transmitted by any means without the written permission of the author.

First published by AuthorHouse 5/24/2007

ISBN: 978-1-4343-0168-0 (sc)

Printed in the United States of America
Bloomington, Indiana

This book is printed on acid-free paper.

Cover design: - Elizabeth Slater and Howard Grigg
Photograph: - Howard Grigg. The Gallery Studios. Uttoxeter.
"Sky's Hat" Dorothy Helen. Quality Ladies Outfitters. Uttoxeter.

Come; let us visit our friends from Eleni Beach once again. They are all there in the sun, waiting for you to join them.

•*INTRODUCTION*•

Welcome to the wonderful Greek island of Skiathos, where today we find Sky Maxwell sitting in the shade of a large raffia umbrella on the marvelous golden sands of Eleni Beach. Lazily she is watching the people around her.

It is the end of September and today only this rather unusual group of friends are here by the sea.

The sun is hot and the breeze gentle. Bliss.

Her sister, the stunning Paris, is swimming in the warm waters with her husband Andros and their friend Vanni. Sky smiles to herself as she watches them splash about and hears their laughter.

In the little taverna built on the beach are Tomas, the owner, and his wife Sofia who together with young Eleni are busy serving not the usual holidaymakers, but Sir Richard Graves and his wife Lady Eleni, world famous photographer Alexi Mandros his wife Athena, and Nicos their son. This is the man who has swept Sky off her feet and who very soon will become her husband.

In fact next week she will become Sky Mandros, her stomach does a twirl at the thought, and unconsciously her face lights up with a wide grin.

As Sky looks around her she tries to get in her mind the connection between all of these people.

Tomas and Sofia are Vanni's parents and they live here on the beach. Their home is just a short walk from the taverna, the two separated by a little kiosk that sells ice creams and cool drinks.

Vanni, and Sky's good pal young Eleni, are also soon to be married, they too will live here on the beach, not with Tomas though, but in their own beautiful villa built amongst the tall cedar trees on the other side of a small car park clearing.

Young Eleni, thinking she was alone in the world traced her father's footsteps from New York to this lovely island, and found not only her half brother Andros, but also this loving group of people to help and guide her.

Andros is the illegitimate son of Lady Eleni and her own father Marco. Regrettably Andros never met his father but has now taken over the roll of protector and financial adviser to his newfound sister. A roll he is more than happy to fulfil.

Marco, sadly killed in a plane crash, was the childhood friend of Alexi, Tomas and his twin, the now Lady Eleni.

All of these people are Greek and very rich, but here on the beach they look like ordinary locals enjoying the autumn sunshine.

Sir Richard Graves though, is like Sky and Paris, English.

Richard was the business partner of Marco, and together they made huge fortunes in shares and gold after starting fresh lives in New York.

He was once very highly thought of by The British Prime Minister and The American President, who often called upon him for advice and guidance.

It is this part of his life that intrigues journalist and author Paris. She has vowed to find out the truth regarding his life. Richard has so far remained silent.

A recluse for many years Richard is now enjoying life to the full after meeting his wife Lady Eleni. A firm believer in the Gods of Mount Olympus she fascinates him and all who listen to her tales. Her title suits her well, but she is more than happy for family and friends call her by the less formal name of "Aunt Eleni."

Swinging her legs over the sun bed and on to the sand, Sky grasps her metal crutches and hobbles towards the taverna where at the little table by the bar the man she loves is waiting.

Nicos, a superb photographer like his father, is very much in demand around the world. A past serial womaniser he is handsome, full of life and oozing sex appeal. Past conquests include young Eleni and surprisingly Paris. He has promised to change his ways and Sky believes him. Paris though, has her doubts.

How on earth did I ever land such a catch Sky thinks to herself as she nears the taverna. My "Jack."

Her pet name for him is very appropriate and comes from her favourite childhood television programme that featured lovely tales and beautiful pictures. "Jackanory."

He has a story for any occasion and almost every picture that he takes.

It is now mid afternoon and time for a glass of cool wine with one of Tomas's superb Greek salads. Full of plump juicy olives and chunks of feta, dressed with herbs and clear virgin olive oil, accompanied by some fresh crusty bread. Perfect. Just perfect.

• C H A P T E R •
1

Nicos gazed down at the bloodied bundle wriggling in his arms and felt an emotion so strong it hurt. His heart thudded in his chest as it missed a beat.

His daughter, only seconds old but already she meant so much to him. He knew at that moment he would love her like nothing else on earth. Cherish her; protect her, die for her if necessary.

Her hands reached up towards his face, a face now wet with tears, she looked straight into his eyes, not with the usual blue of a new born child, but with a searing fiery amber that reached deep into his soul.

His daughter.

"May I hold my baby Jack?" Sky said softly from the bed, "or do I have to wait until she is old enough to talk?"

Nicos slowly walked towards the bed that held his precious wife. The woman who only a few days ago had almost driven him mental by her incessant tidying of the house, checking her overnight bag time and time again, washing things that were already clean, she hadn't sat still for more than a few minutes, and even though she was handicapped by her twisted leg, she had in fact seemed to be everywhere. Occasionally she had also turned into this devil like creature whose temper was at the end of a very short string.

At one point things got so bad that he had gone to seek out his friend Vanni, whose wife Eleni was also nearing her time to give birth, together they consoled each other.

They spent hours sitting at the little table by the bar in Tomas's taverna, grumbling, moaning and drinking.

Between them they downed three bottles of red wine and numerous glasses of ouzo. Sofia, Tomas's wife, and also Vanni's mother, carefully informed Sky and Eleni of the drunken state they were in, and it was left to Tomas to put them to bed.

Vanni and Eleni actually lived in a beautiful villa only a few yards away, but Tomas and Sofia had thought it best if they looked after the men in their home for this particular night, it was after all even closer, being almost next door to the taverna.

Sofia was convinced that there would only be trouble if they attempted to go to their own homes in their current state and decided to do her best to stop any arguments before they had even started.

Tomas found it all very amusing, grown men incapable of walking properly, until Sofia reminded him that it was not that unheard of for him and Alexi to end the evening in a similar way. He grimaced at the thought of the hangovers they would be nursing the following day, pleased that on this occasion it would not be him suffering.

Vanni was put to bed in his old room and Nicos left to sleep it off in the room Tomas once used to let to holidaymakers.

Just like when they were children, Sofia sighed.

It felt good to have her son home again, even if he knew nothing about it in his alcoholic stupor, but her motherly instinct to look after her child whether he was drunk or not had taken over, to be truthful she was actually quite enjoying it.

A breakfast of Tomas's special strong coffee, some of his fantastic pastries and fresh fruit awaited the delicate pair, who still continued to complain about their wives even though they felt so awful, but before long they knew it was time to leave, their night of freedom now a thing of the past.

"And not to be repeated." Sofia said sternly. "Not until those babies are safely delivered. Now go and make your peace with the girls." She kissed them each twice and waved them on their way.

Nicos sheepishly returned home to find nothing had changed. Sky's appetite was huge one minute, and sparrow like another, just like her temper. His normally placid and happy wife was turning into an ogre.

His mother Athena, had said Sky was nesting, whatever that meant in woman speak, and that the birth would not be far away. He couldn't wait. At least then he would have his wife back to normal, hopefully.

Athena was right; Sky went into labor two days later. Her disability meant that she was used to pain. Pain in her arms from walking with crutches, pain in her legs from stumbling into things, and pain in her back from the effort of moving. The onset of labor had passed unnoticed until suddenly her waters had broken as she was once again checking her overnight bag.

It had been planned for her to have the baby in hospital on the mainland where a room had been booked for her, but time was obviously now running out and a flight to Athens completely out of the question.

Nicos shouted to his mother, who was at that moment enjoying a glass of chilled wine on the terrace of her marvelous villa only a few yards away.

Then in a state of panic he telephoned the island's doctor.

Athena calmly ordered Nicos to get Sky into bed and set about helping the young woman relax, gently stroking her brow and softly singing to her.

Alexi, Nicos's father soon joined the trio, with as usual a camera at the ready.

Alexi Mandros, the world famous photographer calmed his nerves by snapping away as Sky slipped deeper into the birth of his first grandchild. It was the only way he could stay sane as he watched her grimace in pain from the contractions that ripped through her body then back to momentary peace.

He, like his son felt useless.

Nicos just kept walking. Over to the window, back to the door, back to the window, all the time chewing on his already short fingernails and nervously sweating as he watch his wife and mother.

"Where is he? Where is that damned doctor?" He was beginning to panic when suddenly he heard a car stop outside. Rushing to the door he manhandled the poor doctor into the bedroom; leaving the nurse to follow on her own.

The nurse ushered the men out, and only Athena, who at Sky's insistence stayed to hold her hand, witnessed the examination that followed.

Sky was grateful for the older woman's company, but the person she really wanted was her sister Paris.

She at present was with her husband Andros and his mother, aunt Eleni, and her husband Richard. They had all recently traveled to England to help Richard find his long lost family after many years of living in New York. Paris, being a journalist had insisted on tagging along and was using her contacts to assist in his quest, plus she was gathering information for her next book. "Richard's Story"

That unfortunately wasn't helping Sky, she wanted her sister with her not hundreds of miles away, she wanted her here, and now. She felt like crying.

Sky was pleased when the doctor had finished his handling of her, she had never been keen on intimate examinations and at this moment just wanted to push. The nurse kept saying no, but the urge was beginning to overwhelm her and suddenly she had no say in the matter. The pain in her stomach took over and the massive contraction that followed made her scream. Nicos and his father ran back into the room just in time to see the baby girl emerge from her mother.

The nurse gave Nicos the scissors and showed him how and where to cut the umbilical cord. His fingers shook as he neared the long bloody strip of skin, but the feeling that he was freeing his baby was one of immense pride and love.

He took the child in his arms, as she was being released and marveled at the sight before him. Her tiny head was covered in a thick mass of jet black hair just like his own, her skin under the clots of blood he could see was white like her mother's, but it was her striking amber eyes that held his gaze. He felt as if she was looking into his soul, already undermining his authority, staking her claim to his heart.

This child was now his center of the universe and he was certain, with that one look, she already knew it.

He remembered the time she was conceived. His and Sky's wedding night, a night he would never forget.

The October day had been wonderful, full of celebration and happiness. The tourists had long left Skiathos and the not so busy locals had time to enjoy the wedding feast. Gallons of wine, and masses of fine food were consumed during the celebrations.

Sky had looked marvelous in her flowing gown of dark cream that shone like gold, with masses of tiny yellow flowers cascading through her long, pale auburn hair. She had even decorated her crutches with matching cream ribbons and pretty yellow blooms.

Paris with her tall slim body and spiky red hair, looked stunning in her dress of bronze. She looked so proud and happy standing at her sister's side. Her past with Nicos put aside for this very special day.

The sight of Sky limping towards him on Richard's arm was something Nicos would never forget. Her smile as she met him at the alter steps, so pleased to have walked this far, so happy that he was waiting for her, it was a moment he would treasure forever.

As darkness fell happy dancing Greeks spilled out into the narrow cobbled streets of Skiathos Town, their long lines bobbing to fabulous bouzouki and violin music.

The day had been blessed with brilliant sunshine that unfortunately got unseasonably hot and stuffy as it neared night. The gentle breeze had stopped and it felt as if the air was being sucked from the earth. Birds stopped chirping and insects invaded the darkening sky, only the swallows seemed to be enjoying themselves. Dipping and darting through the still air in their pursuit of the now abundant food that was on offer.

Even the many cats and kittens that had been waiting patiently for food suddenly disappeared from the streets.

Everyone knew what was to follow, but no one expected the fantastic display of nature at its violent best that they were about to witness. Electrifying, was the word used by everyone, as the storm began.

Aunt Eleni swore it was the Gods marking the occasion, not wishing to spoil things by saying they were actually showing their disapproval.

She was a true Greek, firmly believing in the inhabitants of Mount Olympus and their mystical ways, she was in fact an expert. Her stories were fascinating to listen to and now a few of the wedding party sat on the floor around her chair as she began to tell yet another tale of Zeus and his family.

The first brilliant flash of lightening lit the sky and the loud rumble of thunder that followed almost immediately told them the storm was close. The lightening was so bright the sea reflected its brilliance as the waves grew from a ripple into a raging mass and the wind began to gain strength. Torrential rain hit the wedding party scattering the dancers and storm watchers as it fell, many going to sit at aunt Eleni's feet to listen to her story.

Nicos carried Sky to his car and drove to their new home on the hill as quickly as the elements would allow. Rain pelted against his windscreen with such force the cars wipers only just managed to clear space for his vision.

Lightening lit up the sky like a massive firework display. It was frightening but so exciting.

Parking his car as close as possible to the door Nicos once again lifted his new bride in his arms and carried her into their home.

Built on the hill top only yards away from his father's villa at first glance it looked typically Greek in style, only this home was pure luxury.

It was very large and spacious with huge floor to ceiling windows in each room. These were not protected by the usual wooden outside shutters, but by long material blinds on the inside. Each room had at least one wall of glass and the view from them all was absolutely stunning.

The inside had been decorated in lovely shades of cream with fabulous pale gold marble tiles on the floors.

Small Greek statues and tall green plants occupied space in every room and of course Nicos's photographs were everywhere.

Their bedroom with a huge print of Sky's angel photograph hanging proudly, and it's wall of glass overlooking the beaches of Eleni and Koukanaries, proved to be a marvelous place to watch the ever-increasing intensity of the storm.

As sheet lightening lit the room as if it were daytime the newlyweds came together with intense passion.

Sky had insisted that she would not make love until their wedding night and now in her arms he knew she had been right.

There had been times when Nicos had found it difficult to keep his hands off of her, but he had somehow managed and was now enjoying the wonderful rewards.

The occasional holidaymaker falling prey to his charms did not really count; they were just his way of managing to keep to Sky's rule.

They felt each other's bodies with tender hands. They explored parts unknown until now. Nicos let his hands stroke every part of her body taking his time to help her relax. He knew he was her first lover and encouraged her to feel his skin and the erection that throbbed at his groin.

She was a perfect student.

It was wonderful as their limbs entwined in wild passion. Her twisted leg now forgotten as she allowed him to enter her and later as she straddled his body.

Their passion was as fierce as the storm outside.

As she lay naked in his arms Sky felt a strange sensation.

"Jack my tummy feels all warm and nice and just then I felt something very peculiar. Perhaps we have made a baby. I do hope so as then all of my prayers would have been answered in one day."

"I hope you are right too my love, but if you are you know what we must call the child don't you?"

Sky nodded.

Her quirky parents, original 60's hippies, had named their children after the places they had assumed conception had taken place. Paris, on the romantic Left Bank when they were students, whereas Sky came during an airplane trip to Thailand a few years later. She often joked that she was lucky not to have been named mile high, but deep down was more than happy with the name they chose.

Her parents who had deserted them in their quest to find inner peace, her parents who could be dead having never made contact since the day they left, perhaps to be grandparents and they would never know. Sky felt sad for them and what they would miss out on, perhaps one day she would try to find out where they had gone.

One thing she did know was that no matter what she would be there for her children, right from their birth until the day she died.

The daydreaming was brought to a sudden halt.

"Nicos!" Sky said sharply, using his proper name for a change.

"Nicos can I please hold my baby."

Brought back to the present moment by Sky's voice he gently laid the newborn child on her mother's stomach. Sky stroked the soft warm skin counting her fingers, then her toes. She let her hands slowly run down the baby's legs and began to cry.

"She is perfect." She said after a while. "Thank God she is perfect."

The fear of her own disability being passed on had grown in her mind as the child had developed in her womb. She prayed nightly to be blessed with a perfect baby and now looking through watery eyes she could see her prayers had been answered.

All through her pregnancy Sky had done everything she could to help ensure a healthy child. No alcohol had passed her lips since her wedding night. She had only eaten fresh salads, fresh fish, and fruits grown naturally on the island.

She had religiously done the exercises explained to her by the doctor, which not only did her tummy muscles good but gradually she noticed also helped to strengthened her leg.

And just the thought of any medicine made her feel ill, her own disability being the result of morning sickness tablets taken by her mother. She had let nature take its course.

Her only craving was for nougat, fresh nut filled nougat. In fact she ate so much it became a family joke.

The strict regime had paid off, not only was her child perfect, but she now looked amazing. Her soft auburn hair and her white freckled skin shone with health. Nicos often teased her about her skin; no matter how much time she spent in the sun it still remained lily white, only her freckles increased in colour and number.

The baby had obviously increased her weight, but she knew any excess would soon disappear if she continued to eat her tasty good Greek diet, and stick to her exercise plan.

Nicos sat on the bed and encompassed them both in his arms.

"Thank you Sky. You have given me the most precious thing in the world. Look at her hair, her tiny body. I just can't get over how I feel. The strength of the love that I feel for you both is frightening. I know one thing though; this little madam here is going to rule our lives. Have you looked at her eyes?"

Sky looked into the striking face of her child who returned her stare with a soft light shinning from deep amber pools.

"She is the spitting image of Paris, her eyes are that lovely amber, well unless she is angry that is, and just look at the baby's legs. In fact all of her limbs are so long it's untrue. Yes she's Paris to a tee." She said softly, thinking of her sister.

"She didn't look at me like that." Nicos said frowning. "It was more of a fiery glare when she looked at me. See there it is." He was right. When the baby turned towards her father her eyes changed to fire.

Sky was even more convinced then that the child resembled her own sister, not just in looks but temperament too.

"You are going to have your hands full with that little beauty." Alexi said noticing the change in the way the baby looked at each of her parents. "She is defying you already son, and only a few minutes old."

Athena came over and gazed down at the lovely child.

"She is so beautiful. Thank you both for our wonderful grandchild." Tears were streaming down her face as she stared down at the baby girl, this beautiful baby girl. How different her own life could have been, but now she hoped this tiny bundle would in some way make up for her past heartache, and looking at her now she knew definitely that she would.

"Have you decided on a name?" She almost whispered.

"Storm." They answered in unison.

"Storm." Nicos repeated. "Storm Mandros."

The baby let out a howl of either approval or rejection, only stopping when she found her mothers breast.

"Storm. That is perfect for you young lady." Alexi said emotionally, uncharacteristically putting his camera down for a moment. "Just perfect."

• CHAPTER • 2

It was a beautiful warm late spring afternoon as Sky lay on a soft and very comfortable sun lounger in the shade of a large umbrella, her precious baby suckling noisily at her breast.

She marveled at the feeling of her daughter's soft skin against hers, only a tiny nappy separating the two of them. All of Sky's inhibitions had gone the day she gave birth and now it felt very natural to lay naked with her daughter out here in the open.

No one could see them on the terrace of her home, high up overlooking the rest of the island, so why worry.

Their only neighbours Athena and Alexi were at the Gallery in town, and Nicos had gone to Kefalonia to take more photographs. Her housekeeper, Maria, was in the kitchen preparing their evening meal, all the other staff had long gone home, so why worry at all.

It was so peaceful, just the two of them she wanted the afternoon to last forever.

The Eagles Nest, Sky had called it the first time Nicos had brought her to this wonderful place. The views from here were outstanding. She could see way down towards the many golden beaches of Skiathos, including the one where her friend Eleni would soon be in the process of giving birth herself.

Sky remembered the pain vaguely, but it was the sudden rush of love towards this tiny being, her daughter, that overrode anything else. Nothing in the world could ever compare to the feeling of being a mother, she thought, and wondered how on earth her own mother could have left her children the way she had.

Her thoughts drifted to her sister, the wonderful Paris, the one who had taken care of her for years after their parents had deserted them. She owed everything to her. If Paris had not been staying on this island and asked Sky to join her, then she would never have met Nicos, and never had this beautiful baby.

How she missed her sister. Sky sighed deeply.

It was as if her thoughts were being read. Her mobile phone jumped into action. It's little screen illuminated and flashing. "Paris".

"Hi sis, how's my little niece doing?"

"Hi Paris. I was just thinking of you, it must be esp. or something. Your little niece is just having her afternoon tea can you hear her?" Sky held the phone to her breast as Storm continued to suckle noisily.

"That was fantastic, I could hear her very clearly. Thanks Sky. Oh look now you have made me cry." Paris stopped talking and clumsily blew her nose. Not an easy task with hanky in one hand and mobile in the other. "There that's better," she continued. "And how are you. Did it hurt?"

Sky laughed and told her sister all of the gory details finishing with how much she loved every second and already could hardly wait for the next one.

"So you would do it again then?" Paris asked quite seriously. "I've heard some women say once is enough. Are you positive?"

"Steady on old girl. Not getting broody are you, asking all these questions? Yes it hurt, yes it was messy, but yes I would certainly do it again. Satisfied." Sky was still laughing into her phone. "Anyway how are you lot getting on, and when will you be back. Storm wants to slobber all over her aunty Paris."

"I can't wait for that experience," Paris was laughing now. "And as for us getting back, well I hope it won't be too long. It has been brilliant though we have had a smashing time."

"Tell me all then."

"Well you know we were hoping to find some trace of Richard's family." Sky nodded even though she was on the telephone. "Not an easy thing I tell you. His family home had been sold to pay off death duties after his parents had died, and no one in the village seemed to know where his brothers were now.

We went to the local church where Richard laid some flowers on their grave and he sat talking to them for ages. It was very sad.

He cried, aunt Eleni cried, I did, Andros just looked uncomfortable.

Richard had lots to say to his parents, and he just sat there talking to their headstone. It seemed to do him good though, perked him up a bit. Aunt Eleni told me he really needed to make his peace, and he had.

Well, whilst we were there an old man came along, he just nodded as he walked past but Richard recognised him as once being their gardener so he stopped him and asked about the family.

It seems that Richards's brothers had left the area and gone to live in a town quite a few miles away. He said he thought his eldest brother Marcus had died some years ago, but his family and other brother Julian were still in this new place.

We found it on the map when we got back to our hotel and set about getting up there. It's quite a distance from London so we booked to go on the train. All very exciting for Richard not having been on a train since the war, he couldn't believe the size of the towns and cities we went through.

I could have done with you being here then though, what with booking trains, hotels and things, in fact doing your old job for me when I was traveling, I promise never to take you for granted again." She laughed.

Back in their London home Sky used to book all of Paris's trips on the Internet. Flights, hotels you name it, she had booked it at sometime or other, but that had all finished when she came to live on Skiathos.

"Anyway I managed to get us up there and booked into a place called The George. What a fantastic hotel and the town is really something else. All very old, with beautiful stone buildings, it's very English, yet rather continental with its wide streets and café life style.

The shops are to die for. I had a whale of a time rummaging through all the antiques and things. Fab. You would love it."

Sky had no intention of ever going back to England again, and so doubted her sister's words, but smiled at the thought of those old knick-knack shops.

"We went to a pretty church overlooking the town bridge, St Mary's I think it was called, and out of sheer luck spotted Marcus's grave. Richard fetched some flowers from a shop across the road and once again knelt and talked to his brother. It made me cry again, and aunt Eleni, we are so soppy. He had no argument to settle with Marcus; it was just his parents who the fall out was with.

The vicar came and spoke to us for a while, and he had a rough idea where we might find Julian. A little village, only about 7 miles away. So we all piled into a taxi and went over.

As we were passing through the village Richard spotted this young lad who was the spitting image of his own father. He asked the driver to stop and spoke to the boy. It turned out he was his brother's grandson. He talked to the lad a little more and asked him to go and see if his grandfather would meet him. Seconds after this lad gone in to a wonderful farmhouse just up the road from the village, out rushed an old man.

Guess who was crying again.

Julian and Richard talked for hours. Evidently their father had spun some tale about Richard going away, and over the years they had really just forgotten about him. The first the family knew that he was still alive came when he had read in the Times of Richard's Knighthood.

The following day the whole family came to the hotel for lunch. Not just Julian and his lot, but Marcus's widow, her children and grandchildren too. What a bunch we made. The noise was incredible as they all caught up on news missed over the years. I tell you I have got so much for my book on Richard I will be writing for months.

So now back to normality. We will be flying back to Athens soon and then after a day or so coming over to Eleni beach. Richard and aunt Eleni want to see the babies before they go over to Alonysos. That's if

Eleni has produced hers by then? I am so looking forward to getting back, Storm can slobber all over me if she wants. Oh Sky I am so excited I can't wait."

Storm was now sleeping contentedly after her feed and Sky herself feeling dozy. Paris had talked for ages.

"How's everyone else?" Paris asked not wanting to use Nicos's name.

The thought of her one night stand with him still churned away in her mind. It had almost wrecked her relationship with Andros, but in the end was the major factor in them at long last marrying. Paris also knew about his affair with young Eleni, and she hoped Sky would never hold it against either of them.

"Well Jack is on one of his photo trips today, Alexi and Athena are at the Gallery, but everyone is fine thanks. All gushing over a certain little madam, but it's great really. I feel so proud Paris; I can't begin to tell you. She is the best thing ever, hurry back I want you to see her this small, she is so cute." Sky felt tears falling down her cheeks. Storm was indeed the best thing in the world, she loved her so much it hurt. The baby sensed a change in her mother's mood and woke. She pulled her head up in a rather wobbly fashion and looked straight at her.

"Say hello to aunty Paris then." Sky said placing the phone near to her daughter, who right on queue gave out a high-pitched squeal.

"How's that for only a few day's old then?" Sky asked her laughing sister. "Not bad eh?"

"No not bad at all." Paris replied still laughing. "Have you got one of those photo phones, can you sent me a picky?"

"Yeah. I forgot that. Hang on." Click, buzz. "There how's that." Almost immediately Paris replied.

"Oh Sky it's brill thanks. I will save it on my screen. Right I'd better go and see what's happening with the others. See ya soon. Kiss Kiss."

"OK. Sis. Thanks for calling. See you. Bye for now."

As she clicked her phone shut Sky heard the unmistakable sound of Nicos's camera whirring and turned to see her husband taking yet another picture of herself and her daughter.

"You must have hundreds already," she laughed. "Enough to fill a thousand albums."

"I can never have enough photographs of my beautiful girls." He replied slowly sauntering over to the terrace. "Fancy a drink?" He kissed Sky greedily, and then landed a smacker on the tummy of his daughter. "And how's my little girl today then?" He asked the smiling child who stared directly at her father yet again. "I always thought babies couldn't focus until they were a little older than she is?" He said frowning. "But she seems to be seeing me no problem and just look at her smiling."

"I think she recognises your voice, that or your camera whirring. I don't think she can really see you yet, and don't be fooled by that smile, that's wind."

Sky was laughing at her besotted husband. With every move or noise Storm made he was more and more convinced she was a genius.

Nicos gently picked the baby up from her mother's stomach and cradled her in his arms. Kissing her soft skin he looked at Sky and noticed for the first time she was naked. He felt a stirring in his groin, God she was beautiful. Her pale skin glowed with health and her long hair shone, her body now almost back to its pre pregnancy days looked inviting. Sky saw him looking and felt the need to draw him close.

Storm had other ideas, she promptly threw milk up all over her father, and then preceded to scream like a banshee, her eyes flashed in temper.

"I think Daddies girl has just put a stop to that idea," Sky said smiling. "It's almost as if she knows what we are thinking and doesn't want to share you."

"Tough." Nicos replied huskily. "I need you now."

He placed the screaming child in her little cot nearby, ripped of his messy shirt and joined Sky on the sun bed. "Now close those eyes you monkey. Let me and your mama enjoy a few minutes together."

Nicos was more than ready to make love to Sky.

The model he had taken to Kefalonia had been nothing more than a tease. His body was taught with frustration. How dare she torment him like that only to walk away laughing. Her photographs would never be developed, no chance of her gracing the cover of Vogue now. No one refused Nicos Mandros and got away with it.

Slowly and gently he stroked Sky's body. His hands touching parts that now throbbed with anticipation.

"Please be careful Jack, remember I have just given birth." Sky said softly.

She could feel the sun warming his back as her hands begin to wander over his taught muscular body. Nicos moved rhythmically and sensually, now licking her breasts as his body arched in passion. Momentarily he fed from her ripe nipples, drinking in her natural juices, filling him with a sexual excitement to surpass all others.

It was a wonderful sensation, out here in the open with the man she loved, eagles flying overhead and the smell of hibiscus invading her senses. Sky could think of nothing better.

They reached the wonderful heights of passion joined together, as the soft warm breeze rippled over their damp skin.

Sunni was on his way.

CHAPTER 3

The shrill ring of the telephone broke in to the peaceful silence of Sky's stylish lounge. Their evening meal now over, and Storm safely tucked up in her cot. This was their time. Sky reached over and answered.

"It's Vanni." She said quickly. "Twin boys. Oh how marvelous. Are they OK? Is Eleni OK? How much do they weigh and what are you calling them? Have they got hair?" Sky was a mass of questions.

"Here let me talk to him." Nicos took the phone from her and calmly spoke to his friend in their native tongue. He had been trying to teach Sky Greek during the previous winter months, but as spring came and he got busier, she got heavier with the baby, the lessons stopped. He knew that Vanni could speak English well, but at a time like this his mind thought in Greek, just as Nicos had done at the birth of Storm.

"Right then here we go." He replaced the receiver and told Sky the news. "The babies are small and both bald, they look like Vanni when he was born according to Sofia, and their names are Marco and Tomas. Marco after her father, and Tomas after his.

"What a nice thought." Sky replied, her eyes all dreamy. She already had the feeling that she was pregnant again, and just like before knew exactly when the child had been conceived.

She also realised that with Storm only just over a week old, she was in for some ribbing from Paris, and perhaps a few of the others. But she didn't care. Her life was now centered on Nicos, Storm and the tiny new being inside her.

"I will take you to see them tomorrow." Nicos said glancing at his sleeping daughter "We can show Storm her new friends."

Not only had Nicos been trying to teach Sky Greek, but also how to drive. He had presented her with a little red Clio automatic on her birthday and spent many hours trundling up and down the single island road with her before she had even dared to enter the narrow busy roads of the town.

At first she had been terrified, but now her confidence had grown and next week she took her driving test. Luckily the examiner spoke English. Tomorrow though he would drive, his daughter was too precious to be allowed in the car with a learner. Unfortunately Sky had always had problems getting in and out of his sports car, but clumsily managed with his help, it never stopped her smiling though, nothing seemed to stop her smiling he thought, so one more trip would not hurt.

Nicos curled up with her once again on the long comfortable sofa that dominated their room, and they returned to watch the sun setting slowly over the sea. The view from high up was incredible as the sea turned deep orange then red. The sky looked ablaze, until slowly it turned into its wonderful nighttime black velvet.

During the summer months they loved to watch from the terrace, but as the nights cooled sometimes with a soft breeze, the huge window allowed them to see the fabulous spectacle and stay warm.

"That was a beauty." Sky said softly as solar lights came to life on the outside terrace. "I can't think of anything nicer than to sit here with you watching that."

"I can." Nicos joked gently stroking her breast. "Lets open a bottle." He nodded towards the ornate iron wine rack in the corner.

"You go ahead," she replied. "None for me though."

Nicos stared at her as she smiled and pointed to her stomach.

"Again and so soon? Fantastic!"

Sky nodded.

"I am sure. That afternoon out on the terrace." She blushed slightly at the memory.

Nicos hugged his wife and felt his eyes mist.

"Please Jack, don't say a word yet. Not even to your mother." Sky knew how close they were and how hard it would be for him to stay silent. He nodded grinning, but deep down she knew there was a pretty good chance Athena would know by morning.

Storm woke from her sleep and gave a little whimper. She stretched, yawned sleepily then began to kick her legs to gain some attention.

"Come and meet your brother or sister." Nicos said as he gently picked her up and placed her on Sky's stomach. The baby girl curled up in the fetal position immediately and began to gurgle.

"She is talking to her already." Nicos was full of wonder. Storm gave a loud yell in protest of something.

"Perhaps she is talking to him." Sky said stroking her baby's soft hair. Storm began to gurgle again. "There you are. It must be a boy." Sky laughed. "She knows already. Just look." Storm was gently stroking her mothers stomach.

"How the hell does she know that?" Nicos was amazed.

Sky shrugged her shoulders.

"I haven't a clue but just remember keep it quiet. Let me get the next couple of months out of the way and then you can tell the world. Promise?" She asked.

Nicos crossed himself.

"Promise"

She knew for certain then that he would, well perhaps.

Down at Eleni Beach, the other new parents were not finding things quite so enjoyable.

Both boys cried constantly.

Eleni tried to feed them hoping for a few minutes peace, but neither would take to her full and aching breasts. The midwife helped her pump enough milk out to hopefully fill the babies, but the unnatural procedure upset Eleni even more. She wanted to feed the babies herself; to have a plastic pump attached to her breast was an insult, she was their mother for God's sake.

That it worked did not make her feel any better, in fact she felt even more useless.

Soon her boys were sucking noisily on the tiny bottles the midwife had filled, Vanni holding Tomas, and Eleni with Marco.

"Silence at last." Vanni sighed. "Just listen it's beautiful."

At last they could hear the sea gently lapping against the shore and the cedar trees rippling in the breeze.

"All this is quite common." The midwife explained. "They had a difficult birth as you know, and it will take a few days more for them to settle down."

She was right Eleni had been in labor for 24 hours before Tomas had arrived, followed only a few minutes later by the smaller Marco. Now she was confined to bed in order to recover.

Having visited Sky after Storm's birth, Eleni was disappointed in the size of her children. Storm looked so well, so bonny, yet her two looked thin and frail.

A knock at the door broke into her thoughts. It was Sofia. She was ecstatic, two grandchildren in one go, she could hardly keep away. In fact she had visited countless times since their birth, which had been only a few hours ago but now seemed like days.

The concerned look on her face changed as Vanni explained the necessity for the bottles.

"As long as they feed well then that is all that matters." She said smiling down at the children. "And they need to be fed well, look how tiny they are, but oh so precious."

Eleni did not need reminding how small her babies were and felt like crying, she felt a failure. She wanted her mother, her father, sadly both now dead, she needed someone to cry with she was desperate.

The following morning Nicos loaded his little family into the sports car and drove carefully down to the beach. It was a beautiful bright clear morning, a little cool but still wonderful as they made their way down the hill. Sky smiled to herself as Nicos took the sharp bends at a snails pace, usually he roared down hardly bothering to slow at all.

They parked in the little clearing and gathering presents for the boys, flowers for Eleni, and of course Storm in her carrycot, headed off to meet the new arrivals.

Sky could see the fear in Eleni's eyes the second she entered the bedroom. Quickly she ushered Vanni and Nicos out and placed Storm in the cot between the boys. They stopped their crying immediately and both turned to meet the stranger who had suddenly appeared in their midst.

Sky said nothing as she watched them for a few minutes, then walked over to Eleni and held her close.

The tears came, the fear came out, and the feelings so far hidden gushed from her mouth. It was the tonic Eleni needed, just to be held and understood. The two women stayed hugging for quite some time as Sky slowly pulled Eleni back from the edge of a deep depression.

"I don't understand," Eleni said at last. "I was so looking forward to having them but now they are here I feel so strange." The eyes that looked pleadingly at Sky were red and swollen.

"It happens you know. There is no need to worry. Me and Storm will come to see you every day from now on and help." Sky was rocking her friend in her arms. "Anything you want to say, say to us OK? Don't keep it all bottled up." She felt Eleni nod against her breasts.

"I know one thing though Sky. Never again. That's it. Two in one go, enough."

Sky smiled to herself, she could think of nothing nicer than giving birth again. In fact she could hardly wait.

Vanni tapped softly at the door and opened it slightly.

"Nicos and I are off to the taverna for a quick drink. Won't be long." He was surprised and a little hurt to see that Eleni had been crying.

"Well just you two behave, and don't do what you did last time." Sky replied laughing. "One drink and no more."

"OK see you." With that Vanni was gone. He felt the need to talk to his friend. The sight of Eleni in so much pain and ripped at his heart.

She was so tiny and the twins had sapped every ounce of her strength. No matter what he would not put her through that again. He blamed himself for getting her pregnant, and blamed his father and aunt for being twins.

There was no doubt in his mind he loved the boys, but the agony they had put their mother through made him angry. Everyone fussed over the babies and their mother; but no one spoke to him about his fears. Nicos would he knew for sure, after all wasn't he going through exactly the same?

Hours later Tomas appeared in the bedroom.

"I will order you a taxi Sky. I am afraid they are drunk again. Don't fret though Sofia and I will look after them tonight."

"Again!" said Sky sharply looking towards the ceiling.

"Don't blame Nicos Sky. Vanni kept filling his glass and talking. I heard him say many times he had had enough, but Vanni can be very persuasive you know. I am a little ashamed of him. Two beautiful babies, Eleni to look after and he does this. Please forgive my son." Tomas looked very hurt that Vanni could behave like he had.

"Forgiven." Sky replied for her friend. "There's no need for a taxi though. We will stay with Eleni tonight. You just look after them."

"Do you mean that Sky. Will you really stay?" Eleni remembered saying those same words to Nicos once.

It had resulted in them being lovers, and much to Vanni and Andros's amusement Nicos had proposed. His reputation as a lover was correct and for a second Eleni was a little jealous of Sky. She knew exactly how he could make a woman feel, fantastic, was the only way she could describe it, no wonder Sky looked so well and happy. Any woman on this earth would be happy with a man like that. Deep in thought she remembered his fling with Paris and wondered if Sky knew that her sister had once risked everything for one night with the man who was now her husband.

That's how good Nicos was, the sort to make you risk everything without a thought for the consequences.

Sky left Eleni with the babies, now sleeping together in a heap, they reminded her of a litter of puppies, and hobbled over to the taverna. She ordered lamb kelftiko for them both and a couple of Tomas's special nighttime drinks. His specialties were made of chocolate and hazelnuts, with a topping of thick cream, and could make even an angry elephant sleep.

She kissed her drunken husband on the brow and then Vanni.

"We will see you in the morning." She wagged her finger at them. "You can bring us breakfast. Thanks Tomas." She said as he carried the tray of delicious smelling food for her. "I will sort the dishes out over there."

It was quite a difficult journey for Sky, only a few yards but with her crutches sinking into the sand her balance was not that good. Nicos ran to her side as she struggled to walk.

"I'm so sorry my love. Please forgive me."

"This time you bad lad, I will. Just don't do it again." She started to stumble, luckily the sand was soft but she fell with quite a bump. "Shit that hurt." She said rubbing her side. "Bugger."

Carefully Nicos lifted her into his arms, the sight of his wife sprawled on the sand sobered him up in a second.

"Lets get you into bed." He said softly. "You and my boy."

Sky smiled at him.

"I only did it so you would carry me you handsome hunk." She laughed, but the ache in her side worried her. "I think we had better call the doctor Jack."

Nicos was now petrified; he had a look on his face of sheer terror.

"Ok. As soon as you are in bed." He replied quickening his pace.

As soon as Sky was comfortable in the spare room and Storm once again reunited with her mother Nicos rang for the doctor. He explained that Sky had fallen, and the fact that they suspected her to be pregnant. Now their secret was out, but he didn't care. All he was concerned about was his wife and unborn child.

Storm fed greedily from her uncomfortable mother as they waited for the doctor to arrive. Eleni's midwife had called in and examined her, but Nicos wanted the doctor to confirm that she was OK.

Suddenly Storm slid from her mother's breast and gave a high-pitched squeal as she lay on her stomach. Sky looked at Nicos and her eyes filled with tears. Did Storm know something? Had she sensed something wrong? The squeal subsided into a gurgle as the baby girl once again stroked her mothers skin. Her parents let long sighs escape their bodies. This daughter of theirs was something else.

The doctor pronounced Sky fit but ordered her to have a scan the following day. He didn't want her going to the clinic tonight thinking that rest was probably the best medicine and a very tired Sky agreed.

Nicos changed and washed Storm carefully before placing her at Sky's side. He kissed them both and then Sky's stomach.

"Never again." He said thinking how close he came to loosing a baby he had yet to meet.

Sky gently stroked his hair.

"Will you stay with us Jack?"

"Try and stop me." He replied glugging down cold water. "I will be here at your side all night. Now sleep, try and sleep."

Sky slid down between the sheets and curled around her already sleeping child. She prayed for them all, asking for a special blessing if that was possible. She said that she knew God was busy as there was so much happening in the world, but please could he just this once give her family precedence, she didn't want to be greedy but please just this once.

She fell asleep asking time and time again for God to help, just this once.

An early scan confirmed her prayers had been answered.

• CHAPTER •
4

"He is so beautiful." Paris said holding the day old baby boy gently in her arms. "A real handsome stunner." Storm squealed. "Yes and you are gorgeous too." She aimed her words towards the fast growing girl. Storm replied with a giggle. "You are so lucky Sky. The mother of two such beautiful children. You must be so proud of yourself." She kissed her sister's cheek. "You certainly should be."

"I can't believe it at times. Here I am wobbly old Sky, married to the most wonderful man." Paris stiffened slightly. "Two healthy children. It's as if God is making up for this." She pointed to her badly twisted leg. "Mind you it doesn't really look like I had anything much to do with it. Storm is the spitting image of you, she has your long legs and even your spiky hair." Paris turned towards the crawling child, Sky was right she did look uncannily like herself. "And Sunni there is just like Jack."

Paris began to giggle. "You will have to have another then, but this time make sure it looks like you."

"I don't think so. These two will be enough. She is a right little madam at times and I can see he is going to be finicky. You know, he won't sleep unless Storm is at his side. She sits by his cot every night until he is fast asleep, and then she gives this funny little whimper. If I try to put her in her cot before he has gone to sleep she gets a right mood on her. It's strange but lovely really; she has looked after him right from the very beginning.

She used to lie on my tummy and talk baby talk to him, stroking my lump. I can see they are going to be very close."

"What about Eleni's two. How is she with them?" Paris asked as Storm tried to pull herself up on her aunt's very expensive designer trousers.

"Similar really. Every time we go they are crying, they are only a few days younger but you would think there is month's difference. As soon as I put her with them to play they go quiet and just get on with it. Eleni has asked if she can borrow her every night to make them sleep. I laugh about it but it must be hell. Storm has only cried a couple of times, and Sunni has yet to do more than gurgle. Mind you they both have tempers but I am so lucky to have two reasonably quiet babies and both of them eat for England."

"Shouldn't that be eating for Greece?" Paris said laughing as Storm fell yet again on her nappy wrapped bum.

"Oh no. These two are duel nationality and I am going to make sure they speak both languages too. I can say quite a lot in Greek now so we have different days with different words. Monday might be Greek and Tuesday English. If Jack is away it's always English though." Sky had a naughty look in her eyes and laughed. "He would not be a happy bunny if he found out." The sisters laughed together.

The rest of the day was taken up with girlie chat. It had been so long since they had been together that the time just flew. They talked about Paris's new book and her living arrangements.

For almost two years, in fact ever since Andros had proposed he had been at her side as promised. He worked on his laptop and only rarely had to visit his business warehouse in Athens.

The trouble was he was frustrated and Paris felt hemmed in. Having been a globetrotting journalist for so many years and now a successful author she had become uneasy herself.

They came to a mutual arrangement. Andros was to spend some of the week in Athens at his mother's house and work as before, whilst

Paris would live at the home they had built here on the island and write. The remaining few days they would spend together. It suited them both, although her mother in law, aunt Eleni apparently thought it rather strange.

She and Richard were inseparable and now happily lived on Alonysos, the thought of a married couple being happier like this amazed her.

"Did you know Richard is eighty this year?" Paris asked. Sky shook her head. "He looks so much younger. Evidently aunt Eleni is throwing a grand party at the beach for him. His brother is coming over from England, with some other relatives, and Tomas has said they can have a couple of his houses in the village to stay in. It's so nice for Richard, everything he went through and now he is so happy." Paris thought of the things she had written in her book. All true. Richard had not had an easy life until aunt Eleni had come along. His Goddess as he called her.

"When is his birthday then?" Sky wanted warning. She knew Alexi and Athena would want to go, so she would need to ask Maria in plenty of time if she would stay with the children. She also wanted to get her body back to its usual shape. She had been doing her exercises just like before and sticking to her fresh food diet so it might not take that long. Hopefully anyway.

"End of April I think. Nicos will know. Where is he anyway?"

"Gone to an island called Kalymnos for a few days. It's a big fresh sponge place so he tells me. Evidently the fallout from Chernobyl killed the sponge's years ago, made them go all hard and useless or something. It's a bit frightening really, all that way down in the water and they died." Sky shivered. "It makes you wonder how it got there and what other damage it did. Anyway they are growing back as normal now and he has been asked to take some underwater photographs. I bet he is having a brilliant time; he loves this sort of job. Makes a mint as well."

Nicos was enjoying himself on the trip, just as Sky had thought, but in a totally different way than she could ever imagine.

He had left Sky resting, hopefully not going to give birth for sometime, but the baby had other ideas and Sunni made a quick entrance as his father flew over to Kos.

Sky had phoned him to tell him the good news and insisted that he stay and do his job. Everything was OK at home and in fact the birth had been much easier than the previous one, only a couple of weeks early. Athena was with her and Paris on the way, so not to worry.

She sent a photograph through her phone of the two children together, the new baby lying in Storm's arms.

Nicos felt so proud although a little sad that he had not been with her, but still he felt at least ten feet tall, first the wonderful Storm, and now Sunni. The photograph brought tears of happiness and pride to his eyes.

Sky my beautiful wife, thank you; he spoke the words in his mind as he stared at his little children.

Nicos had arrived on Kos and was met at the airport by the owner of a diving school on Kalymnos. They shook hands and introduced themselves.

Nathan Green was a wealthy English man and used to mixing with the elite, but even he felt a little star struck at meeting the world famous Nicos Mandros. He could hardly believe that he had agreed to do this assignment, but Nicos assured him that if he could help Greece in any way he would.

The two men were of the same mind, if they could do anything they would, but only if the locals allowed them to.

Knowing how proud the Greeks were, Nathan had offered his services for a nominal fee, to charge nothing would be seen as an insult, he soon realised that, but a small fee was quite acceptable. The islanders had suffered through no fault of their own and he was more than pleased to help.

A little warily Nathan asked Nicos if he thought this promotional scheme they had come up with would help. Nicos replied that he didn't think it would, he knew it would.

He also knew the islanders would be grateful for Nathan's help by providing the boat and breathing apparatus the men needed for the dive.

The photographs Nicos would take were to be sent to newspapers and magazines throughout the world. Hopefully some of the sponges in their natural environment some already cut and bleached ready for sale, plus some shots of the island.

The pretty little island would be in the news and that could not be a bad thing.

Nathan thanked Nicos over and over as they made the journey from the airport to the quaint little harbor at Mastihari.

Normally the trip over to neighbouring Kalymnos would be made by ferry, but today the two men went over in Nathan's private speedboat.

Sky would love this Nicos thought as they bounced over the waves, the sea spraying them with misty drops. He remembered how she yelled when he took her on his motorbike. He loved to ride and she had caught the bug herself one day when he had taken her to Kefalonia. Completely forgetting she used crutches he had hired a bike to take her round the island. He had been mortified at his mistake; Sky on the other hand had thoroughly enjoyed it. He could almost hear her whopping with joy as they rode the waves, and smiled to himself. How he loved her, and now she had given him a son, what more could a man want?

As little town of Pothia, the islands capital came into view, Nathan slowed the boat and Nicos began to take photographs. His camera whirred away as they neared the pretty buildings of the ancient town, with its backdrop of tree covered hills and occasional white church showing through the greenery. If the rest of the island were as pretty he would have some fabulous shots to give the locals, and hoped he would have time to look around after the dives.

He could see Pothia was just like any other Greek harbor. Full of colourful fishing boats, tourist day trip boats, and the occasional rich man's yacht.

Pretty tavernas lined the streets and shops displayed their goods across pavements. The air was full of wonderful smells and lots of noise.

He had never ever arrived at a Greek harbor where there was silence and wondered what they all found to actually shout about.

Nicos's reputation had reached Pothia before he had, and a group of men accompanied by some onlookers waited to greet him as he stepped ashore.

Some of the men were the divers from the sponge factory, the ones he would need to know well in order to stay alive in the depths of the sea. Nathan assured him they were among the best divers in the world and he would be perfectly safe. Some English, some Italian and the rest

Greek, Nicos greeted them warmly and was pleased to meet his diving buddy, a man of similar age and stature to himself.

Paulo was an Italian who had fallen in love with the island whilst learning to dive and had never gone back to his native Naples, in fact his family had all come to live here years ago, well all apart from his brother. Stefano had stayed in Italy to pursue his career as a top-flight footballer. Now sadly only Paulo and his younger sister Giovanna were left on the island.

They lived in the village of Myrties, close to where Nicos would be staying. Paulo said he hoped the two men would have time to get to know each other well ready for the dive in a couple of days.

Nicos began to feel excited; all of this was new to him. It had been months since he had dived, but then it was for fun and not nearly so deep.

There was a feeling of danger about it as Paulo began to explain their diving and safety procedures during the bumpy car ride to the village.

Nicos had always been a keen diver, although not that regular, and knew the rules well, but he let Paulo speak anyway as he gazed through the taxi window.

The pretty little village of Myrties was made up of one road, the road to Massouri, with small white houses, tiny shops and busy tavernas along each side of the pitted tarmac.

Paulo asked the driver to stop just outside a small hotel, which stood precariously on the steep cliffs that led down to the sea.

"Come," he said to Nicos. "This is where you will stay my friend."

Nicos was quickly shown his room, the open windows framing wonderful views over to a tiny island across a narrow strip of water. Nicos sighed at the beautiful sight before him.

This island was really something else, yes, it was typically Greek, with a little bit of a touristy thrown in for good measure, but wonderful and peaceful, so tranquil, so marvelous.

A quick glance told him that the room was basic, but as with all Greek hotels, spotlessly clean.

He stepped out on to his balcony and noticed half a dozen other hotels that littered the cliffs, all looking much the same as his and smiled, he wondered what made them choose this one when they all seemed so similar.

He unpacked quickly and phoned Sky. He wanted to know all about his son and how she was. He was so sorry to have missed the birth, but pleased that his mother had been there. They talked for a long time and blew kisses to each other down the line. Storm took the phone from her mother and tried to speak, only baby gurgles came from her mouth, but they were enough to make Nicos's heart fill with pride. His daughter, and how he loved her.

He looked once again at the photograph Sky had sent, she was learning fast. She was not yet a natural with a camera and always short of time, but she no longer took what he called cheesy snaps.

Her hobby these days was designing pretty shoes and with the help of the town's cobbler was doing a good trade in nice footwear for disabled people. Nicos was very proud of how hard she worked.

Paulo knocked at his door interrupting his daydream of home.

"Everything OK Nicos?" He asked a little shyly. He knew only too well that this man must be used to a higher class of accommodation, but this was the best hotel in Myrties. Nicos nodded.

"Fine thanks. Look my new son, born as I was flying over." He showed Paulo the phone screen.

"I think we should celebrate then, it is also time to eat." Paulo smiled widely as he spoke. "I am famished after today."

He and the other divers had already been down to the seabed to find the best place for Nicos to take his photographs. "I hate to tell you though, some of the girls in the village have heard that you are hear and are hoping you will take their photographs. They say they want to look like an angel."

Nicos laughed. The photograph that he had taken of Sky at the underground lake on Kefalonia had become the advertisement for an expensive perfume and shown on TV all around the world. It had been named her angel picture, made him famous, rich, and much sort after. He was already wealthy enough to never work again, but he loved his job and took the assignments that appealed to him now. This one did.

The sponge farmers had been hit very hard by the death of their crop and if he could help he would. They must have collected a fortune in order to have his name on the article they were going to produce, but he already knew he would return half of his fee to the islanders as a donation to their campaign.

Athena would not be too pleased, she did his accounts as well as Alexi's and frowned upon giving money away. Her aim in life was to make as much as she could, and then to spend it with just as much enthusiasm, a task she never seemed to tire of.

Nicos however was like his father; the stunning locations and the photographs they allowed them to create were payment enough.

Pride was payment enough.

"Come on then let's go." Nicos nodded and followed Paulo out into the warm evening air.

He had never been to Kalymnos before and could smell a slight difference in the air but was unsure what it actually was, probably the trees, he thought. Now what were they eucalyptus? He took another deep breath. So fresh, so nice.

The island over the water looked wonderful now it was nighttime, lit with hundreds of tiny lights around its shoreline and in the tavernas. If he stopped walking and listened hard he could just make out music and laughter coming from over the water. He would have to visit before he left, that was one thing he was certain of.

Paulo led him to a busy taverna on the cliff edge having booked the best table earlier in the day.

"This is a good place for fish. I hope you like fish?" He asked again a little uncertainly.

"I should do. Brought up on Skiathos how could I not." Nicos replied with a laugh.

They began their meal with an assortment of local dishes, all smelling wonderful and tasting delicious. Paulo ran through the safety regulations again as they ate, Nicos listened and learned.

As the taverna started to fill more and more people came to their table to shake hands with this man who was going to help them.

The owner introduced himself and assured the two that their meals were on the house, as was any wine they required. He had brought with him a superb smooth silky red and a bottle of retsina, upon hearing of Nicos's good news about his son shook his hand and slapped his back.

"Have which ever." He shrugged his shoulders. "In fact have them both." He laughed placing the bottles down. "Enjoy your meal."

Paulo could hardly believe the amount of girls who flocked to their table. They all introduced themselves to Nicos then walked on seductively. This man was a real magnet to females, he thought as yet another stunning girl came to say hello.

"One of the perks of the job." Nicos said laughing. "Not bad eh?"

"You can say that again." Paulo said his eyes shinning as a young Swedish girl sashayed past. "I can hardly eat."

The taverna owner began to feel a little uneasy, every time he looked up Nicos was being disturbed. Eventually he put one of the waiters on guard just in front of their table to ward off any more intruders.

The two men enjoyed the peace and at last had time to eat their meals.

"Ah here is my sister." Paulo stood as she came over. "Nicos, please may I introduce Giovanna."

Nicos looked up at the most stunning girl he had ever seen. She had a mass of long wavy black hair, huge deep brown eyes, and beautiful olive skin. Her breasts were more than ample and her tiny waist lead to nicely rounded hips. A real Italian woman. For a moment she reminded him of a young Sofia Loren.

He stood clumsily and held out his hand.

"Please join us." He gestured towards the empty chairs, hoping that she would take the one closest to him. "Have you eaten?"

"Thank you," she replied in Greek but with a strong Italian accent. "I have had my meal at home but I would love a glass of wine."

Nicos's hand shook slightly as he filled her glass with the red.

He could hardly keep his eyes off of her for the rest of the night. He loved the way she giggled, the way her voluptuous lips spread as she smiled, and the way her eyes shone whenever she looked across at him.

"Giovanna doesn't dive but she will be with us when we do. She looks after the food and drinks on board. Nathan stays on board too, he pilots the boat and sees to the air pipes." Paulo said to break a long silence.

He could see Nicos staring at his sister and felt a little angry. This man was married, his wife had only hours ago given birth to a son, and here he was obviously making a play for her.

"Perhaps it would be better if you didn't come this time." He said to Giovanna, hoping to keep the two of them apart but knowing he really had no choice.

"Oh no Paulo. I must come. Who will feed all of you hungry divers if I am not there?" She smiled at her brother and patted his arm. "I always come with you I am your good luck charm."

The following morning Nicos joined the other divers on the tiny jetty at the bottom of the cliff. Their boat was ready and the equipment safely stowed, Nathan waved them aboard.

Nicos watched as Giovanna busied herself towards the back of the boat and took a couple of photographs as she worked. He always found that the best shots were taken when the subject was unaware of the camera and hoped that it would be similar in this case.

Although he was a master of his work he always had that nagging doubt that he would at some stage take a bad photograph. This slight fear kept him on his toes.

As the little boat slowly chugged away from the island Paulo once again began to talk Nicos through the diving procedure. Today they were just going down to look and practice, tomorrow, if all went well, Nicos would have his underwater camera with him.

Giovanna came and sat with them, turning her face up towards the sun, eyes closed. She looked so beautiful as the breeze swept her hair back from her incredible features. Nicos watched her for a while and eventually managed to speak. He asked huskily about the tiny island they were passing.

"It is Telendos Nicos, a beautiful place." Her voice sank deep into his brain. "If we have time I can show you. Would you like that?" He nodded, not daring to speak.

Paulo frowned; he knew only too well what would happen if Nicos went with her alone, he could feel the sexual waves from where he sat.

"That is a good idea Giovanna. We can show him some of the lovely beaches." He included himself on the trip for her own good and was trying to make himself feel slightly better. After all it was he who had introduced them and when the inevitable happened it would be solely his fault. Paulo felt slightly sick.

Nicos understood and felt a little ashamed of himself. All he could think of was getting her naked and he realised Paulo knew that too.

"Ok that's a date." He smiled, thankful in a way to have temptation taken away, for now anyway.

He had often bedded holidaymakers and never gave them a second thought, but he knew once he had tasted this woman he would be in big trouble.

He took out his phone and looked at the photograph, hoping to get some support from his children. Sky had sent another one, this time with her holding both of them, his heart jumped. He felt slightly sick as he saw Storm's eyes flashing from the screen it was as if she knew his thoughts.

The dives they did that morning were short but superb; Nicos was amazed at the abundance of the sponges on the seabed, and the amount of brightly coloured fish that swam amongst them. More than once he put his thumb up to Paulo, indicating that he had found a good place to shoot. He noticed how the suns ray filtered through, lighting the clear water to an amazing depth and he knew the photographs would be wonderful.

Paulo gestured that they should start the ascent, and slowly they began to inch their way towards the boat. Having been to quite some depth, the journey back was slow and frustrating, Nicos wanted to see Giovanna again as quickly as possible, but he knew how dangerous going up too fast would be and followed Paulo's instructions to the letter.

Breaking though the surface they pulled off their diving masks and gasped the clean clear air, both men began laughing.

"Brilliant." Nicos shouted. "That was brilliant. There are so many places for me to go tomorrow I can hardly wait." He felt exhilarated; the freedom of the water and the wonderful sights he had seen made him feel so alive.

Giovanna, true to Paulo's word, fed the divers well. She had made fresh salad baguettes, some with feta cheese, some with tasty chicken. There was delicious soft honey cake, juicy fresh fruit, and lots of fresh water. Nicos could hardly believe how much water his body seemed to need, but looking around he saw all of the divers were drinking plenty.

Next day the little boat followed the same path in the sea, but this time Nicos was attached to Paulo by a rope during the dive. This was to enable him to be as still as possible in the water whilst he took his photographs. Paulo was acting as his steadier as he stopped swimming and held his breath in order to prevent water movement or air bubbles showing on his lens.

The sun was even brighter today and the under water world came alive with fish of all shapes and sizes, their bright scales reflecting the rays as they darted between the sponges. There was so much for him to capture the time past very quickly and he was disappointed when Paulo tapped on his shoulder and pointed towards the bottom of the boat.

The water today was so clear it looked as if the little boat was floating. Nicos could not resist taking a shot from below.

Once again they ascended slowly, this time Nicos didn't care. He knew he had taken some stunning shots but he also knew this afternoon Giovanna was taking him to Telendos. OK Paulo was tagging along, but surely he would not be with them all of the time, I would be Nicos thought, if she was my sister. He smiled to himself and wondered if Sunni would be as protective with Storm, but knowing her she wouldn't need protecting from anyone. Her personality was already beginning to show and she was definitely going to be a handful for anyone.

Giovanna had prepared similar food to yesterday but this time included a delicious wine.

"It is from the island," she said pouring Nicos a glass. "I thought if you liked it I could show you the winery and you might take some pictures of that too?"

"Of course I would, and yes it is superb. In fact if you have time I would like to see as much of the island as I can. As you know I am here for the rest of today and tomorrow." Nicos was unable to fly for at least 24 hours because of the dive.

"I will make time if it will help the campaign. In fact I think a little tour would be better this afternoon and then tomorrow we will have all day to see Telendos." She replied smiling and went on to give the other divers their food.

Later that day the three of them sat quietly as Paulo drove his battered old car along the windy road through Myrties and then up into the hills. The scenery was magnificent as they went higher, tall cypress trees bent by the winds, an abundance of tiny flowers in the fields, the usual goats and hundreds of rabbits scampering about in the bright sunshine.

"It is so pretty." Nicos said aiming his camera through the open window. "Your island is going to look wonderful in the article."

They stopped in a tiny village for lunch, where once again the taverna's owner insisted on them not paying. Nicos was quite a celebrity even up here in the hills, something he found rather amusing and more than a little pleasing.

As before their meal was constantly interrupted by locals wanting to thank him, it made for a very long lunch break, but a very happy one. Constant chatter and backslapping mixed with good food and wine helped them all relax even more. Nicos felt very much at home.

Next stop, the winery, which was typically Greek with its crumbling white walls, baskets full of grapes waiting outside, and hundreds of wasps filling the air with noise.

As usual no one seemed to be working other than the insects. Large colourful butterflies fluttered amongst the huge red poppies in fields nearby. Nicos stopped to take yet more photographs.

They were invited inside the winery for a tasting, and offered large chunks of feta before each glass of clear fresh wine. The trio bought a few bottles of the red, although Nicos was not allowed to pay for his.

The wine took effect and their laughter echoed around the hillsides, it was a fabulous afternoon that Nicos did not want to end. He had enjoyed Paulo's company more than he had at first thought; he was funny, knowledgeable and very happy to show off this island that he had loved at first sight.

Giovanna was obviously devoted to her brother and watched proudly as he pointed out yet more sites of interest.

Nicos noticed that the wine had given her face a lovely healthy glow, which unfortunately made him want her even more.

The journey back to the village was a noisy happy one. The trio sang old Greek songs, thumping the cars floor with their feet as if dancing.

Giovanna sang a beautiful Italian song that told a tale of unrequited love. Her voice was so soft and clear it made the hairs on the back of Nicos's neck stand up, and shivers run down his spine.

Please let me get off this island quickly, he thought as he listened to her song.

They dropped him off at the hotel and arranged to meet later that evening. Paulo asked where he would like to eat and he pointed to the taverna on the island across the water.

"If it is possible?" He asked then added. "It looked so magical last night and I could take some really good shots of Myrties from there."

"Of course if that is what you wish. I will go and arrange a boat for later." Paulo parked the car and ran down to the jetty.

At last Nicos had Giovanna to himself and for the first time in his life was totally speechless.

"We will see you later then." She said climbing out of the back seat. Nicos held her arm to help and felt her breast touch his arm. Gently he pulled her to his chest and kissed her. The lips that he had watched for so long were so soft and warm, they tasted a little of the wine that had past through them earlier, and he melted. He felt her body press against his.

"Go to your room." She whispered.

Nicos didn't need telling twice.

Paulo ran up the steep stone steps and found her alone. "We can go over about 8," he said breathlessly. "Can you go and tell Nicos, Nathan has just asked me to help down there." He pointed back to the jetty. "I would tell him myself but it would be great if you could."

"Ok then see you later." Giovanna kissed her brother's cheek. "Be careful and remember you have had some wine so no diving." He returned her kiss and ran off waving.

She had been racking her brain for an excuse to go to Nicos but Paulo had just handed it to her on a plate. She smiled to herself as she walked along the dusty road, well aware of what was to come.

His body was ready as he opened the door. He stood there totally naked and silently led her into the room. The window shutters were wide open and a gentle breeze swept through.

Neither spoke as he slowly undressed her, kissing each part of her body as it was revealed, her simple cotton dress and underwear soon a pile on the floor.

He carried her to the bed and buried his face in her soft warm breasts. They were so wonderful to touch and so delicious to taste. He licked her large dark nipples that were already erect, letting his hands gently massage the large round surround. He licked her stomach and saw as she arched her body when he moved lower. He drank greedily as she writhed in passion. He could wait no longer. Roughly he plunged himself into her over and over. Using her muscles she gripped him tightly as he climaxed, not letting go until every drop of his juice had gone.

"God almighty." He gasped. "Where did you learn that? It was fantastic."

"It is natural." She sighed rolling him over and pinning him to the bed, his arms stretched wide. "Don't move an inch."

She took his shirt from the back of a chair and ripped the sleeves off, then used the tattered material to tie him to the headboard. "Now it is my turn." She purred as she left the room.

For a few moments she left him trussed and unable to move before returning with a bowl of ice cubes. Taking some in each hand she held them tightly, allowing the cold water to drip on his hot skin. He groaned. She placed a cube between her teeth and began to trace over his body, the warmth of her lips and the coldness of the ice as she moved aroused him like never before. Being unable to move was torture, fantastic torture. His body writhed and arched as she cupped his manhood in her now freezing hands before allowing her lips to part. She took him as deep as she could. Nicos the one time Casanova was enjoying the most amazing experience he had ever known.

He could hardly breathe, instead short useless gasps of air entered his lungs, he felt as if he were fainting with pleasure, his head began to spin, then blackness.

Slowly Giovanna untied Nicos and left him to sleep. Writing a note of the meeting time and place for later she left the room silently.

The piercing ring of his phone broke into his exhausted sleep.

"Hi babe." It was Sky. "How did the dive go?" She wanted to know all of the details, but Giovanna had turned his mind to mush and his ability to speak had almost deserted him. "You sound awful." Sky said as he stuttered on about the dive. "You had better stay a little longer. I don't want you flaking out on the plane. Stay for another day. Oh my poor boy." She was so concerned her tension passed to the children who both began to cry. "Sorry Jack I'm going to have to go. I will phone tomorrow. Bye."

"Thanks Sky. Sorry, but I think you are right I will stay another day. See you soon." He just about managed to blow kisses to her.

If only she had known, her concern would not have been about his health, but for her marriage, her sanity and her children.

CHAPTER 5

"Why do you bother with him Mum?" Storm said sharply. "Bastard!"

"Storm don't speak about your father like that!" Sky replied sternly. "He is your father whether you like it or not."

"Not." Came the harsh reply.

Storm marched out of the room in a huff, she would have slammed the door if there had been one, but the lounge and dinning room were open plan and connected by an arch way, it only added to her anger and frustration.

Why her mother bothered to phone Nicos every week was a mystery to her. She had listened on occasions and was surprised to hear how relaxed and civilized Sky was. She would have spat fury down the line if she ever spoke to him.

Sunni couldn't care less; he had never even met his father, so why should he bother about a man who could not even come to see his son?

Storm on the other hand remembered him well; she remembered being tossed into the air, having her tummy tickled, bath times with him were always wonderful. They would drench the room as they played in the warm soapy water.

And as for his fairy tales, well she could still remember listening to his lovely soothing voice even though she had been so young.

She had only been just over nine months old when the awful telephone call had been made and didn't really understand. Yet she could still remember the sight of her mother crying silently as she listened to him try to explain, it was an image that was etched in her mind.

Over the years Sky had done her best to reassure her that daddy still loved them, some love, she thought. Walk out on his children and wife just like that, yeah he loved them all right. Bastard.

Storm just wanted to ask him one thing. Why? Then she would chin him. She felt her fingers clench into a ball at the thought of Nicos and that other woman. There was a pretty good chance that if she ever met the two of them she would chin the woman as well. What the hell had she done to him to make him leave everything just like that?

Her mobile sprang to life.

"Hi Matt." She listened for a while. "Yeah that would be brill. When?" Silence again, just her feet tapping on the marble floor. "Great see you later then." She blew a kiss. "Byeeee."

She waited until she heard her mother replace the receiver and went back into the lounge.

"Well?"

"He is OK thanks." Sky said sadly knowing her daughter would not ask politely about her father's welfare. "Sends his love." Her voice was quivering and Storm knew at any minute her mother would be crying.

"Matt has just called." She said quickly changing the subject. "He wants me for an ad. He is picking us up tonight and we are off to London. Great eh?" She tried to sound excited but the sad face of her mother upset her greatly. "Oh Mum. Why don't you just let it go? You are still young, and very good-looking. I'm sure you could find another man."

"And I'm a cripple. You forgot that bit." Sky replied sharply. "And as for young I think not, fifty is not too far away and anyway I don't want another man. Your father is the only man for me, always has been and always will be." She wiped her tear filled eyes. "How long will you be away this time then?"

"Only a couple of days. Matt wants to shoot and then come home. He hates the cold weather they get as much as I do. Better go and pack. Where's Sunni?"

"Gone to the gallery with Alexi. He said he would be back for dinner though, why don't you call him?"

Storm just nodded, her mind already sorting out which clothes she would need for the trip. Her make up had a case of its own, but her clothes needed some thought. Although it was only early spring the temperature on Skiathos was already in the mid twenties, but London would probably only reach low teens at a push. I'll freeze, she thought, shivering unconsciously.

Up in her room she packed a good mixture, then went through and added some more. Knowing her luck the English would have a heat wave if she only took warm clothes. Mind you she could always buy some more, well Sunni could.

The shops in London certainly made up for the awful weather, and the music scene was the best in the world. All of a sudden she felt excited. London here I come!

Storm now nineteen was a much sort after top model. At six feet tall, slim and bronzed, with short spiky dark hair, she had the body that would look good in a sack. She walked with grace, strangely almost manly, and could turn on the most amazing looks from her flashing eyes; it was as if she was looking directly at you from the page. Men loved it, they found it sexy and threatening and talked about the things they would do to her given the chance. But, given that chance anyone who met her turned to jelly. She had this frightening air of superiority and an invisible wall that allowed very few through.

Despite her height and beauty Storm's best asset was her feet. Toes long and shapely, nails expertly manicured, with skin so soft, they were truly amazing. They were her fortune and she looked after them well.

Her career had begun when she had modeled some shoes for Sky. Her mother's business of designing glamorous footwear for the disabled had taken off in a big way and orders came flooding in. Most of the time she modeled them herself, but as the business grew and the demand for children's nice shoes rocketed Storm was enlisted to help.

Sky had her own web site on the Internet and with Alexi's help advertised her wares around the world.

Storm was a natural. She loved to dance around in front of the camera and show off, but she could also take things seriously. Alexi saw the potential and got in touch with a friend who he knew had the right contacts.

Matthew Morgan, an English man now living in Athens, realized the minute he saw the stunning child that she was a winner and began to turn her into what the media called a " child supermodel."

Her face lit the covers of many magazines and her feet were in just about every catalogue on the market. She met pop stars, other top models and all the best couture houses were queuing up to sign her for their labels.

Sky and Paris decided that she should stay freelance, that way she could model for anyone at any time, but only if she wanted to. At first they traveled with her but as the years passed only Sunni accompanied Storm.

Sunni had appointed himself manager to his sister and insisted on traveling with her wherever she went. He advised her on her clothes; make up, which assignments to take, and which to turn down, finally where she should go and who with. He not only had exquisite taste but also could hold his own amongst the much older men who wanted to poach Storm for themselves.

No one would mess with his sister whilst he was around.

Sunni had also inherited the Mandros magic with the camera.

His photographs were the ones advertisers used. Being totally relaxed with her brother behind the lens Storm's talent shone through. The brother, sister, partnership was born, and with Matthew as their agent, the sky was the limit.

At one stage Nicos had phoned and offered to advise them, but Sunni had in no terms told him where to go. The telephone conversation they had was like two strangers arguing, as in fact it was. Nicos had never returned, even to see him once and deep down Sunni felt desperately hurt.

Not only had his so called father upset his beloved mother and sister, but also had rejected him from the day he was born.

This woman had a lot to answer for, this Giovanna monster.

"Hi bro." Storm had decided to phone Sunni at the gallery. "Matt has just called, Wants us in London tomorrow." She waited for his reply. "Yeah that's right. He's coming here tonight to pick us up." Another break as she listened. "Yes I have packed a mixture, yes some nice things." She laughed as she spoke.

Her brother would go through her luggage anyway so why he asked she didn't know. Not one item would go with them if he did not approve. On some assignments she had taken an empty case, Sunni insisting that nothing she owned was appropriate. Instead upon their arrival he would scour the shops for the things she needed and her once empty case would return full of fantastic clothes.

His reputation for spending huge amounts made him very welcome by the designer labels. If he bought something and Storm wore it, you could guarantee it would be in demand. Sunni latched on to their enthusiasm and now insisted the goods should be free. In fact most of the things she had now were freebies.

Now instead of waiting for Sunni to come to them the likes of Versace, Gucci, Dior, and D&G sent Storm their latest fashions without charge. It was to them a cheap and successful way to advertise, but much to their annoyance she would only ever wear shoes designed by Sky.

Hardly a day went past without a parcel containing a fabulous outfit being delivered, with an invitation to a swanky do also inside.

Sunni chose which of these she should attend, which would give his sister most publicity, the ones where he knew the "in crowd" would be, and never once did he let her go alone.

He always picked the best "do's" and his own reputation as a superb manager grew. He was very successful and daily showered with post containing photographs of budding young models desperate for him to manage them, but Storm was the only one he wanted to be with.

His secretary replied for him with thanks, but rejection.

Sky was so proud of her offspring but sad that their father was not with them to enjoy their success. She thought of him often, and wondered where she had gone wrong. For many months she had blamed her twisted leg, her parents had deserted her and now her husband, and in a deep depression took a kitchen knife to her own flesh. Paris arrived just in time to stop any further mutilation, and insisted upon staying at the villa until she was certain Sky was safe to leave.

Athena and Alexi called every day and between the three of them helped Sky over the darkest days of her life. A nanny was brought in for the distraught children, and over the week's life settled down slightly.

As before Andros wanted to kill him. His list of reasons for hating Nicos seemed to grow regularly. Firstly he had taken his sister's virginity, he then seduced Paris, now he had left Sky broken hearted.

There was a time when their childhood arguments had been put to one side as Andros enlisted Nicos's help to win back Paris. It was strange that the man who had caused the split, was the very one to reunite them. He knew his sister Eleni held no grudges, always insisting Nicos had helped her grow up, but he would gladly rip his head off for the other two. Anytime, the sooner the better, Nicos had been a thorn in his side for long enough.

Alexi had been so angry with his son he went over to Kalymnos in an effort to make Nicos return, but the meeting of father and son had not gone well. Alexi was full of anger after his flight and boat ride, punching his son to the floor the moment they met. They argued and cried as Alexi pleaded for Sky and her children, then used threats of a change in his Will, but Nicos would not budge. He loved Giovanna; he also loved the island, and would never return.

Alexi travelled home alone, a tired old man, now determined that any energy left would be channeled towards his grandchildren. They were his reason for living, his own son a thing of the past, someone he no longer recognised in his life.

Athena felt torn and miserable, her son, how could he, but then she always knew he was easily tempted. He always had been and always would be. One day she knew he would leave this woman who had shattered his family for a new model, younger, perhaps prettier, something would make him stray, and then Giovanna would feel just as broken as Sky. She felt a little sorry for the woman, knowing with certainty what was in store for her. Nothing could ever make her hate her son but at times like this she felt as if she had given birth to a monster and blamed herself for indulging him as a child.

Nicos had however been generous to his deserted family. The villa on the hill had been signed over to Sky, solely in her name. He placed a million euro in each of his children's bank accounts, and regularly sent Sky a substantial allowance cheque for their upkeep. She called it his guilt money and never touched one cent.

Her family used the money from her own business to live; his money went straight to the children, their million euro growing rapidly. She wanted nothing from him but his love and prayed nightly that one day he would return.

"Hi aunty Paris it's Storm. How's things?"

"Fine thanks. What's the matter or should I ask what are you after?" Paris replied cautiously, Storm usually phoned when she needed a favour. Once again she was right.

"Well Sunni and I are going to London for a few days. A photo shoot jobbie. I just wondered if we could borrow your house for a while?"

"Of course you can. Why didn't you ask your mother, its her house as well."

After Paris and Sky's parents had left them at the ages of 21 and 17, their house in London became the property of the sisters. Paris ever hopeful that their parents would return had never wanted to sell, but Sky hurt by their desertion had other ideas. Let them come back to nothing, she had once said, that's if they come back at all. The house had stayed and was now used regularly by Storm and Sunni. Many of their assignments were in London and it was proving to be a great asset. Both of them hated hotels they liked to feel at home even though they were in a different country, this place was perfect.

Photographs of their mother and aunt decorated the lounge. Some of their clothes still hung in wardrobes, and their bedrooms had stayed exactly as they were the day they had decided to live on Skiathos.

Paris had returned regularly during the years, but Sky had never come back.

Richard and aunt Eleni had even used it when they attended a Royal Banquet some years before. Rumor had it that an informal meeting between The British Prime Minister and The President of The United States had taken place in the lounge the following day, but Richard would never confirm this.

Paris's mind drifted for a moment. Richard, how many times had she talked to him, and yet still not found out all of his secrets. She remembered him tapping his nose and saying For Queen and Country, when her questions got a little too close to the mark. Now he was dead and she would never find out the real truth. Bits and bobs had immerged during the time she had written her book about his life, but not everything and it had annoyed her immensely.

She felt a little sad thinking of him now gone, and aunt Eleni, Tomas and Sofia. How Alexi and Athena kept going was a mystery, both well into their nineties and still going to the Gallery on a regular basis.

Storm interrupted her thoughts.

"You know why I haven't asked her. She only gets upset and anyway she's upset enough today. She's been talking to him again." Paris knew only too well who" he" was and sometimes despaired of her sister. She shared the same view as Storm. He was a bastard!

"Well its OK by me. I'll phone the housekeeper and warn her. No all night parties my girl."

Storm giggled.

"Who me?" She replied childishly. "Never."

The last time Sunni and Storm had stayed half of London's in crowd had descended on the house and Paris had received a flood of complaints from the neighbours after a party that had lasted two whole days.

"Just one more thing aunty." She continued to use her weak voice. "Can you keep an eye on mum for us please?"

"You know I will. When do you go?"

"Tonight." Came the excited reply.

"Well I'd better get my things and come over. Let me phone Andros to let him know where I will be if he wants me for anything and then I'll be round."

"Thanks aunty you're the best." Storm blew countless kisses into her phone.

"Only when you want something. Now go away and let me get sorted. See you in a short while you monkey."

Paris was almost as close to Storm as Sky was. She was the one the little girl had turned to when her mother fell ill with depression. She couldn't understand why her loving mummy had suddenly turned into this strange being. Hobbling around their home as if in a daze, not bathing, not eating, and hardly ever speaking just mumbling, her leg a mass of cuts. Storm was frightened for herself and her brother, their father was missing, their mother looked like a robot, Paris had pulled them through and she loved her for it.

Even during school Storm had consulted her aunt, and once the modeling jobs had begun to arrive, it was Paris the girl turned to for guidance.

Her sex education had also come from Paris and they often spoke as two adults when discussing contraception and men.

Paris treated Storm as an equal and for that she was rewarded with a truly devoted niece.

The terrace outside The Eagle's Nest was tonight full. Sky had decided earlier that the air was warm enough for them to eat in the open. Matthew had arrived, and so with Storm, Sunni, Paris, Alexi, Athena and herself the evening air was filled with talk and laughter. It made a nice change and gave her a much-needed lift.

She watched her children as they ate, knowing she would miss them dreadfully during the next few days, but would never admit to them how lonely she would feel. Their lives were for living, not like hers, still on hold.

"Right then you two time to go. It's over to Athens then straight through to London. We should be there about 2ish if everything is on time." Matthew kissed Sky on both cheeks. "I will call when we get there, I know these two will be out clubbing as soon as they can, but don't worry I'll look after them."

This time Paris had insisted Matthew stayed at the house with them. She wanted no repeat of the party, for her sake as much as the neighbours. It had taken an unwelcome winter visit and lots of flowers to pacify them before, plus numerous bottles of whiskey with very expensive labels.

Not that Paris was short of money, married to one of the richest men in the world and successful herself, she had more than enough, but still, she didn't like to throw it away.

In fact after the party she had stopped the secret monthly allowance she gave Storm and Sunni, only for one time though, and that had made her feel so guilty she had doubled the next months contribution to their "nightlife fund" as they called it.

"Right then brov. Let's hit London." Storm kissed everyone around the table and went to collect her cases.

As expected Sunni had thrown out many of her things only to replace them with what he considered more suitable. Next time he can do it himself from scratch she thought.

They left in Matthews's car waving wildly until the road curved and their view of the villa became obstructed.

First stop Skiathos airport and a short flight to the main land.

The change over in Athens went smoothly and before long the trio were in the air bound for London.

Sunni settled Storm in her luxury first class seat. A cold eye shield was put on her face, and a blanket wrapped around her, a pillow under her head. The chair was tilted back to almost flat and her bare feet doused in thick cream. Next he turned out her light and asked the stewardess not to disturb them until half an hour from landing, and then he would appreciate it if she brought two large bottles of cold still water. He gave his orders and thanked her, smiling sincerely as he spoke. Manners cost nothing he thought, and always brought the best in people. He knew from her reaction that she would do exactly as he had asked.

At last he settled back in his own seat.

Soon be in London again he thought. How he loved it, especially when Storm was with him. She attracted people like bees around a sunflower, he smiled to himself, let the partying begin. Great!

• CHAPTER 6 •

Just as Matthew had predicted Storm and Sunni dropped their cases in a heap, changed quickly, then headed for the nightclubs. To him it was well past bedtime, but they saw things differently, in their eyes the night was still young.

3am and London was just coming to life.

He shouted a reminder of the photo shoot at 11 next day as they ran towards the waiting taxi. He waved farewell and said a quick prayer that Sunni would be sensible enough to limit Storm's alcohol intake.

No point in coming all this way for an assignment if she turned up looking bedraggled and hungover. Not that she ever did. At nineteen, the time of recovery she needed from a night out was very little. Matthew envied her stamina. It seemed to take him days to get over a good night out now, instead of the hours of his own youth.

He lay in bed unable to sleep, wondering where they were but he had no doubt that he would be reading about it soon enough.

Usually as soon as the glamorous pair entered a club the journalists would pounce and stories would be told of all manner of outrageous doings. Most of them they laughed off, but sometimes they hurt. He could always tell when a newspaper article touched a sensitive spot, usually when their father was mentioned, Storm would be quiet for days.

At last he heard the front door shut and listened as they stumbled and giggled their way up the stairs. The names of famous people were mentioned as they discussed their night, Kate, Jordan, Robbie, even Wills and Harry along with a host of high profile footballers. It must have been a good do. At least now he could sleep after all it was nearly 7am and his alarm was set for 9.

Matthew sighed as he realised this trip was going to do him no good at all.

Breakfast was a quiet affair. Paris had notified her housekeeper of their stay and the lovely lady had prepared a full English breakfast for them all. Storm just looked at hers and picked about with her fork. Sunni tucked in as if he hadn't seen food for months, Matthew stuck to the toast.

He may have been born in Kent but he had never been a big fan of English food, give him the fresh Mediterranean diet any day, but one thing he did enjoy was a good roast dinner. Beef was undoubtedly his favourite. Lots of dark crispy roast potatoes, light fluffy Yorkshire puddings and thick tasty gravy. His mouth watered at the thought and in his mind he could almost smell the meat cooking.

Get this shoot over in time and he would treat himself in one of the pubs close by. The hotels he had stayed in over the years had all tried to produce a roast lunch, but he found the best ones were always in old pubs.

A roast with a pint or two of best bitter, nothing better.

At least this morning the marmalade was tangy and bitty waking up his tired taste buds a treat. Licking his lips he noticed Sunni finish Storm's almost untouched meal, she was now downing strong black coffee with that much sugar in he could smell the sweetness from across the table. It must have been a real good night!

"She met a chap last night." Sunni broke the silence. "Sis is in love." He teased.

"No I am not. We just had a nice talk and a few dances that's all." She punched her brother's arm.

"Allesandro Fagioli. Sounds a bit flowery for me, what is he a Spanish footballer?" Sunni spoke through a mouthful of toast.

"No actually he is a photographer and Italian by the way. He asked if he could pop along this morning if it's OK. I said it would be." She replied calmly, knowing very well they would not be very happy

"You said what?" Matthew was angry, his mind whirred. No one came to shoots just like that. He could be anyone. Perhaps hired by one of the designer houses to tempt Storm away from him. "I don't think so Storm."

"Look he is desperate for a break. He said one photo of me would be all he needed to be taken seriously so I said OK. Right." Her eyes flashed at Matthew. "It's my body OK."

Sunni could be right Matthew thought, he had never seen Storm quite like this before perhaps it was love. He watched as she flounced out of the room. Sunni hardly noticed as he buttered another round of now cold toast.

"Oh I like it like this. Burnt and cold. Wonderful." His teeth ripped a huge chunk from the slice and his tongue licked at the butter on his lips. "Umm."

"What is this chap like then? Come on spill the beans." Matthew was concerned and surprised that Sunni was not more interested.

"Well he spoke to her at the bar first, then I noticed them dancing and after that they were sitting talking. I joined them for a while and he seems OK, but I felt like a gooseberry so I left them to it. I know I should have been keeping an eye on her, but I found a nice young lady myself. These things happen you know." He could see a surprised look on Matthews face. "But at least I didn't invite her along like madam and her Italian stud." He laughed. "Stop worrying, we will be back home this time tomorrow and she will have forgotten all about him."

Allesandro was impressed, not only was she fun to talk to but even more beautiful in the flesh than her photographs gave her credit for. Now as he stood outside of the Knightsbridge house he felt a little nervous, out of his depth. She had told him she was staying at her aunt's house and wrote the address down, but the way she had talked led him to believe that it was just any old house, not this lovely Victorian building that stood before him.

He took a deep breath and walked up the short pathway that led to some steps, and then to the door. This door stood between him and success. If today went well his name would be noticed, if not then he would be back taking holiday brochure shots and postcard pictures.

It had to go well with Storm too.

Unconsciously he crossed himself before pressing the doorbell, even that was impressive, a round brass plate with a little white stone center, but he had preferred to use that than the huge brass lions head knocker that seemingly glared at him from the centre of the shiny green door.

He swallowed hard as Sunni opened the door after what seemed like hours.

"Hi Allesandro. Come in we're just finishing breakfast. Storm has gone to get ready." Sunni ushered the terrified young man into the kitchen. "This is Matthew her agent. He has said you can come along. One photo only though OK."

Matthew frowned, he had said nothing of the kind but knew now he was well and truly beaten. What with Storm's invitation and now Sunni, he stood no chance in banning this Allesandro whatsis name. He shook the young man's outstretched hand.

"Sunni is right. One photo only OK." Matthew said menacingly Allesandro nodded still looking and feeling terrified.

"It is so good of you to let me come along." He said in faltering English. "I know it is not what they call the right thing to do but I took my chance. It may be the only chance I get. Thank you. Grazi." He almost bowed to Matthew who was beginning to feel like a very old man as he looked at the handsome youngster.

Allesandro was tall and slim, but with just the right amount of meat. Not huge bulging biceps, but nice tight skin over obvious muscles. His hair was longish, just past his shoulders, and sun-streaked blonde, he had the most amazing large almost black eyes edged with long thick lashes and a face that could have been chiseled from stone. His looks excited Matthew. Here was a find if ever I saw one, he thought. Not behind the camera but in front of it. He had an idea.

The shoot that morning was for a well-known jeweller in Bond Street. They wanted to launch a new range of gold and diamond pieces;

luckily they had decided Storm was the one to do it for them. It was all very hush hush and even she would not be told until the last minute what exactly she would be modeling. Matthew knew of course and the exorbitant fee he had negotiated made sure he was the only one to know. The shots were to be published in all of the top class magazines on the same day, shots of the whole range, pages and pages of Storm just wearing gold and diamonds.

And maybe, just maybe Allesandro in the pictures with her.

It would be sensational.

The four of them arrived at the studios just before 11 and were shown into a large dark room. Security guards came in and searched their bags and an angry Sunni demanded an explanation. Matthew told them why. Storm was going to be modeling millions of pounds worth of gems over the next couple of hours. It was hardly surprising that security was tight. Sunni nodded happy now with the reason.

"Why didn't you tell us before Matt?" Storm asked in a huff.

"They couldn't risk the place being raided. The stuff today is worth a fortune and they asked me to keep it quiet. You just wait and see."

Sunni and Allesandro began to set up the studio. Working well together Matthew noticed. They had been given a backdrop of black silk and strips of the same material to drape over Storm.

"This isn't going to cover much." Sunni said laughing as he held a thin piece of the silk up high.

"That's the idea. The jewellery is on show, not her body." Matthew replied.

"You mean I'm going to be naked." Storm butted in. Allesandro swallowed hard.

"Well nearly. You will have this." Sunni took great delight in holding another strip of silk in the air. "Just about your size." He giggled. "What do you say Allesandro."

The young Italian could hardly speak, just the thought of Storm with only that on her made him feel quite dizzy.

The banter was interrupted by the arrival of the jeweller and a group of heavy looking security guards. They dramatically marched across the room and placed a large black box on the table, it was still attached to the man's wrist by a thick metal chain and handcuff.

"This is it then." He said unlocking the cuff and handing Matthew a key. "You know what we want." Matthew nodded as he clipped the cuff to his own arm. "Are you sure I can't stay to observe?"

"No. Sorry. As I said when I accepted this job, no one but us in the room. I must protect my girl from prying eyes." Matthew could see the man was excited just thinking about Storm and felt disgusted. He didn't want to see his jewellery at all, just her, dirty old man, Matt thought.

Sunni waited until they had left.

"Right then Matt what exactly do they want?"

"Well," he began. "The jewellery must be shown at its best obviously."

He went on to explain how he thought Storm should pose. Sunni walked around the room nodding occasionally, a finger at his lips, deep in thought. The others watched in silence. Eventually he stopped moving.

"Come on sis. Lets make a start." He took Storm's hand and led her to the set. The strong light made her blink furiously.

Allesandro watched in awe as Sunni moved his sister from one pose to the next, thinking to himself that it was a good job she was still fully clothed. She just let him do what ever.

"Allesandro would you mind helping for a moment?" Sunni asked without looking at him. "Just grab that clip board and write a few things down for me."

"Si." Came the rather shaky reply.

"Write down number 1. Across the rug." Sunni had thrown a fluffy sheepskin rug across the floor and Storm was now lying on her back spread-eagled. "Number 2 from behind." Allesandro dare not look. "Number 3. Damn something is not quite right. Matt what's missing?"

Still Sunni didn't turn round. He was totally focused on Storm's body. Matthew did not reply, he knew Sunni would see what was missing, just as he could.

"Allesandro give that board to Matt and come here." He took the young man's arms and placed one across Storms breasts and the other down towards her crotch, spreading the shaking mans fingers to form a fan. "That's it. Brilliant."

62

Again he walked around the room. Looking at the two entwined bodies and thinking. "Storm turn your head and look away from him." She did as she was told. "Allesandro, can we call you Alex it's much easier." The young man nodded, they could call him anything, his brain was spinning out of control. "Look over her head towards me. The black eyes stared straight at Sunni. "Fantastic. Right then strip off and cover yourselves in this." He handed Storm a large jar of gold tinted body cream.

She began to take her clothes off and could see Alex begin to sweat; she noticed the bulge in his jeans.

"Come with me." She whispered to him and then spoke a little louder. "We are just going through to the shower room, make up and stuff. Back in a few mins." She led Alex through into a little shower room. "Can't have that on the photos." She said undoing his fly and caressing his now painfully throbbing manhood. "Just look at the size of that." She smiled, Alex was extremely well endowed. "Let's get rid shall we?" She kissed him hard and pulled herself up on to a table. She spread her legs and tugged at the surprised mans shirt." Oh God I've been waiting for that." She breathed as he thrust himself harder and faster. "Stop oh God stop." He had hit her g spot and would not slow down, as her body bucked in orgasm. "No don't its wonderful."

The table groaned and shook as their passion took over. Storm squealed as another ripple of ecstasy overcame her body. They kissed breathlessly and held each other close for a moment as their heartbeats slowed from racing to near normal.

Storm smiled up at him, her beautiful amber eyes glowing like flames, her face damp with perspiration.

"That is one dangerous weapon you have there." She said laughing. "One hell of a weapon."

Between them they managed to cover their bodies in the gold cream, not an easy thing when all they wanted to do was make love again. They put dramatic black lines around their shinning eyes, and a ruby red shimmer on their lips. Storm ruffled her hair, then reached up and did his.

"Right lets look at you." She smiled at his huge member beginning to rise again. "I think you had better wear these." She handed him a pair of skin coloured panties. "I usually use them myself but I think today you can." She laughed as he struggled to get all of himself into the small undies. "Don't split them."

Eventually they were ready.

"Ok bruv what's first?"

Matthew opened the black box and produced a thick yellow gold bracelet, a matching necklace and earrings, all decorated with a mass of inlaid diamonds that glistened as their many facets caught the light. Storm put them on.

"Right both lay on the rug, Alex go behind that's right. Now put your left arm over her breasts." Sunni draped a strip of silk over her lower stomach. "Look as if you are going to nibble her ear. Perfect."

Storm could feel Alex's warm breath in her ear and immediately felt turned on, it showed in her eyes.

Sunni stood behind the large camera. "Matt put the wind on please." Matthew turned on the machine and waited for Sunni to say stronger or not. "A little more." Matthew turned the dial slightly.

A gentle breeze rippled on the silk and Storm thought she would burst. Here she lay, naked, a superb specimen of a man at her back, his soft breath in her ear and silk fluttering over her stomach, and to cap it all she was draped in over a million pounds worth of gold and diamonds. She felt her body reach the height of ecstasy as Sunni's camera whizzed into action.

"Fantastic. Right number 2." Sunni issued his orders from behind the camera.

The two models worked well together, their bodies molding as one and giving off sexual vibes that transmitted to the film. Sunni was more than pleased.

Eventually Matthew picked up the last piece of jewellery. It was a huge diamond ring.

"How the hell are you going to do this one?" He asked twisting the massive ring in his fingers. "Any ideas?"

"You bet I have." Sunni replied. "Fetch that table from the bathroom will you." Storm giggled, Alex prayed the wet patch they had left was now gone. "Just there that's it." He pointed to the center of the set and stood thinking, his finger once again over his lips.

64

A sheet of black silk was draped over the table and Storm placed on top. "Knickers off Alex." Sunni ordered "Don't worry we will only see your back." Alex turned his back and rolled the tight underwear off, his penis immediately sprang to attention at being released. Storm giggled again.

"Keep looking at me," she ordered. "Don't turn round whatever you do."

"Storm open your legs and wrap them around Alex. Yes that's right, now look at me over his shoulder and put your hand on his bum." He twisted the ring to the front and moved a couple of lights. " Great. I tell you what sis your eyes don't half sparkle today."

Sunni was unaware that Alex had once again entered his sister and was flexing his penis muscles rhythmically. It was driving Storm insane.

Sunni took the best photograph of his career as his sister climaxed silently on the table.

"I think you can forget about being a photographer after this little session." Matthew said to the still joined pair. "It's modeling for you from now on Alex. Want a manager?"

"Yes please." Alex replied shakily, he was still flexing inside Storm. "But only if I can pose with this one."

She felt him explode once again.

"Sunni pass those gowns will you?" She pointed with a trembling hand to her case. "Yes both of them."

Luckily she always carried two of everything when on a shoot. Two lots of spare undies, two sets of makeup and thankfully two wrap over gowns.

She placed one over Alex's shoulders and wrapped herself in the other. "Time for a shower. Won't be long." She took Alex by the arm and led him back into the small room, his hands fought to keep his gown closed as they walked.

This time the shower was witness to their love making. Soft and slow as the water poured over they're heads.

Storm was in love for the first time in her life.

Allesandro was in trouble.

Big trouble.

• CHAPTER •

Allesandro was quiet as he watched Sunni work in his studio. Matthew had persuaded him to return with them to Skiathos, just in case any of the shots needed redoing. Matthew knew they wouldn't but he wanted to keep an eye on this new member of his stable, once the contract was signed he could relax, but for now he wanted Alex close by.

Storm had been over the moon to take her new lover back home and quickly installed him in the spare room next to hers.

Sky knew why, she was so much like her father at times; sex was their favourite pastime.

One by one the photographs shone from the computer screen and Sunni took time to inspect each of them. Zapping out a blemish here and there, highlighting Storm's skin in places and doing things to Alex's muscles that made him look as if he worked out regularly.

"You don't really need a model." He laughed as Sunni changed some more details, "You can do any thing with this."

He was right; the computer could indeed make a subject look completely different just with the touch of a button. Sunni smiled and went on with his work.

"There that's the last one done. Now we are ready to print."

Noticing how keen the young man was he had generously shown Alex each step he took to arrive at the perfect shot. The printer buzzed into action and the first of the photographs came into view. Alex watched as Sunni laid it flat in an old wooden frame and laughed as he gently blew hot air from a hairdryer over the damp sheet. He then held it up high and inspected it again.

"Do me a favour will you?" Sunni asked. "Just hold it like this and stand over there." He pointed to a space in the cluttered studio. Alex did as he had been asked.

"Perfect." Sunni said after a while. "Just right. Come on let's have a look at the rest."

What was left of the afternoon was now taken up blow drying shots and holding them up high for Sunni to inspect. Alex enjoyed every second of it. He had originally gone to London in the hope of taking photographs himself, just one of the right person at the right time, or wrong time, depending on who it was, would have put his career into gear. Instead he had landed this modeling job, and was now in the company of a true master.

Sunni Mandros had a reputation that far outstripped his fathers and grandfathers, and Alex intended to learn as much as possible but he also knew once these shots were published he was in deep trouble. Matthew would tear up his contract, that's if he had signed it by then, Sunni probably never speak to him again, and as for Storm; well he dare not think what she would do.

"Fancy a trip over to London?" Sunni said without glancing from his computer screen. "I think these are too good to let someone else take and in any case it will do you good to have a break from my sister." He laughed.

Storm had almost worn Alex out with her constant demands for sex. Not just ordinary wham bam, but full blown Olympics. Sunni could hear them from his room and felt a little sorry for his new friend. His sister was certainly something else.

"That would be great, but," Alex started to speak, Sunni interrupted him.

"Don't worry it's on the house as they say. Tickets etc out of the business and as for spends, well I'll draw you an allowance. It's about time Matthew got that contract in order then we can start to pay you properly. Come on let's go tell the others."

Alex felt gutted as he walked with Sunni back to the villa. These people had welcomed them into their home; their lives and now they were giving him money. This was here he wanted to be, not the place he had left, he had no wish to return ever.

"Oh Sunni why can't I come too?" Storm made her lips quiver childishly. "It's not fair."

"Stop being a baby. Like I said we are taking the photographs, having a look round then coming home. We will only be a couple of days so stop nagging. You can do without him for a couple of nights can't you?" She shook her head and turned on a sad face. "Grow up sis." Sunni patted her bottom, knowing it was something she hated. Within seconds they were wrestling on the floor just as they did when children.

"Stop that this minute!" Sky said sharply. "Will you both grow up."

They lay on the lounge floor laughing, friends again. Storm bent over and tickled his ribs.

"You minx." He giggled. "Always have to have the last word, well just watch this." With one swift movement Sunni had tipped Storm over his shoulder in a fireman's lift. "Right it's the fountain for you."

"No. Mum save me!" Storm yelled as Sunni stomped out on the to terrace where, slightly to one side, a large white marble fountain shot water towards the clear blue sky. On a sunny day like today, a rainbow could just been seen in the falling spray.

"Sunni put her down please." Sky was in no position to chase after them but did her best hobbling along at as fast as she could. "Disturb my fish and I'll thrash the both of you."

Years ago when the fountain had been built Sky had insisted that the base be large and deep allowing her to keep pretty fish that flashed bright colours as they darted amongst the water lilies and plants.

Sunni dangled his screaming sister over the edge of the fountain wall before turning and gently placing her on the floor.

"Quits?" He asked breathlessly.

"Quits." She replied grabbing a handful of water and throwing it at him.

"Right now you're for it." He chased her back into the villa where once again the wrestling began.

"Anyone would think they were still kids." Sky sighed. "No one would believe me if I told them."

Alex laughed.

"I used to be like that with my brother, but that was years ago. I haven't seen him for a long time." He said a little sadly. "I would love to fight with him again."

"Well why not. Families should always keep in touch." Sky said gently patting his arm and gesturing for him to sit by her. "Do you write to him?" She poured two glasses of smooth red wine and handed him one.

"Grazi." He raised his glass to salute her. "Chin Chin. No I haven't, not for ages. You know what it's like. Time just goes and before long years have passed, but perhaps I will do one of these days." He sat silently for a moment. "What is left of my family live in Naples or are dotted around here in Greece. Yes you are right, I should keep in contact."

He smiled at Sky knowing full well that he would not write to any of them. They were poor fishing families living on the coast, either still in Italy or here in Greece, he wanted better than that and had no real wish to be in contact with any of them. He wanted to be at the top, not as a photographer, as was his first plan, but now his mind was set on modeling. How he had enjoyed that day, not only because of Storm, but the way he was treated, it made him feel like someone, someone special.

He sat back and sighed, sipping his wine he remembered the fabulous time they had enjoyed.

Matthew had included in his price for the shoot, meals at The Ivy, where anyone who is anyone ate, nightclub entries and even tickets for concerts. Clothes arrived at the house by the box full and invitations galore to cocktail parties. What a shame they were only going to be in

69

London such a short while, Alex wanted to go to them all. Sunni had sorted through the invitations and discarded most, and much to Alex's amazement, accepted just a couple.

"These will do." He had said waving thick gold edged cards in the air. "We must get you the right gear Alex. Pass me that tape measure Storm. Ta." Sunni expertly measured Alex then picked up his mobile, and after a few minutes of chat and laughter switched it off with a flourish. "Armani do you?"

Alex was astounded when less than an hour later the most wonderful assortment of Armani clothes arrived; the boxes all had his own name on.

"Mouth shut Alex or you will be swallowing flies." Storm teased. "Let me have a look?" She went through the fabulous clothes as if she were at a jumble sale. Holding items high for inspection and eventually choosing for him.

That night Alex wore a dark Armani suit and a sensuous deep pink silk shirt with matching tie. He had Storm on his arm in a black Dior cocktail dress and for the first time in his life ate at The Ivy.

This was definitely the life he wanted.

The meal was surprisingly good, he had expected tiny bits of this and that, but no it had all been delicious and plenty of it too.

He did however, find it hard not to stare at the numerous celebrities that came through the door, and when the Beckhams strolled in he almost spluttered.

"Better get used to it Alex. Once those shots are printed you're face is going to be known all over the world." Storm said softly.

"Well his bum will be." Sunni laughed.

"I don't care what part of me they all see." Alex replied laughing with them. "As long as I can live like this forever."

"Well stick with me and you will." Matthew joined the conversation. "Come back with us, that's if you can, and I'll get a contract sorted as soon as possible. Then let's see the jobs arrive."

He was certain he had come across the best male model to hit the scene for years and had no wish to share him with anyone else.

After the meal came visits to nightclubs and wine bars, the names of which Alex had read about but never dreamed he would see the insides of.

It was definitely a night to remember.

A taxi arrived first thing the following morning containing a very excited Allesandro and his belongings in one tatty case.

"Is that it?" Storm asked looking at the disgusting luggage. "All your life in that?" He nodded, she laughed. "Come on join us for breakfast and then it's off home."

She took his arm, led him through to the kitchen and his new life began.

Allesandro shook his head in disbelief. It all seemed so long ago, yet it had only been a couple of days, now here he was in this fantastic villa high up in the hills. He could see the beautiful beaches shining white, and the sun glistening on the sea below. He was sharing a bottle of delicious wine with Sky Mandros, well known herself for her fabulous shoes; the famous Storm and Sunni were still fighting in the lounge.

"I feel I should pinch myself, I can't believe this is really happening to me." He said softly to Sky.

She was such a lovely woman, so understanding, so kind, yet another who he knew would be hurt badly. It made him feel very sad. Why did life have to be so complicated? He would enjoy the next couple of weeks and then go quietly, it was the only thing to do, and he knew it.

It made a nice change for Sunni to have someone to talk to on the flight to London. Usually he was with Storm and Matthew, she would be resting and Matt reading a book, but this flight was different. Alex talked to him about Naples and Sunni decided that he would use parts of Pompeii in his next shoot. Athens was his favourite city backdrop, then Paris, but why not try Naples, he thought.

Sunni talked about his life on Skiathos and his family, Alex could tell he loved his grandfather very much. Whenever Sunni spoke of him his eyes softened and his lips smiled.

The two young men enjoyed a couple of drinks, something Sunni had told Storm she should never do. " It will dehydrate your skin," he had said. "You must only have water." And with him being in charge that is all she ever got.

The in flight meal was not too bad either; in fact the whole journey was quite pleasant.

"We will be staying at aunty Paris's again." Sunni told Alex. "Hope you don't mind?"

"I think it is a lovely place." He replied not minding one bit to be sleeping in such a fabulous house.

"And we have a table at The Cipriani tonight and then on to Stringy's." Sunni added.

Alex could hardly believe his ears; a table there was like gold dust. The waiting time was months not hours or days, and as for Stringfellows well how many times had he dreamt of walking in there, he had got to stick with these people no matter what.

The jeweller had sent a Silver Shadow Rolls Royce to pick them up at Heathrow, and Alex felt as if the dream was getting to be a little overpowering.

"He wants to see them first." Sunni said pointing to his briefcase on the floor. "Wants to have an ogle at Storm, dirty old man." Alex felt a pang of disgust. "I could see that day he wanted to get a glance of her naked." Sunni continued. "So could Matt that's why we threw him out. Ugh. I can't stand creeps like that."

The jeweller silently confirmed Sunni's words, taking a long time to view each shot, letting his fingers wander over Storms image and licking his lips.

"You must take the lovely lady something nice." He said turning to Sunni, Alex spotted the film of perspiration on his brow. "Let me find something very special. What is her ring size?"

"L" Sunni quickly replied, he could not wait to get away from this horrible man. He would pick the most expensive ring he could find he decided as he watched the photographs of his sister being manhandled once again.

The man switched on his intercom and asked for a tray of rings to be brought into the office and Sunni had a good look through. He pointed

72

out a large gold ring with diamonds set in the shape of a flower. Alex nodded. It was a stunning piece. Sunni knew Storm would probably never wear it but it served the old man right for being such a letch.

"You have good taste my friend, that is an exquisite ring. Please have it ready for my guests when they leave." He instructed his secretary.

"And we must leave you now Sir." Sunni said stiffly. "We have much to do this visit." He nodded to Alex."Got everything?"

"Sure have" Alex replied gathering the photographs from the desk. "Let's go."

Sunni collected the ring from the secretary and the two young men left the shop. Once outside they both let out a huge sigh of relief.

"What a horrible man." Alex stood shaking his head.

"Unfortunately all part of the job." Sunni replied. "God I need a cigarette." He patted his empty pockets. "I'll just pop over there and get some then we had better take these sharpish over to the publishers. Normally I wouldn't bother bringing the photos myself, but I get the feeling these are very special, and anyway I have enjoyed it." Alex smiled as Sunni went towards a kiosk.

It all happened so quickly. One second Sunni was paying for his cigarettes, the next he was being pushed over and his wallet taken from his hand. Alex ran to his side as a young woman grappled the mugger to the floor. Sunni brushed himself down and went over.

"Call the police," the woman said breathlessly. "I'll be your witness I saw everything." She was struggling to hold on to the scruffy kid on the floor.

"Let him go." Sunni said gently. "I can't do that to him and anyway I've got my wallet back."

"You mean I've got your wallet back for you." She replied angrily. "All this for nothing." Her stockings were laddered, her coat covered in dust. "And no sign of a thank you." She said standing up and shaking her self like a cat.

"Thank you very much. Please let me make amends." Sunni was immediately smitten. This tiny woman who had wrestled the kid to the floor was so pretty. Not beautiful, not stunning, just pretty.

Her hair was a wonderful rich brunette, cut into a shoulder length bob, she had large pale green eyes and a generous bow shaped mouth. He could see she was not skinny, but nicely rounded, such a lovely change from the string bean shape of many of today's women.

He took a note from his wallet and handed it to the shocked kid still on the floor.

"Think yourself very lucky pal. Next time just ask nicely." He said waving the precious money in his face. "Get some food with this. OK."

"OK," the lad replied. "Thanks mister." He mumbled before running off.

"Now young lady let me thank you properly. Sunni Mandros at your service." He bowed slightly and smiled at her not really knowing what to say next. Alex spoke for him.

"Let Sunni here take you out to lunch, that is after he has bought you a new coat and stockings. If I were you I would make him buy you a new dress and shoes whilst you are at it. In fact I would make him buy you a whole new wardrobe full of things." All three of them began to laugh.

"Steady on Alex. You will have me buying everyone in the street something next." Sunni turned to the woman and bowed slightly again, taking her hand he brought it gently to his lips. "As I said, Sunni Mandros at your service. Thank you for your help, and where would you like to start. Shopping or eating."

"Shopping." She replied shyly, not really sure if he meant it or not. If he did then it would probably take longer than her hour's lunch break, but who cares, she thought. The one and only Sunni Mandros was taking her for some retail therapy, it was a once in a lifetime treat. If she lost her job, well tough, she could always get another one.

Sunni raised his arm for a taxi; it took quite a few attempts before one actually stopped.

"I hope you don't mind but I've just got to drop these off and then the afternoon is all yours. Sorry I didn't catch you're name."

"That's because I didn't give it." She smiled at him. "It's Emily, Emily Hulme." He just grinned back at her, what a lovely name, so feminine, just like its owner.

True to his word once the photographs had been taken to the publishers and Alex dropped off at the house, Sunni was all hers. He took her to the most fabulous shops, Gucci, Versace, Louis Vitton, she could hardly believe it, and the way he was greeted in each absolutely amazed her. Anything and everything she looked at for more than a split second was bought or just handed over as a freebie.

"You must stop this." She laughed. "Or I won't look at anything else, and in any case how on earth am I going to get this lot home?"

"Ok." He replied, but continued to carry on as before, her pile of bags growing rapidly, anything that required a box was being delivered directly to her home.

As they walked arm in arm along Kensington High Street gazing into the shop windows Emily stopped and turned towards him, resting the numerous bags on the floor for a moment.

"Did you mention lunch or am I being greedy?" She asked softly. "But I'm starving after all of that and I really don't want this dream of a day to end."

"Lunch it is." He said feeling the pangs not of hunger but of something strange "Where would you like to dine?"

"You choose." She replied picking up as many bags as she could. "This has been fantastic thank you. Something I shall remember for the rest of my days. It's the sort of thing girls like me dream of. Shopping without a care in the world what it cost."

"Emily are you married or anything?" He asked after a moment.

"No. Young free and single. I live with my parents, how's that for being old fashioned." She giggled nervously wondering if she was going to pay for her things in another way.

"Snap. I live with my mother and sister."

"Storm's your sister isn't she?" He nodded. "She is so drop dead gorgeous. So slim and beautiful."

"Not a patch on you Emily." He looked at her seriously. "If I ask your father would you like to come back to Skiathos with me. I know it is rather sudden but I really want to get to know you better. If he wants me to court you properly I will, I will do anything believe me." His eyes said everything.

"Then let's skip lunch and go straight home. He is on shifts this week and should be at home this afternoon." Emily could hardly believe she was acting so hastily but an offer like this didn't come along every day. "Come on let's go see what he says." She added with an excited giggle.

Sunni had no idea what shifts were, but felt so happy she had not turned him down flat.

Emily's parents were more than a little surprised to see a taxi stop outside of their neat little terraced house.

"I wonder who it could be," her mother said peering around the net curtains. "George it's Emily. She must be ill or something. Quick."

The red painted door flew open as Emily and Sunni struggled up the path with her bags.

"What's the matter? Are you ill love?" Her mother was quivering with fear.

"No Mum. I'm OK thanks. This is Sunni, just look at all of the things he has bought me."

George peered at the man who had treated his daughter to so much from over the top of his spectacles.

"And what did you do to deserve them?" He asked sharply, hoping that the reply would not be what was spinning around his mind.

Emily sat down and told the story of Sunni being mugged and how he had asked her to go to Skiathos for a holiday. Sunni looked at her quizzically, he had never mentioned a holiday, he wanted her there forever.

"Well I'm not sure. It's a bit quick." Her father was puzzled. He could see how happy his daughter looked, and liked this man who he knew from the newspapers to be very rich but not bloshie. He looked to his wife for guidance.

"Please Sir. I will look after her I promise. I will make her phone home every day and if she feels homesick or anything I will bring her back straight away. I live with my mother and sister, so there will be no funny business. Promise. If you and your wife would like to come too, just to make sure, then please say." Sunni was pleading and had his fingers crossed that they would refuse his last offer.

Emily held her breath, hoping exactly the same.

George made them wait a few moments in silence before giving his reply.

"You just make sure you do look after her my lad or you will have me to answer to."

"Oh Dad thanks." Emily flew across the room and hugged her father. "Thanks Mum." She knew it was her mothers doing; Emily had seen her nod slightly when her father was stuck for words. "Well I don't suppose there's any need to unpack this little lot." She looked at her bags now scattered on the old woollen carpet.

"Yes there is." Sunni said, "Don't forget I still owe you a meal. Pick you up at 8. Laghan's tonight."

Emily gulped.

"You don't really mean that surely?"

"I never say or do anything I don't mean." He replied. "Best dress and all that." He shook her fathers hand. "Thank you Sir. You have made me very happy."

It was only a day later when Sky greeted the rather dazed young woman like a long lost friend; it was great to have an English girl to talk to for a change.

"This is your room." She led Emily inside. It was similar to all the other rooms in the villa, very fresh, very spacious and had a fantastic window at the end. "Settle yourself in and come out to the terrace. You can get this way." She pushed a button on the remote control that sat on the bedside table. The huge window slid open silently. Emily just stood still, her mouth open wide. "It's this one to open it and this one to close." Sky showed her the buttons. "Oh and this one for the TV." She pushed a little red one and a huge plasma screen sprang to life. "Anything you want just say. Please don't be afraid to ask. You are very welcome here. Oh and your little bathroom is through here."

"And don't forget to phone your parents." Sunni shouted from the lounge.

Emily unpacked her things and explored the room. It was everything she had ever dreamt about, read about in the glossies, and unbelievably for now it was now her room. OK just for two weeks, that was all her father would agree to, but she knew deep down she would be back, and soon.

Sunni was such a lovely man, he may be rich and at the top of his profession, yet he seemed so normal. So nice and caring, quite ordinary in a way, homely and lovely, but having met his mother Emily could see why. She had certainly brought her children up well.

Having changed out of her traveling clothes into shorts and a top she nervously stepped out on to the terrace. Sky noticed her face peering from the window opening.

"Come and join us my dear. I bet you could do with a drink after that long flight."

It was only about four hours from England, but Sky realised for a girl like this that could well be a long flight. "It is so hot today, come and sit here in the shade." She patted the seat next to hers. Sunni stood as she neared the table.

"Everything OK Emily?" He asked. "If you need anything just say."

"I have already told her that Sunni. Emily we really do mean that." Sky said gently

"Thanks Mrs. Mandros but everything is fine."

"Please call me Sky, everyone else does."

It was hard at first for Emily to get used to calling her by her first name, but a couple of drinks gave her confidence and soon they were chatting like old friends.

"Did you ring your father?" Sunni asked as he refilled their glasses.

"Oh I forgot." She put her hand to her mouth. "Blast I'd better do it now before I have any more of that." She giggled slightly tipsy from the wine and her wonderful surroundings.

"Here use this." Sunni handed her his mobile.

They listened whilst Emily talked excitedly to her parents; she described her room and the terrace she was now sitting on. She told them all about the wonderful views, and finished with "love you lots."

"Sorry it was a bit long, I tend to get carried away sometimes." She felt embarrassed by how long she had been on the phone and dreaded how much it must have cost.

"Don't worry about that." Sunni laughed. "You haven't got to worry about the cost of anything whilst you are here. Believe me anything can be yours, your wish is my command."

78

Emily blushed not used to such a romantic thing being said in front of parents.

"In fact tomorrow we will go into town and have a scout round, just in case there's anything you have forgotten. We could pick up the magazines at the same time." The photographs would be in the latest fashion magazines and Sunni could hardly wait to see them.

"Tonight though we are all going to the beach to eat. Eleni would go mad if I didn't take you down. She loves a good natter." Sky said, reverting to her almost forgotten London accent. "It's a dress down place so trousers will do." She knew Emily would not have the first idea just how basic the taverna was.

Even though Marco and Tomas, the twins, now ran it they had left almost everything as old Tomas had built it. The floor still sand, the grapes falling though the bamboo roof, and the little table by the bar, used only for relatives, remained in its original place.

The customer's furniture had been updated though, and now fifteen tables with their new whicker chairs stood in the sand, the old swinging chair had long gone making way for the extra room needed.

The boys had turned Tomas's quiet taverna into THE place to be at night. Youngsters visiting the island flocked there in droves, and quite often music could still be heard as the sun rose over the sea.

What an evening it was, Emily felt like pinching herself as she looked around the table. There was Sunni at her side, Sky, Storm and Alex, Paris, Eleni and Vanni. Unfortunately Athena felt a little poorly and she and Alexi had stayed at home, they were so old now anything to do with their health seemed to scare them stiff.

Emily listened to them all chat and took a liking to Paris immediately. The woman, whom she had only known as the author of good books, was sitting there talking to her as if they had known each other for years. Emily laughed as Paris teased Storm about something, and then watched as she spoke seriously to Sunni. They were discussing the shoot and Sunni was telling his aunt all about the photographs.

"You will see them tomorrow anyway." He said.

"Tomorrow you say." Alex said coughing in shock.

"Yeah. The mags should be at the Gallery first thing in the morning." Sunni replied rubbing his hands. "Can't wait."

The meal was superb and the wine free flowing, sitting there in the warm night air Emily unconsciously let out a huge sigh.

"Are we boring you?" Sky said amused by the young girl.

"Oh no Sky. It's just that everything is so nice. I want tonight to last forever."

Alex thought the same but dare not say anything.

"Come on let's have a little walk." Sunni stood and held Emily's chair. "Won't be long." He called to the others.

He took Emily's hand and walked her slowly along the beach. The sun had long gone, but the lights from the taverna lit the way.

"Happy?" He asked after a while.

"You bet I am. Thanks for a lovely meal and everything. I've really enjoyed it. Wait till I tell my friends back home who I dined with tonight." She laughed.

"Well I did promise your Dad I would look after you and I will." He looked out over the sea. "You are so different Emily." He looked into her eyes. "I want to look after you."

Emily blushed and was pleased for the dim lights; she knew her nose always shone bright red whenever she got embarrassed. But this was not embarrassment; she was falling for this lovely man, and knew he felt the same. The blush had come from happiness.

They walked past Eleni's villa and right to the end of the soft sandy beach before turning to go back towards the taverna.

"Look up there." Sunni pointed to the top of the hill. "That's our home you can see." Her eyes followed his finger, and sure enough right up high she could see tiny lights twinkling. "Mum put those lights in the trees three Christmases ago and never got round to taking them down."

"Well I think they look fabulous and hope she leaves them there. It looks so pretty." Emily said softly. "Suppose we had better go back to the others."

"I am afraid so. I could walk with you for hours." Sunni was looking at her again. "But yes let's get back before I break my promise to your Dad and seduce you here in the sand."

Emily giggled, but thought how marvelous that would be. She didn't know if she would be able to stop herself from going to bed with Sunni, as she too had promised her father, it was like torture already. She looked towards the stars, Dad why did I say such a stupid thing?

"Come on," he pulled gently at her hand. "Let's go back."

"Here come the lovers." Storm teased as Sunni and Emily walked slowly in the sand. "I bet you move faster than that tomorrow." She added. "Once those mags arrive just you see him run." They all laughed.

Storm was so proud of her brother, not just because he was her brother, but he was the best in the business and yet still got excited like a little boy when his photographs were published. She knew he would not sleep tonight, his excitement keeping his brain active, and as for breakfast, no chance. He would sip a coffee in his hurry to get to the Gallery. Once he had seen them in print then he would relax, but only if they came up to his expectations, if not then he would be like a bear with a sore head for a week. She crossed her fingers and said a little prayer.

"Come on time to go home." She said to Alex. "It looks as if this place will be full soon."

Young holidaymakers were now beginning to arrive and the music had been turned up. Marco and Tomas were busy at the bar and just waved as the family group left.

"Stop fretting brov, you know they will be great." She could see a frown on his face and knew what he was thinking. She gently patted Sunni's back. "Come on, home with you." She linked his arm and walked with him to the cars, leaving the others to follow behind.

"He usually gets worse than this Emily. He can be very uptight. But you being here has helped him no end." Emily was flattered by Sky's words. "And you must be excited too." She said to Alex.

"Oh very." He replied a bit flatly.

Yes he was excited but also scared to death.

Tomorrow would be the end of his dreams.

81

• CHAPTER 8 •

Sunni picked Emily up and whirled her round and round laughing as he held her tightly, he had been unable to sleep with excitement and had brought her to the Gallery almost as soon as it was light, now he knew it had been worth every shred of his stress.

"Just look at those. Brilliant!" He shouted. "Look."

A pile of magazines were laid open on his desk, all showing different photographs of Storm and Alex. "That has got to be the best shot I have ever taken." He pointed to the one where Storm had the diamond ring on her hand, her eyes shinning brightly over Alex's shoulder looking straight into the camera. "I don't think I have ever seen her look so sexy."

Alex also looked superb as the light caught the contours of his body, a slight film of sweat glistening on his tanned skin.

Luckily Sunni had no idea why, only Storm and Alex knew exactly what was happening between them at the precise moment the shot had been taken.

Telephones began to ring wildly and Sunni tried to answer them in turn. Each conversation held congratulations and an offer of work, and all of them taking much longer than he really wanted.

Everyone wanted to talk, ask about his new model, who was he, how had he found him. Sunni tried to give little away; he knew Matt wanted Alex for himself. One wrong word and they could loose him to a higher bidder and that would be catastrophic. The amount of work he was bringing in would keep them busy for months, everyone wanted him, Levi's, Armani, Gucci, you name it they wanted this new, very sexy, man to model their goods.

Sunni hoped Storm would not be jealous, he wanted them to work together and the best results were always when the models were good friends. He knew they were lovers, but with Storm's past history that could end at any time, experience told him she soon got bored with a man, he said a quick prayer hoping for their relationship to last at least six months, then she could do what ever she wanted.

Soon Emily too was answering the phones. She wrote names and numbers down and promised Sunni would get back to them as soon as he could.

The feelings Sunni had for her grew deeper as they glanced at each other and smiled before yet again picking up a ringing phone.

The morning flew past as they worked comfortably together.

At one point Emily got up to make them coffee, Sunni reached for her hand as she passed, kissing it gently. He could not speak as he was taking a call but his eyes said everything, Emily loved the fact he had bothered to pause at all and smiled at him. He handed her a 10-euro note and pointed through the door towards a patisserie. She just nodded, understanding without a word being spoken.

Within minutes delicious warm honey pastries and a steaming mug of strong coffee were placed in front of him. He blew her a kiss and smiled watching as she battled with a crumbling pastry of her own. They both burst out laughing together as the honey ran down her chin and the pastry broke in half, crumbs and goo flying all over her cream silk top.

"What a mess." She cried trying to wipe the food from her chest only succeeding in leaving large marks where the honey had soaked into the fabric.

"Never mind. Pity I can't lick it off but a promise is a promise. Your Dad hasn't got the first idea of how tempting his daughter is, especially covered in honey." Sunni pulled a face making her laugh even more.

"I know the feeling," she answered letting him know just how much she thought of him. "Roll on next visit, then he can't say anything." She paused for a moment. "That's if you want me here?"

"You bet I do." He replied gently. "That would make me so happy, I mean that. Oh Emily these two weeks are going to be a nightmare."

"What he can't see can't hurt him." She sighed temptingly.

"No, I said no monkeying about and I meant it so stop tormenting a poor soul. I think the best thing would be for you to go home now, and then I won't be tempted at all." He tried to sound sad.

"No chance pal. I'm stopping here!"

"Thank goodness for that, I was only teasing anyway."

He knew it would be hard to resist her, especially now he knew she was willing, but he was a man of his word and the thought of facing her father knowing he had broken his promise was worse than not being able to treat Emily as he wanted to.

Emily's phone rang again.

"Sunni it's Matthew for you. He says it's very important." She handed him the phone and watched as his face showed various emotions, horror and shock amongst them.

"What." He shouted. "Storm will kill him." He put his hand to his forehead. "How the hell did they find out so quickly? Oh Shit. I think I'll kill him to save time, cut out the middleman." He paused and sighed. " Matt do you think we have been set up? Now what are we going to do? I've got all these jobs in the pipeline. Help!" Sunni listened some more. "Don't be silly Matt, she won't go for that. Ah well. I thought it was too good to be true." Another break while he listened to Matt speak, Emily was unable to keep still, what on earth had happened. She stood behind Sunni's chair and waited for the call to finish.

"Well what was that all about?" She asked massaging his taught shoulder muscles. It was obviously something bad they were like concrete.

"That's wonderful thanks." Sunni stretched his neck from side to side. "Wonderful."

84

"Well?"

"You're not going to believe this, in fact I don't think I can really." He sighed. "Matt says he has had a phone call this morning from an English tabloid. Evidently Allesandro Fagioli is the husband of Gina Farnidi." He said sarcastically, Emily shook her head and shrugged her shoulders, no she didn't understand. "Gina Farnidi is the daughter of Giovanna Farnidi and Nicos Mandros, my father." She held him as he cried. "That bastard has made love to my sister, the half sister of his own wife. God, Storm will rip him to pieces, mother will be so upset. Help me Emily I don't know what to do." She held him tightly in her arms and let him cry, rocking him back and forth, stroking his brow and kissing him gently.

"There's only one thing you can do Sunni, and that's to tell them before it hits the papers. Don't let them find out from gossips or anything. Let's go and ask Alex if it's true first, then we will go and tell Sky and Storm. That's if you want me to come or would you prefer to tell them alone?" Her voice was gentle.

"No I want you with me please. I need you to be there. You know that man who calls himself my father has never even laid eyes on me." He told Emily the story of Nicos and Giovanna. "Why mother speaks to him every week I have no idea. Storm gets really angry about it, I just feel so sad."

"It might help if you met him you know. Find out from him why he didn't come back."

"No chance! I would kill him on sight." He replied sharply.

"No I don't think you would, but for now let's go and see Alex." Her voice was soft and soothing.

They left the office, the ringing phones and the now cold coffee, got into Sunni's car and headed for the hills. Emily drove, she had just taken the keys from him and he had let her. He needed someone strong and she was proving to be just that.

He sat in the stationary car, now parked outside of his mother's villa and thought. What the hell was he going to say, this was going to break his mother's heart, sister's heart and greatly upset his beloved grandfather. What a bastard his father was. No one knew he had a second daughter, he had never said a single word to anyone.

Emily walked round to his side of the car and opened the door.

"I'm with you don't forget." She said gently. He looked at her and smiled.

"Thanks Emily. What would I do without you?"

"Allesandro." Sunni called as he entered the villa. "Allesandro I need to speak with you."

Sky appeared from the terrace.

"Sunni what ever is the matter?" She asked.

"Where is he mother? I need to see him urgently." Sunni was getting angrier by the second.

"For some unknown reason he has packed his bags and left. He thanked me and just went. I expect your sister has been up to her tricks again." Sky said in a motherly fashion.

"The bastard!"

"Sunni you know how I feel about swearing. Now come on through and sit down." Sky returned to her seat on the terrace. Sunni and Emily followed; he held her hand, playing with her fingers for comfort. "Come now sit down and tell me what has happened. What has she done this time?"

Sky was convinced her crazy daughter was at the bottom of the trouble.

"I don't know where to start really." Sunni's eyes filled with tears, this was going to hurt his mother so badly. "Alex is married according to Matthew." He began.

"Well nothing new about married men and young women." Sky said sarcastically.

Sunni took a deep breath, there was only one way to tell his mother the news, that was straight and to the point.

"Yes but mother his wife is Gina Farnidi. Giovanna and father's daughter." He stopped and watched his mothers face begin to contort, then crumble as tears flowed down her face. "I'll kill him mama honest I will."

Sky just about managed to control her voice.

"He never said one word about a daughter, not once in all of these years. All of my phone calls, not once." She paused. "Have you seen Storm yet?" Sunny shook his head. " Did she even bother to ask if he was

86

married, I don't care who to, but did she even ask?" They both knew the answer to that, once Storm set her eyes on a man she didn't care if he was single or not. "She will be hurt and I imagine very angry, but she should have asked." Typically of Sky she was trying to see both sides. She smiled weakly. "No wonder he has gone, she will tear him to shreds."

Sunni nodded and returned his mother's smile.

"I would not like to be him when she catches up with him, that's if she bothers to look." He said with a sigh.

"I wonder where he has gone?" Emily asked rather quietly.

"Back to his wife no doubt." Sky replied. "Men like that always run back home with their tail between their legs." She thought about Nicos. "Well mostly they do anyway."

"Then I think Sunni and I should go and find Nicos. Make sure all of this is true." Emily said. "I think it will do Sunni good to meet his father at long last."

Sky looked at her, momentarily deep in thought.

"You are wise beyond your years Emily. I think that would be a very good idea." Sunni glanced from his mother to Emily, both women were smiling; perhaps it was a good idea after all.

"Right then I will see Storm first, where is she by the way?" He asked.

"Gone to see Eleni and the twins at the beach. She said she fancied a swim, no wonder Allesandro didn't want to go with her." Sky replied. "When will you go over to Kalymnos?"

"Probably tomorrow. I need Alex back for some shoots, it's just a pity I won't be able to use Storm as well. I can't see her wanting to work with him again can you?"

Sky shook her head. Not a cat in hells chance of Storm ever working with him again. Sunni would have to use one of Matthews other models, ah well a first time for everything.

"Come on Emily I think we had better go to the beach before the jungle drums start and Storm finds out about all of this." Sunni rose and kissed his mother's cheek. "Won't be long Mama. Perhaps you had better ring father and tell him, I think he ought to know a war party is on its way."

87

Sky waved them off then hobbled over to Athena's villa, she would tell them before they too found out from gossips. Alexi would be angry she knew, and Athena very upset. She had another granddaughter that she had never met. It would be harder on her than any of them. Storm would find another man, Sunni would get another model, but Athena would never be able to make up for lost time with this girl Gina.

Once they knew, then she would phone that rat of a husband, because that was what he was, a rat but still very much her husband. Sky had never contemplated divorce, she had always held on to the faint hope that he might just return.

She wondered how Nicos would feel when he too found out, not too pleased with Allesandro. I bet, she thought.

Sky still loved him no matter what. He had given her pride in herself, love and two precious children. She had more money than she knew what to do with, a fabulous home, her own business, and it was all down to him. Yes there had been a time when she hated him for leaving her, but now as she got older it didn't seem to hurt so much, she still loved him and would welcome him back with open arms as if he had just returned from a weekend away, not the almost twenty years that had past since he had left.

You are one crazy woman, she thought to herself, totally crazy.

She wondered what he looked like now, probably gray, or even bald, no; Greek men seldom went bald, so gray it was. Chubby, or at least not as slim as he was, lined around the eyes, yes definitely.

I'll go with Sunni and Emily she decided, it's about time we spoke face to face. During her weekly talk with him on the phone she imagined him as he was years ago, yes, she would go and see him for herself. It might be better for Sunni if she were there too.

There were so many questions running through her mind.

The one thing she would ask though was why? Why did he not return to see his son, what had kept him from looking at the baby he had fathered?

As Sky had envisaged Athena was more upset about Gina than the fact Allesandro had had an affair with Storm. Alexi too was predictable, he just got angry, Storm, his precious little granddaughter had been tricked, or so he thought.

In fact his precious little granddaughter, was at that moment swearing and cursing like a trooper. Sunni and Emily had found her sitting at the little table by the bar; she was looking absolutely gorgeous as usual. The twins were making a big fuss of her, and holidaymakers asking for her autograph. She stood up and smiled as she saw her brother and Emily walk across the sand.

"Hi." She called. "Fancy a drink to celebrate? Those pics are superb bruv." She kissed his cheeks. "Truly great. Is Alex with you?" She looked behind them to see if he was there.

"No sis. I think you had better sit down." Sunni pulled up a chair for Emily and nodded as Marco asked if they wanted ouzo. "Allesandro has gone, we think back home." Storm looked surprised. "He is married Storm, married to our half sister."

Sunni just blurted the bad news out in one go. He told her exactly what Matt and told him and waited for the eruption, it came. Storm by name, storm by nature. She went ballistic. Not because he was married, but because of who he was married to.

She cursed her father, his trollop, and just about everyone. Sunni waited for her to settle a little.

"Did you ask him Storm?"

"Ask the twat what?" She replied, her eyes flashing fire plus many other danger signals.

"If he was married of course."

She was silent for a second.

"No. I never thought. Mind you what difference would asking that have made. We had the hots for each other and that was that." She paused for a moment, thinking. "He must have known his wife was my half sister. The Mandros name is known by just about everyone. He must have known who I was, why didn't he say something?" She hissed getting angrier by the second.

"Well, he wasn't going to tell you was he. Just landed himself a modeling job, and got the worlds best supermodel on the end of his dick. Sorry Emily I shouldn't have said that. Well Storm what do you think he was going to say."

"You are right as usual I suppose. So he's gone has he, well that's the end of that." She said rather sadly for Storm. Sunni realised she must

89

have thought a lot about this man. Usually she just shrugged when an affair came to an end, but not this time, she seemed genuinely upset.

"Well not really, you see lot's of have jobs have come our way this morning and most of them involve you and him."

"No chance!" She spat. "No way!"

"I had to ask. I had better use one of Matt's others then." Sunni looked at Emily for help.

"Don't you dare? You can use me with someone else, not him." Storm was angry with her brother now.

"Look Storm it's him they want. So think about it, you and him, or one of the other girls and him. That's that I'm afraid."

"Judas." She said nastily. "You are supposed to be my loving brother."

"And I am but just think about someone else will you for a change." He hissed. Emily gently took his hand; she could see this argument was upsetting him. "Anyway me and Emily are going over to Kalymnos tomorrow to see him and father."

"What! You are going to see that bastard!"

"Mind your language in front of Emily. Yes we are. If I can persuade Alex to come back for these shoots then I will, if not at least I will have met father. That is the end of it." Sunni knocked back his drink and stood. "It's up to you Storm. Work with him, or not at all."

Emily walked quickly after Sunni as he made his way back to the car.

"You were so masterful then Sunni. Made my spine tingle." She said gently. Sunni stopped in his tracks. He took her face in his hands and kissed her softly, then harder. Their breathing came in spurts as the kiss went on and on. Emily could feel herself getting moist as his hardness pressed into her stomach.

"Oh God. Roll on your next visit." He said breathlessly looking into her beautiful green eyes. "Roll on."

Emily just laughed, never before had she met a man with so many principles, she was pleased in one way, but it left her feeling very frustrated.

"I have an idea Sunni. Take me somewhere no one else goes." She stared back at him. "And now please." It was almost an order.

Sunni drove part of the way up the hill and turned off down a dusty cliff road. He parked under an old eucalyptus tree and turn towards her.

"Kiss me again please." She slid towards him. "Now!"

He did as she asked and soon they were locked into a passionate embrace. Emily's hand wandered down to his zip, as she bent towards him Sunni slid his hands down the front of her blouse and felt the warm softness of her breasts, he felt a gushing release almost immediately.

"I love you Emily," He sighed as she raised her head. "I love you so much." He kissed her again. "Now it's your turn." Slowly he undid her still honey-stained blouse and began to kiss her ample breasts. His hand slid up her short skirt and to his surprise found no sign of underwear, his manhood rose again at the discovery.

"Stuff your Dad." He said lowering the back of her seat and entering her in one swift move. "I can't wait a moment longer."

With the roof of his car down Emily could feel the sun on her face and breasts, she could hear the sea splashing against the rocks below, feel the warm breeze in her hair, and she could feel the man she was rapidly falling in love with thrusting himself into her body.

Sunni was right, stuff her dad, sorry dad but this is heaven.

"Shit. I haven't used anything." Sunni unknowingly ruined a perfect moment by being practical. "Are you on the pill?" Emily shook her head. "Good." He replied making amends for his last comment. "Now I shall have to do the right thing and you will have to marry me whether you like it or not." He laughed, "Will you?"

Emily just stared wide-eyed with shock at his request.

"Don't you think it's a bit sudden for that?" She replied after a long pause.

"We tend to do things quickly in our family. Just ask mama and Eleni." He laughed. "So will you?"

"I might, but you will have to wait. I'm not a speed merchant you know." Emily felt slightly confused everything was moving so quickly.

"Oh I don't know about that." He giggled. "But don't worry I will wait."

• CHAPTER •
9

"What a pretty looking place." Emily stared in wonder as the ferry chugged its way into Pothia harbor. "I don't think I have ever seen such a lovely town."

"Nearly as nice as Skiathos." Sky replied laughing as Emily blushed. "But you are right it is lovely."

The trio watched as the thick anchor chain rattled it's way into the deep swishing waters of the harbor.

Emily took Sunni's hand and gave it a squeeze. He had been almost silent since the beginning of their journey that morning. She knew he was scared, excited but scared, and even a little angry. He turned and smiled at her.

"Thanks Emily. Sorry if I'm a bit strange today. I will make it up to you promise."

"Don't be daft, it's a big thing is this. Anyway we are there now, the hardest step has been taken. Don't forget I'm with you." She reached up and kissed his lips gently. "I'm here for you."

92

As they waited until the other passengers had left the ferry Sunni leant on the white railing scouring the harbor for the first sight of his father. Not that he had any idea what he looked like. Sky had removed all of the photographs of him after his desertion and never once shown him his face. Just look in the mirror, was all she had said to him.

Just like his son Nicos too was scouring the sea of faces, he spotted them. It was the brilliance of Sky's hair shinning in the sun that had first caught his eye. He studied her face; he could see that she had hardly changed. He felt a lump in his throat as he watched her steadier herself with the crutches on her arms. Suddenly he felt like crying, what had he done. This beautiful woman, his one and only Sky, still his wife. All the love came flooding back as he watched her hobble onto the harbor side, not an ounce heavier than she had been all those years ago. Her lovely hair still long, and her white skin flecked with hundreds of freckles. He felt like running up to her and taking her into his arms, he felt as if time had stood still. His injured little lion cub, his angel of the lake, the mother of his children, now he wept.

Giovanna was a wonderful sexual partner, very daring, very athletic, but that was all. As a person she was very shallow. She wanted everything, and wanted it now. At first he found her exciting, the way she buzzed everywhere spending his money. If ever he said no she threw a tantrum fit for a three year old, then made him change his mind with the most wonderful sex session she could dream up, and if it was one thing Nicos could not refuse it was sex.

Sky on the other hand had never asked for anything. It had always been him who suggested she had new things. She never complained, not like his lover. The woman who now sat at home stuffing her chubby face with honey and nuts. Sky had brought his son to him, something Giovanna would never have done he knew only too well.

One of the reasons he had never returned to Skiathos was the thought of leaving Gina alone with her, that and the almost unbearable guilt of the hurt he had caused.

The day his father came to see him was etched upon his mind; it was a day he would never forget.

Gina his daughter, was so pretty and fragile, so even tempered, most of the time, and if it weren't for the fact she looked like Giovanna, and himself, he would have doubted her parentage. How could he have left her alone with her mother, she wouldn't have lasted a week, his heart was torn.

By the time she was born he was already beginning to despise his mistress; it was Gina who needed him now. His family on Skiathos would be well looked after he knew, but she only had him and Paulo to guide and help her.

What he should have done was to take her and beg Sky to let her stay with them. It would have been a long shot, but at least he would have tried instead of giving in from the word go.

He had never been keen on Allesandro, but Gina had persuaded him to let them marry, something she had regretted from day one. He wanted to say I told you so, but held her many times as she cried, staying silent. He wanted to thrash him for hurting his daughter with his constant affairs, but she refused his help and just cried even more. It must be her fault, she used to say, but Nicos knew different. Now he had not only hurt Gina, but Storm too and in the process Sky and Sunni. How he would like to get his hands round his neck, but no chance, the sly son of a bitch had disappeared off the face of the earth. Gina had no idea where he had gone, and Sky said nor did they.

Allesandro had just packed up and gone leaving both of his daughters heartbroken.

His daughter's husband was just like him in his younger days, if it moved, shag it, was his motto that was until Sky had come along. Nicos smiled lopsidedly to himself, even then he had picked up the occasional holidaymaker, some things never change he thought, wishing more than anything that he had been different.

His eyes brought him back to the present. Sunni, and there was no mistaking his son, standing on the harbor looking around, the mirror image of himself in his younger days. The girl with him must be the one Sky had told him about, Nicos thought as he watched the trio move to a roadside taverna.

He watched as Sunni took out his mobile and waited the few seconds it took for his own phone to spring into action. Nicos's heart dropped as he saw Sunni pass the ringing phone to Sky, he had come all of this way, and yet he could not speak to him.

"Kalimera Sky." He said softly. "Yes I can see you." He noticed all three of them immediately look around as Sky relayed the news. "I will be with you in a moment or two. Bye." He clicked his phone off and stared at it, suddenly feeling very nervous.

Nicos walked slowly towards the taverna where the trio now sat sipping hot coffee. He hoped that Sunni would spot him and run into his aching arms, but no they were talking and no one noticed his arrival.

"Hello Sky." He said shakily.

Sunni immediately stood knocking his chair over onto the cobbles; Nicos could see that his hands were clenched.

"Nothing would give me greater pleasure than for you to strike me. I know I deserve it, but please not in front of the ladies." He tried to smile. "Perhaps tomorrow when we are alone."

"Hello Jack." It had been so long since he had watched her lips say his pet name; he stared at her face and began to sob. "Come on sit down." She put a comforting arm around his shoulders. "Here." A clean handkerchief was produced. "Come on cheer up or we will be on the next ferry back. Fine old greeting that." She smiled at him; her own heart flipping as she looked into his lovely eyes once more.

"What can I say but sorry." He began. "It is not enough I know, but I am so sorry."

They spent a very long lunch talking and getting to know each other all over again. Sunni watched as his mother's face brightened as she spoke, her eyes flashing, he knew then she still loved him.

He listened to his father try to explain and miserably fail, but something made him warm to this man.

Emily just sat and watched the others. After being introduced she let them get on with it. After all hadn't she been through something like this before, she thought to herself. Not many people knew she had been adopted; an orphan at six months old, but it was her grandfather she had met as a youngster, not a father who had deserted her. Her situation was different but she knew exactly what Sunni was going through, the main fear now was one of rejection. She could see he was watching every move Nicos made, listening to every word he spoke, he was already hooked upon this man, and rejection again would crucify him.

Staring at Nicos, she realised her fears were unfounded. Nicos looked towards his son often, smiling nervously with his mouth and eyes, he was now the one in fear.

95

They had chosen to stay at a hotel in the town, Sky not being over keen to be too close to Giovanna. She realised that at some stage they would probably meet, but that could wait as far as she was concerned, forever if it was left up to her. Nicos carried her bags as they made their way along the harbor road.

"Just like old times." He said lightly.

"No Jack. Those times have gone. I have come here for two reasons. One to see my son meet with his father, what he does after today is up to him. If he decides he never wants to set eyes on you again so be it. Secondly to warn you about your parents." She stopped and sat on the sea wall. "They are both in their nineties, in poor health and I feel you should see them before they die." She saw her words had shocked him. "You did not return for the funerals of Tomas, Sofia, aunt Eleni or Richard, but please Jack do not leave this too late. I am begging you on their behalf, not mine or yours. Athena needs to see her son before she dies, and I know Alexi would be angry with you at first, but he needs you too. Please come and see them, if only for a few days. Promise me that if nothing else?"

Her eyes watered at the thought of loosing the old couple but recently she had noticed how suddenly both looked so old and fragile. Ninety was a fine age to reach but it was beginning to take its toll. Sky hoped Nicos would agree.

"I will try." He answered patting her hand.

"You will do more than damned well try. You will come home you heartless pig." She thumped him hard in the chest.

"Yes I will then." He laughed. "I am too old myself to take any more of that." He rubbed the spot she had hit. They both laughed together.

"Mother is everything OK." Sunni was at her side in a flash.

"Yes thanks it's alright. We were just having one of our spats." Sky and Nicos smiled at each other. "Anyway he is going to do as he has been told so don't worry."

"Your mother could always get her own way." Nicos said. "Especially when she used violence."

The years rolled back in a split second as they all started to laugh.

For the next couple of days Nicos took Sunni around the island, he took him diving and showed him his studio. It was amazing how alike their photographic techniques were, but both having learned from Alexi, it was easy to understand why. As they bent heads together over one particular shot a crying young girl interrupted them.

"Papa come quick." She said rapidly. "Quick, quick."

"Hey Gina. Slow down." Nicos held her in his arms. "Slow down. Now tell me what is the matter?"

"It's mama." She wailed. " She is so ill."

The two men rushed from the studio and followed the running girl up the dusty road. Sunni hung back slightly as they both ran into a little white house.

"Come, perhaps you can help papa." Gina took Sunni's hand and pulled him inside.

The cool and dark of the room hit them all suddenly; Giovanna had not even bothered to open the shutters, the air was smelly and stale.

Nicos quickly ran round the room, he needed light. All he could see at the moment was a heap on the floor. Sunni held Gina close as Nicos examined the prone body of his mistress.

"She is so cold." He said shakily. "I think she is dead." Gina gasped and began to sob. Sunni held her closer.

"If only I had called by sooner." She cried. "I waited until now because I know she usually likes to stay in bed late."

Nicos nodded, Giovanna had been turning into quite a slob recently. Stopping in bed until lunchtime, not cleaning the house or doing the washing, not even bothering about her own personal hygiene. The only thing she had been interested in was food, piles and piles of food.

Turning her over gently he could see it was food that had killed her; it spilled from the side of her grotesquely full mouth. Quickly he covered her face with her shawl. His daughter need not see that. Let her remember her mother as she had been, not as she was now.

Sunni handed his phone to Gina.

"Call for the doctor."

She nodded her thanks and pushed the numbers before speaking rapidly in Greek. He heard her say her thanks and goodbyes before watching as she pushed more numbers.

"Uncle Paulo. It's me Gina. Please come to mama's it is an emergency. Yes now." She cried in Italian this time.

Paulo beat the doctor to the house by seconds pushing his way through a throng of wailing women standing on the pathway. Giovanna's friends and neighbours had already begun to gather having guessed something terrible had happened.

The doctor examined the body and called for the undertaker.

As her mothers body was taken from the house Gina once again held on to Sunni, crying into his already sodden shirt.

"Come let us make coffee." He led her into the kitchen and began to look in the cupboards.

"Here." She said softly. "It's in here."

Whilst the two young ones busied themselves preparing a tray of coffee and cakes Nicos and Paulo sat in silence. One had lost his sister, the other his mistress. Paulo was almost distraught with grief, his sister, the beautiful Giovanna gone.

Nicos on the other hand thanked her under his breath. Her death had given him the chance to return to Skiathos, and hopefully Sky. It was about the only good thing she had done since they met, this and give birth to Gina. What a horrible man I am, he thought, and began to grieve along with her brother, grieve for the woman he once knew, not the Giovanna of today.

Emily felt a pang of jealousy as she watched the young girl get out of Nicos's car and take Sunni's hand.

"This is Gina." Sunni introduced his half sister. "She has had a terrible shock this afternoon. Her mother has died suddenly." Emily immediately stood and held the girl in her arms.

"Come and sit with me Gina." She said as Nicos and Sunni went over towards Sky. "Do you want to talk?"

The young girl nodded and told her all about the tragic afternoon. Her English was quite good, but in her shocked condition Gina often reverted to Greek, and at times Italian, Emily tried hard to keep up with what she was saying.

She told her how good Sunni had been in helping her make drinks for all of the people who had called at the house and how he had even helped her wash the cups up afterwards. Both girls giggled.

"I cannot go back Emily." Gina looked down at her hands. "My husband has disappeared and now my mother has died. I cannot go back to that village." She wept. "My life is such a mess."

"I'm sure Nicos and Sunni will sort something out. Don't worry please." Emily placed her hands over Gina's in a comforting way. "Please don't worry."

In fact Nicos was at that moment booking both Gina and himself into the hotel. The further away from that house the better for both of them. Sky had agreed when he asked for her opinion. Gina smiled when he told her of his success.

"Do you want to fetch your clothes and things?" He asked tenderly.

"No. I never want to go to Myrties again." She replied.

"But you will have to my darling, everything we have is there and you will need to go for the funeral."

"Let me come with you." Emily said gently. "Together we can get your things and then come back here."

"OK. But tomorrow." Gina replied. "Not today. Now I am so tired."

Emily helped Gina to her room and sat talking whilst she showered and got into bed. It was still early evening as far as Greeks were concerned but the young girl was shattered. Emily sat and stroked her brow.

"Thank you Emily. You are a great comfort." Gina sighed. "I hope all goes well with papa and Sunni, then we can be friends." She smiled.

"I would like that." Emily answered. "Now try to get some sleep."

That evening Nicos joined Sunni and Sky for their meal. He was subdued but still managed to have Sky laughing more than once.

"You never change do you Jack." She said giggling over one particular comment.

"Why do you call him Jack mother?" Sunni asked frowning. She went on to tell her son about how they had met, the tales he told and the reason for his nickname. They laughed about their times on the motorbike and relived their early days as the night went on.

"You never did get to make me look like a mermaid." She said poking him in the ribs. "You promised remember?"

She told Sunni about the trip to Melissani lake and the story behind the photograph in her bedroom. He had heard that one before but said nothing. He could see his mother was really enjoying herself as she chatted.

"There is time yet." Nicos replied. "A mermaid you will be." He was flirting with her openly and Sunni was unsure whether he liked it or not, but she seemed to be having fun so why not. Nicos's phone rang.

"Yes Paulo." He paused and listened. "OK. We will see you tomorrow." He went on to explain that he was bringing Gina and Emily to collect some things the next day. "Thank you my friend. Until tomorrow then."

"Paulo has arranged the funeral. As I am not her husband the priest thought it best that he did it. It is the day after tomorrow. Will you stay until then please?" He touched Sky's hand. "Please. Gina needs someone and Emily will be a big help to her I know. They are friends already I can see that." Sky looked to Sunni to reply. It was entirely up to him, this trip was for him.

"Yes we will stay." He faltered at almost calling him papa, and blushed slightly as he realised.

"Thank you Sunni. That means a great deal to us both."

"What will you do after?" Sunni asked. "Gina says she will not go back to live there again. Where will you move to?" It had dawned on him that once again he might loose touch with his father.

"Your mother thinks I should go to see my parents, and she is right. I think Gina and I will come back with you if we can?" He looked directly into Sunni's eyes not daring to look at Sky.

"Mother what do you think is best, after all Storm might just kick up a bit over having Gina there."

"Storm will be over Allesandro by the time we get back. She is probably out somewhere tonight with some poor unsuspecting chap. So I don't think Gina will be a problem. It is you Jack who her anger will be directed to." She turned to Nicos. "She is very much like you in lots

100

of ways, and one of them is her temper. She will not be a push over, but if you are prepared to try then it is up to you. I'm sure Athena will be thrilled to see you."

"Talking of Storm I had better let her know we are staying a little longer." Sunni said punching the numbers on his phone. "Hi sis." He listened for a moment then nodded towards Sky smiling. "Mother said you would have some chap there." He laughed at her reply. "Listen for a second will you. We are staying a few days longer than planned." Pause. "Yes that's right. No Alex isn't here, he's disappeared." Pause. "Probably three." Pause. "Yeah. A funeral." Pause. "No I haven't killed him." He laughed, Nicos and Sky smiled at each other. "Ok see you then. Bye." Sunni clicked his phone shut.

"You are right mother, she has another chap already. Plenty more fish in the sea, she said, Alex can go drown for all she cares." He laughed and looked across at Nicos "She thought I'd done you in and when I said no she said pity. You see you will have your work cut out with her all right. Anyway I'd better say goodnight. Emily will wonder where I am, it's a good job I sent them some food up the restaurant has closed now. See you in the morning." He kissed his mother and shook Nicos by the hand. "Will you be alright getting to your room?" He asked his mother, who nodded her reply.

"I will see she is." Nicos spoke for her. "Goodnight."

They watched in silence as Sunni strolled across to the hotel entrance.

"What an awful day you have had." Sky said tenderly. "I'm sorry about Giovanna." She meant it even though there had been times when she had hated the woman. It was no way to die, choking on food, very undignified, and something no one deserved. Nicos agreed.

"It has had its good points though. I have really enjoyed tonight, just the three of us." He replied. "I think Sunni has too. He seems to be thawing a little. You know that first day I took him out alone I asked him to hit me and he refused. He said he would save it for another day, I hope that day never comes."

"Not with Sunni it won't, but Storm I would not be so sure about. Anyway it's time I got to bed." She went to stand. Nicos took her crutches just like in the old days and walked with her, both were surprised at how quickly they matched their strides, he felt comforted and pleased but said nothing.

101

"Goodnight." He said and kissed her cheek. "See you at breakfast."

Sky nodded, she dare not say a word; she knew any thing she said would give the game away. How she would have liked to ask him to join her, how she longed to feel his touch, how much she wanted him to make love to her just like before.

She stood by the half open door and watched as he walked away, head down, hands in pockets, and wondered if he was thinking the same, hoping for all her worth he was.

Lying in bed unable to sleep she thought about her time on Kalymnos. She had come here with the excuse to ask him to return for his parent's sake, and it had been an excuse. She wanted him to return for her sake, she knew that now.

Could she really love him again? Yes.

Had she ever stopped loving him? No. Came the reply from her brain.

Was she doing the right thing in agreeing to let him return with Gina? That would mean he had no ties on this island to return for. No. Came the truthful reply.

Was she happy knowing that? Yes.

Would she regret her hasty decision, would he desert her again? Who knew, but at this moment Sky didn't care.

Did she feel any guilt? Perhaps a little but not enough make any difference in the way she felt towards him.

At last she felt into a deep sleep.

• CHAPTER • 10

The day of the funeral was unusually gray and overcast. The skies seemed to mirror the feelings of the group that stood by the fresh grave.

Gina had cried for hours, she still had this terrible guilt that if only she had called at her mother's house earlier Giovanna would have still been alive. She had a deep sense of failure that at the present time no one could help lift from her.

She stood in the middle of Emily and Sunni, each of them holding her trembling hands as she muttered farewells to her mother.

Nicos stood with Sky, Paulo stood alone. Pain was etched upon his face, age had been good to him but today he looked all of his years, and more.

The little village church had been full to overflowing as the people of Myrties paid their last respects. Most had now gone on to the taverna were the funeral lunch was being held, leaving the family to spend their last few minutes alone.

103

It was time they needed before getting on with the rest of their lives.

Nicos had decided that the best thing was for him and Gina to go to Skiathos as Sky had said. Not only to see his parents, but to live.

Paulo wanted to remain on Kalymnos but had promised Gina he would come over to see her whenever he could.

The poor girl was torn. Should she stay with her uncle and be close to her mother's grave, or go with her father to a new life with these people that she had only just met? Her friendship with Emily was going strong, but the fact that she was returning to London shortly made Gina feel even more uncertain. Emily had promised that she would be back soon, and even offered to take Gina with her.

The young Italian girl had never left the tiny island she now lived on and had no wish to be in a huge city, even for a day, or did she? The fear of the unknown outweighed her curiosity at the moment. All she could think of was her mother, and only if she had been that little bit earlier in calling.

Sky noticed how Gina kept going as if in a trance. She knew that the young girl was blaming herself, but Sky felt that she too had played a part in Giovanna's death. If only she hadn't come to the island perhaps she would still be alive. Perhaps if Nicos had not been preoccupied with his son he could have saved this woman who Sky had never met. She knew how much Giovanna had wanted Nicos to marry her, but Sky had refused him a divorce. She insisted that they had married until death us do part, and that was the end of it as far as she was concerned. If only she had let Nicos marry his mistress perhaps things would have been different. Thinking back though, Nicos had never actually said he wanted to re marry; in fact it had been Sky who mentioned divorce not him.

Still, for a few moments she blamed herself.

Standing at the side of Gina, both Sunni and Emily were blaming themselves. Emily because she had insisted that Sunni meet his father, and Sunni because he had.

Paulo as deep in thought as the others had decided that it was his fault. He had known all about Nicos when he first came to the island but had still let his lovely sister fall for his charms. He should have put a stop to it from the beginning, it was his fault, he should have stopped it. That however had never been an option.

He hadn't let Nicos fall for Giovanna, he had stage managed their meeting.

Encouraged it, all for his own personal gain.

Yes it was definitely his fault.

Nicos knew it was his. He had treated Giovanna badly. OK she wasn't the best housekeeper in the world, but his constant nagging for her to run after his every whim was perhaps excessive, he took his guilt on leaving Sky out on her, and he knew it. She had been fantastic in bed, on the floor, in the bath, wherever she could make love in fact, but that was about it really. He knew she had always wanted to marry him, and once Gina had come along, her constant nagging about him getting a divorce had sent him into the arms of many holidaymakers. He felt safe with them, only here for a week or two then back home. No chance of getting serious, just getting laid, and that was all he wanted. No ties sex. Wonderful.

But for once in his life Nicos felt guilty.

The little group slowly left the flower-strewn grave yard and made their way towards the taverna. Gina held on to Sunni as she stumbled along. Sky and Nicos walked together as they used to many years ago. Him holding her crutches and she hobbling along, both instep as if they had always walked this way.

It left Paulo to accompany Emily. In his faltering English he tried to make conversation but failed. Emily understood though, she told him; to loose his sister must have left a huge hole in his life, but time was a great healer, and one day he would get out of the black hole that at the moment threatened to swallow him. He stopped and stared at her.

"You understand very well Emily. It makes me think you have been through something like this yourself." He said slowly.

"I have Paulo. I lost my parents and grandmother when I was only a baby. So yes I do know how you feel." She replied.

He nodded and asked nothing more; he could see now how the funeral had affected her. Her face looked tired and sad, her eyes misty, not for Giovanna, but the for people she had lost so early in her life. He decided there and then to buck himself up. If this young girl could live with such a tragedy, then he could too.

His mood had lightened immediately; he took her arm and smiled.

"Thank you for sharing that with me. You have given me hope," he said with a grin. "Let us celebrate Giovanna's life, and not be so sad. Come on let's catch up with the others."

His stride increased and Emily had a job to keep up with him at first, so sudden had his step changed, but she soon found his rhythm and managed to stay by his side. They did in fact reach the taverna before the others and were handed full glasses of ouzo as they walked into the shaded bar.

Paulo made a little speech thanking all of the villagers for coming today and then began to toast his sister.

"To Giovanna." They all raised their glasses and repeated his words. "My sister would not like us to be sad, so let us enjoy this afternoon. Please eat and drink, let us give thanks for her life even though it has been such a short one. She would like us to be happy."

The villagers felt the change in his mood and as told, began to enjoy the afternoon. They drank and talked, ate and talked, then drank some more, and as evening came started to dance.

Paulo led the line and Nicos stayed at the other end. They smashed plates and sang, it was quite some party, very fitting for a girl who had once been so full of life. Giovanna would certainly have enjoyed her funeral; it lasted until the early hours of the following morning.

"I hope mine is as good as this." Nicos said gasping for breath. He had left the dancers and come to sit with his family.

"When Storm gets hold of you it may well be sooner than you think." Sky replied laughing.

Her daughter would certainly make him suffer for deserting her, and in a way Sky wanted Sunni to react, but no. He had at first looked as if he might, but Nicos had won him over almost immediately, and now they were friends.

Storm, she knew would not be so easy. In fact she was looking forward to seeing the scrap that was sure to unfold. It would be interesting, but hopefully not as bad as she imagined. Perhaps Storm would be like Sunni, no she knew there was not a chance, but maybe, eventually, she would accept her father once more.

It is all going to be very interesting, I shall have to wait and see, Sky thought.

As dawn broke over the tiny island of Telendos just across the water Nicos piled his family into a taxi.

"Back to the hotel I think." He said as they all climbed in wearily. "Hopefully we can get breakfast, then its to bed for a few hours." No one answered, but all agreed in their minds.

"That looks lovely Jack." Sky said pointing to the tiny island with the sun just rising behind its hilly center. "So pretty." She sighed.

"If you like I will take you there tomorrow. Let us have just one day alone together before we return to Skiathos. Let me show you some of the places I have loved for these past years. Give me the chance to explain. Please Sky, say you will." He paused waiting for her to reply. "Sunni may I borrow your mother tomorrow?" He asked, hoping his son's approval might sway her.

"If mother wants to go then it's OK by me. It will give Emily and I a chance to have a look round too." Sunni really meant it would give him chance to go to bed with her. Who wanted to look around when they could be making love all day? "I think you should go mother, it would do you good." He added hoping as much as Nicos that Sky would agree.

"Yes Jack. You can take me out tomorrow." She said eventually, trying to ignore the blush that crept up her son's neck.

Men, she thought, they are all the same, but then so are we women. The chance to be with Nicos alone had made her feel excited once again. She remembered their youth and the trips they had back then. Nicos always made days out such fun, and treated her so well, she felt like a teenager again just at the thought.

"Are we having a motorbike Jack?" She asked laughing.

"If you want one then we will." He replied, remembering the way she always screamed during past trips. It was a wonder he hadn't been deafened by the noise. "Telendos is very small." Before he had finished speaking he remembered her problems in walking. "So maybe not a motorbike, but I will find something. Trust me. Something much better." Nicos began to giggle to himself.

Back at the hotel they all did as he had suggested. Breakfast and then sleep. The day was already warming as the sun continued to rise and it was a shame to miss it, but all four of them were thinking of tomorrow, all in very different ways and for different reasons, at least they could have this afternoon by the pool. Today was certainly a day to rest. After the dancing and talking at the funeral, everyone needed a day of rest.

They all met later, feeling much livelier after a good sleep. Sunni was first to appear by the pool, his mind firmly set upon how he was going to spend the next day. Then came Sky, who would be shocked if she could have read his thoughts, and just after her came Nicos and Gina. Emily was last to reach the group, yawning and stretching as she lay down on the sun bed.

"I'm not sure if that has done me any good or not," she said yawning widely. "I can't seem to wake up properly."

"Perhaps this will help." Sunni picked her up and jumped into the water with her in his arms.

"Oh you!" She cried as they surfaced laughing and spluttering. "Take that." She splashed him over and over, flicking water high into the air. Sunni just dived under the surface and swam away. "Come back here you and take your punishment like a man." Emily, always a good swimmer, raced after him.

They played for quite some time, mostly under the surface where Sunni could kiss her without being seen, and run his hands over her almost naked body. Her tiny bikini had been the true reason for his actions, the sight of her in such small pieces of cloth had sent his penis into orbit and the only way to stop his mother noticing was to get into the pool as quickly as possible.

Nicos had however noticed and smiled, his son, just like himself, he felt rather pleased.

Eventually Emily climbed out of the pool and dropped on to the sun bed at the side of Gina, who had hardly moved. The emotion of the funeral had exhausted the young girl who now dozed in the sun.

"He was right, that's much better." She said a little breathlessly.

Sunni was in trouble again as he watched her rub cream on her legs and modestly stayed in the water. He leant his head on his arms at the poolside and smiled, roll on tomorrow he thought as the sun cream was now being rubbed into her stomach and breasts. His problem now was how to get rid of the animal in his trunks, only one thing for it. A long cold shower.

"Won't be long," he shouted getting out on the opposite side of the pool. "Just going for my ciggies." It was a good job he had left them in his room; it gave him the excuse to disappear for a few moments.

Nicos smiled to himself, had that been him he would have taken Emily with him even if his parents had been there. He knew exactly how Sunni felt; in fact his own body was beginning to react at the sight of Sky in her miniscule costume. She didn't wear a bikini, but a very sexy black one piece that had more cut out than was actually there. She looked fantastic but he knew he had to tread carefully were she was concerned.

"Won't be long. I've forgotten my ciggies too." He said rising suddenly.

Nicos met his son as he made his way towards his own room.

"Ciggies." Was all Nicos could say before bursting out laughing. The two men cried with mirth. "Like father like son." Nicos managed to gasp as tears fell from Sunni's eyes. "See you in a minute or two." He left his son doubled up laughing.

The women could not understand why every time Nicos and Sunni looked at each other they began to laugh. In fact a one point Sky felt a little angry.

"Tell us the joke Jack." She said sternly.

"It's between father and son." He replied. "And not for your ears. Right Sunni." Who nodded his reply, not trusting his mouth to say anything coherent.

Luckily his phone sprang to life.

"Hi sis." He waited whilst she spoke. "Yeah, tomorrow then home." He decided against telling her Nicos and Gina would be with them. "Brilliant, not like a funeral at all, more like a party." He felt a pang of guilt as Gina raised her head slightly. "It was a celebration of her life, and the villagers certainly did that. She must have been very popular." He saved himself just in time and was pleased to see the young girl smile at his words. "You OK then and the gramps, they OK?" He listened while his sister spoke. "That's good. See you soon. Just behave. Bye." He blew kisses into his phone and heard his sister giggle.

As youngsters it had been Storm who had been the leader, but now she always turned to her brother for strength. It was as if she acknowledged he was the sensible one and needed him to lead her, he had in fact taken the place of Nicos in her life although neither of them realised that.

"Is she OK?" Sky and Nicos asked in unison.

"Yeah. As usual she got a bit of man trouble, but other than that everything is OK. Athena is a little better, but Alexi has got her cold now. Those two they just pass thing back and forth."

"You didn't tell me mother was poorly." Nicos sounded concerned.

"She has just had a summer cold." Sky replied. "But one of these days she will be really poorly Jack, and that's why you must come back." Nicos nodded.

"Gina and I have talked it over and we will come back with you. Can we have the guest rooms to start with? I don't want to just turn up at mama's door it wouldn't be fair. Let them get used to me being there again first I think, plus they need to get to know Gina. I hope they won't reject her, I don't care about myself, but she doesn't deserve that." He looked very sad at the thought.

"I'm sure Athena will welcome her with open arms Jack, don't worry." Sky gently touched his shoulder. "You have more to worry about than that don't forget." She didn't have to say her daughter's name; they both knew what she meant. "Anyway let me rest. I get the feeling tomorrow will be quite some day." She smiled at him with shinning eyes.

Things are really looking up, he thought, there's hope for me yet. Nicos sat silently as the others dozed in the sun, his mind active making plans for his and Sky's trip. He would make it a day to remember and he knew exactly how to do it, a couple of phone calls should do the trick, he thought as he made his plans smiling to himself. If this didn't help him get Sky back, nothing would.

They all stayed at the hotel to eat that night and took a stroll along the harbor road before bed. Sky and Nicos stopped for coffee and cake whilst the other three continued towards the still open shops. Sunni had a pretty girl on each arm and a big grin on his face as they wandered around. He purposely stopped outside of a jewellers.

"That's nice." He said pointing to a tiny diamond ring.

"Oh no I like that one." Gina tapped the glass by a huge sapphire. She looked at Sunni and winked quickly.

110

"Well I like that one." Emily pointed to a solitaire diamond ring that sparkled in the center of the display. "It's fabulous. Just look at the way it shines." Her eyes took on a similar sparkle. "Not that little thing." She pointed to the one Sunni had first gestured to. "Yours isn't too bad though Gina, but mines definitely the best."

Sunni smiled at her and then towards Gina, she had read his mind, but after all she was his sister wasn't she. That little wink had told him so much, they were brother and sister and he felt proud, then a little guilty, she would be on her own tomorrow.

"What will you do with yourself whilst Nicos takes Sky?" Emily asked, she too could read his mind. What was it with women and minds, he thought to himself, and then hoped Emily would have a good idea of what he had planned for their day alone.

"Uncle Paulo is coming to take me out. We can say our goodbyes and talk about mama." Gina looked very sad. "He has promised to visit Skiathos so hopefully it won't be too long before I see him again. It seems such a big step for me, but with your help I know I can make papa proud."

Sunni was touched by her words.

"I will look after you from now on. Don't worry about that." He put his arm gently around his sister. " Gina can help you with the wedding arrangements can't she." He looked towards Emily.

"I haven't actually said yes yet Sunni." She laughed. "But if I do, then yes she can help."

Of course she would marry him; she had loved him from the moment she had laid eyes on him. The forlorn look on his face as he got up from the ground, the hopelessness as he had tried to dust himself down. The way he had refused to call the police and had given the youth money for food, had all played a part in her falling head over heels in love.

"Come on let's go and find the others. I'm ready for a coffee now." Sunni led the girls back towards the harbor road. "They will be in one of these." He nodded towards the row of tavernas. "Keep a look out."

Gina spotted them first and pointed.

"It's a lovely night." Sky said looking towards the twinkling stars. "Thanks Jack." She smiled at him and then towards the others who had just reached their table. "Did you buy anything nice?"

"No but we saw lots of lovely things. Tomorrow I think we will have a good shop." Emily replied with enthusiasm.

Sunni and Nicos just looked at each other and smiled. Both knew she would get her shop, but not until Sunni had finished with her.

They lingered over delicious liqueurs and coffee, soft cream filled cakes, and tiny pieces of nutty chocolate for quite some time.

Just sitting and relaxing in the warm night air, all thinking about tomorrow and listening as Nicos told a lovely story about the night sky. His voice was almost hypnotic as he spoke.

It had been so long since Sky had heard one of his stories, she sat back and listened, and as he talked she could feel her whole body begin to relax. Slowly her eyelids became heavier.

• CHAPTER •
11

Sky slept well, better than she had hoped.

The excitement of a day out with Nicos had at first kept her mind active as she lay in the cool bed, but the day of the funeral was still taking it's toll and before long she was sleeping deeply.

In fact all five of them had a good night and said as much as they chatted over breakfast.

Nicos was pleased to see that Gina was beginning to get a little less tense about her move to Skiathos and he listened as she asked Sunni a stream of questions.

It felt good to hear his son talk of Eleni beach, Marco and Tomas, Koukanaries beach, and all manner of well-known people and places from his own youth.

The Gallery, he could hardly wait to walk through its door once again, it had been far to long since he had. Strolling through the narrow cobbled streets of the town, eating at one of the tavernas and watching a film at the open-air cinema, or listening to a visiting orchestra.

113

He could hardly wait to get home, and that is what Skiathos was, home. He even smiled at the thought of the crowded buses, how he had missed them, and his car, I wonder what happened to that, he thought.

"Did you sell my car?" He asked without realizing he had spoken out loud.

"Er no Jack. It's in the garage." Sky squirmed slightly in her seat.

"Tell him the rest." Sunni laughed.

"Well it's in the garage a little bent and scratched, but basically OK." She giggled. "I had a little accident." The look on Nicos's face was one of horror.

"My lovely car, what happened?"

"Well I know you always said I shouldn't drive it, but Storm had taken mine and Alexi wanted to go to the Gallery. He is far too old to drive himself so I took him in yours. I did all right, I got into town but those narrow streets are meant for donkeys, not sports cars. Anyway I dropped him off, phoned Storm and asked her to pick him up later and headed for home." She paused and looked at Nicos, screwing up her face in the knowledge of what was to come. She took a deep breath. "I hit the tree by Athena's house, you know the one on the bend just down the hill a bit." Nicos nodded, how many times had he come close to hitting it himself. "Well the tree survived, and so did I, but your car got a bit bent. Serves you right anyway, you should have been there to take him yourself." She prodded his ribs and smiled.

She was right he knew, and he felt so glad she had not been hurt, he kissed her nose, just like he used to. Sky was a little shocked, she hadn't expected that.

"I'll forgive you but don't do it again." He wagged his finger. "Come on time to go, our taxi is here. Where is your bag?" He had given her a list of items to take.

"It's in my room." Sky handed him her door key. "Will you fetch it for me, you will be much quicker. It's on the bed."

He ran up the hotel stairs taking them two at a time. Finding her room he opened the door and looked towards the bed. The bag sat in the middle just as she had said, but it was the picture on the bedside table that caught his eye. It was the one she had sent to his phone the day he first made love to Giovanna, his heart lurched. He picked up the frame and took it to the window. He held the photograph towards the sunlight.

114

Three smiling faces stared back at him, Sky with baby Sunni on one knee and little Storm on the other.

For a few moments the pain in his chest was searing. Nicos stood and cried.

"Papa what is wrong?" Sunni walked into the room.

"Can you ever forgive me my son?" He showed him the photograph. "I can never forgive myself." The two men hugged and cried together, Sunni because he could feel his father's hurt, and Nicos because he had just heard the word papa come from his son's mouth.

"We had better go." Sunni said softly. "Mama will wonder what has happened to us." They dried their eyes and took deep breaths.

"Right I'm ready." Nicos said with a big grin, but deep down he still felt sad. "And what are you doing today?" He punched Sunni gently knowing full well what his son had in mind.

"Hopefully persuading Emily to marry me." Came the reply. "The best way I know how." The two men laughed and patted each other's backs.

"Here's to today then." Nicos shook his son's hand "Best of luck, she is a lovely girl."

"Thanks papa."

"What have you two been up to?" Sky asked as they returned with her bag.

"Talking men talk mama, now off you go and have a good day." Sunni kissed his mother's cheeks as she left and watched her hobble along, her arm firmly held by his father. "Be good." He shouted as he saw them reach the taxi.

Sky waved through the back window as the car gathered speed.

"It's just you and me then Jack." She said softly.

"About time too. Thanks for letting me take you out today, I know it can't be easy." His voice was full of concern. "And thanks for not despising me." He patted her hand and gazed out of the side window afraid to look at her, his emotions were still raw from seeing the photograph.

"I don't despise you Jack, I just feel hurt and bewildered." She said quietly. "Very bewildered."

115

For a while they sat in silence as the car traveled along the dusty winding road.

"I hope you don't mind but I have planned a couple of things for today." Nicos said eventually. "First we are going to Masouri. It is a little village just past Myrties, very pretty but very small, it won't take long but I want you to see just a little of the island."

Sky nodded, still looking through the side window. The road began to dip and rise as it wound around the rocky hillside.

It always amused her how many of the Greek roads were built around trees, instead of cutting them down to make the road straight, they went around and put a hairpin bend in. Great if you were a tree, but awkward if you were a driver.

She watched as they passed through Kantouni, yet another pretty village, mind you, was there a village in Greece that was not pretty, she thought to herself.

They traveled through Myrties and on to Masouri. As Nicos had said it was only tiny, and very quaint but it was the view from the cliff that he had brought her to see.

"Look over there." He pointed to the little island across the water. "That is where we are going to have lunch." Her eyes followed his finger to a little taverna right on the corner of the rock. Slightly saddened she studied the path from the harbor to the taverna.

"It looks lovely Jack, but how am I going to get round there?" She waved one of her crutches.

"Trust me you will." He laughed.

"No motorbike!" She replied with a huge grin.

"No. Not today."

They stood and admired the wonderful scene for some minutes and she listened as Nicos told her about the places she could see, and then watched as he tied a white handkerchief to a bush on the roadside. She looked at him puzzled.

"Don't ask, not yet anyway," was all he gave as explanation. "Come on back to the car."

He led her back to the waiting taxi whose driver quickly stubbed out his cigarette in the dusty ground and held open the door.

He took them back along the road and down to Myrties harbor where together with Nicos they gently helped Sky onto a brightly coloured fishing boat.

"This is one of Nathan's." Nicos said as he sat down beside her. "One we used to go out on to dive."

The little boat chugged its way out of the harbor and across the narrow stretch of water to Telendos.

As it neared Sky could see this was just like any other harbor, only so tiny. It had tavernas along the shore, lovely little houses and a smattering of shops, only everything looked so small. Even the fishing boats looked tiny, it must be the effect of the island, she thought, looking up to the top of the hill in the center.

As the crew busied themselves anchoring the boat, she looked along the harbor road and suddenly burst out laughing.

"Jack you have got to be joking!" She exclaimed. "No way."

"Well you did say no motorbikes." He laughed with her as they gazed at an old man holding the ropes of two donkeys. "It's the best way believe me."

The boat crew helped a laughing Sky over a little wooden walkway, which was actually no more than a wide plank, and on to the tarmac.

Nicos spoke quickly to the donkey's owner and between them they hoisted an almost hysterical Sky on to the back of one.

"Jack don't leave me up here." She squealed as he let her go and went to mount his own.

"Stop wiggling about. I'm only here."

The crew tied her crutches to the back of his donkey and off they went.

Nicos led the way, holding on tightly to the rope attached to the bridle of Sky's mount. He smiled to himself as her heard her squeal, just like on the motorbike he thought, feeling slightly sorry for the poor animal.

Gradually Sky got the rhythm as the donkey walked along. It seemed to be quite docile and daringly she leaned forward to pat its neck.

"This is great Jack, I can see over everything." Sitting back up as straight as she dared Sky actually began relax. It was so easy to look around and she soon began to enjoy the ride, even if at times strange smells seemed to be coming from her animal, plus the odd weird sound as it steadily walked along the stony track.

"Bend down slowly." Nicos shouted as they came to a curve in the path where an ancient olive tree had right of way, its fruit laden branches falling down low in front of them. "Don't get up until I say."

He could see Sky do as she was told, lying almost flat against the animals back, he knew she would regret going quite so low. "Ok up you come, but slowly."

"Phew. Thank goodness, I don't think Red Rum here has bathed this week." She wrinkled her nose against the smell and dust that had come into her nostrils.

"Whoa," she heard Nicos call. "Right Sky call to him to stop and pull back slightly on the reigns."

"Whoa." She said softly.

"No, let him know who is boss. Louder."

"Whoa!" She yelled, the animal came to an abrupt halt. "Hey I can drive a donkey." She laughed and put her arms out for Nicos to lift her off. "That was brill thanks Jack." She said slipping down the animal's side and almost kissing Nicos as he held her tightly. She stopped herself just in time and quickly turned her head away. "Why have we stopped here?"

Sky gazed round at the pretty deserted beach just below.

"I think we need to talk." He said scooping her up in his arms and carrying her over loose stones to the sand, where she was amazed to see two sun beds with a table to one side, a bottle of wine and two glasses stood on the top. He placed her gently on to one of the beds. "I want you to ask me anything, and I mean anything. I think I owe you some answers."

Sky looked towards the sea in silence, accepting a glass of wine she nodded but still said nothing. Eventually she looked towards his frowning face.

"Why Jack. That's all I need to know. Why?"

Now it was his turn to be silent as he thought about his reply.

"When I came over here," he began. "I was a celebrity. I couldn't believe it. Wherever I went the people had heard of me. Nicos Mandros, the man who was going to save their island. From the main town, to the smallest village, wherever I went people brought me drinks, food, little gifts. They were all so pleased that I had come to save the sponge industry.

Paulo and Giovanna took me all over the island, I was a star, and it went to my head." He paused and looked at her, she continued to sip her drink and stare out to sea. "Giovanna was beautiful then and reveled in my status as much as I did." He glanced sideways to see if there was a reaction. Nothing. "I fell for her charms, I was putty in her hands. During the day I went diving with Paulo and took my photographs, and at night she was waiting.

Nathan set up a gallery in town to sell my photographs and everything seemed rosy. Only I didn't feel right. I wanted to come home. That photograph in your room back at the hotel has been on my screen since you sent it, look." He held his phone up for her to see, and true to his word the original was there. "I have had many phones since then but always transferred this, I could never really let go you see. I loved Giovanna in a way, but nothing to the love I felt for you and the children." He saw her head move slightly. "The reason I stayed was Gina and my father. The day he came over and we fought was the worst day of my life. To have my father strike me like that made me realise just how many people I had hurt and when I got back to the house Giovanna told me she was pregnant. I knew what she was like, bad tempered and very spoilt, how could I leave. My father said he never wanted to lay eyes on me ever again, nor mama, and if I tried to see him he would ignore me as if I were a stranger. He said I was out of his life for good." His voice wavered with emotion. "I knew I had done you wrong Sky, and the children, but what could I do. I had no idea if you would have me back or not, would you eventually turn the children against me, and how could I live so close to papa and not speak to him? I was in such a mess, only your phone calls kept me sane, those and Gina. At one point," he turned to look at her. "I almost packed up and came back bringing her with me but I did not have the courage. So I decided to stay and help her as much as I could, be a good father to her at least if not to my other children.

Giovanna had more or less ignored her from the day she was born I had to do everything. All she was interested in was us getting married, I tried to tell her I would never divorce you, but she kept on and on. It was my name and money she was after, not me I think in the end.

Poor Gina grew up loving her mother so much, only to be hurt by her time and time again, yet she still came back for more. Oh Sky I just didn't know what to do."

For a few minutes he sat and sobbed.

Sky kept her eyes fixed on the white handkerchief he had tied on the cliffs the other side of the water. She dare not look at him; she knew very well what would happen. How her arms ached to hold him, her body to feel his weight, to feel his naked soft skin, but no she kept on staring at the little white speck and took another sip of wine.

Eventually Nicos continued.

"When Gina met Allesandro I had this strange feeling, I knew it would all go wrong. To have my little girl in the hands of this man was like torture, you see I disliked him from the word go. He was handsome, cocky and so full of himself I wanted to hit him, but Gina fell in love so what could I do? I talked to her and had to admit defeat, so I gave her the best wedding I could and tried my hardest to like her husband.

I will admit he tried to learn from me. His ambition to be a photographer had been with him since childhood, he had read about papa and me and was more than willing to learn. The fact that he had married my daughter made him feel very important. I think like Giovanna he was after my name and status.

The day he left to find his fortune, as he put it, I held my baby as she cried, and vowed to get my revenge, but it looks as if he has done more damage to himself than I could ever inflict." He laughed. "You know I could never hurt a fly let alone another human."

Sky looked him in the eyes.

"But you hurt me Jack, very badly." She said and turned to stare across the water once again.

"I know I did and I am so sorry. Would you have turned us away, me and Gina? No don't answer that. I could not bear it if you said no. I would have wasted so many years I think it would finish me off."

He was right, Sky would have taken the two of them in, it was in her nature to forgive, to be kind. Could she have turned the love of her life away?

No never.

"I have no idea where Allesandro is now and I don't care." He added. "I just hope Gina will see what he is like and forget him."

"She is young Jack, her heart will heal. It will take time, but she will heal believe me. She already looks so much better, given the fact her mother has just died, she looks remarkably well in fact. Sunni is very fond of her, and as for Emily, well I think they will be good pals. I hope so anyway for both of their sakes.

I think Sunni wants to marry his young lady, and if Gina lives with us, then it will be easier for Emily to leave her family.

As for Storm, I have no idea what her reaction will be. She has always been top dog, well in her own eyes, and to share Sunni with another sister will hit her hard. I think you are in for a bumpy ride with her Jack, so please take it slowly."

"I will do whatever you say I promise. Thank you Sky, thank you so much." Nicos smiled at her his eyes misty with tears, he knew now where his heart really lay, with her, and to be truthful it always had. "We will return with you and be happy I know."

And so will I, Sky thought, very happy.

They lay on their sun beds, both deep in thought, sipping wine and nibbling at the olives mixed with tiny pieces of feta cheese and sprinkled with lovely aromatic herbs that Nicos produced from a cool box by his bed.

"Fancy a swim?" He asked, his eyes now shining happily. "Come on I'll carry you just like in the old days. Get your cossie on."

"What here?" She giggled. "There's no where to change."

"Can you see anyone else?" He asked, she shook her head. "Well then no one can see you can they."

He watched as she shyly began to take off her blouse and shorts, wriggling about on her sun bed in order to keep her feet out of the sand.

"Don't be so silly Sky. You are making it very difficult for yourself. Here let me help." He stood and held out his hand. Sky looked up and blushed but nodded.

"Let's not bother with cossies Jack. Let's pretend it's years ago."

She remembered the times they had swum at Eleni beach totally naked, the moon and stars lighting the little waves as they rolled slowly to shore. Nicos just nodded and began to remove his own clothes cursing his body for giving his feelings away.

"That looks good." She said eyeing his obvious excitement. "Very good."

Gently he lifted her from the bed and carried her in to the warm sea. Holding her close they began to kiss, long lingering kisses that touched the core of her soul.

"I though we were supposed to be cooling down Jack, not getting hotter." She laughed.

Now they were in waist high and the waves gently knocked their bodies together. Sky felt him hold her legs and wrap them around his middle; he held her close. He kissed her breasts, her nipples erect from the touch of the water, then he kissed her neck, and let his hands massage the cheeks of her rear. It felt as if time had been rolled back as he gently lifted her slightly before entering, the force of the waves helping him to go deep.

"Oh God that feels good." She breathed. Letting her head fall back she could feel the sun on her face as her hair fanned out in the water. "It has been such a long time Jack. No one has touched me since you left." Slowly she pulled herself upright and kissed his lips, she could feel the stubble on his chin rubbing her skin. "Don't ever leave me again."

"Never ever my love. Oh Sky I love you so much. It took me all these years to realise, but you are truly the only one for me. My soul mate, my angel of the lake, and now you are my mermaid."

Sky felt waves of pleasure exploding in her body as he thrust deeper and deeper, his hands gripping and pulling her close, seconds later he reached the point of no return. He gave her every last ounce of his being, crying out her name as he at last came to be still.

They stood silently, arms wrapped around each other, letting the water lap against their bodies.

Sky pushed herself away gently and swam off, she may have been unable to walk properly, but once in the water she could swim as well as anyone.

"I'll get you." Nicos called and suddenly burst into a crawl. "I'll get you." He repeated, then spat out the seawater that filled his mouth.

"Bet you can't catch me." She replied laughing and speeding up.

"Bet I can."

And he did. Grabbing hold of her ankles and pulling her back through the water.

"I said you wouldn't get away that easily. Come on time to dry off before lunch." He picked her up in his arms and kissed her gently.

"What's for afters?" She giggled kissing him back.

Sky felt like a youngster again, not the mother of two almost twenty year olds, her eyes shone with happiness.

"Anything you want." He replied lifting her from the water and placing her gently on the sun bed. "Anything at all."

They lay dozing in the sun, its rays warming and drying their skin.

"I don't suppose I will ever understand it all Jack." She said quietly. "I doubt Storm will ever forgive you but I know Sunni will and I certainly will, but please never again." She looked over towards him. "Promise."

"Yes I promise." He replied and reached out to hold her hand. "More wine before lunch."

"No thanks." She giggled. "I've got to drive that thing again." She nodded towards the donkeys sheltering under a nearby olive tree.

"Come on then let's get going." Nicos helped her stand and dry any damp bits before dressing. He whistled to the donkeys that reluctantly left their shaded cool spot and ambled towards them.

"They are very well behaved." She said as he lifted her on to the back of hers. "Well that was until I got on board." Her donkey had rapidly turned and was heading back to the shelter of the tree.

"Pull back on the reigns Sky. Show him who is boss." Nicos could hardly speak for laughing; her face was a picture of terror. He quickly jumped onto the back of his and rode after her and taking hold of the rope lead they set off towards the taverna, the one he had pointed out from the other side of the water.

Once they got going it was quite a pleasant ride over the rocks, and only very short, something Sky was more than pleased about. The wine was now sloshing about in her stomach and not mixing very well with the seawater that had been drunk during their lovemaking.

As they neared she could see that once again they were expected. A small wooden table had been set for two, just a little apart from the others. It was closest to the sea and shaded by a pretty vine covered arbor. On its pristine white cloth sat fresh crusty bread, dishes of tzatziki, black olives and large bowl of fresh salad, an open bottle of red wine, a large bottle of water and four sparkling glasses.

I shall be plastered if this keeps up all day; she thought to herself, but who cares, I certainly don't. She concentrated on the bread and water to begin with just to be safe.

After a while plates of chicken breasts, lamb souvlaki and slices of beautifully soft creamy garlic potatoes arrived. It was a meal made in heaven.

"Why did you put the handkerchief over there Jack?" She asked nibbling none to ladylike on a chicken breast and licking her fingers.

"To show you I surrender. I wanted it to be a symbol of my humbleness I suppose." He replied softly.

"I'm glad you did for what ever reason, it gave me something to concentrate on when you were talking. I think I would have cracked if I hadn't had that." She felt silly as now the tears fell from her eyes.

"Oh Sky." Was all he could say; instead he knelt on the floor and buried his face in her lap, her tears falling on to his shirt spread as the cotton soaked up the moisture. Gently she stroked his hair, hair that was once jet black, now mottled with gray, once so thick, now thinning slightly.

"I love you." He said at long last.

They lingered over their lunch chatting and laughing, relaxed and happy in each other's company. Gone were any doubts Sky had felt in taking Nicos back, not straight away as her husband, she had to let the children get used to him being there first, but gradually she hoped they could pick up their lives together.

Although the meal had lasted for hours Sky felt quite sad when Nicos called for the bill, but she had to giggle when he asked for the donkeys to be brought to them at the same time.

"That's a first Jack." She laughed as the waiter nodded and shuffled off. "You know I shall remember this day for ever. What's this place called again?" She turned round in her chair looking for a sign.

"What do you think it would be called?" He replied. "See if you can guess."

Sky looked around the cobbled courtyard where the tables were laid; she looked at the pretty pots of flowers, their blooms bright against the white stonewall. Still shaking her head she looked further afield, out over towards the sea where the water splashed against the rocks on the shoreline, then behind the taverna where the land rose steeply towards the summit of the island's only hill.

"It could be anything really." She sighed. "All I know is it has been wonderful."

"I shall tell you then. It is called The Café on the Rocks." He smiled.

Never had a place been so aptly named.

The donkeys arrived with the bill, and soon the laughing pair were heading off towards the harbor where Nathan's little boat waited swaying lazily on the gentle waves of the sea.

Nicos slid from the saddle of his donkey and went to help Sky. He was shocked to see her kiss its neck and pat it fondly.

"Bye bye Dobbin. Thanks for looking after me today." She whispered in its ear.

"After all of your screaming and shouting I don't believe what I just heard." Nicos stood hands on hips.

"Well a girl can change her mind can't she?" Sky replied. "And he had been good really I suppose."

As the boat chugged out of the harbor he was even more amused to see her waving to the dumb creature.

"Bye." She called. "Bye."

They sat close to each other and watched in silence as they got further and further away from the little island.

"What a fabulous place that is. I bet not many people have even heard of it, but then if they had it wouldn't be so special. I hope it never gets crowded and touristy." Sky said softly.

"I doubt that very much. Holidaymakers like things easy I don't suppose many would like the trek we have had today. Taxi, boat, donkey, boat, taxi."

125

"When you put it like that I suppose not. But I have loved it all." As she smiled at him he noticed her nose had turned slightly red from the sun.

"Well that is the first time I have ever seen you change colour. Your nose is pink." He laughed as she quickly put her hand up to cover it.

"It must have been because I was closer to the sun on the back of Dobbin," she giggled. "I'd better put some cream on once we get off this."

Now that Nicos had mentioned her nose the rest of her skin began to tingle as if burnt. So much had happened since breakfast she had completely forgotten to put on any sun cream. I'm going to suffer for this, she thought to herself, not realising just how much.

The crew moored the boat and came to help her from her seat, carrying her once again over the wooden plank walkway.

She thanked them and waited whilst Nicos collected their bags and shook hands with the men.

The narrow jetty was quite busy, as a little further down a tourist boat had moored at the same time as they had.

Evidently the holidaymakers had been on a trip to Pothia and the sponge factory. Sky looked at the wonderful specimens they were carrying as they walked by chatting loudly.

Suddenly a loud splash and a cry drew her attention towards the sea. A little girl had slipped and was now flaying her arms about wildly as she panicked in the water. Sky's heart filled with pride as she saw Nicos was first to react. He dropped their bags and smoothly dived straight into the water seconds before the girl's father clumsily jumped in.

With the help of the boat's crew Nicos managed to haul the girl out and hand her back to her distraught mother, then between them the men dragged her father from the water.

Sky watched as the girl's father shook Nicos's hand and patted his back, she couldn't hear what was being said, but she could well imagine. The mother then came up and obviously thanked him, kissing his cheeks to emphasize her point.

A smiling Nicos picked up the little girl and hugged her, he kissed her and wagged his finger in the air, telling her off but also being very gentle. He waved as the family walked away, the little girl gripping her mother's hand for all she was worth.

"Just look at me." He said coming over to where Sky stood, his clothes dripping water and his sandals squeaking as he walked. "But it doesn't matter, she is safe now." His eyes once again looked towards the family.

"I was so proud of you Jack. And now I understand so clearly. I think I understand everything, I must have been blind not to realise before." Nicos frowned as she spoke. "Come on I'll tell you in the taxi."

By the time they had reached the waiting car Nicos had almost dried off but he still placed one of their beach towels on the car seat just in case. He looked at her and waited, a little worried as to what she would say.

"I know now why you stayed here." She began. "You need to feel wanted, needed, rather than to be just accepted for what you are." He frowned even more. "I think it all comes from trying to be like your father. All through your childhood you wanted to take photographs as good or better than the ones he took.

You wanted to be as good at running or swimming as Andros, but failed, so you fell out with him instead.

You could see Eleni needed you when she first arrived, and then a very lonely Paris." She heard a sudden intake of breath. "Yes I know all about Paris, but in splitting her and Andros up he then needed you to help mend the rift, so once again you became friends.

You met me and I needed you to help me walk, but once we had Storm you could see I was quite able to cope and when the job came along to help Kalymnos you jumped at it. You helped to put the island back on track and in the process fell for the charms of Giovanna, but she too needed your help. She was a little unstable I feel, and when Gina came along she could not cope. I don't think for one minute she didn't love her, I just think she was scared.

Gina of course has needed you all of her life and that is why you stayed. Then today without a thought for yourself you saved that little girl." Sky patted his knee. "You are just one very caring person, but you need to be more confident Jack. You are a wonderful photographer; you are a loving man, a very kind man. Just try to be more confident in yourself." She felt her eyes fill with tears. "Just do me a favour and don't

127

fall for any more sob stories." He wrapped his arms around her and kissed her brow.

"I promise, never again." At that moment he meant his words more than anything in the world.

They sat holding each other until the car stopped outside of their hotel.

"Do you want to eat out tonight?" Nicos asked a yawning Sky, "or shall we stay put."

"Stop here please I feel shattered." She replied. "And I feel so cold." She began to shiver. "Oh God I feel sick."

Nicos carried her quickly to her room, the taxi driver following behind with their bags and her crutches.

For the first time in her life Sky had sunstroke.

• CHAPTER •
12

Nicos stayed at her side throughout the long night. Every time he gave her water to sip she was sick, every time he tried to wrap her shivering body she threw off the clothes sweating almost immediately the sheets touched her skin.

He listened as she rambled in her troubled sleep not quite being able to make out the jumble of words that came from her mouth.

Eventually exhausted and slightly more stable she slept.

Nicos willed himself to stay awake just in case she needed him, but eventually exhaustion got the better of him and he too fell asleep, his legs curled up underneath his body as he let his head fall on to the bed.

"Jack wake up." She said shaking his shoulders. "I need the loo again."

He woke in a split second, but his legs took longer. He sat rubbing them to bring back the circulation.

"Hurry up I'm desperate!"

129

He did his best and after what seemed an eternity managed to carry her into the bathroom. Her stomach had emptied from the top at first, now the other end was beginning to react. Feeling as low as she had ever known Sky sat and cried, Nicos knelt at her side and held her close.

"It must be love if you can do that whilst I'm in this state." She blubbed. "Oh I feel so poorly."

"I said I love you and I meant it Sky. I'm so sorry this is all my fault. I had completely forgotten about you and the sun. I should have made you wear a hat and plenty of cream. I'm so sorry my love."

"It was such a fantastic day. Trust me to spoil it all." She wailed.

"Come on back to bed."

He helped her back into the bedroom and was pleased to see that she dragged the sheets across her body; the fever was beginning to die.

"Join me Jack. Give me a cuddle." She pleaded. "I need a cuddle."

"Only if you promise not to throw up on me." He replied, pleased to see her smile.

"Sorry but I can't promise anything at the moment."

Nicos slid under the sheet and held her as she cried herself to sleep.

That was how Sunni found them next morning, wrapped around each other fast asleep. He stood and looked at his parents, it was the first time in his life he had seen them together like this and found it a little strange. Nice but strange.

Then he noticed the smell.

"Ugh." He said out loud waking his father. "What is that?" He whispered, his nose wrinkled.

"Your mama has been very poorly in the night. She won't be going back to Skiathos today. Come here I will explain."

Nicos managed to slip from the bed without waking Sky and beckoned for Sunni to go into the corridor where he told him all about her illness.

"So you see you will have to take Gina back with you. Please look after her for me and make sure Storm understands it is me her anger should be aimed at not Gina. I will bring your mama back in a day or so. She will need to rest and drink plenty of water, I will make sure she

130

stays out of the sun." He laughed. "You should see her nose its bright red." Sunni smiled he had never seen his mother anything but white. "We shouldn't laugh really." Nicos said still smiling. "She had been so poorly."

He gave Sunni the keys to his room and told him where the travel documents were. "Tell the others not to panic, a couple of days and she will be OK believe me." He turned to go back into the room. "Do me a favour son, order coffee and pastries for me I'm starving, oh and more water for your mama please."

"Of course I'll get them to bring it up straight away. Anything else?"

"No thanks. Just look after Gina."

The two men hugged and patted each other's arms before parting.

"I'll give you a ring." Nicos said softly. "Let you know when we should get home."

Sunni raised his arm acknowledging his father's words and went off in search of a waiter.

Closing the door quietly Nicos tiptoed into the bathroom and treated himself to a long hot shower. The bad night and worry about Sky momentarily forgotten as he revived himself under the stream of water, in fact he relaxed so much he began to sing softly to himself.

"That sounds nice." He heard Sky say from the bedroom. "Not just your singing but the sound of the shower."

With a towel wrapped around his waist he stood in the doorway rubbing his hair dry with another.

"If you want one I'll help you if you think it will make you feel better. Do you?" He asked.

"Oh please I feel so sticky and grubby." Sky swung her legs over the side of the bed and reached for her crutches.

"Hold on wait for me." Nicos ran across the room and caught her as her weak legs gave way. "Now hold on." She wrapped her arms around his neck as he lifted her from the floor. "Waste of time me getting dry I think," he laughed pulling the towel from his waist and once again stepping into the shower. "Now hold on to the rail whilst I get the gel and turn the water on."

131

Hot water poured over Sky's head as he rubbed shampoo into her long sun bleached hair. Expertly he rinsed it well and instructing her to hold on to the wall rail again began to soap her body with fresh smelling gel.

"That feels so nice. I don't think I have ever felt so awful in my life. Next time I shall wear the biggest hat I can find." She said spitting out water as she spoke. "What time are we leaving today?"

"We're not." He said quite sternly. "You are staying put for a couple of days and I am going to wait on you hand and foot. I have already spoken to Sunni and he is going to take the girls home. Me and you will have a couple of days to ourselves and you can get properly better."

He was kneeling and rubbing her legs with gel, his face level with her bush of soft pubic hair. In any other circumstances he would have made the most of his position, but not today. Sky had been far too ill, perhaps next time, he smiled to himself at the thought. Yes, definitely next time, and of those there would be many. Never again would he wander from this lovely woman. He stood slowly and reached for the showerhead taking time to rinse her body thoroughly, gently rubbing his hand over her skin to help the suds slide away.

"Much more of that and I won't be responsible for my actions." She laughed. "I could stand here all day with you doing that."

"No naughty thoughts for you today my girl. Rest and water, some honey and perhaps a little bread. That is it. Tomorrow will be a different story though." He grinned at her before turning off the shower. "Right wait there." He stepped from the cubicle and wrapped himself in his damp towel quickly rubbing his hair with the previously discarded smaller one. "Right then here we go." He covered her body in a soft dry towel and rubbed gently.

"You will need to wrap my hair up or I shall keep dripping on you." She laughed. As quickly as Nicos rubbed her body droplets of water fell on parts he had just dried, and on himself.

"Good thinking." He replied and put her hair up in a towel turban. "That's better." The dripping stopped almost immediately. "Now for the rest of you." Once again he tried to dry her but a knocking at the door interrupted him. "Don't move I'll just be a minute." He rushed to the door not wanting to leave her for a moment more than was necessary.

It was the waiter with breakfast.

"Right. Let's try again."

By this time Sky was in fits of giggles.

"I wonder what he thought. This is my room and you just answered the door dressed like that." His damp towel had stuck to his body leaving nothing to the imagination. Nicos looked at himself in the mirror in shock before bursting out laughing.

"I bet he thought what a lucky man I am." He kissed her gently. "Now back to bed for you."

He scooped her up in his arms and carried her back to the bed puffing up the pillows before letting her sit back. He fetched her hairbrush, deodorant and face cream. "Put plenty on your nose." He teased handing her a little mirror.

"Oh God just look at it." It was the first time Sky had seen her burnt face with her nose like a red beacon stuck in the middle. "Thank goodness we are staying here. Can you imagine if Eleni saw me like this she would laugh for a week."

Once the grooming had finished Nicos fetched her clean underwear from the drawer and then dressed himself.

The room looked like a bomb had gone off, but first on his list was to get Sky drinking. He poured her a large glass of water and some strong coffee for himself, he even allowed her to nibble on a honey soaked pastry before he attacked the mess of discarded clothes and wet towels.

"You will make someone a good husband one day." She sighed, but before he could think of a fitting reply he noticed her eyes had closed and she was fast asleep. Very gently he lifted her from her sitting position and laid her flat then covered her with the sheet. He pulled the shutters closed but left the windows open slightly to let some fresh air circulate the room.

Sky woke as the waiter brought Nicos his lunch. She watched as he took the tray from the man at the door and thanked him. Greek salad, crusty bread some chips, fresh peaches and tiny sponge cakes, bottles of beer and water.

"Are you running up my room service bill?" She said gently so as not to make him jump and drop the lot.

"Nice to see you awake my love. How do you feel?"

"Very thirsty actually."

"Well there's some fresh water here." He poured her a glass from the newly opened bottle. "Hungry?"

She shook her head.

"Not really thanks, just so dry." She gulped at the glass.

"Steady on that will come straight back if you do that." He warned. "Now sip it slowly." Nicos took a long drink of his cold beer and smacked his lips. "That's better." He sighed and began to eat.

"Perhaps a little cheese please." She asked. "And some of that salad it smells so fresh and clean somehow."

In the end they shared his meal eating slowly so not to shock her tender stomach. The only thing he would not let her have was the beer.

"Maybe later." He said when she asked. "But only if Dr. Nicos thinks you are well enough."

Sky was surprised how tired she felt after lunch and once again Nicos made her comfortable in the bed. Just before she had let her eyes close his mobile phone sprang to life, it was Sunni. She listened as Nicos asked about the journey and his answers to Sunni's questions about her health but she shook her head when Nicos gestured for her to speak, she felt too weak to even talk to her son.

She found it hard to believe that sun stroke could make her feel so ill, she had heard of it obviously, but this was the first and definitely the last time she would get caught out, mind you, she thought, it has given me time alone with Nicos. Her eyes had closed before he had finished his conversation, this time she slept with a smile on her face.

Two days later she felt well enough to go outside. Nicos made sure she was under a large poolside parasol, that she had plenty of water and a large bar of her favourite chocolate with some fresh bananas at her side.

"Now don't move from there," he said wagging his finger at her. "I will only be a short while I have some shopping I need to do." He kissed her gently and waved as he left.

She watched him go and sat back to relax in the warmth of the day. It was so nice to be in the fresh air once again so she took some deep breaths as she looked around the pool. Most of the faces were new, the holidaymakers from before she was ill now gone home. She looked at her

134

body a good half stone lighter than a few days ago and let her hands run over her hipbones that now jutted from just below her skin.

At least her face was a decent colour, the redness had turned into a soft golden brown, and the only downside was the fact her nose had begun to peel.

She nibbled on the goodies Nicos had left and felt her body react to the energy they provided. She heard her stomach growl and smiled to herself, at last she was getting hungry.

Nicos returned with an assortment of bags.

"You OK?" He asked immediately and noticed that a couple of bananas and most of the chocolate had gone.

"Yeah I feel great thanks. What have you got there?" She sat up straight and started to open the bags.

"Just a few presents for home." He replied lifting out his purchases one at a time. "A large sponge for Storm and one for Paris. Some local wine for papa and local honey for mama." He sighed. "I want to take something for Gina to remember her mother by but I don't know what." He frowned.

"How about a photograph of the church you know the one where she is buried. Not a morbid one of the grave or anything but a pretty one of the church." Sky replied.

"Brilliant. I'll go now the light is just right." Nicos stood up quickly. "I'll just get my cameras."

"Let me come with you?" She asked with a whine. "Please. It would do me good and I promise to keep out of the sun."

"Yes you can come and I know you will keep out of the sun because I have brought you this."

From one of his bags Nicos produced the most beautiful fine straw hat she had ever seen. It had a huge cream brim decorated with a fabulous matching feather. It was exceptionally glamorous, very flamboyant and totally unsuitable for a sun hat, but Sky loved it.

"Anyone would think I'm off to Ascot." She giggled and promptly plonked it on her head.

They laughed together for a long time it was a wonderful moment in their lives. They hugged and kissed, and laughed some more, any tension between them long gone.

"I love you so much." She managed to say unsteadily. "So, so very much."

He kissed her again.

"Come on let's get you dressed, we had better get going before the light changes." Nicos said eventually, tears still streaming from his eyes from the laughter.

Sky changed into a pretty pale green sundress and fabulous matching sandals. The delicate colour made her very hard won tan look even better.

The highlights in her hair sparkled as she brushed it before placing the huge hat once again on her head. Sun cream was rubbed liberally on any bare flesh and after a squirt of her perfume she was ready.

"Got your cameras Jack?" She called to him from the bathroom. "I'm just about ready."

Nicos clicked his phone off, having just booked their taxi and looked up as she entered the room.

"You look great my love. Good enough to eat." He rose from the bed and launched himself at her.

"Steady on you animal." She laughed. "Don't you damage my feather."

"OK. I'll behave for now. Later I can't promise." He grinned, that lovely boyish, roguish grin that she knew so well. "Taxi's waiting madam." He held out his arm and together they walked slowly back out into the bright sunshine.

Sky had to admit that the hat was brilliant on an afternoon like this, no more squinting as her eyes were now permanently in the shade. It will do wonders for my wrinkles, she thought as she hobbled along.

As Nicos had said the taxi was waiting at the hotel steps.

"After you." He held the door open and helped her into the back seat.

She patted his hand gently as he nervously asked to be taken to the church at Myrties.

Soon they were bumping along the dusty road leading out of the town. As they passed through the village of Kantouni Sky noticed a group of people eating at one of the tavernas in the square.

"That looks nice Jack." She said as they passed, noticing how pretty the little place looked. Pots of flowers were scattered amongst the tables, a couple of marble statues and a little water fountain in the center made it look very inviting. The delicious waft of garlic and herbs entered the car and her stomach gave a mighty rumble.

"I think you are getting better." He teased and rubbed her tummy with his hand. "We can stop there on the way back if you would like?"

"Please." She replied. "It looks so nice."

"But you can't have your desert there. If you can manage it I will take you to have the best ice cream in the world."

"Can't we just skip first course and go straight for that?" She asked giggling. One of Sky's diet killers was homemade ice cream she just loved it.

"No." He answered firmly. "You must eat something first."

"OK spoilsport."

They went back to watching the countryside pass as the taxi wound its way along the road. One minute they were high up on the hillside and the next traveling down towards the sea, eventually the road leveled off mid way between the two but it was still very bendy.

Sky felt Nicos stiffen slightly as they passed the sign to say they had reached Myrties and realised that this was going to be hard for him. He must have felt something for Giovanna, even if was only a little, and she had given him his lovely daughter. Not knowing quite what to say she patted his hand again and smiled. His eyes replied his gratitude; no words were needed for her to see how thankful he was for her to be there.

The taxi stopped at the church gates and Nicos helped her from the car. He asked the driver to wait and then took Sky's arm. For a second he hesitated and unusually looked at her for guidance.

"What about from over there." She pointed to where a cluster of poppies swayed in the breeze just to the side of the ornate church door. "You could get a lovely picture from there." She was using her tourist's eye, as Nicos called it, and not an artist's, but it did the trick by jump-starting his mind.

"No I can see a much better place. You sit here, I won't be long."

He helped her on to a cool stone bench and ran off around the perimeter wall of the graveyard. She watched as he disappeared for a moment or two only reappear in a space where the old stonewall had crumbled.

She could tell that from his position he would be able to get the full church in his shot, along with Giovanna's grave, plus the poppies. The broken wall would act almost as a frame. She smiled to herself, it would be one more of his stunning shots and she hoped Gina would be pleased.

For a while she sat and watched as he prepared to take the photograph, but feeling sleepy in the heat she pulled down the brim of her hat and snoozed. He might have said it would only take a minute, but she knew better, he would be there until he had taken the perfect photograph.

His footsteps in the gravel roused her from her sleep.

"Thanks Sky that was a great idea Gina will love it. Sorry it took so long." She pulled her hat back straight and looked into his sparkling eyes, they once again told her everything she needed to know. Her idea had scored a lot of brownie points.

"Time to eat I think." He held out his arm to help her stand and kissed her quickly on the cheek. The suddenness took her by surprise.

"What was that for?" she asked.

"Just to say thanks again." He seemed almost shy. "And I love you." She smiled at him warmly.

Things had gone so much better than she could ever have imagined. To be back with him had been beyond her wildest dreams. She was soft she knew, and Paris would no doubt tell her off, but she loved him and always had. So that was that as far as she was concerned, they loved each other and sod what the others thought.

The sun was slowly sinking when they reached the pretty taverna in Kantouni. It was still early for Greeks to eat, but a scattering of holidaymakers were already at some of the tables.

Nicos ordered a mixture of dishes not wanting to upset Sky's stomach with one large meal, and allowed her to have an ouzo, although he did ask the waiter to put in plenty of lemonade. It was the first alcoholic drink she had tasted in days and was pleased after a sip or two that it was only a weak one. She could feel it go to her head immediately but nibbling on the delicious food that had been brought soon made her feel less tipsy.

They took their time to savor the fabulous meats and salads that had been presented and chatted for longer than planned. The sun had gone altogether by the time they had finished and pretty coloured lights lit the cobbled eating area of the taverna.

"This really is nice." She sighed gazing round. "And I feel so much better to have a full tum." She patted herself gently.

"It's a pity really but just down there on the beach is a marvelous steak house, well bar come restaurant really. It would have been too much for you tonight, but if we ever come here again I will take you." He said. "On the other hand if you fancy a little walk we could go for that ice cream."

"You bet." She replied laughing. "One thing I always have room for is ice cream." She licked her lips in anticipation.

If Nicos said it was the best in the world then it would be. He called for the bill and helped her to her feet; he stood holding her crutches and waited until she was steady.

"Right then this way it's not far through the village." He pointed down a dimly lit dusty road towards the sea. "But the easiest way to get there is along the beach." She scowled at him; sand and crutches had never gone well together." Don't worry I'll carry you."

They walked slowly towards the sound of the sea leaving the pretty village square behind. Only a few villas and low apartment buildings lined their route, some with olive trees and thick bushes of pink hibiscus in their sun scorched gardens, still alive with bees even at this time of night.

As Nicos had said the beach was only a short walk away and before long Sky was hoisted up in his arms as he tramped over the sand.

"Hold on to your hat. And those." Her crutches were swinging dangerously close to his treasured parts.

Sky could see that many bars and hotels had their frontages leading straight out on to the beach. Most having steps from the poolside directly down to the seashore.

Music from the steak bar could be heard before Sky could actually see the place that Nicos had mentioned, but as they neared she was able to make out coloured lights reflecting in the waves, smell delicious aromas from the restaurant and hear laughter from the wooden terrace.

"Next time you can definitely bring me here it looks smashing." She said as he took a breather, letting her stand in the sand for a moment.

From the chatter Sky realised that it was a "locals" eating place, and if the Greeks ate there then it would no doubt be as excellent as Nicos had said. She could hear a smattering of English spoken but no other language and then remembered back at the hotel it was mostly English holidaymakers. Perhaps this tiny island had yet to be discovered by the other Europeans, and she hoped that would not be for many years, to keep it unspoilt like this would be marvelous.

Once again Nicos gently lifted her into his arms.

"We won't come back this way." He said puffing slightly. "But I wanted you to see all of this." He nodded towards the sea.

"Thanks Jack it's lovely."

As he left the sand and was able to walk on tarmac he slowly let her slide to the floor.

"Lets get a seat." He pointed to the sea wall where a few people were already sitting, Sky looked at him in surprise. "You have to wait your turn here I'm afraid. About one in the morning the queue will be right along this wall, but it will be worth it believe me." He led her towards a vacant part of the wall.

Sitting down she looked across the tiny road to what looked like someone's home, only at the front of the house were a few rickety wooden tables where people were eating. A few dim light bulbs hung from a wire and an assortment of candles were the only form of lighting. As a table became empty the people nearest to her got up and walked across the road.

"Shouldn't they go next?" She asked him pointing to a group further up.

"It's an unwritten thing, everyone seems to know who they follow and wait their turn. That group were just in front of us so once they go across we won't have too long to wait."

"But what if they have a big meal or something." She said childishly.

"It's usually only desert people come for so don't panic. Most people have already eaten elsewhere, have a stroll and end up here. Now just sit still and wait."

140

Sky watched and waited, her crutches at her side, she was ready to move the moment a table became vacant. The group took their turn.

"Us next Jack. Oh this is quite exciting I can't wait." The lights from across the road reflected in her eyes.

"You look gorgeous." He said bending over and kissing her softly.

"Nicos my friend you are so welcome." Came the cry from an old woman who stood in the house door way. "I have a table for you here."

They walked to where the woman was indicating.

"Celia, Kalispera. Please my I introduce Sky, my wife." He noticed how the woman scowled at his introduction. "I know it's a shock for you, but I never did get divorced. Gina is quite happy I hope you can be for me too?"

For a few awkward moments Celia looked Sky up and down.

"Welcome Sky. You must be a very forgiving woman to take this rogue back and so soon after Giovanna's death. I would have thrashed him to within an inch of his life, not that a man with such thin principles is worth thrashing." She said with a toothy grin. "Just please look after Gina for me. She holds a special place here." The old woman patted her ample bosom.

"I certainly will you can count on that." Sky replied trying not to feel nervous under the woman's gaze, her words had stung slightly. Sky knew she should feel some guilt, but why? If Giovanna hadn't taken Nicos in the first place then perhaps she would still have been alive. Sky also knew that was a weak excuse. "As if she were my own." At least those last words seemed to please the old woman.

"Come and sit, let me fetch your desert."

"But she doesn't know what we want yet." Sky whispered to Nicos.

"There is only one to choose." He laughed as Celia returned with large dishes of homemade vanilla ice cream melting quickly under a boiling mix of large black cherries soaked in Kirsch.

The smell was amazing, the taste pure heaven.

Nicos watched as Sky attacked her portion and laughed as she wiped her finger around the soon empty bowl.

"Fantastic, superb, out of this world." Sky licked her lips. "You certainly got that one right Jack. I have never had anything like it in my life. Can we come again please."

"Well I do have to come back at some stage to sort out Giovanna's things I would love it if you came with me." He reached over and held her hand. "I would really love it."

"I'll come. Just leave me here for a few days I would be quite happy." She laughed "Oh I am so full now. I shall dream of that tonight. I wonder how she makes it taste so delicious?"

"You will never find that out I'm afraid. The recipe is a secret passed down through the generations. Only the women of the family know what goes into it other than the cherries and Kirsch, but I bet they could make a fortune if they sold the recipe."

"I hope they never do Jack. It would be such a shame." Sky sighed deeply. "This is more than a desert, its an experience." She looked across to the sea wall where now hardly a space could be found to sit. "I suppose we had better let them have the table."

Nicos paid the bill and once again helped Sky to stand. He waved to a taxi waiting a little further down the road and within minutes they were on their way back to Pothia and the hotel.

They made love slowly and sensuously, the heat of the night putting anything energetic out of the question. Afterwards Nicos stroked her body gently, sighing as he explored the parts that years ago he knew so well.

"Celia is right you know. You must be a very forgiving woman to have me back."

"I can't help myself Jack. I know I should be ranting and raving at you, and thrashing you like she said. But I love you I always have. You hurt me deeply but I got on with life and slowly the pain subsided. Our chats every week helped, I made myself think you had just left, not been gone years. But come to think about it she is right I should thrash you." She slapped his bare bottom with her hand spread open. The noise echoed around the room, along with his surprised yelp.

"Look you have marked me." He howled, quite shocked by the suddenness of her movement, and sure enough an imprint of her fingers could be seen on his skin. "You husband batterer."

"Stop being such a wimp, you deserve worse than that so stop complaining." She replied laughing.

They giggled together for a while then quietened as they fell into each other's arms and made love again.

"Home soon I suppose." Sky said, her fingers walking over his chest shinny now with perspiration. "I had better get back and see what sort of mess my shoe business is in. I bet there are orders by the hundred to be sorted and you," she prodded him hard with her finger, "have got to make your peace with your daughter and your parents."

"You are right but it seems such a shame, these past few days have been so nice, just us. You will come back here with me though won't you?" His brow wrinkled into a frown. "I want you to be with me wherever I go from now on."

"Yes I'll come but only if you take me to Celia's again, no other reason."

"Great I'll get things sorted in the morning. Better warn the kids we are coming home."

He carried on talking for a while before realising Sky had closed her eyes and was fast asleep.

The past few days had taken more out of her than she knew, he would have to make sure she had time to rest once they did get home.

Nicos smiled to himself in the dark as he lay thinking of his old island and the people waiting for their return.

• CHAPTER •
13

Sky woke to hear water tinkling and the soft sound of Nicos singing to himself in the shower. She stretched lazily, yawned and spread herself out over the disheveled bed letting her eyes close once again.

"Kalimera my love." Nicos stood in the bathroom doorway with only a towel around his waist. "Sleep well?"

"Wonderfully thanks. You?"

He sat on the bed and nodded. Sky began to stroke his arm gently.

"I have got to go and get our tickets sorted or we will never get home." But it was too late. Under the touch of her fingers his body had decided for him, the tickets would have wait for now.

They made love as only old lovers could. Slowly, softly, knowing each other's bodies likes and dislikes, where to kiss, where to nibble. Their hands wondered over each other gently. He shuddered as she teased his skin with her nails, gently but firmly scraping them along his body. It was a wonderful torture. They rocked together slowly, their bodies fitting one another's so well.

144

Nicos lay down on top of her breathing deeply, his body glistening in the morning sunlight that flooded into the room.

"I shall have to have another shower now you little devil." He said kissing the tip of her nose. "Might as well get you done at the same time."

He lifted her from the bed and stood her in the shower unit.

Her scream must have awoken most of the hotel guests as he turned to water on full blast, and cold.

"That will teach you," he laughed. "Now lets get you clean." He turned the dial and slowly the water began to warm as he soaped her body.

"That's nice Jack."

"Now leave me alone woman." He slapped her wondering hands. "Or I shall leave you in here to do this yourself. Now just hold on to that rail and behave."

At home Sky had a seat fitted in the shower but here she needed help to stand under the stream of water. She thought about her lovely bathroom and her home. All of the fittings she had put in to make life easier suddenly seemed to beckon. She missed her own bed, her own things around her, but most of all she missed her children. This was the longest she had been away from home since Nicos had left. Sunni and Storm had been on assignments, but at least in her own home somehow she still felt close to them.

"You OK?" He asked, a worried look on his face. "Only you've gone very quiet."

"I feel homesick. Don't know why it's just come over me. See if you can get us a flight today Jack. I want to go home."

"I'll do my best angel."

Nicos rinsed her hair and body with a long spray from the shower then gave himself a quick scrub before turning off the water.

Having learned over the past few days he wrapped her hair into a towel turban first, then rubbed her body with a soft dry towel.

"Breakfast first then I'll go into town. You start packing and we will be on our way before you know it." He smiled down at her then held her close in a comforting hug. "Come here you look all sad, soon get you home don't worry."

145

They chose to sit by the pool to eat breakfast this morning, both wanting to make the most of their last day as if it had been a holiday coming to an end. Sky could feel the sun on her back as she sipped at a cup of steaming coffee. The now ever present hat was quickly placed on her head.

"Can't get burnt today of all days," she said as Nicos laughed. "It's a good job you got this for me."

They sat silently for a while just happy to be in each other's company, but Sky realised things would have to change slightly once they reached The Eagle's nest. She saw him watching her and read his mind.

"I know you want to move back in but you will have to wait," she said replying to his unasked question. "Firstly you have got to get to know Storm again, and I am sure your mother will want to make a fuss of you for a bit. Let's just take it slowly Jack. No rushing into things. We can still have our time together, but as for you moving back, not yet. It's for the best believe me." She covered his hand with hers and gave a comforting little squeeze. "It won't take long."

Nicos sighed. He had really hoped to return and live with Sky, but deep down he knew she was right. He had to tread carefully with his eldest daughter and his father. Perhaps he would stay at the beach. Eleni and Vanni had plenty of room, at least he could ask, if not Paris might let him stay. On second thoughts he doubted that, it was her sister he had abandoned and by all accounts she and Storm were big chums. No Eleni or somewhere in town. He would only be a few minutes drive away wherever he stayed, but then he had to get his car fixed first. Perhaps I won't bother, he thought after all it was old now; no I shall buy a new one.

His mind was in a whirl. New car, new life, it was exciting but slightly frightening.

"You stay here and I'll go and see about those tickets." All of a sudden he felt the need to get back. As Sky had said she felt homesick, he too now felt the real need to get home. He rose and kissed her cheek. "If you can manage to pack your things that would be a great help. Won't be long."

She waved as he left the hotel gardens and sat back treating herself to one more coffee before hobbling back to her room.

With difficulty she pulled the suitcase from under the bed and threw it on the top falling over it herself with the effort. Well that's the worst bit over, she thought, now to fill the damned thing. Luckily she had not brought too many clothes for the trip, as originally their stay had only been planned for a couple of days. Most of her things now were new, ones she had been forced to buy as the stay got longer and longer. She didn't bother folding them neatly knowing that Maria would soon have them all in the washer.

All the time as she collected her things she was praying Nicos would be successful in his search of tickets.

Being on Kalymnos it wasn't going to be that easy. Firstly they had to get the ferry over to Kos, and then a taxi to the airport before getting a flight. Timing was of the essence, unless one of the dolphin water taxi's was going to Skiathos, but she knew that was a long shot and the thought of being cooped up inside one of those for a few hours was not that appealing anyway.

She shrugged her shoulders and carried on packing.

After closing her case and checking the drawers she realised that if Nicos was unable to get them tickets her things would have to come out once again. Now she wished she had taken more care, everything would be creased to high heaven. Uncharacteristically Sky sat on the bed and cried. The aching in her chest to see her children and home again had now got quite painful.

"Hey, what ever is the matter?" Nicos came through the door to see her weeping, "Come here," he sat at her side and held her close. "What is it my love?"

"I just want to get home," she blubbed. "Did you get the tickets?"

"No," he replied and saw her face crumble. "But I met Nathan in the harbor and he said he will take us over to Kos and then fly us in his plane. I told him how generous that was, but he said it was the least he could do. After all I saved his diving business once people started visiting the island again."

"But that was years ago." She sighed.

"We have stayed good friends though. In fact I have seen more of him than anyone. He knows all about me and the torment I went through."

"When do we go?" Her voice trembled slightly. If someone could have spirited her home this second it would not have been quick enough.

"He is waiting outside now."

"Oh Jack that's brilliant." Sky threw her arms around his neck and kissed him with a smacker. "Come on get moving then. Where are your things?" Nicos pointed to his battered suitcase standing in the hallway. "Great. Come on then."

Sky stood, took her crutches from the bed and hobbled out of the room as quickly as she could. She paid her hotel bill adding on a hefty tip, well you never know they might be back one day, she thought, and wanting to go ASAP she also paid Nicos's bill. The staff waved as they left shouting their thanks and hopes that they would soon return. Sky waved back and added that they hoped so too.

At the bottom of the hotel steps Nathan stood at the side of his car moving quickly to help Nicos as the two of them emerged from the reception.

"I shall miss you my friend," he said slapping Nicos's back. "I have enjoyed our talks over the years. Just look after that little girl eh."

Nicos nodded, he was feeling emotional now. He was glad to be going home at last, but sad to be leaving friends and the beautiful island that had become his home.

Sky could see it in his face and touched his arm gently. There was no need for words as they looked into each other's eyes.

Their journey home began.

"Nothing seems to have changed much." Nicos said as they sped through the old town of Skiathos and out towards the hills. He looked like a child trying to see everything at once, his head moving from one side to the other in the hope of spotting someone familiar.

"Some things have." Sky replied. "Wait to you get home." She was right.

Nicos could hardly believe the difference in his home. She had built on several rooms, one for her office, one for Sunni's studio, two more guest rooms, for the children's friends, she explained, and of course the beautiful fountain.

Sky watched as he walked around the building taking in every detail, she saw his shoulders heave as he took in deep breaths, and his head shake from side to side.

148

"Home." It was the only word he could manage before breaking into racking sobs. She hobbled over to him through the dusty ground.

"Home at last Jack." One arm went around his shoulder protectively, the other holding on to a crutch to keep her balance.

She waited until he had composed himself before saying anything more.

"Now to go and see your mama, I'll be waiting on the terrace. Go on." She urged, then watched as he walked slowly over to his parent's villa.

"Maria I'm home." She called through the kitchen door and was immediately engulfed in the huge bosom of her maid.

"Oh it is so good to see you. Just look you are so thin. Sunni said you were unwell. Come let me get you something." The old woman fussed over Sky and made her sit on the terrace whilst she fetched pastries and coffee, and as expected the dirty clothes were quickly bundled into the washer.

"Thanks Maria. Oh it is so good to be home. What time are the children due back?" But before Maria could answer Sky heard the roar of Sunni's car and the tyres skid as he brought it to an abrupt halt.

Within seconds the unmistakable voice of Storm hit her ears.

"You sod. You knew he would be there. Don't tell me lies." She hurled at her brother, her amber eyes flashing with anger.

"Storm I really had no idea. It's Matt you should be shouting at not me." Sunni said with a grin.

"Children, stop it." Sky called.

"Mama your home." Storm ran out on to the terrace and once again Sky was engulfed in a bear hug. This time though the mountains of soft flesh were missing. Storm didn't have one ounce of fat on her.

In the excitement of seeing her mother Storm had forgotten her argument with Sunni, and even that her father might be there, but it only lasted for a millisecond.

"Is that bastard with you?" She spat.

"Storm if you mean your father, yes he is here, and at the moment talking to your grandparents. Now what was all that racket about with Sunni?" Sky quickly changed the subject; it was Nicos's job to make his peace with her, no one else's, not even hers.

149

"Well Matt phoned and had an assignment for us but what he didn't say was that bloody Allesandro was in the photos too. Evidently he's been staying with Matt all this time. Got a contract and everything. Twat."

"Storm! Mind your language." Sky said sharply. "Did you do the shoot?" Storm nodded. "Did it go OK?" Again her head bobbed. "Well what's the problem?"

Sunni spoke for his sister.

"It was brilliant mama. Her eyes were like fire and as the shoot was for make up it went fantastically well. I'm off to get these developed and I hope you calm down before I get back. Flaming sisters nothing but a pain in the backside." His voice trailed off as he walked away to his studio. Sky looked at Storm who immediately burst out laughing.

"Poor Sunni. I do give him a hard time," she giggled. "But he should have warned me."

"Perhaps he is telling the truth and he didn't know. How many times have you known Sunni to lie? No, I think he would have been as surprised as you. Anyway talking of sisters, where is Gina?"

"Gone with Paris and Emily. Evidently Emily's grandfather is ill and as Sunni didn't want her traveling alone he asked Paris to go, then she invited Gina so that she wouldn't be on her own here."

"How do you get on with her?" Sky was concerned that her headstrong daughter might be a little too much for the gentle Gina.

"She's OK I suppose, a bit old fashioned but nice enough. It's not her fault her father is a bastard, sorry mama, a pig. I like Emily too; I think she is just right for Sunni. I wish I could find someone like that. All I ever seem to get is hassle from the men I meet, they all seem frightened of me I suppose it's because I'm rich and famous." It had been a long time since Storm had opened up to Sky like this.

"You will one day love. He's out there now not realising what is in store." Sky sighed. She could remember feeling just this way when she was young.

Who would want a cripple like her she used to think. No fame or riches for her, just a gammy leg. Her heart stopped for a second as she heard Nicos's footsteps in the gravel. Storm looked up, her eyes showing the anger ready to spill out. As he neared her fists clenched and Sky could see the disappointment flood over her as Sunni called to his father. She had been ready to pounce, to fight, and now nothing.

"Hey papa. Good to see you. Come and look at these." Sunni's voice deflated Storm in a second but the wait for him to come got too much and after a few minutes she ran over to Sunni's studio.

Standing silently in the doorway she watched as her brother and father examined the photographs that had been taken of her over the past few days.

"Papa." It was no more than a little whimper. Nicos turned and looked at his beautiful daughter. "Oh papa." Unexpectedly she flung herself into his open arms and cried. Nicos held her for a long time, rocking her gently as she sobbed.

"You disappoint me Storm I thought you had more fight in you." He laughed stroking her hair and face. "I thought out of everyone you would have at least slapped me."

"I wanted to." She said softly. "I wanted to punch you, kick you, all sorts of things. But as soon as I saw you there I knew I love you. I have waited so long for you to cuddle me again."

"Come on then let's cuddle some more." He wrapped his arms around her gently. Sunni tactfully left the room and joined his mother.

"Don't look so worried mama. They are having a hug would you believe." Sunni could see the fear in this mother's eyes. "Even papa said he was disappointed in her. I think he thought he was in for a fight or at least a good telling off. But nothing."

"Thank God for that. You know I had been dreading a show down. I thought at one point I would maybe have to choose between them and that would have been a nightmare."

Sunni tilted his head to one side

"Who would you have chosen?" He asked quietly.

"My daughter of course. My children come first and always will do." She said quite seriously. "Anyway let's have a glass of wine and you can tell me about Emily's grandfather." Sky rang a little bell that sat on the table. "Would you bring us some wine please Maria." She asked politely. The old woman scuttled off only to reappear moments later not only with wine but also a plate of delicious nibbles. Sky laughed, "You are serious about fattening me up aren't you." The old lady just smiled and nodded before shuffling off back to the kitchen.

151

"Well." Sunni began. "Emily's father phoned the other night to say her grandfather had been taken ill. Evidently he is in a home and the matron had called him. He is her only true relative you know," Sky shook her head. "When she was a baby her father, mother and grandmother were all killed in a car accident, six months old I think she said. Anyway her grandfather who was already getting on a bit tried to bring her up but found it all too much so he had her adopted. The couple that had her agreed that they would keep in touch, and let him know how she is doing. They liked him so much he started going on holiday with them and at Christmas he went to stay, so you can see she is still very close. It was good of them don't you think?" Sky nodded. "Well Storm and me had to go off to Athens on this shoot so I asked Paris if she would go with her. She agreed and insisted that Gina go as well, evidently she has never been further than Kalymnos in her life. But the best of it is when Emily was telling Paris about her grandfather it turns out he is the man she has been looking for about a story. Something to do with Richard." Sky's face now wore a frown. "Luke Gould his name is, doesn't mean anything to me, but Paris was so excited she could hardly sit down."

"If it's the same man, then it was he who saved Richard from the Japanese prisoner of war camp. I can just imagine Paris." Sky said with a smile. "I bet she could hardly wait to get over there. I hope it's the right man; it could well be someone completely different. Haven't you read her first book on Richards life?"

Sunni shook his head.

"Never seemed to have time. Perhaps I will now, especially if Emily has a connection."

"Are you going to marry her?" Sky asked completely out of the blue.

"I hope so. She has said she will but insists on making me wait, and getting a job to earn her keep. I ask you, I have more than enough, but she insists. It won't be easy though, she can't speak a word of Greek yet so I don't know what will happen."

"She can work for me." Sky smiled at her son. "She can work in the office with me. I have been meaning to get someone for ages and now your papa is back I'm hoping to spend some time with him. If she agrees then that would be brilliant from my point of view. Talking of which I had better go and see how many orders have come in. Can't be idle much longer." Sunni helped his mother stand and handed her the crutches.

152

"Thanks mama. I will tell her when I phone later."

Sky hobbled off to her office and had a quick glance into Sunni's studio as she passed. Nicos and Storm were sitting on the floor still wrapped in each other's arms. She could hear the mummer of their voices but annoyingly was unable to make out what was being said. She smiled to herself, at least blood had not been spilt, and she had really expected that to happen.

She settled herself down at her desk and logged on to her own web site. Within seconds e-mails from around the world were appearing on her screen. Yes she definitely needed some help with her business.

Nicos peered through the door to see her head bent over her keypad as she furiously typed replies.

"Busy?" He stupidly asked.

"You bet. Just look at this lot." She waved a sheaf of papers in his direction. "So many orders I have had to print them off. Mind you Carlos will be happy." She saw Nicos frown. "You know the cobbler in town. Well he makes my shoes up for me and sends them out. They go all over the world. It's very good for his business as well as mine, he has had to take on three men just to look after my side of things."

"You have done so well Sky, I'm proud of you. Not only have you brought up my children single handedly, but also become successful in your own right. I am so proud of you." He kissed her head. "Now put that away until tomorrow. Tonight I think we should all go and eat at the beach. I'll ask mama if they want to come too."

"How did it go with them?" Sky stopped typing and looked directly at him.

"Very well with mama but I think I shall have to work on papa for a while, once he sees me with Storm I think it will help. He was so worried about her and Sunni growing up without a father, but when he realises she has forgiven me I think he will too. You know I can hardly believe I am here, home again. Thank you so much." His voice quivered slightly the emotional day was beginning to take its toll. "I can't go out tonight in these." He let his hands wonder over his creased grubby trousers and shirt. "I wonder if Sunni will run me into town to get some new things?"

"I bet he will. Go and ask. I'll finish up here and go for a nice soak in the bath. I fancy getting dressed up tonight, I feel so happy." Her voice

153

was light. "Do you know I'm really looking forward to it I shall ring Eleni now and ask them too. The boys are bound to enjoy cooking for a good family get together." She clapped her hands with excitement. "Go on, you go into town and get something nice to wear."

In the end both Storm and Sunni went their father. They helped him choose some new clothes, not that he really needed any help, Nicos had always been good with style, but he let them anyway.

As they walked through the narrow cobbled streets he spotted The Athena Gallery sign above the old shop and his heart jumped. Unable to resist passing without looking in the window he was surprised to see colour photographs on display.

"They are mine." Sunni said proudly. "I don't do many black and white these days." When Nicos and his father had shown their photographs they had all been monochrome.

"They are very good my son." Nicos was in awe of some of the shots Sunni had taken. "You have certainly inherited your grandfather's eye for detail."

"And my father's." Sunni said with a wide grin. "You can have a good nosey round another day, come on." He had to pull at his father's sleeve to get him to move.

"Yes come on papa let's go for a drink before we go home." Storm spoke softly; she had been very quiet so far.

The three of them sat at a table in the taverna Nicos used to go to for lunch all that time ago. Sunni ordered, his father was too engrossed taking in the surroundings.

"Here's to us and a new beginning." Nicos raised his glass. "My wonderful children. Thank you for letting me back into your lives." They raised their glasses to the toast.

"Here's to mama for bringing you back." Storm said softly as a tear rolled down her cheek. They raised their glasses once more.

Before anymore could be said their table was surrounded with Nicos's friends from the past. There was a huge amount of backslapping and shaking of hands, loud chatter, and more drinks. It could have turned into quite some party had time allowed, but Sunni ever watchful of his father's wine intake as well as the time, eventually announced that they should go home.

"Time for more stories another day papa."

"True son, very true. But just give me five minutes. I will meet you back at the car." He saw the look of concern on Storm's face. "Don't worry little one I shall probably be there before you are. I just want to get a present for your mama, don't worry. You two finish your drinks and meet me in a few minutes. OK."

"OK." She agreed reluctantly and waved as he disappeared back into the shop-strewn streets.

A short while later, true to his word Nicos was waiting at the car.

"OK papa?" Storm called as they neared.

"Yes thanks." Nicos replied patting his shirt pocket. "Take me home to your mama."

They piled into Sunni's car and sped off through the streets. Home, thought Nicos once again, why the hell did I ever leave?

The meal that evening turned out to be nothing like Nicos had imagined. His homecoming so far had been slightly fraught with his father but other than that everyone had been pleased to see him once again, until now.

Alexi decided that a noisy night out would be too much for the very frail Athena and so they remained at the villa.

Eleni was OK if a little frosty, but Vanni had the look of a volcano waiting to erupt. He was angry with Nicos for not returning for his parent's funerals, as well as for deserting Sky and the children. He sat through most of the night with fists and teeth clenched. He had been under orders from Eleni not to start any arguments, but as the night went on he found his promise harder and harder to keep.

He had wanted to punch Nicos the second he laid eyes on him, wanted to fight, only the fact that they had been such good childhood pals, and Eleni had ask him to behave, stopped him wrestling Nicos to the floor. Instead he steadily downed the ouzo and wines on offer. Not a good mixture with a temper that was itching to get out.

Sky looked lovely in a deep cream silk dress, her tan had certainly given her a healthy glow, although Nicos could see her eyes were tired. It had been a long and very emotional day for her so it was hardly surprising, he thought.

155

She loved the little gold necklace he had given her earlier with its pendant of a smiling sunshine and now sat quietly twisting her fingers around the chain.

"It looks like you when you smile," he had said when she opened the box. "You are my ray of sunshine."

"Don't go telling another one of your stories Jack," she giggled. "It's a little too soon, but thank you I love it." She kissed him as he reached around her neck to do up the clasp "I love you too."

Whilst they ate Sunni and Storm continued their argument about Allesandro, but with less gusto than before. Storm was slowly beginning to believe her brother and now wanted to have a shout at Matt.

"Why didn't he tell us that worm had crawled to him?" She asked spearing a piece of squid with her fork that she held like a dagger.

"To let things cool down I expect. You can't blame him really, I mean Alex is going to make a lot of money for Matt whether you are in the shots or not. I think we should all forget what has happened and start again." Sunni replied in his laid back way.

"Don't forget Gina in all of this." Sky said softly. "You are not the only one who is hurting Storm, think of her as well."

For the rest of the time Eleni talked to Sky, Storm continued to batter Sunni with her questions, and Vanni, Nicos could see, was trying hard to keep himself in check.

The twins had laid on a lovely meal and the only friendly reaction Nicos got from Vanni was when he complimented them with the words.

"Your grandfather would be very proud of you. That was delicious."

It had at first been quite a shock for Nicos to see how the old taverna had been changed. Only slightly, little things here and there, but still it was different, and as for the flashing lights and disco music later in the evening Nicos doubted that old Tomas would have approved. He was surprised to see just how many young people came to spend the night drinking and eating, dancing and watching Sky TV. In the old days Tomas would close as the sun went down, very few people had even heard of Eleni beach let alone found it.

In a way he admired the boys for turning it into THE place for holidaymakers to spend their Euro, but hoped it would not turn out like some of the nightspots he had read about in the newspapers. Greece was becoming the trendy place to get drunk and that he did not want to see here on this beach.

At last the evening was over. They waved goodbye to the boys who were now very busy with their younger guests and politely kissed Eleni and Vanni goodnight. The four of them piled into Sunni's car and headed for home.

Home, Nicos loved to hear that word. Home he repeated in his mind.

It was an automatic thing to enter the villa and kiss his children good night, then follow Sky into what had once been their bedroom. He sat on the bed a little unsure what to do next. Should he stay or go to his parents, it was obvious there was no way he could stay with Eleni and Vanni, and in a way wished Vanni had fought with him, at least it would have got rid of the tension. As he sat thinking Sky appeared from the bathroom leaning against the frame of the door to steady herself.

"It is up to you Jack." She said reading his mind. "The children seem to have accepted you back and I certainly have, but it is up to you."

Nicos stood and walked over to where she had balanced herself and scooped her up into his arms.

"What a silly question my love. I want to wake up with you tomorrow and every morning until I die."

"Now don't go getting all dramatic Jack. If you want to stay then that's OK." Nicos put her gently on the bed and went into the bathroom to wash. Sky could hear him humming to himself, pleased now that she had left his things untouched in the cabinet.

All of a sudden it seemed so natural, she thought to herself as her very heavy eyelids closed.

"Sleep well my little angel?" Were the first words she heard as she woke. "I had forgotten your little snore. It's lovely."

"I do not snore." She said laughing and gave him a punch.

"Oh I think you do." He replied and raised his arm to allow her to slide her head onto his chest. They lay in silence for some time just watching as the sun's rays broke through the slats of the curtain blinds.

157

"This is heaven," he said kissing the top of her head. "Do you remember that day?" Nicos pointed to the large photograph of Sky as an angel.

"I certainly do. It was one of the best days of my life and for that reason I have never taken it down. I'm sorry to say I took all the photographs of you down I just couldn't bear to see your face. It hurt too much." Just the memory of the pain she had felt made her want to cry. "You broke my heart you know and boy was it painful."

"I am so sorry Sky. I know I can never make up for that but let's start from scratch shall we."

"I think we should at least have a try." She replied smiling up at him.

They lay with their arms gently draped around each other both gazing at the photograph that had meant so much, and happily still did.

• CHAPTER •
14

Gina, sitting nervously at the side of Emily, was unsure if she felt excited or just plain terrified. Never having left Kalymnos in her life before to be in an aeroplane seemingly floating over the Swiss Alps was an experience that was bordering upon the unreal.

At the beginning of the flight she had been between Paris and Emily and had spent most of her time leaning over Emily's legs to get a better view out of the tiny window, but now they had changed places and her eyes had not moved from the fantastic scenes below.

She could hear Paris and Emily talking about the grandfather, who it seemed Paris could hardly wait to meet, and left them to it, quite happy to watch and marvel as they flew over the snow covered mountains.

"He has an old shoe box full of photographs." Emily told Paris. "I used to look at them when I was little. He had a tale for each one. Oh I do hope he is the man you are looking for. It will make him so happy to have someone who is really interested in that part of his life. I think I was a little too young to understand most of it."

159

"I hope so too." Paris replied. "It will finish this book on Richard off properly. To get another view of what actually happened will be great. I always had the feeling that Richard was holding something back. You know, not spilling all the beans." She sighed and looked over towards Gina. "I'm glad we have come away before Nicos got back, I don't think I want to face him just yet." She hoped for Sky's sake she would be able to forgive him too. "And I don't want to hurt her any more than she already has been." She nodded towards Gina.

The young girl was pleasant enough and turning out to be a good friend to Emily, but it was Nicos who Paris's argument was with and no way did she want Gina to feel uncomfortable.

Nicos, however, was a different story all together.

She remembered how she had sat for night after night holding Sky as she sobbed, helped when the two young children got too much. Watched as slowly Sky had pulled herself out from the depths of despair and got on with her life. The way she felt so proud when her shoe business took off, the way she watched her sister guide her children into adulthood.

She was so proud of how Sky had not let her disability ruin her life, but she felt savage towards Nicos who had almost wrecked everything. He was a selfish pig and Paris itched to tell him how she felt.

She had hoped Storm would have reacted with a similar feeling, and had been very surprised when according to Sunni nothing of the sort had happened. In fact Emily had been almost as shocked as Paris when during a phone call Sunni had said father and daughter just fell into each other's arms. Emily had retold her conversation and it turned her stomach; it was if he had been a hero returning from war the way Storm had greeted him.

At least Andros would be spared a meeting with his one time friend. Now old and ailing he no longer traveled to Skiathos it was left to Paris to go to him in Athens. Their marriage had been in name only for many years now but their friendship would last forever. Old age had mellowed his temper, and as far as sex was concerned, well he had enjoyed more than his fair share in the past.

Paris was so much younger than him it had been inevitable that living apart, all be it their choice, the age gap would one day catch up with the cosmopolitan couple. Paris smiled to herself at the thought of her husband. Lovely Andros, now so gentle, almost a father figure instead of a husband, how she loved him and always would. He was her mentor, her guardian, yes she loved him.

A slight difference in the level of the engines noise made Gina jump and Emily took her hand.

"We will be landing shortly. There's nothing to worry about. The pilot is just slowing down a bit." She said comfortingly and smiling into the worried face of her new friend. Emily was right. In less than no time they were rushing along the runway at Heathrow feeling the pull on their bodies as the plane slowed suddenly. The roar of the engines made Gina hold Emily's hand even tighter. That part she did not like one little bit, the taking off had been exciting, and the floating peaceful, but that, no, coming in to land was a different matter.

The trio waited until the plane was almost empty before standing and getting their bags from the overhead lockers.

"I can never understand what the mad rush is all about when a plane lands." Paris said as she lifted their hand luggage down. "They won't get away any quicker, look the suitcases are still being unloaded. It happens every time, especially with holidaymakers."

They walked along the plane, through the drafty tunnel and into the buzzing airport. Planes from all over the world were landing every minute or so and the arrivals hall was stuffy and cramped. They saw from a small TV screen which carousel their cases would be coming on and had a little giggle as they spotted people who had rushed from the plane were now standing impatiently awaiting their luggage.

"See I said there was no need to rush. The cases have only just started to appear." As Paris spoke a few battered suitcases began their journey on the jerky and slow moving carousel. It always amused her to see at least one case go round and around before being claimed. Whether people had forgotten which was theirs she never really understood, and there was always a beach umbrella left on it's own to continue the slow and bumpy ride to where ever forgotten beach umbrellas went.

They collected their cases and made their way through Passport Control. The officer had a good look at Gina's photograph, making her feel even more nervous than before, but eventually he smiled and handed her the document back.

"That made me feel scared," she said in her heavily accented voice. She could speak fluent Italian, courtesy of Giovanna and Paulo, obviously

Greek, but only English with a lot of thought. Her words were slow, but she managed in the end. Sometimes she spoke all three languages in one sentence, but only when she was excited or angry, it was an experience to hear her on these occasions. Her hands would fly wildly, her eyes shine with passion, and her words a mixed up jumble. Anyone who was witness to one of these outbursts immediately fell in love with the pretty passionate girl.

Paris found them a taxi, giving the address of her London home first.

"I thought we could drop our stuff off and then come with you if that's OK Emily?" She asked.

"Yeah, course it's OK. Then I can take my things and have a quick chat to Mum and Dad before we go over to the home."

"Do you want to see him on your own?" Paris asked hoping Emily would agree for them all to go.

"It depends on how poorly he is really. Mum will know. I don't suppose he will want too much excitement if he's not well, but she will know best." Emily replied.

Gina remained silent, now looking out at the huge number of cars and buildings that they were passing. This was certainly going to be a trip she would never forget, so much to see, and all of it gray. Even the sky was gray, full of lighter gray clouds; it made her shiver just looking at it, and this was supposedly summer.

She was more interested in the shops though as they made their way through the streets to Paris's house. She wanted the car to slow so she could get a better look and got frustrated when the only time it did was outside a row of houses.

"Never mind Gina." Emily had noticed the look of disappointment. "We will show you the shops another day. The three of us can have a good nosey round then."

Eventually they reached Paris's beautiful Victorian home where they quickly dumped their bags and cases before whizzing off to Emily's parents.

Her mother hugged her close before greeting the two women standing behind.

162

"Come on in my dears. I'll put the kettle on." She showed them into the front room, which was to Gina like something she had never seen before. Too dark and full of furniture for her liking, everything seemed so different, but she did like Emily's mother.

Round and soft, like mothers should be. Fussing over Emily and the others as if she had known them for years and it was the most natural thing in the world. Not like her own mother who found it hard to say anything nice, very rarely cuddled her daughter, and spent more time worrying about herself than anything else. Still the memory of Giovanna brought a tear to her eyes, she was, or had been her mother and nothing could take that away.

They sat and chatted over cups of strong tea and slices of a delicious soft cake until Emily's father appeared. He had changed his shift at work today in order to go with Emily to see her grandfather.

"I think it's just old age myself," he said after greeting the other girls. "He is getting on now you know."

Paris had the feeling he was warning Emily slightly that the old man was one step nearer death, but at least he agreed that Paris could go with them. Gina could stay, if that was OK, and have another cup of tea with Emily's mother.

Feeling quite comfortable and slightly warmer than in the taxi, Gina agreed readily to wait, and no it was no problem at all, in fact she felt quite pleased to be staying put. The journey was beginning to take its toll, and she was ready for her siesta.

Within minutes of waving the others off Emily's mother had made a fresh brew, as she called it, and cut Gina another slice of the delicious cake. She told Gina to call her Doreen and said her husband would be pleased if she called him George.

"No need to stand on ceremony ducks." She said to the bewildered Gina, who had no idea what that meant, but smiled in the knowledge that it must mean something nice. She could tell by the wide grin on Doreen's face that it was something good.

After finishing her drink Gina asked to go to the bathroom and when she returned was greeted by the noise of the television. She could only understand a little of what was being said, but found it fascinating anyway.

It was obviously a programme about the English countryside, which amazed her how green and pretty it all was. As she sat enthralled by the pictures her eyes slowly closed, Doreen gently placed a blanket over her and left her to sleep. She looked so young and bewildered all Doreen wanted to do was comfort her.

She had heard from Emily how Gina had recently lost her mother, other snippets about her father, and now had the urge to hold the girl in her arm's, instead she made sure she was warm. It was the next best thing to an actual cuddle.

Whilst Gina slept the others were arriving at the old people's home where Luke was now living. It was an old mansion house that had been converted and these days housed old soldiers and women who had served in the forces during the war. Many had limbs missing, but mostly Paris could see that their only problem was old age. She smiled to them as they walked through immaculate gardens and up the old stone steps to the front door. George pushed on the modern doorbell, which looked slightly out of place on the magnificent oak frame; it should be a big brass ring or something Paris thought as they waited for a reply. It was not long in coming.

A young girl in nurse's uniform greeted them all warmly, and walked them through the maze of rooms and corridors, to where Luke now lived.

Paris waited on a chair outside whilst George and Emily went in to his room. She heard as Emily greeted her grandfather and then as George spoke to the old man. She could hear the mumbled reply and noticed a distinct wheeze as the old man struggled slightly for breath, but she could tell he was very happy to see Emily once again.

The minutes ticked by as they chatted and Paris began to feel frustrated but guilty. She wanted to get in to question the old man, let them talk niceties some other time. She knew is was wrong to think like this, but was more than happy when eventually George called her in to the old man's bedside. He introduced her to Luke and explained why she wanted to talk to him, but only if he felt up to it.

Paris noticed a glint in Luke's eye at the mention of Richard and knew immediately this was the man she had been searching for. She saw how he straightened his back and how his fingers began to dance on the

164

white cotton sheet. He was as excited as she was. This meeting would hopefully be the first of many.

Luke pointed to the chair at the side of his bed, and asked her to sit down. He told her how pleased he was that someone was writing about Richard.

"He was such a lovely man. So brave." Luke said softly. "A real unsung hero if ever I knew one. No airs and graces, just sleeves rolled up and muck in with the rest. A true gent." It was obvious to Paris that Luke truly admired the man he was speaking of.

"Pass my box Emily please." He asked and before anyone could say more he was delving into his past. "This was the day I found him." He held a badly creased, almost brown and white photograph out towards Paris. She took it gently not wanting to cause any further damage and heard a strange noise as her own breath was involuntarily sucked in.

There true enough stood a very young Richard. So skinny you could almost see through him, his ribs and kneecaps standing out from almost transparent skin tainted dark with the blood of his comrades. His hair thick with blood and leaves, standing to attention as if gelled into position, the clothes he wore were no more than tatters, and his shoeless feet were black with grime. His young face a mask of pure bewilderment, as terrified eyes looked into the camera's lens.

Tears trickled down her face as she remembered the lovely man in the picture. He had described this moment to her himself, but to actually see it before her spoke a million words more.

"This was taken a couple of days later. Nabia had been to work on him then." Luke smiled as he passed this picture over.

What a change. Richard looked so different. He had proper clothes on, his hair was flat and clean, his eyes had the beginnings of a twinkle, and he no longer had that haunted look.

"You loved him too then young lady." Luke said softly. "I can tell from your face." Paris just nodded, she was unable to speak, her body wanted to explode with grief for the lovely gentle man who looked back at her from the picture.

"I got to know him very well and did an article on him when he was knighted." She managed to say after a while. "He told me all about this you know but seeing it here makes it ten times worse than he described. I am writing a book on his life, I did one some years ago that was based mainly upon his wife, Lady Eleni, but I always wanted to know more about him. He was so fascinating, yet I always felt he was holding something back. Tell me Luke, do you know why he was knighted, and don't tell me it was for his charity work. I know that was just an excuse. Do you know the truth?"

The old man smiled a knowing smile.

"You bet I do," he began to cough. "Tell you what come back tomorrow and we will go through what I know," he winked at her making her giggle. "I'll let you treat me to a drop of something medicinal for my trouble."

"Of course. Any preferences?

"Bells, Teachers, not fussed really. It all does me good." He winked again.

"Is that OK with the nurses then grandpa?" Emily asked innocently.

"Oh yes." He replied laughing, knowing full well if they had any idea Paris was bringing in a bottle it would be confiscated and dished out in dribbles, not in a good glass full that he could feel down to his toes. He glanced at Paris who understood immediately, she just nodded slightly. "Until tomorrow then my dear. I shall look forward to it." He held his hand out; Paris took it gently and was surprised when he kissed hers instead of the shake she had expected. "Until tomorrow my dear."

Paris left the room first giving George and Emily the chance to say their farewells in private. If the truth was known she couldn't wait to get home. She needed to put as much down in her notebook as she could, and the sooner she got to bed, the sooner tomorrow would come.

Paris was silent on the journey back to Emily's parent's home, but her brain was working overtime. She saw Luke's photographs in her minds eye and remembered seeing that frightened look on Richard's face the day he had been knighted. If it had not been for Aunt Eleni there was no way he could have gone through with the ceremony. She was his backbone, Paris realised that now.

He had waited most of his life for this gentle but very strong woman, and boy had she been worth waiting for. Not only did they marry within weeks of meeting, but also she had introduced him to life outside of his home.

Paris said a little prayer of thanks to her.

Once in the taxi Emily and George chatted on about the health of Luke, and then about her life on Skiathos. George was happy that she had found love, but a little wary of her living so far away.

"At least we come over quite often." Emily said as he voiced his concerns. "And the wedding will be over here."

"You've said yes then?" George interrupted.

"Well I did in a way, I just said he would have to wait a bit, but after seeing granddad today I think the sooner the better."

"And then you'll go and live all those miles away." George said sadly, he was pleased Emily was happy but oh how he would miss her.

"You know there's nothing stopping you two coming over to inspect where I live." She giggled, knowing full well how impressed they would be with Sky's villa and the beautiful island. "In fact I think you should."

"Yes." Paris interrupted. "That is a very good idea. Sky has plenty of room so you needn't worry." She would have asked them to stay with her, but wanted to get on with her book, the less interruptions the better. "Thank you for taking me today George I have been looking for Luke for years now, I couldn't believe it when Emily told me about her grandfather. Fate, that's what I call it. Pure Fate."

She had the knack of saying one thing and thinking something else. Already her mind was concocting questions to ask the old man the next day, and the fact that she must not forget to take the whiskey.

"Home," announced George slowing the car to a standstill outside of their house. "What's the betting Doreen has got the kettle on already."

As they walked up the concrete path Doreen appeared, her finger to her lips.

"Ssh," she whispered. "Gina is asleep. Little duck."

They followed Doreen past the lounge door and into the kitchen. Paris smiled to herself as she noticed how they all walked on tiptoe, almost creeping past the open door.

"Kettle's on." Doreen said busying herself at the sink. "How was Luke?"

167

They told her about their meeting over tea and even more cake, well Emily did. She was so pleased that he was not as poorly as she had thought, and the relief could be heard in her voice.

"Paris is going back tomorrow. I think they have a lot to talk about." She added. "I will call in again before we go home though. Tomorrow afternoon we are taking Gina shopping."

"Just you take care of her." Doreen said sternly. "She has been through a lot recently and it looks to me as if she is worn out." Now she sounded all motherly.

Paris smiled and thought of her own mother, was she dead or alive, no one knew, and probably never would.

They all turned as a very sleepy Gina arrived in the kitchen.

"Sit down ducks, let me get you a cuppa." Doreen was already on her feet.

"No thank you. I have drunk enough I think," came the slow and very polite reply. "Please excuse me for sleeping."

"Oh don't worry about that child. You must have needed it." Doreen said and unable to resist any longer pulled the young girl into her arms. "Feel better?" she asked looking down into the smiling face, pleased to receive a nod in return. "Good".

"I think we had better go." Paris said eventually. "It's been quite a day for all of us. Thank you very much, both of you." She shook George's hand. "Emily would you mind taking Gina shopping on your own tomorrow I don't know how long I shall be with Luke."

"No course not." Emily replied. "We can go earlier now, pick you up about 10?"

"Yes OK." Gina smiled but Paris could see she was worried and waited until they were in the taxi home before questioning her.

"Don't you want to go shopping with Emily?" She asked as the car crept through the rush hour traffic.

"Of course, but I have no Euro." She replied shyly. "I didn't see papa before we left. I only have this." She held out a skinny leather flip top purse.

"Don't worry about that silly girl. I will give you both enough to have a good time." Paris pulled her into her arms. "And don't go fretting I shall get it back off Nicos when we get home." She would do no such

168

thing but did not want to hurt Gina's pride. There was no way Paris would ask Nicos for anything, ever. "And in any case it's not Euro over here, not yet anyway." She felt the tension drift away from the girl as she spoke. "Tonight I think we should stay in and have a take-away, what do you recon?"

"What is that?" Gina asked puzzled. She had heard so many words already today that meant nothing to her, and now Paris was saying more.

"We order a meal and someone cooks it, brings it to the door, and all we have to do is eat it. Brilliant. No washing up or anything. Now what shall we have? Chinese? Indian?" She could see from Gina's face that she had not got a clue what she meant. "Tell you what I'll choose. Umm. Chinese. I hope you like it."

Gina gave a bemused smile; what ever it was it would go down well, she was famished.

They reached Paris's home and both slightly wearily unpacked their things. Paris sat Gina down in front of the television and ordered their meal. She chose a variety of dishes, hoping at least one would be liked by the girl. Poor kid, she thought, what a time she has had, and now to cap it all food she had never heard of.

Paris was pleasantly surprised as she watched Gina take a little taste from each of the silver dishes, nodding and pointing her fork to the chicken chow mien as her favourite, she herself didn't care. Tiredness was beginning to over take hunger in her body and not long after their meal they both retired to bed exhausted.

Gina dreamt of her island miles away, Paris of the photographs she had seen.

The following morning over a full English breakfast, cooked by Paris's housekeeper the two women talked about the day ahead. Gina was excited and thanked Paris over and over again for the strange money she had given to her.

"Spend the lot if you want." Paris said smiling. "If you need any more get Emily to pay and I will sort it out with her later. OK."

"OK and thank you."

Paris was amused to see how Gina was dressed, first on her list would be a jumper, she thought to herself. The young girl had mistakenly assumed that England would be as hot as Greece, wrong, very wrong and this morning wore a sleeveless t-shirt, knee length jeans and sandals.

As they chatted and ate a knock at the door announced the arrival of Emily.

"Ready Gina?" She asked pinching a slice of toast. The young girl nodded. "Come on then."

"Look after her Emily." Paris asked, then told her about the money as she walked them to the door. "See you later."

At last she was on her own, well with the exception of the housekeeper who was busy washing up the pots.

"I'll be in my office." Paris called to the woman and disappeared upstairs. Her office, her haven, now to work.

She quickly got into her stride scribbling down notes on one pad, and writing down questions that arose in another. Her meeting with Luke could well be the last and she wanted to make sure she missed nothing.

She heard talking from downstairs and looked at her watch. Surely the girls were not back so soon, but realised there was one only female voice, and that sounded fraught. Leaving her desk she stood at the top of the stairs and called to the housekeeper.

"Is everything OK down there?"

"Oh Miss Paris. Would you mind having a word with this young man." Came the nervous reply. Paris ran down the stairs, her long legs making short work of the steps.

"Can I help?" She asked automatically and then gasped. Before her stood a youngish man, probably mid twenties, very smart in his navy suit, slim and slightly balding.

He was the spitting image of her father.

"I am looking for the owner of this house," he asked in English with the strangest accent she had ever heard. "Can you help me?"

"I am the owner. What is it you want?" Her voice was trembling.

"Are you Paris or Sky?" Came the uncertain reply.

"Who is asking?" She could see very well, but wanted to hear him say.

170

"I am Gabriel Maxwell. Your brother."

"I think you had better come in and explain yourself." She said more sharply than she had intended. "Coffee?"

The young man nodded and followed her into the lounge. Paris pointed to the sofa.

"Please sit. By the way I am Paris."

"I have waited so long to meet you," he said clutching at her hands. "So many years." Tears streamed down his face. "Look." He held out a photograph. It was of her, Sky and their parents taken at her university graduation. "Mother gave me this a long time ago."

Paris stared into the eyes of her family and listened as Gabriel explained.

Once her parents had left England they had traveled through Europe and eventually settled in a Kibbutz just outside Jerusalem.

"That is how I got my name." He smiled at her. "After the angel Gabriel." Paris nodded; knowing her parents and their liking for unusual names it did not surprise her one bit.

He told her how they had lived there for a few years before moving to Thailand. "They never seemed to settle," he said sadly. "I loved Jerusalem, but they always had this urge to move. We stayed in Phuket, but then after a while went to Cairo. There were times when I felt I had no roots, it was as if as soon as they had made a home they wanted to move on." He looked up at her. "Eventually we went back to Phuket. They were very old and had decided that they wanted to spend their last days there." Paris could sense what was coming next. "They died in the Tsunami, they died together." She could hear the sadness in his voice.

Now she could feel tears on her cheeks, but what for. These were the people who had abandoned her and Sky so many years ago. Not one word, one letter, nothing in all those years, but they were her parents and even now she missed them. She wanted to ask why, that was all, why did they leave, and now she would never know. Paris realised she was crying for herself.

"I took this to the people at the Oxfam tent and told them what I knew, names and everything I could." He shook his head remembering how hard it had been, his eyes darted around the room as if searching for something. "At first no one knew anything but a BBC journalist recognised you. He said he had known you years ago when you worked on

171

a newspaper together. He told me this was the last place he remembered you living at and so I came to London to track you down."

"Where have you been living?" Paris asked shakily.

"Over the restaurant I work in. It's just around the corner that is how I knew someone was here. Last night when I passed on my way to the shop on the corner I saw a light on, but I dare not call then. I waited until this morning so I could present myself in a proper fashion." His hands stroked his suit jacket. "I did not want you to be disappointed in me." He paused. "I have brought you this." It was her mother's wedding ring. "You should have it being the eldest."

Paris held the ring in her fingers for some time before gently sliding it on. It was slightly too big and a little bent, but all of a sudden it meant so much.

"Thank you." She whispered.

"And I have these." Gabriel passed over his birth certificate, her parent's death certificates, and some more photographs. "And I am willing to take a DNA test if you want." He sounded desperate. "You are my only family now. You and Sky, where is she?"

"Sky lives in Greece, so do I actually, I'm only here on a flying visit." She looked into his sad face. "You must come to Skiathos one day, I can't wait until Sky sees you." She was thinking out loud. "She is disabled you know." She warned him.

"Yes mother did say something. She said it was all her fault. She could never forgive herself. It was the reason they left, she could not bear to see her like that."

"Please be careful what you say to Sky about it. I don't want her blaming herself for any of this." Gabriel nodded as Paris spoke. "She has been through enough. Oh Gabriel I have so much to ask you but I need to go out soon." She looked at the old grandfather clock in the corner.

"Don't worry. I can come back. I have to work until midnight tonight so I will call in the morning if that is OK?"

"Yes." Then on impulse she added. "And bring your things. I go back to Skiathos tomorrow I want you to come with me."

"I would love to." His eyes shone. "Thank you for accepting me like this I don't know what to say."

"There is no doubt in my mind you are who you say you are. The minute I laid eyes on you I knew you were family. You are the spitting image of father. There is no doubt in my mind at all."

Gabriel left with a huge smile on his face.

He had found his sisters at long last.

The meeting with Luke went as well as she could have asked for. He produced more photographs and answered all of her questions, but her mind was elsewhere. What timing, she thought to herself; here I am with the man I have looked for for years and all I can think about is the brother I never knew I had.

She thought about Sky and wondered what her reaction would be, hoping that she would welcome him too. It was strange to think she already had feelings for this man who was really no more than a stranger, yet she felt this bond.

It was in his eyes, they were the exact colour now shared by herself and Storm. That fiery amber glow, no, there was no doubt in her mind; Gabriel was who he said he was.

Paris thought about her father once more, how his eyes used to glow and felt sad that she would never look into them ever again.

Still she managed to make a lot of notes, many of which would be included in her book.

"You are not the same as yesterday." Luke said as she scribbled down some more. "Something bothering you?"

"Not really thanks. I'm just tired." She wanted to keep the news to herself for now. Emily and Gina would have enough questions when they met him in the morning without someone else bombarding her with why's and wherefores, but one thing she must do was warn Sky. She would phone her as soon as she got home. Once that was decided she felt better, it was almost as if she was sharing the problem with her sister even though she was miles away. After that she bucked up and spent the last few minutes with Luke going over her notes.

"You know that still doesn't tell me why he was knighted." She said frowning.

173

"If he wouldn't tell you then nor will I." Luke replied with a sigh. "I thought about it last night and that was something only he should tell anyone."

Paris felt deflated. Where did she go next? Richard was dead. Luke would not say. Perhaps she would make something up. That was it, she would do as much research as she could and fill in the gaps with her imagination.

She said her farewells to Luke and thanked him for his help.

"I'll leave that for you." She said as he went to hand her the remainder of the whiskey "Medicinal purposes only mind you."

"Promise." He replied winking. "I have really enjoyed our meeting, thank you for coming." He kissed her outstretched hand. "Don't suppose I'll see you again."

"You might at the wedding, that is if you are well enough to go." She sighed thinking really, if you are still alive. "Just look after yourself and behave." She bent and kissed his cheek. "Just behave."

Paris felt a little sad on the way back home. Luke was right she would probably never see him again and when he died Richard's secret life would go with him, he was the last link in her chain, but she admired his loyalty to the man who had meant so much to them all.

It was useless, she couldn't concentrate. The notes she had taken listening to Luke were now just a jumble of words, at this moment they meant nothing. The only thing on her mind was Gabriel, no that was wrong, the only thing on her mind was her parents.

Absent-mindedly she wandered back down stairs and picked up the photographs that had been left on the coffee table. One by one she inspected them, looking deeply into the aged eyes of her father and then her mother. They both looked as if they had shrunk, but that was probably old age, she thought. They both looked thin, but oh so happy. The little boy holding his mothers hand and waving to the camera with the other had a huge grin on his face.

Gabriel, so young and so innocent looking, and so much like her father. His original birth certificate was in Hebrew, but a translated copy had been folded neatly and placed inside the plastic folder.

174

Carefully she slid out the other documents, death certificates. Drowning. On both of them it said drowning. Her heart seemed to stop then jump with a thud. She had seen the awful images of the disaster on the television with eyes glued to the screen, like countless thousands of others, but to realise that whilst she was watching she could well have been seeing her own parents perish, the thought made her feel sick.

Poor Gabriel, what he had gone through, it must have been hell.

The certificates informed her that it had been he who identified them, what an awful thing to have to do, but at least it was better than not knowing. So many people still had to find out the truth, although after all of this time hope would surely be waning. But did you ever give up, she thought to herself, deep down you hoped that one day they would walk back through the door, that was how countless others must be feeling. Never give up hope.

Suddenly Paris understood Sky. She had never given up on Nicos; yes she had cursed him over the years. Threatened this and that, but always she had said, when I lay eyes on him again, never if I do, but when I do.

Sky had never given up on Nicos, Paris knew then that neither had she with their parents.

Emily and Gina bounced through the door their bags full of goodies banging against the walls as they rushed into the lounge. Both stopped dead and stared. Paris was sobbing into one of the cushions as if her heart had been broken.

"God Paris what's happened? Is it granddad, is he ill, or Mum? Tell us please. What's the matter?" Emily had dropped her bags and was kneeling at the side of her distraught friend.

"No nothing like that." Paris sniffed. "Fetch us a cuppa and I'll tell you. Sorry, I should say please."

"I'll go Emily." Gina said not really knowing what to do. "You stay with Paris I won't be long."

Over tea and biscuits Paris told her rather amazing story.

"Gabriel will be here in the morning. He's coming back to live with me for a while and then he can decide what to do with his life. God knows what Sky will say but I don't care. He is our brother and we should look after him, that's if he wants us to. He may not like us once he gets to know us I suppose."

The idea of the young man leaving her life was something Paris had only just thought about and it hurt.

He was the last link to her parents and she felt like she owed him something, she was not sure what, but time would tell. "I'd better see if I can get him a seat on our plane." She said suddenly panicking. "Then I'm off to bed. I feel exhausted. Gina I'm sorry you'll have to amuse yourself tonight."

"Don't you worry Paris. I'll take Gina home with me; Mum can make a fuss of her. You know how she loves to do that." Emily smiled. "You get to bed and we will be here first thing in the morning."

Exhausted Paris might be but sleep was beyond her.

The images from Luke's photographs were mingling with those from the television coverage of the Tsunami disaster each time she closed her eyes. She tossed and turned; eventually she gave up and decided to pack her bags ready for the morning. Carefully collecting her clothes and placing her notes in her briefcase she noticed her mobile phone on the desk. No time like the present, she thought as she looked at the clock. 6.30am, would Sky be up yet, she didn't care, she needed to talk to her.

• CHAPTER •
15

The shrill tones of the phone made their way into Sky's dream startling her into consciousness. She sat up quickly and grabbed at the receiver.

"Hello." She said urgently. "Paris is something the matter."

Sky had always believed people only phoned during the night if something was wrong. Sleepily glancing at her watch she realised it was in fact early morning, and not really that early.

She had overslept again; just lately her body had felt so tired. She yawned and listened before leaning over and punching Nicos. "Hang on a minute Paris." Nicos sat up and stretched. "Tell me again."

Nicos could see from the concerned look on Sky's face that something was amiss. He watched as her fingers wrapped themselves in the corner of the sheet and then let go again. Her feet were moving up and down, she was obviously agitated. "OK See you later. Thanks for warning me. Bye."

"Well what was that all about?" He could tell from the frown on Sky's brow, and the tears glistening in her eyes it must have been bad news. He reached over and pulled her close. "Come on tell me what's wrong."

Sky tried to remember the exact words Paris had used but it felt strange. Nicos sat with his mouth open as he listened, a brother, and coming to live here with Paris. It didn't seem to make any sense, but listening to the rest of Sky's words he supposed it was possible.

If Paris was certain then it must be true. He had never known any one pull the wool over her eyes; she had always been very shrewd when it came to knowing what to believe, or who to believe.

"Well let's wait until they get here before making any snap judgments." He said softly, trying to sooth Sky who was now even more fidgety than before. "Paris is usually right you know."

"Yes Jack she is my sister, I think I know her well enough." She snapped. "Sorry. It's just been such a shock." Her voice said more calmly. "It's not just him, it's the fact mum and dad are dead."

"I'm not completely heartless Sky. I was only trying to help." He sounded hurt.

"Come here you lovely hunk," she held him even closer. "Oh No!"

"What's up now?" Nicos held her slightly away.

"I've gone all hot and prickly, I feel so sick, it must be the shock. Quick help me into the loo." Sky held her hand over her mouth as Nicos scooped her up into his arms and made a dash for the bathroom. He knelt at her side stroking her back as she retched.

"You know I still feel rough from that sun stroke. I can't believe how it's affected me," she said crying. "Sod the shoes today I think I'll just rest. Just look, even my legs are swollen." Sky let her hands wonder over her puffy ankles as reality kicked in. "Oh Jack are you thinking what I'm thinking." He nodded. "For God's sake I'm almost 50. It can't happen. Its not natural I'm too old." Her tears came in great sobs.

For a couple of years now her periods had been erratic and thinking it to be the menopause had decided she was no longer fertile. It had been depressing to think she was that old but a blessing to get rid of her monthlies. They had plagued her life since her early teenage years and the thought of getting rid for good kept her going. Some women suffered terribly during the change of life, but Sky actually looked forward to the

178

day when she could kiss goodbye to sanitary towels, painkillers, spots and greasy hair for good.

"What are we going to call this one?" Nicos was so excited.

"Cherry if it's a girl silly." She smiled remembering the delicious desert on Kalymnos.

"And for a boy?"

"Dobbin. How's that? Like it?" She thought of the donkey and laughed.

"Sounds great to me." He replied sarcastically. "Now if you've finished in here I'll fetch breakfast and we can celebrate in bed."

Nicos felt so good he wanted to tell the world, shout it from the terrace. Me, to be a father again, fantastic. Now he had the chance to prove himself and this time no messing up, he thought.

He carried Sky back into their room and gently placed her on the bed before kissing her long and hard.

Breakfast could wait a little longer.

Nicos slowly kissed her all over taking great care to lavish plenty of attention on her tummy. He stroked her skin in a tantalizing way, and sensuously teased her body with his tongue until she felt she could stand no more, but he was in no hurry and made her wait until she was smoldering.

After, Nicos lay with his head on her still flat stomach letting his fingers wonder over her skin.

"I can hear it," he said with a big grin. "Gurgling away as happy as a lamb."

"Those are hunger pangs Jack. What happened to my breaky?"

"I'll go now madam, this minute. Just you lay here." He leapt off the bed and opened the blinds, letting the sun stream into the room.

"Oh and Jack. Let's just keep this to ourselves for a while. I'm a bit old and you never know we could well be barking up the wrong tree, perhaps it is still the sunstroke." Sky prayed that she was wrong, how she would love another child.

"OK my darling. You're the boss but it will be hard you know and as for being wrong, what do you really think?"

179

"I realise that it's going to be difficult to keep quiet, but until we know for certain its schtum all right." Sky put her finger to her lips emphasizing her words. "I'll give Athens a call. Perhaps we could pop over to the hospital next week to see the doctor."

"Good idea. We can call and see Andros whilst we are there." He said cheerfully.

"I don't know if that is such a good idea, but we can see." Sky knew the depth of Andros's anger towards Nicos and feared they would have one almighty row. "But if I don't get food soon I won't be going anywhere!"

"Hang on one tick." Nicos ran out of the room.

Sky sat back against the pillows and stared out over the hillside. What a day this was turning out to be, a brother appearing in a few hours and perhaps a baby in a few months. Never do things by halves do you girl, she said out loud to herself.

She spent much of the day lying on her sun bed in the shade of her huge umbrella, but she might as well have been at her desk, her mobile phone seemed to ring constantly. Her drawing pad, usually for sketching her shoe designs, was a mass of notes and orders, but there was no time for new ideas today.

Nicos on the other hand was busy in Sunni's studio. He still had the photographs taken at the little churchyard on Kalymnos, and a few he had sneakily taken when Sky was not looking to sort out. He knew she would be pleased that once again she was the subject of his lens and hoped his shots would do her justice.

He smiled to himself as the images began to appear on the computer screen. This modern room of Sunni's was certainly a delight to work in and the photographs could be seen so quickly. No more soaking of film and waiting hours for the photographs to dry like in the old days. He thought about the times he had spent with his father developing reels of films, and then together choosing the best shots to be framed and put on display in The Gallery.

He decided once these shots were completed to his satisfaction he would walk over and have a chat with his father. He knew Alexi found it difficult after what had been said, but if Nicos could persuade him to talk even just a little it would be a major breakthrough. He so wanted to be pals with him again.

180

Thinking of his parents brought him back to how shocked he had been on seeing them again after all these years. They had aged so much in that time his stomach had lurched at that first meeting. Their voices were the same, if a little softer, but their bodies were totally different. Their eyes were not so bright, their skin wrinkled. Alexi once so tall and handsome, now looked slightly shriveled. His mother the glamorous Athena, slim, stylish, and graceful of old, now like many older women, slightly chubby and shrunken in stature.

That first meeting brought back all the loving feelings he had for them, not that he had ever forgotten this love, just that over the years his mind had other things to dwell on. Now he felt so guilty it hurt.

He needed a nice frame to put Gina's photograph of the church in and decided to ask Alexi if he fancied a ride into town. At least it would be a start if he agreed, and he knew how much his father missed The Gallery, that at least was one thing they had in common.

"Sky would you mind if I went into town for a while. Thought I might ask papa to come along?" He said strolling out on to the terrace as once again she put her mobile down.

"That bloody phone hasn't stopped all morning." She sounded exasperated

"I know I've heard it from in there." He laughed. "So do you mind?"

"Of course not silly. In fact whilst you are there would you call in and get me some nougat I just fancy a nibble."

"That's it then. Confirmed." Nicos rushed over and kissed her tenderly.

"Confirmed." They giggled together.

The only time Sky ate any sweets other than chocolate was when she had been pregnant, and then only nougat.

"Wait Jack. Let's go and see them at the hospital before we get carried away, and remember say nothing. Promise."

"Ok spoilsport. Won't be long."

"It would be good if you were back when Paris and the others arrive. I want you here when this so-called brother appears. I need you with me for that Jack."

"I'll be back don't fret. You try and rest." He replied blowing her yet another kiss as he left the terrace to walk the short distance over to his father's villa.

Nicos was quite surprised with the speed that Alexi agreed to come with him. It was as if he could hardly wait to get away, even if it was for just a short while.

"I hate being cooped up like this. Old age is not my best friend I'm afraid," he said as Nicos helped him into Sky's car. His own was still sitting in the garage battered and bumped. "Thank you for asking son."

Nicos smiled but said nothing, it was the first time his father had called him that in years and he felt a little emotional.

He drove down to the town slowly in order that Alexi could have a good look around. It felt comfortable having his father at his side even if it was for only a short time.

Nicos parked the car in his old spot in the town, under the shade of a lovely grape vine not far from the cobbled street where The Gallery was situated. It reminded him of his first meeting with Eleni and her surprise that they owned similar cars, red Audi coupes. What a lot had happened since that day and what a lot he now had to look forward to. He felt so good; his life was at last back on track.

The two men walked slowly through the narrow streets, stopping now and again for Alexi to talk to old friends. He looked happy and relaxed greeting those he had not seen for many months.

The villa was a marvelous home, but it could be quite lonely stuck at the top of the hill with no one but Athena to talk to.

His grandchildren called most days, but it was a case of "hello" and minutes later "bye then," but still he was grateful that they bothered at all. He knew how busy Storm and Sunni were, and envied their youthful vitality. His own body was crumbling before his eyes and he hated it.

Athena seemed quite happy to potter about their home and garden, but Alexi felt he still needed company, but most of all he needed a purpose in life. What was the point in breathing if there was nothing to aim for?

As Nicos opened the door to The Gallery Alexi stood and took a deep breath, back at last, his domain.

The smart young lady hired by Athena to run the shop stood behind her desk and greeted them warmly. She recognized Alexi but wondered who the man was with him.

"My son Nicos." Alexi introduced him. "This is Olivia our secretary. Well she does everything really here at the shop. Sells the photographs and does all the paperwork. A little treasure she is." Olivia blushed at the glowing reference Alexi gave.

"My pleasure Mr. Mandros you know how I love being here." Her smile showed she was speaking the truth. "What can I do for you today?"

"Nicos here wants a frame. Now lets have a look at what we have got."

Alexi strode over towards the back of the shop where an assortment of frames was lined up against the wall. "Come son let us choose together." He beckoned Nicos who could feel a lump of emotion in his throat.

They knelt on the floor side by side placing the photograph in one frame then another. Eventually they chose a thin white wooden frame. It highlighted the whiteness of the little church and emphasized the wonderful graveside flowers; the wild poppies and the broken stonewall.

"Actually papa I need two frames. Here look at this, it's a present for Sky."

Nicos held out a shot of Sky sitting in the sun, her huge hat pulled down over her eyes and a large glass of wine in her hand. "I think a bronze frame for this."

"That is one hell of a shot Nicos." Alexi said holding the photograph at arms length. "A real beauty." Praise indeed from the master, thought Nicos. "You are nearly as good as your own son." Alexi punched his arm jokingly, but Nicos knew Sunni was as good as Alexi, if not better. His eye for detail surpassed anything Nicos could see and Alexi's words made him glow with pride.

The old man insisted that Nicos take the frames "Put them on the shop's account Olivia please."

"But father I should pay." Nicos replied quickly. "This is Sunni's shop remember."

During their quarrel on Kalymnos Alexi had insisted that Nicos was now out of his Will and everything would go to Sunni.

"Words that I spoke in anger my son. I have never changed anything I could not." Alexi's old eyes misted over. "You are still my son." The two men hugged.

"Fancy some lunch papa?" Nicos said eventually.

"That little taverna round the corner?" Alexi asked. "It's ages since I have eaten there." His smile told Nicos he was enjoying this outing as much as he was.

"If that's what you want then we shall go there." He replied.

They slowly sauntered back through the narrow streets and out towards the harbor.

"I won't be a minute papa. Sky wants some nougat she'll go mad if I forget." Nicos ran into the sweet shop returning moments later with a large bag stuffed full of Sky's order. "This should keep her quiet for a while," he laughed shaking the bag. "Now for lunch I'm starving."

They found a nice table just in the shade. The sun was beating down and these days Alexi quickly felt uncomfortable if he got too hot.

"Not like when I was young." He said slowly. "Marco, Tomas and I would be outside no matter how hot it got. We would always jump into the sea when it got too much, very often totally naked. Oh those were the days."

The next couple of hours passed by quickly as Alexi told stories from his youth. Nicos was an avid listener even though many of the tales he had heard countless times before. It was good just to sit and listen, and to see the smile on his father's face as he relived those happy days.

They ate and drank well, although Nicos was a little wary of his father drinking too much wine. He knew his medication allowed him to drink a little, but glass after glass may well be overdoing it.

"I think three is enough papa. Don't forget I have to drive home." Nicos made it sound as if it was he who was ending their little session; he knew how proud his father was.

Alexi nodded, he could sit here all day reminiscing and drinking, he felt happier than he had in ages, but he also knew Athena would not approve. A tongue lashing from her would spoil what had been a lovely trip, and if he behaved perhaps Nicos would bring him again. He felt like a little boy wanting approval and for a second it hurt.

Nicos threw a bundle of Euro onto the table and helped his father stand.

"I'm not that decrepit yet son." Alexi said sharply, but with a smile, and in a way he was happy to feel Nicos's strong hands grip his arm. "Not just yet anyway."

Back in the car Alexi turned to Nicos.

"Thank you I really enjoyed that. Perhaps if you are not too busy we can come again? Hopefully Sky will want some more of that." He pointed to the now scrunched up paper bag. "Have you something to tell me?" His eyes glistened.

Alexi knew how Sky had eaten nougat seemingly by the ton during her two previous pregnancies.

"No pulling the wool over your eyes is there." Nicos laughed. "But don't say a word Sky will kill me if she thinks I have said anything."

"You won't have too my boy. It will be around the town before we get home. Everyone knows how she was before so I bet in the shop they put two and two together before you had reached the door." Alexi laughed. "But isn't she a little old?" He added with a concerned frown.

"That's just what she said. Let's just pray everything is OK." Nicos patted his father's leg comfortingly, but deep down he shared the fear that something might go wrong. He had heard of women giving birth late in life, quite often in fact, but still he felt a little niggling fear.

As the car pulled on to the main road a taxi whizzed past.

"That's Paris and the others." Nicos said speeding up. "I promised Sky I would be there when they arrived." He told Alexi all he knew of this mystery brother.

Try as he might Nicos could not overtake the taxi containing Sky's family and had to be content with seeing Gina wave to him through the back window.

"She's a lovely girl." Alexi said waving back to his newfound granddaughter. "So is that Emily. I hope she and Sunni marry before I die. I would love another good knees up before I go."

"Don't be daft papa. You've years left yet." Nicos said not really believing his own words.

185

"I don't think so son. In any case what is the point when you can't enjoy yourself anymore." Alexi was serious. "I have had my fun, my share of women, my beautiful wife and my child. I have lived to see my grandchildren grow, and now I feel I have almost had enough. You know some days it is hard just to carry on, but today was fantastic thank you. It has given me a real boost."

Nicos smiled at his father, he would make time to do this again, he thought to himself. Nothing could ever make up for lost time, but he would do his best to make sure his father's last years would be enjoyable. No more running round here and there taking photographs, his time was now to be used looking after Sky and his parents.

They came to a stop just as the taxi spilled its contents of people out on to the courtyard of the Eagles Nest.

"Papa, grandpapa." Gina ran over and hugged Alexi then Nicos. "I have had such a lovely time. Paris has been so kind, oh I had to borrow some money I hope you don't mind." She laughed nervously.

"No I don't mind at all." He replied and looked over to where Paris stood. Her eyes said everything, they shone with anger and hurt. "I'll sort it out with her later."

"Nicos." Paris nodded towards him.

"Paris good to see you. Thank you for taking care of Gina."

Their words were sparse, their voices sharp.

"She's a lovely girl Nicos," came the reply. "Don't worry about any money. Call it my treat." Paris would rather go with out herself than ask him for anything. Not that there was any chance of that. Andros had turned Richard and Eleni's fortunes into billions, and her own success meant money was no object.

Nicos might be wealthy but his own fortune was greatly overshadowed by the obscene amounts Andros talked of. It had been his life's work since being given the task of overseeing young Eleni's inheritance, and the fact that Richard had given Andros all of his shares made him even more determined to do his best.

Always a good businessman, he relished the fact that now he could play with the best. He had learned from Richard the tricks of the trade regarding share dealing, and the already large amount of funds grew rapidly.

186

It spelt the end of his life with Paris, apart from the odd weekend here and there, but all he needed now was the daily thrill of the stock exchange. To outsiders it seemed a lonely and rather sad existence, but one, which Andros enjoyed wholeheartedly; it was his life, his mistress.

"Would you mind if Gabriel and I went to see Sky alone?" Paris asked the little group "Just give us a while please."

"They can all come to us." Alexi spoke up. "Athena would love to hear about London from the girls I'm sure."

"Thanks that would be great." Paris was already leading a shocked Gabriel towards the villa.

"This place is huge." He said gazing in wonder. "Does Sky own both villa's?"

"No that one is Alexi's, but this one is Sky's. The terrace is through here." Paris pointed to an archway at the side of the kitchen. "It overlooks the hillside and down to the beaches." They stopped walking for a moment. "Down there is Eleni beach, our friends own a taverna on the sands." Her arm moved slowly as she pointed to the white shinning strip of shoreline way below them.

"It's all so fantastic." He replied breathlessly. "Paris I feel so nervous."

"Don't worry Gabriel. I'm the scary one, Sky is a babe." Paris laughed.

They carried on walking towards the front of the villa where Sky was asleep on her sun bed.

"That's a fine greeting sis." Paris called out loudly waking her immediately.

"Oh sorry. It's Jack's fault. He promised to be here. Typical, I bet his is in some taverna in town and has forgotten."

"No, he's next door with Alexi and the others. I asked them if they would give us three some time alone." Paris ushered Gabriel in front of her own body. "This is Gabriel."

Sky's breathing stopped for a second, her heart jumped hard in her chest.

"Hello Sky." Not knowing what to do he held his hand out as if to shake hers.

187

"Silly boy come here." Sky clumsily grabbed her crutches and pulled herself upright. With one hand she shakily touched his shirt, then his hair and lastly his face. "You are so much like father I can't believe it. Paris told me you were but until now I had no idea. There is certainly no doubt you are family." She pulled him close and gave him a hug. "Come and tell me all about yourself." She gestured towards the table at the end of the terrace.

Gabriel and Paris followed as she hobbled over and sat down.

"Just one thing." Gabriel looked puzzled. "Who is Jack?" The sisters burst out laughing.

"It's Nicos. That's his nickname, always has been from the day we met." Sky told the story of how it came to be. "I only call him Nicos if I'm mad with him." Sky was laughing quite hard. "Now let's forget about the others for a while it's you I'm interested in."

Sky rang a little bell and within seconds Maria appeared. "Wine please Maria and a few nibbly bits if that's OK."

The trio sat listening to the water tinkling in the fountain for a few moments.

"I don't know where to start really." Gabriel was so nervous he felt quite nauseous.

"Tell Sky what you told me." Paris egged him on as she filled their glasses with wine.

So he did.

Starting with his earliest memories and finishing on that awful Boxing Day, which not only devastated him but the rest of the world.

"Here. I've got these for you to look at." He handed Sky the photographs. "They are a bit tatty I'm afraid, but then they have done a few thousand miles in my pocket."

Sky looked at her mother and father smiling at her from the center of the shots. The little boy standing in front of them held his hand high as if waving. There was no doubt that it was Gabriel. She stared at them for some time as if willing her parents to speak until eventually all of the questions in her mind had been asked, but once again she received no reply.

"Gabriel is going to stay with me." She heard Paris say from the end of the tunnel that was now in her mind. "I promise to bring him here

188

often. I think we all need time to get to know each other." Slowly her voice came out into the open. "Sky are you OK."

"Yeah." She sighed. "I was just asking father why." Sky started to cry. "Oh Paris that's all I wanted to know and now I never will." Paris went over and knelt at her sister's feet.

"It's all we both wanted to know and never will. But we have got each other and that's all that counts now. Each other and the children." Paris said calmly as Sky sniffed loudly and looked into her sister's eyes hoping to see some comfort. "And Gabriel is part of our world now." Sky nodded.

"We ought to have a party then." She smiled at her brother. "I think we should all go the beach tonight and have a nice meal there. We can introduce you to Eleni and the boys. Pass my phone Paris I'll give them a ring." As she pushed the digits on her phone she heard a car pull up in the courtyard followed by the unmistakable sound of Storm and Sunni arguing.

"Never mind them Gabriel it's just my children. They always fight but let anyone try to come between them and then they stick together like glue." She cancelled her call. "Better wait and see if they are coming too."

In the end they had a party of twelve, including Alexi and Athena, who had decided on this occasion to come with them.

Only the twins would be missing from the table, but then someone had to do the cooking.

• CHAPTER • 16

What a party it turned out to be. Eleni and the boys made them all so welcome and greeted Gabriel as if he was an old friend.

"I can hardly believe them." He whispered to Paris. "They are crazy."

He watched as the twins made cocktails for the holidaymakers throwing silver shaker cups to each other from one end of the bar to the other, flamboyantly bowing to the applause each time. "And the food is delicious and I should know being a chef."

"I didn't know that." Sky said putting down her knife and fork.

"Oh yes. Back in London I was head chef at the restaurant. It was a little different to this." He laughed.

Paris could see the worried look in his eyes had now gone, in fact he seemed more relaxed all round.

"My boss was not over happy for me to leave so suddenly but I told him it was a family matter." He smiled at her. "And it certainly is that eh?"

190

Paris nodded.

"Hey Marco," she called. "Hear that. Gabriel is a chef so if you need a hand you know where to come."

Marco ran over to the table.

"Do you mean that? I know you have only just arrived but as you can see we are full tonight and have been all day. The season is in full swing and boy could we do with some help. Come down to the beach tomorrow and we can talk."

"I never expected that." Paris said more than a little surprised. "Perhaps I shouldn't have said anything."

"No it's great." Gabriel had the biggest smile on his face. "I would love to work here and I can't sponge off you can I. It will be a little different to what I'm used to but I'll soon get the hang of it wait and see."

As Emily looked around the table a frown came over her face.

"What's the matter sweetheart?" Sunni asked a little concerned. "Please tell me. Is it your grandfather?"

"No nothing like that. It's just a bit difficult really." She paused, looked straight at him and took a deep breath. "Here goes then. Well, you know you have been asking me to marry you for some time now." Sunni nodded and smiled. "Well I really want to." He gave a cheer. "Ssh! But how is my father going to put on a do for all of these rich people. Your family talks in amounts that mine can only dream of. You all spend money as if means nothing. I mean just look at the lovely gold jewellery your mother has on tonight. It must have cost a fortune." She paused again and sighed. "How can we ever live up to your standards?"

"Oh Em, don't worry. I will go and speak to your father as soon as I get the chance. Between us we will come to a solution and don't fret I won't make him feel uncomfortable. Promise." He kissed her nose. "Now cheer up and have a think."

"What about?"

"When. When shall we get married? The sooner the better from my point of view but I know how you ladies like to spend lots of time getting ready for weddings." He looked longingly at her. "Just don't make it next year or something stupid. It's almost a tradition in this family to get done and dusted rather quickly. Like I said before you ask mama some time, or Eleni for that matter, neither of them hung about for long. Once you have met the right man." He pointed to himself. "Why wait?"

"Silly. I can't wait myself really but you are right mother would love to do it all properly, so how's about the beginning of September, that's if we can get a church and everything, if not Christmas. That do you?" She replied softly, hoping no one had overheard their conversation.

"September would be great. Can I tell the others?" He asked grinning widely.

"No not yet. Let's go and see father and get the church booked first."

From the smile on her son's face and the obvious excitement of Emily, Sky knew exactly what they were talking about. She hoped they would be happy.

As all mothers of son's knew, their boys were better than the rest and Emily had certainly got THE best in Sky's eyes.

She turned her attention to Storm. Tonight her daughter seemed to be a little bit quiet, yes she was answering when spoken to, but not once during the evening had she started a conversation. Instead her eyes flashed as if she felt angry about something, and Sky noticed her looking at Gina very thoughtfully. Allesandro. It could be nothing else that had made her daughter like this. Sky knew she had fallen for him big style and to have his wife as her half sister must be tearing her apart. A mother/daughter chat was needed Sky thought to herself.

Next she looked over to where Paris sat near to Gabriel. Not only was he a dead ringer for their father but of Paris and thinking about it Storm too. He seemed such a nice young man, tall and very handsome, quite witty, and not at all out of his depth with all of these new people. He would fit in well, she would need time to really accept him as her brother, but it was obvious that Paris had taken to him immediately. She saw her sister throw her head back and laugh, as he spoke, no doubt a tale from his time at the restaurant.

At her side Eleni and Vanni were deep in conversation with Alexi and Athena, Nicos was joining in now and again. As usual they were talking about photographs, computer equipment and cars.

Both Vanni and Nicos had a passion for cars and although they could afford to have any make or model in the world, here on the island it was such a waste, but they could still dream and talk about Ferraris and

192

Porches. Why not? At least they were talking now, still a little strained but things were getting better.

The only ones who were not talking were herself and Gina. Sky looked over and watched the young girl. Sometimes she looked like a frightened rabbit, as her eyes seemed to dominate her lovely face, only now her eyes were following Marco as he worked his way around the taverna. A little smile lifted the corner of her mouth as he turned and gave her a nod. Well well thought Sky perhaps a budding romance is on the cards, she caught Eleni's eye who nodded her answer to the unasked question. Wouldn't that just make things easy? Gina with Marco would leave Allesandro for Storm, but life was not that kind, or was it?

She let her hands stroke her tummy. I wonder what is in store for you, she thought to herself, whatever it is I just hope you will be happy.

What a strange day it had been. First the prospect of a baby, then the meeting of her brother and seeing photographs of her now dead parents. Sky sat back and thought about them becoming more than a little guilty not to feel sadder than she did.

It was her parents all right in the pictures, but they might as well have been two strangers standing there. What did they actually mean to her, not much really and that was the saddest part of all.

Not long after midnight Alexi asked for a taxi to be called.

"I am sorry everyone but our bed is calling. Thank you for the best day I have had in ages Nicos, and thank you all for a lovely evening." He held out his hand to Athena. "Come, let us leave the young ones to enjoy the rest of the night."

Nicos saw a glimpse of the old Alexi and Athena as they held each other and danced a few steps; it brought a lump to his throat.

"Wait papa. Sky and I will come with you. Any one else ready to leave?" He asked looking around the table.

"I think I will if that's OK with Gabriel." Paris answered, she was feeling tired. It had been a very emotional last few days and her body was asking to rest.

"You go on. Don't worry about me I can get a taxi back or sleep here on the beach. It is such a warm night I might just do that." He laughed as he spoke.

"You will do no such thing." Paris said quickly. "Just think about all those mosquitoes. They would have a field day on your skin."

"Paris, Paris I was only joking. Just remember I was brought up in a tent, mosquitoes have already had enough of my blood I think." Then more seriously. " Listen I will come back later promise but if the others are staying I would love to as well and have a dance."

"He can stay here." Marco came over to say the taxi had arrived. "Save him coming back in the morning."

"Thanks Marco." Gabriel shook Marco's hand. "So you see there is no need to worry about me."

"OK then see you tomorrow. Bye everyone." Paris held her hand up and waved. "Tomas. Bye see you soon." She called to Marco's twin who was busy chatting to a leggy blonde by the bar.

Eleni and Vanni walked along the sand with the others and said their goodnights. One of the advantages of living here on the beach was that they were home within minutes of leaving the taverna.

"Fancy a nightcap?" Vanni asked putting his arm around her waist. "We can sit on the veranda for a while." Eleni knew what this was leading to.

Every time Vanni held her like this he was feeling manly as he put it. A shiver of anticipation ran down her spine, silly old thing, she thought to herself, but smiled anyway. Their love life had hardly dwindled since they had first met. Only the arrival of the twins had meant a slight lull, but now both in their fifties with no pressures or children to worry about, they were once again like teenagers in fact better than that.

Lately they had enjoyed experimenting, nothing outrageous, just a little spicy, using a few toys and oils to bring some extra fun into their lovemaking.

"Crème de Menthe on ice please." She answered.

Vanni rubbed his hands together and clapped.

"Anything you want, won't be long." He replied already knowing his message had been read and understood.

Within minutes Eleni could smell the wonderful aroma of lily and jasmine scented candles, she knew she was in for a very good night indeed.

They sat for some time in the warm night air, sipping their drinks and listening to the music from the taverna. They could hear the youngsters laughing and occasionally a splash as one either ran into the warm sea or was thrown in by boisterous friends.

"It sounds as if we are in for a noisy night." Vanni said softly as yet another peel of laughter made its way along the beach. "Let's go and make some of our own."

He took her glass and placed it on a little wicker table before gently leading her into their huge bedroom, which led straight from the veranda.

The villa had been their pre marriage project and every room had been designed to their specific tastes, all of it reflecting their considerable wealth.

Cream marble floors with slightly darker cream walls, the blinds were of a deep gold, almost bronze, as were the wall lights and a huge central chandelier. This hung over the biggest bed they could find, its foot and headboards a tangle of bronze grape vines. A large bronzed framed mirror hung on one wall and at each side of the bed stood cream cabinets. Marble statues of Greek Gods, both naked, posed in opposite corners of the room, and that was it. So simple yet so effective.

Vanni reached into the drawer of his little cabinet and produced three beautiful gold-topped crystal bottles.

"My choice tonight I think." He said with a slightly wicked grin.

What more could a woman ask for, Eleni thought as Vanni carefully chose one of the wonderfully scented oils, but it's a shame about my dress.

Vanni slowly removed his clothes teasing her by trailing some of the items across her body and knowing what was about to happen Eleni began to breathe deeply and took a last glance of his taught muscular frame.

A gold silk scarf was placed over her eyes seconds before he ripped her dress from her body. The sound of tearing material and the pull as the threads gave way made her gasp.

Then came the coolness of scented oil being trickled over her warm skin as Vanni got to work. Eleni loved this part of their game; the feeling of his hands gently massaging the oil into her body was so relaxing, so sensual. He was fast becoming a master of the art.

195

Vanni took his time to cover each and every part of his lovely wife. Her toes, knees right up to her neck, which twisted and strained in ecstasy, even her fingers were massaged. He continued until he was satisfied she was completely at his mercy.

He saw her lips curl into a smile as he reached into his bedside cabinet once again.

Now, which toy should he choose tonight?

Sometime later they lay in each other's arms, content.

"God Vanni that was superb. Pity about my dress though I only bought that the other day."

"Never mind my darling you can have a dozen tomorrow." He sighed and kissed her nose. "You can have as many as you want if I can do that to them."

"Beast." She hit him with her pillow. "Gorgeous beast."

• CHAPTER •
17

Up in the Eagles Nest things were a little calmer.

"I enjoyed tonight," Nicos said as he washed before bed. "In fact I have enjoyed all of today. Gabriel seems OK. I wonder what Andros will have to say?"

"Not a lot I suppose. He is a right miserable old man these days. All he thinks about is making more money. You'd think by now he would have enough. It's as if he can't think of anything else. I feel sorry for Paris in a way. She's married to a man who is married to his work, but that's life I suppose." Sky yawned and stretched. "I'm shattered. Hurry up let's have a nice cuddle."

Nicos slipped between the sheets. "That's a bit boring."

"Tough." She replied and kissed his brow. "Tough luck matey."

They snuggled up and kissed for a while but it took only minutes before Sky was asleep in his arms. Nicos lay listening to her soft rhythmic breathing and sent a word of thanks up to God. Why he ever left this

197

lovely woman he would never know. He dozed off holding her close, a little smile on his lips, his mind happy.

Breakfast next morning was a noisy affair. Sunni seemed to have his mobile phone permanently stuck to his ear. He was trying to rearrange photographic shoots in order to be able to fly to London with Emily.

"Don't worry about my career will you." Storm said spitefully. "Just you go and sort everything out to suit yourself."

"Storm don't be so awful. Sunni needs to see Emily's father about something." Sky shot her a sharp glance and then smiled at Emily. "Think about someone else for a change."

Uncharacteristically Storm burst in to tears her beautiful eyes clouding over with grief.

"My baby what's the matter?" Sky reached over and held her hand. "Come on let's go to my room and we can talk." She picked up her crutches and hobbled along the terrace, Storm followed still crying. They sat together on the bed and Sky wrapped her arms around her daughter. "Come on darling tell me what's wrong?"

"Oh mama it's not fair." How many times had Sky heard that one in the years of Storms life? "Sunni has got Emily, you've got Dad back but I haven't got anybody." Sobs racked her body.

"Is this about you Storm, or you and Allesandro?" Sky asked very gently.

"He's just a pig." She spat back.

"Now you know you don't really mean that. Do you love him Storm is that what the problem is?" Sky gently stroked her daughter's hair.

"I did but not now." That was no surprise; Storm had constantly loved and disguarded men since she was a youngster. "It's just I feel so lonely at times."

Those last words hurt Sky. She had always tried to involve her children as much as possible in everything she did. They had family meals, family trips and how many times did they all go to the beach. Countless.

And yet she understood.

198

"But you are still so young darling. You will find someone one day just wait and see. Just don't rush into things like a bull in a china shop, you could frighten the right man off you know. You will find him one day, believe me."

"Do you think so mama?" Came the childish reply through quivering lips.

"Of course I do. Just wait. I mean I was much older than you are when I met your father." Sky smiled at her daughter. "There is someone out there for you but you have just not met him yet, or perhaps you have and can't see it. Anyway if I can find a man, you surely can."

"Suppose so."

"Now let's go and finish our breakfast and see how Sunni has got on. Be happy for him Storm."

"I am mama. I think Emily is great for him but I get a bit jealous at times. She comes between us, we always did everything together but now he tags her along too."

So that was the problem Sky thought, not Allesandro or some other man, but Emily. Her daughter was jealous of Emily. Sky sighed softly to herself.

"My darling don't worry. No one could ever come between you two in fact isn't that what he trying to do now. Making sure he's with you on these shoots, sorting them out so it's you two together." Storm nodded. "Well then stop being silly and let's see if we can help with these secret plans of theirs."

They shared a nice comforting hug before going back out on to the terrace, Storm's hand resting on her mother's shoulder as she hobbled along on her crutches.

It was a beautiful morning; the sun had risen in to a cloudless sky. The birds were singing and countless bees were going about their work amongst the fabulous flowers that were now in bloom. Above them an eagle soared on the thermal drifts, squawking with pleasure as it rose.

"Hey Storm fancy being my best man?" Sunni called, he was unaware of his sister's conversation yet felt it had something to do with him. Sibling's intuition.

He knew he shouldn't really say anything until he had spoken with George but he desperately wanted to cheer her up. He could see immediately his request had.

"Me? I thought you would have one of the twins anyway didn't know you were getting married." She replied with a big grin.

"Well we are and as you are my best mate it's your job."

"Well then yes. Thanks Sunni, Emily."

The mood lightened immediately and Sky smiled across at Nicos. Another upset in her daughter's tempestuous life smoothed over. She certainly was Storm by name and storm by nature, Sky thought, everything was either fantastic or awful, no gray patches in between where things were just OK.

Sunni was successful in rearranging a shoot for lipstick, not that Storm ever needed much, but on her the bright colours looked amazing.

Millions of girls bought these cosmetics hoping in some strange way that they too would look as good, but Sunni knew only his sister could make a product look so sexy. In a way he felt sorry for these women, but this was his job to make things look as enticing as possible and with Storm as his model even a paper bag could be the height of fashion.

"Right then the future Mrs. Mandros, we had better get a flight sorted." He smiled over at his pretty girl. "I for one can't wait."

"Nor can I. I'm so glad you are going to be best man Storm I know it means so much to Sunni." Emily said softly and Sky noticed her daughter's chest fill with pride. "What will I do about bridesmaids? I've got my best friend and I know she will be pleased to bits when I ask her but I had always hoped for more. Gina will you do me the honor?" Gina looked up from her breakfast, the discussion so far had not involved her but she had been listening.

"Oh I would love to Emily. Thank you so much, you must help me though I expect an English wedding will be very different from a Greek one."

"Of course I will help silly. Just remember I've never done it myself before so it's all new to me too." Emily replied laughing.

The group finally finished their coffee and pastries and having decided upon their day's tasks left the table.

Only Sky and Nicos remained.

"I shall have to get something really nice." Sky said thinking out loud.

"Well why don't we have a good look round when we go to Athens. Have you booked that appointment yet?"

"No!" Came the reply rather sharply, followed by a more gentle, "I'm scared to. What if it's all in my mind and there is no baby. I've heard of phantom pregnancies, and what if there is something wrong?" She slammed her coffee cup down in frustration.

"Sky calm down." Nicos knelt at the side of her chair. "I'll be with you and no matter what the outcome is as long as you are alright then I shall be the happiest man in the world. I think we should phone them today. OK?"

"Go on then, you do it." She felt relived to have got that off her chest, but until she knew for certain the niggling doubts would remain in her head.

"I'll go to your office now and see what I can come up with."

Nicos left Sky with a kiss and a smile, but in his heart he too had doubts. Please God don't let there be anything wrong with her. If it is a baby then I shall promise to do everything I can to be a good father, but please don't make Sky ill. Like so many men he knew very little about the workings of a woman, but even he realised Sky was rather old to be pregnant. With his mind in a whirl he opened the office door and jumped back in surprise. Emily sat behind Sky's desk tapping away on the computer.

"Sorry did I startle you?" She looked up over the screen.

"No, well yes actually." He stammered. "I had totally forgotten you work here now. How is business these days?" He wanted the room to himself but felt that he needed to be polite.

"Very busy." She replied. "I never realised there were so many people in the world who wanted odd sized shoes, or just one shoe, mind you some of these beautiful sandals can hardly be called shoes. It doesn't do them justice, have you see these?" She held a catalogue out towards him.

"Yes I had a look the other day. My wife is a very clever lady." Nicos had a proud smile on his face. "I'll see you later then." He turned to leave.

"Did you want something from in here?" Emily asked gently.

"Not really I just wanted to use the phone. Don't worry I'll go next door."

He waved as he left.

Next he tried Sunni's studio, which like the office was occupied. This time his son was busy with the photographs of the last shoot.

"Just look at these papa. Storm looks brilliant."

Nicos walked to the back of the desk and leaned on Sunni's chair. The two men gazed into the screen and Nicos felt slightly shocked. There in full colour was his daughter with hardly a stitch of clothing on draped over a very sexy looking Allesandro.

"It's for aftershave." Sunni informed him.

"Then why hasn't she got any clothes on?" His reply was quite sharp.

"People want to see her body papa. It sells things by the bucket load." He carried on scouring the image for any impurities.

"Have you booked your flight yet son?" Nicos asked wanting to change the subject as jealousy raged in his chest. His little girl looking like a femme fatal just to sell aftershave, but then he had to agree she did look fantastic.

"Yeah. We go tomorrow. I shall have a word with Emily's dad, I fancy The Savoy for the do, but she is worried about him not being able to afford it. I've told her not to be silly so I will have to work on him a bit." Sunni continued to tap on the computer as he spoke.

"You realise your grandparents are too old to travel, and so is Andros come to think of it." Nicos said watching Sunni's fingers glide over the keyboard.

"Yes and that is why we have decided to have two weddings. The proper one in London, a church do with all the trimmings, and then one here, Emily said she would like to have a blessing down at the beach so I agreed. It makes life so simple don't you think? In fact she is going down there this afternoon to speak to Eleni and the twins. Now the secret is out we might as well get on with things."

"Good idea." Nicos patted his son's back gently. "Well I'll be off. See you later."

Nicos ended up going round in circles. Every room he went in someone else was already working, the cleaning maids, Maria in the kitchen, Storm in her bedroom and Gina in hers. Each time he stopped to talk for a while, and before long he realised the morning has passed him by.

Right, he thought, only one thing for it. Walking quickly he went over to his parents villa where he was slightly dismayed to find both of them wanted to chat.

"Papa," he said eventually. "Do you mind if I use the phone in my old room for a few minutes."

"Go ahead son but is something wrong. You must have a dozen phones over there." Alexi nodded towards The Eagles Nest.

"Not up to your old tricks again are you?" Athena asked with a scowl. "Not another woman already Nicos?"

"No mama I can't believe you could think such a thing." Mind you it was hardly surprising with his track record, but he felt sad that his mother had said those words. "I need to phone someone for Sky, but it has to be private and all the rooms in the villa are occupied or noisy."

He left the room quickly so Athena would not see the disappointment on his face.

Another shock was in store as he opened his old bedroom door. All of his things were as he had left them on the day of his wedding; even an old bottle of aftershave stood exactly where he had put it down.

"I thought you would be back." Athena said from the doorway making him jump. "I imagined your marriage would only last a short while so I left everything as it was."

"Oh mama did you have no faith in me at all?" Nicos was close to tears, had his mother doubted his love for Sky.

"Nicos you were a pig with women just like your father. I know all about his ladies and put up with it, but I always thought Sky was stronger than me. I was certain the first time you strayed she would throw you out."

"Well you were wrong. I love Sky and always have, but before you start on me about Giovanna let me say one thing. I have made my peace with my wife and she has forgiven me so please mama can you forgive me too?" Nicos walked over to where Athena stood and looked into her wrinkled face. "Please mama let us forget about the past."

Mother and son embraced.

"Look after her my son." Athena patted his shoulders then held his face in her hands "Just look after her."

Nicos nodded as his mother left the room.

Sitting on his old bed he dialed the hospital number. Eventually he managed to speak to Sky's doctor and after making an appointment phoned the airline and arranged for them to fly over in the morning.

The appointment was for the day after but he knew how much Sky wanted to go to the shops and a little retail therapy might help her to relax. If she went to the hospital all tense and stressed the doctor would not be too pleased.

He booked a suite at the Athens Hilton, making sure that their bedroom would have plenty of yellow roses, Sky's favourite, and champagne on ice waiting for their arrival. He sorted out the taxis and then decided to give Andros a call.

He knew he would be in for a right good telling off, but might as well get it over with sooner rather than later.

In fact Andros seemed pleased to hear from him and surprisingly invited him and Sky to eat at the house.

"Paris is coming to see me with some chap who says he is her brother." Andros said quite calmly. "So we can make a party of it."

After their chat Nicos put the receiver down and sat staring at the phone. What a surprise that had been, he had really been shocked by Andros's manner. Over friendly if anything, but perhaps old age had mellowed him at last.

Andros had always been a little strange, one minute palley, the next as if in competition, but perhaps their childhood friendship did count for something after all.

Next Nicos phoned Paris who was as surprised as he to hear about Andros's invitation.

"It seems a little odd to me Nicos. Last time I spoke to him he was all for ripping your head off, mind you so was I at one point, now he wants you to go and visit, it's a bit strange but never mind. Why are you going over anyway?"

204

Damn, thought Nicos, I had better think of something fast. His mind went a total blank so instead he told the truth.

"Promise me Paris you won't let on." Now he felt nervous. "If she knows I've said anything she'll go crazy."

"Don't worry I'll stay quiet." Paris was now as worried as he was. "She's a bit old don't you think?"

Nicos spilled all his fears out to Paris and felt the now familiar panic as he spoke.

"Thanks Paris I needed to talk to someone." He said eventually. "I felt like I was going to explode with worry."

"I'm just glad I've found out." She replied. "Now we can both keep an eye on her. Which flight are you on tomorrow?"

Nicos gave the details and was pleased to learn the four of them would be traveling together.

"See you tomorrow then." Paris said cheerfully. "And stop worrying Nicos. Sky is as strong as an ox, she'll be OK." Her words did not echo her own fears but she felt Nicos needed some reassurance.

After more chat with his parents Nicos finally made it back to the terrace as the others returned after their days work, only Sky was missing.

"Where is your mama?" He asked Storm sharply. "Is she OK?"

"Stop fretting papa she is in her office just finishing off isn't that right Emily?"

"Yes. She won't be long." As Emily spoke Sky hobbled around the corner.

"So the wanderer returns." She said with a smile and gave Nicos a kiss on the cheek "What on earth have you been up to all day?"

"I went to use the phone over at papa's and got talking and you know what my parents are like for being chatty, well time just flew. By the way that shopping trip I promised you, well we are going tomorrow." He could see from her face she understood his meaning.

"Oh I can't wait." She clapped her hands in relief. "A wedding outfit how exciting."

Both she and Nicos knew the wedding outfit was second in their thoughts, but for now let their children think otherwise.

205

"Right," said Nicos feeling much more cheerful. "Who's for a glass of wine?"

Hands shot into the air as the group sat back and began to discuss their day.

• CHAPTER •
18

As their taxi pulled up at the tiny airport building Sky spotted Paris and Gabriel, she could see they were deep in discussion, and wondered what it was that seemed to be so interesting. A little pang of jealousy crept into her mind.

This young man who had appeared from nowhere had almost taken over her roll as Paris's confidant. She continually talked about him, what he was doing, where he had been, and on more than one occasion Sky had to stop herself from asking her to shut up. But, thinking about the changes that had happened so suddenly in his life it was no wonder Gabriel had much to ask and so much to tell.

Paris had always felt that her parents would return someday and this was the nearest thing to that Sky supposed, she on the other hand had hardly given them a thought. It was them that made the decision to leave their home and children not hers or Paris's, it was they who had a son without bothering to let the girls know, why should she care, but Sky knew she did, just a tiny bit.

"Penny for them." Nicos said looking into her face.

"Oh its nothing really. I was just wondering what those two were talking about that's all. Don't worry so much Jack you'll end up with an ulcer." She patted his leg and smiled. He was terrified and she knew it. Whatever they found out tomorrow she prayed that he would be strong enough to help her get through it.

Cancer. That was her greatest fear. She had read somewhere that cancer of the ovaries could sometimes do strange things to the body. It upset the hormones and could well give the impression of being pregnant when really the prognosis was much worse.

"Come on then let's go." The car had stopped completely now and Nicos was already collecting their cases from the boot. Sky followed as he wheeled them towards where Paris and Gabriel stood.

"Kalimera Paris, Gabriel." She called brightly. "It's a beautiful morning to go flying." Her beaming smile hid her fears well.

"Kalimera." Paris turned and kissed her sisters cheek. "You OK Sky?"

"Yes thanks. A little tired, but nothing a bit of retail therapy won't put right."

"I think that's a good idea. We can all go together if you like. I need something for the wedding, so does Gabriel. What about you Nicos?"

"I phoned Armani yesterday, they should have my suit ready this afternoon." He replied casually.

One of the good things about being as rich as these people was the fact that they just had to ask and things were done, and done well.

Although the ladies measurements were held at a number of shops Paris and Sky always wanted to go and look first, the men though much preferred to phone their orders through.

"Top hat and tails I was told. Light gray suit and darker waistcoat, white shirt and maroon cravat." He nodded as if coming to the end of a list. "Sunni's is exactly the same." He laughed. "Evidently Storm is having that too. I'll wager she looks better in her get up than I do. I don't think I have had that many clothes on for years but I suppose it will keep the cold out."

"That's a point Sky we had better make sure we have something with sleeves. Goose pimples won't look so good on the photographs."

Paris said seriously knowing they quickly forgot how chilly England was compared to their little island in the sun.

Sky smiled and nodded, that was her idea of a floaty number out of the window. If she was pregnant then a tiered chiffon dress could have hidden her bump, but now she would have to think again.

"Tell you what." Sky said a little over excitedly. "Why don't you take Gabriel to get measured Jack while me and Paris go to Dior, then we can all meet up for lunch before going over to see Andros."

"Good idea." Nicos had never really liked shopping that much. He always felt like a spare part in the ladies outfitters, and on occasions slightly embarrassed when the mannequins paraded the clothes, especially the underwear. These tall slim beautiful women made him hot under the collar, and quite often in other regions of his body too, as they floated about in front of his eyes. "We'll go and get you sorted." He nodded to Gabriel.

"Put it on my bill." Paris said to Nicos. "They already have the card number." Yet another plus of being well known and rich.

The flight to the mainland wouldn't take them long this morning, which was a good thing, as Sky's constant fidgeting was already shredding Nicos's own fragile nerves.

Paris pointed out the marvelous antiquities to a spell bound Gabriel as they circled the city waiting to land.

"Some say it is the only way to really see Athens." Nicos added to her continuous commentary. "And I can certainly understand why. It is so beautiful, I never tire of the view from up here."

"There is our house." Paris pointed through the window to the wonderful white marble villa on the hillside. "That is where Andros lives it used to belong to his mother Lady Eleni, remember I was telling you about her."

"It looks stunning." Gabriel was breathless at the sight below. "Absolutely stunning."

Paris had told him about her marriage to Andros, well some of it, and she had been pleased that he did not asked too many questions, her private life was just that, private even to her sister, let alone her new brother.

209

They left the airport and walked into the heat of Athens in summer.

"I'm not going to enjoy trying that suit on today." Nicos said wiping his brow.

"Don't be such a sissy, they will have air conditioning at the outfitters." Paris giggled. "Men! Why does a little thing like shopping always put them in a spin."

Thankfully the dark windowed limousine sent from the hotel was air conditioned, and Nicos soon cooled down, in fact within seconds the hairs on his arms had stood to attention.

"That's better." He sighed breathing in the cool air.

"And you are worrying about wearing a suit in England." Paris was still giggling at him. At least it was better than fighting with him, she thought. Sky seemed happy enough to have him back, although a little quiet today, so that was good enough for her, but if he ever did anything like that again then she would be down on him like a ton of bricks. She nodded as if agreeing to her own thoughts.

Sky stayed in the car with Paris whilst Gabriel and Nicos checked in at the hotel.

"He has ordered this for the day." She said as they reappeared. "Where to first then Jack?"

"I thought if we dropped you two off first then it will give you a little more time. I will phone when we have finished at Armani and see how you are getting on. I can always take Gabriel on a tour round if you aren't quite ready."

"Good thinking batman, Dior it is then."

Nicos gave the driver instructions through the intercom on the back seat and off they went.

Gabriel sat for most of the journey with his nose up against the windows gazing at the fabulous sights here on ground level. Not only did Athens look stunning from above, there was much more to see at street level as well.

Eventually shop frontages took over the view, but even then they had an air of something very special, and the sight of the blackened windows of the Dior emporium made him snigger.

"Don't they like to show off their things then?" Gabriel asked with a giggle.

"It's not that but people don't like to be seen. Many of the top designer shops have blackened windows. It stops everyone looking through at the rich ladies inside." Nicos said mirroring his mirth. "Very rich people don't want to share with the normal people of this world. Isn't that right Paris?"

"It doesn't bother me much but I know many of the ladies I used to interview wouldn't step inside a shop with ordinary windows. They hated to be seen, thought it was slightly vulgar. It's also a security thing, not only does it protect those inside, but helps to stop designs being copied."

Gabriel nodded trying to understand; he had never had much and found all of this slightly bazaar.

After seeing the women into their shop, he and Nicos went to Armani.

A tall well-built man who Gabriel decided he would not want to fall out with under any circumstances guarded the door. He gave off a slightly menacing air that made the young man feel a little nervous.

"Good morning Mr. Mandros. Please take a seat and introduce your guest if you would be so kind." He almost growled as he spoke, his face lighting up with a smile as Nicos explained this was the brother of Mrs. Paris Yannisos.

The names Mandros and Yannisos brought the head assistant scurrying to the waiting area, two of the richest families in Greece, today the service would be second to none.

"This way if you please gentlemen." The assistant bowed slightly. "Your wedding attire is ready Sir." He gestured to a male mannequin who stood in the middle of a small viewing area.

"He's got your suit on?" Gabriel whispered.

"No silly. That is a replica. Mine will be over there." Nicos pointed to a curtained off room. "I'll go and try it on." He nodded to the assistant. "That is fine. Mr. Maxwell requires similar please."

The assistant nodded and clapped his hands, within seconds another man appeared.

211

"Please come with me Sir I will take your measurements." His breath smelled of mints as he spoke to Gabriel. "This way."

Nicos smiled to himself as Gabriel was led away looking like a lamb going to the slaughter, and no doubt he would feel like it when he was asked to undress. The good thing about this type of emporium was once measurements had been taken they were kept on file and unless the person put on, or lost weight, this was the one and only time they would be taken. It was a long and arduous process, where even the length of Gabriel's fingers and toes would be measured as everything even his gloves and socks had to fit perfectly.

Eventually he reappeared to find Nicos sipping cold champagne and reading a magazine.

"Can I offer you a drink Sir?" The assistant asked as he came from behind the heavy velvet curtain.

"Please." Gabriel replied and sat down quickly next to Nicos. "They even measured my ears." He said stifling a laugh. "I'll never want earmuffs."

"No but you want your hat to fit properly." Nicos replied. "These people do a thorough job." He paused and took another sip of his drink. "My suit is fine but I'll leave it here for now, they can send them all over together. Evidently Storm is coming for her fitting soon along with Vanni and the twins so they might as well ship them all over at the same time. The men in England are going into Armani in London for theirs so we can all pick them up together." He smiled. "I wonder how the ladies are doing? I think we should stay here for a while and enjoy some hospitality it will give them a bit longer. I bet Sky hasn't even chosen a colour yet let alone an outfit."

"Did you say pick them up in London?" Gabriel took a glass from the assistants silver tray.

"Yes. Once the fittings have been sorted they will send them over to London. It's all part of the service." Nicos replied.

Gabriel realised he had a lot to learn now he had entered the world of the wealthy elite.

As the two men sat sipping champagne and watching as mannequins paraded before them in the next season's outfits Nicos's phone sprang to life.

"Hi Jack. How's it going at your end?" Sky sounded excited.

"Great in fact we've nearly finished. What about you?" Nicos replied.

Sky's voice echoed slightly as she told him how they were going to be a little late.

"Paris has tried on so many things I feel confused." She laughed. "Mine is done and dusted but that sister of mine is going through everything they have got."

"Tell you what then. Why don't Gabriel and I go straight to Andros's and I'll send the car back for you two. We can have a manly chat before you arrive."

"Sounds good to me. See you later then. Bye."

Nicos ordered himself a few things from the new collection and also decided to treat Alexi whilst he was there. A couple of beautiful soft cashmere jumpers and various other items were added to Nicos's bill.

"I can see papa in those." He said to Gabriel. "They will help keep the winter chill out of his poor old bones." Alexi had always been slim but muscular, now though he appeared to be paper thin, it was something that worried Nicos greatly.

"They will be delivered tomorrow Sir." The assistant bowed again as he spoke. "May I get you anything else?"

"No that is fine thanks." Nicos replied as he led Gabriel from the shop.

"Don't you have to pay?" Gabriel said quietly.

"They just charge my card. Nothing as vulgar as paying in cash." Nicos whispered back. "Don't fret they will get their money." He smiled, handed the doorman a hefty tip and thanked the assistant who bowed again slightly as they left. "And his tip will go on top. I always give 2 per cent of what the total is. He has done well this afternoon. Right off to see Andros. This could be quite an afternoon."

Had he had known how true those words were as they sped through the streets, Nicos would have stopped the car there and then.

• CHAPTER •
19

Once again Gabriel sat with his face seemingly glued to the window as the wonderful sights of the city passed before his eyes. Before long though they were on the road leading out of Athens and up into the surrounding hills, now his eyes feasted upon the wonderful villas partly hidden by tall cypress trees swaying in the warm breeze.

"There are the most fantastic views from the house." Nicos said as the car negotiated the narrow roads. "You can see almost all of Athens from high up."

Gabriel was now looking through the back window as if trying to catch every last glimpse of the city below.

He turned as the car slowed to a stop in front of some very impressive old metal gates; they opened gracefully allowing them to pass into the stunning gardens.

"You can breathe you know. It is allowed." Nicos had noticed how the young man had been holding his breath as they swept silently along the drive. Gabriel smiled.

"I don't think I have ever seen anywhere like this in my life." He said in awe of the large white house at the end of the drive.

"Wait until you see inside then." Nicos replied.

The butler came to open the car doors, his dark tailcoat suit looking out of place on this very hot day.

"Mr. Yannisos is expecting you Sirs but unfortunately he has an unexpected visitor at present and will be slightly delayed. Are the ladies not with you?" He asked peering into the limousine.

"No they will be along a little later." Nicos answered then instructed the driver where to collect Sky and Paris.

"This way then gentlemen allow me to show you to the conservatory." Like the assistant in the shop, the man bowed slightly.

"Thank you. This way Gabriel." Nicos walked towards the house. Gabriel followed, his head spinning as he tried to look at everything around him.

"May I offer you drinks?" The butler enquired as he seated them in the large cool and airy conservatory where the view over the city stunned Nicos even though he had seen it many times before.

"Please. Ouzo OK Gabriel?" Nicos asked and upon receiving a nod also asked for one himself. "A hot day like this calls for ouzo there is nothing quite like it for cooling you down."

A smartly dressed waiter served the drinks and left a dish of assorted olives on the table, the two settled down to wait.

"What is that over there?" Gabriel asked pointing down the sloping lawn to a smaller white marble building.

"That is the swimming pool." Nicos replied. "Fancy a walk down?" Gabriel nodded yet again.

The doors of the conservatory were slightly open allowing them to walk directly out on to the steps leading down to the lawn.

Nicos pointed out buildings of interest and the busy harbor at Piraeus in the distance, as they walked he talked, trying his best to remember as much as he could about the city below.

Suddenly raised voices interrupted his commentary.

"Don't even think about it!" They heard Andros shout. "Never let me hear you say that again."

215

"But it is true. I'm leaving your employment." The reply came from a familiar voice making Nicos's face crumple into a frown as he tried to remember who it was. "I want nothing more to do with you." They heard a thump as if someone had slammed their fist into something.

They both began to run towards the veranda and together dashed through the open doors of Andros's office.

"Allesandro!" Nicos recognized the owner of the voice as he and Gabriel burst into the room. "What the hell are you doing here?"

"I have come to tell this bastard I have had enough." He spat towards Andros who stayed seated behind his large mahogany desk a moment before rising. His eyes shone in a strange manner and his lips curled into the most peculiar smile.

"Nicos. How nice to see you again." Andros said sarcastically. "And this must be Gabriel the cuckoo, after my money are you cuckoo, well I'll tell you once and only once. No chance."

"What do you mean Andros? This is Paris and Sky's brother how can you be so rude." Nicos was appalled by his old friend's behavior.

"Why else would he appear out of the woodwork, if not to get his grubby hands on my money?" Spittle trickled down Andros's chin. "You say you are their brother, I say you are after my money. Well you won't get it."

He pushed a tiny gold button on the desktop and within seconds they felt a presence behind them.

"Trouble boss." Another voice familiar to Nicos.

This time it was Paulo. He stood in the open door blocking the sunlight with his bulk.

"What the hell is going on Andros? I don't understand." Nicos was bemused to see the two men here in the office.

"Sit and let me tell you then." Andros pointed to large deep leather chairs that stood to one side of the room. "Now if you please." He clapped his hands impatiently.

Paulo didn't move, instead he stood by the window arms crossed over his chest, a gun in one hand, legs slightly opened, and a menacing look on his face.

216

Once the three stunned men had taken their seats Andros walked back behind his desk and slowly poured himself a glass of water before sitting down.

"Now let me see where shall I begin. You know this is going to be more fun than I could have ever imagined." His eyes had that strange light in them again. "I have dreamt about this moment Nicos and often wondered how I could get you here, and then out of the blue you phoned and now you have walked into my little trap." Andros rubbed his hands together in a childlike manner. "Now where shall I start? Let me think." He continued with the strange motion of his hands, it was as if he were washing them. "I know how's about when you screwed Paris Nicos. That is as good as a place as anywhere."

Nicos squirmed in his seat as a trickle of sweat ran down his back. Andros looked totally mad, what the hell was going on, a shiver of fear swept down his spine.

"Ever since that day I have plotted my revenge and today is the culmination of years of waiting." He tapped a gold pen on his teeth. "The night you screwed Paris changed my life Nicos. How do you think I felt every time she wanted me to make love to her knowing you had been there eh? Well I'll tell you it made me feel sick. One of the reasons I live here is so that I don't have to see her disgusting face, the face of a whore."

"Don't you call my sister a whore!" Gabriel went to launch himself at Andros only to be struck to the ground by the butt of Paulo's gun. He fell to the floor with a thump; Nicos could see blood oozing from his cut brow.

"But that is what she is." Andros said as if talking to a child.

"She is also your wife." Nicos added helping Gabriel back into his seat.

"Is that what you think my friend. Well let me tell you how wrong you are." Andros paused and grinned strangely at Nicos, his fingers now busy tapping a weird rhythm on the desktop. "I divorced her years ago and the only reason I let her come to me when she feels it is her duty to perform, is because I hate her so much. You may think that is strange but I know it is only duty that brings her here to me. You see she has another man. I told you she was a whore." His voice rose alarmingly.

217

"But why Andros I still don't understand any of this. I thought you loved her?" Nicos cried even more confused than before.

"I will admit that once I did love her, I worshiped the ground she walked on, every hair on her head, and that is why I mistakenly let you help me to win her back. Yes, when I married her I thought I was in love and for two years I did nothing but be by her side whilst she wrote her books, but every day the feeling of disgust got stronger. Every time I saw you and Sky together I wanted to shout out that you had screwed my wife, and let us not forget my sister. Poor little Eleni also fell under your spell you bastard. How Vanni can stay with her I will never know.

But then you had Storm, a beautiful baby girl, the one thing I could never have, a baby of my own, something to do with an illness when I was a child."

For a moment Nicos thought Andros was going to cry.

"For Sky to announce within weeks of the first baby that another was due well it shattered my already broken heart and that is when I decided to get even." He laughed uncontrollably for a few minutes, tears streaming down his red cheeks. "And you fell for my plot just as I expected. Couldn't keep it in your pants could you once you laid eyes on Giovanna. Mind you she was pretty good at putting it about too, or didn't you know that?" He smiled at the puzzled look on Nicos's face. "Let me show you something, but I don't think you will enjoy this."

He pressed a button on the desk and one of the priceless paintings on the wall silently slid to the side revealing a blank TV screen. "Or, perhaps you will enjoy this." His finger pushed hard onto another button and the screen sprang to life. "I like to look at it when I'm feeling a little low." Again the strange laugh escaped his lips as Nicos and Gabriel stared at the screen. "Like what you see?" He asked as the images of Giovanna and Andros appeared, naked on her bed and obviously making love. "I can stop it anywhere you like Nicos just ask." Instead of waiting for a reply he paused the action as Giovanna rode him with passion.

"You foul pig." Nicos shouted and rushed towards the desk. He felt the blow of Paulo's gun as it hit against his head and blood trickle down his cheek.

"Oh and how's about this." Andros fast-forwarded the film to show a very small Gina asleep on his chest. Her podgy little arms curled around his neck, Andros was still naked and his arousal obvious to see. "Pretty little thing Nicos. Very nice." Andros licked his lips in a disgusting manner.

"You filthy bastard. If you have done anything to her I will kill you." Nicos tried again to reach behind the desk only to receive yet another blow from Paulo's gun. "And how can you stand there and see this without it turning your stomach Paulo. She is your niece for God's sake. Giovanna was your sister. What the hell is going on?"

"Paulo has a naughty little habit with young girls Nicos didn't you know? I've bailed him out on many occasions or he would not be standing there now but rotting in jail. He also has a taste for the white powder and that can be rather expensive. Right Paulo?"

He looked over to the man who was at his beck and call. Paulo didn't move.

Andros continued. "How many men would sell their sisters? I am afraid he is one very sick man." He gave a cackling laugh.

"You mean you blackmailed him?"

Nicos was aghast. Paulo was his friend or so he thought, not some blackmailed drugged up pervert, but then Andros had been a friend at one time. His head was in a spin.

"Correct my friend. I got him to introduce the sexy Giovanna to you knowing you would not be able to resist. I knew you would have an affair and then some of the many photographs and films I took would have made their way to your wife, Sky would ditch you and I would have had my revenge, but I had not bargained for you staying with Giovanna. Nor did I expect to learn that stupid woman, your wife, has had you back, she wouldn't even look at me." He nodded towards Nicos. "Yes I tried on many occasions but no, the pathetic woman became a nun."

"She is not stupid or pathetic." Nicos shouted ignoring the throbbing pain in his head. "She is a lovely woman."

"And according to my spy's a pregnant one. Nicos you disgust me. How could you impregnate her at such an age? It is more than disgusting." Andros screwed his face up then spat at Nicos. "That is what you deserve." He paused as if thinking. "And if you are wondering where poncy Allesandro fits in well watch this." Again he pushed the button on the desk. This time the screen was filled with images of Storm and Allesandro. "Such a slut just like her father, sex mad. Just look Nicos, see how your beloved daughter performs for a man."

Nicos could not help himself but look at Storm. Her marvelous body naked for all to see, her legs entwined around the shinning body of

Allesandro. He felt deflated and let a long sigh flow from his lips. Andros had gone too far, he needed to act.

Looking at the other two captives he tried to gage their fitness, he could see Gabriel was finished, but there was a sparkle of light in Allesandro's eyes. He too was digusted by the images on the wall, but then Gina was his wife, and Storm had been his lover.

This was Nicos's ally and he quickly realised that. Now if only he could make the young man even angrier then perhaps together they could launch an attack on Paulo and Andros.

"What are you blackmailing him with the Andros?" Nicos asked and looked straight into Allesandro's eyes.

"Money, lovely money. I met him when he first started courting Gina and we got talking." Came an unexpectedly soft reply. "He just wanted money to get away from the island and become a photographer, I said I would help. The only trouble with him was he has very expensive tastes and soon he was in debt much deeper than he ever imagined." Andros gave his strange laugh. "So I sent him to London on the express orders to bed Storm, told him I would wipe his debt clear if he did certain things for me. How was I to know he would be instantly successful and now the silly man thinks he can walk away from me just like that." He clicked his fingers to emphasise the point. "No chance. I can ruin him in the blink of an eye. How did you all think the press got hold of his story so quickly?" Andros smirked. "Oh I'm so clever." He looked directly at Nicos. " He might be in with that man who is my wife's lover. Oh did you not know Nicos? Paris and Matthew have been lovers for years. I knew the day it started, look." Now the images of Paris and Matthew came on to the screen. "They met when Storm began her career." The film moved but only Andros was now watching.

Nicos was trying to signal to Allesandro with his eyes, Gabriel sat in stunned silence and Paulo stood once again by the door.

The telephone on Andros's desk broke into the eerie silence.

"Oh good. Show them into my office please and bring a magnum of champagne." Andros sat back and rubbed his hands. "The ladies have arrived so no silly business when they come in, right Nicos?"

Nicos nodded but his mind was battling with thoughts of how to keep Sky and Paris from entering the room.

"I have this trained on your dick my friend." Andros waved a revolver in the air before his hands disappeared under the desk. "Right on your scummy dick Nicos." He laughed. "And as for you two, well Paulo here will take care of you." The two young men nodded, both too stunned to reply in words.

The butler knocked before entering the room and announced Sky and Paris, the waiter a step behind with the ordered champagne, both leaving once their jobs had been done, but not before Nicos noticed how the butler gazed around the room. He must have noticed the blood on their faces, why oh why didn't he say or do something. Perhaps he too was being blackmailed by Andros?

"Come in ladies. Please take a seat we were waiting for you before we started the celebrations." Andros stayed seated but spoke in a polite calm voice. "Unfortunately you have missed my little speech, so I will have to start again."

Sky hobbled towards Nicos and immediately gasped at the cuts on his head. She looked over to Gabriel and saw the blood now drying on his face.

"Sit down Sky." Andros brought his gun from under the desk. "And you slut, pour us all a glass of champagne." He aimed his words and the gun towards a visibly shaken Paris. "Come on chop chop. We all want a drink, today if you please."

As Andros concentrated his eyes on Paris Nicos leapt from his chair and launched himself over the desk grabbing the champagne bottle for a weapon as he slid. The heavy bottle burst on to the head of Andros splattering pieces of blood, hair and flesh over Nicos and the desk. Andros slumped to the floor stone dead.

A shot rang out quickly followed by a second. Sky screamed as Allesandro flew in slow motion across the room, a huge hole in his chest and as Paulo admired his handy work Gabriel took him by surprise. A solid marble statue smashed onto his head leaving an imprint of the Goddesses breasts on what was left of his face.

For a few seconds no one noticed Sky slumped on the floor. A rapidly growing pool of blood surrounding her body as it poured from a gaping wound in her head.

An animal like scream left Nicos's lips.

• CHAPTER •
20

"No just listen." Nicos was talking into his mobile phone, trying to calm a distraught Storm down.

His fingers ran through his already ruffled hair as he spoke, his handsome face now gray and wrinkled with worry.

"It is too long a story to tell you now, but yes she has been shot and she may loose the sight of her right eye, perhaps even both, but thank God she is still alive." Nicos paused listening. "Yes she is still having an operation but they are doing their best. Paris is OK and so is Gabriel although he has had a few stitches in a wound." He paused again. "Yes so have I, but that is nothing. Listen Storm poor Allesandro is dead." He waited for her reply. "He was trying to help us. He gave his life to save ours. A very brave young man."

Nicos felt so sorry for the youngster who had launched himself upon Paulo's gun. He had his life before him but gave it up in that split second of confusion when Andros had slumped to the floor. "Please tell Gina he was very brave. I know you loved him once too, but he was her husband. Please try to help her Storm, just for me. I cannot be with you

222

for some time yet. I refuse to leave Athens until Sky comes with me and the doctors say that will not be for some time, weeks maybe months, but I am not leaving her alone."

Nicos continued his disjointed conversation explaining as much as possible. He wanted to give Storm the details, as he knew full well the press would print all sorts. It would be the leading headline around the world tomorrow and his children needed to know the truth but they also needed to be protected.

"Look if that's what you want then come over but do me a favour bring Gina with you, oh and can you phone Sunni. I can't get in touch with him I assume he is still on the flight to London. Would you call him for me." He nodded and smiled as Storm replied. "Thanks love. The police need to see me and once your mother is out of theatre I want to be with her." He waited again whilst Storm spoke. "See you soon then. Please be careful. Love you." Nicos blew kisses down the phone, it was the closest he could get to hugging his distraught daughter at the moment, but he felt slightly better to hear her giggle and reply with kisses of her own.

Nicos clicked his phone shut and stared at it for a few moments. His head was in a whirl. Thank God the butler had seen Andros pointing the gun at Nicos on the office security camera and called the police.

How ironic that the obsession Andros had with security would be his downfall. Every room had security cameras recording the movements of the household, something he had obviously forgotten in his mentally unstable frame of mind.

The police upon hearing what the butler had to say also alerted the ambulance service and both arrived together just as the first shot was fired.

Too late to save Andros, Allesandro and Paulo, but there just in time to help Sky.

What would he have done if she too had died? It was something he could not imagine, life without her. Even though he had lived with Giovanna all those years his telephone conversations with Sky had been the highlight of his week. What a stupid man I have been, he said out loud, bloody bloody stupid.

223

The police had interviewed Paris first and were now speaking with Gabriel, my turn next Nicos thought as he walked slowly along the white hospital corridor.

Occasionally he passed by a window where he could see from the darkening sky night was beginning to fall; unfortunately he could also see the world's press at the hospital gates.

Bright flashes from the photographer's cameras were lighting up en mass every time a car came into the wide gravel drive. They wanted to miss nothing, even nurses were being photographed and asked questions, but this was one of the best hospitals in the world, and one where the staff were used to protecting their wealthy patients. The journalists failed miserably in their quest for news.

Nicos took a deep breath and straightened his back, what a peculiar day this had been. It had started out so well and now it was as if he were in a nightmare. Let's get this interview over and then I can concentrate on Sky he thought then said a little prayer for her in his mind.

The police had already confirmed that they would not be prosecuting anyone there was no point. Andros was dead. It meant less paper work, but they needed to hear his side of the story for their records.

The butler had handed over the security tapes and everything Paris and Gabriel had already told them tied in with the video. At least that was one man Andros did not have a hold over, the butler would be rewarded handsomely for his quick thinking.

Nicos walked to the very end of the corridor and out in to the cool night air. He stood by the security doorman, one of many guarding the hospital, and lit a cigarette. He took a long drag and felt the strong smoke enter his lungs; he held his breath for a couple of seconds to get the full effect. How many times had he tried to give up this habit, but at this moment he could think of nothing nicer as the buzz from the nicotine hit his brain. He took another deep drag of poison into his body.

Nicos jumped as a hand appeared from nowhere on his shoulder.

"Would you like to come this way?" It was one of the policemen. "We have taken over a room down here." Nicos threw what remained of his cigarette on the floor and ground it in to the gravel before moving. "We just have a few questions for you Sir. Please follow me."

The two men walked back down the corridor and into one of the side rooms where another policeman and a uniformed woman sat behind a hastily converted table. Usually used for flowers now a computer and various pieces of paper littered its surface, empty polystyrene coffee cups and, Nicos was pleased to see, an ashtray sat amongst the debris. He lit another cigarette.

They talked and asked questions, showed photographs and scribbled down notes. The uniformed woman tapped speedily on the computer keyboard as Nicos relived his nightmare visit to Andros. It wasn't until the policeman sat back that Nicos realised the interview was over.

"Thank you Mr. Mandros I think we have everything. You may go to your wife now. We all hope she recovers quickly." His face smiled and his lips moved but Nicos could tell his brain was still sifting through the information.

Slowly Nicos rose and shook the man's hand. He felt exhausted, drained and suddenly very old. The effects of the day along with a constant stream of cigarettes and no food saw him crumple to the floor in a faint.

"Jack, are you there?" Nicos woke to the soft sound of Sky's shaky voice. "I can't see you Jack. Please are you there?" Now she sounded frightened.

"Yes my love." Nicos quickly collected his thoughts and sat up in what appeared to be a bed.

One minute he had been talking to the policeman and then nothing. Just darkness, now here he was in a room with Sky.

"They told me you had collapsed. Oh Jack are you alright?"

"Don't worry I'm OK." Nicos swung his legs over the side of his bed and walked slowly over to where, through the darkness he could see Sky. Her face and head were a mass of thick bandages. "What has he done to you my darling?"

He took her hand and kissed it gently.

"Hold me Jack I'm so frightened." Her voice trembled as she spoke. "They think I might be blind." Nicos took her into his arms. "What about our baby?" Fear filled her voice.

"We shall have to wait and see my angel but you are alive and that is all that matters at this moment." He kissed her chin, virtually the only

225

part of her face showing and held her close as she fell once again into a drug-induced sleep.

As the light slowly crept into the room Nicos stirred. His back ached from sitting at an angle with his arm around Sky. He could hear her breathing and thanked God she was alive. His hand slipped down towards her stomach and prayed that if a baby were in there the little mite would be OK.

As Nicos gazed at his watch he heard a tap at the door and looked up to see a nurse slowly enter the room. She smiled at him and looked over at Sky.

"She woke in the night but only for a few minutes." He whispered.

"Yes we know we were watching." She replied and pointed to a tiny camera high up on the wall.

"Thank God for those things." Nicos muttered. "Now tell me the truth. Is she going to be blind?"

He listened as the nurse gave him as much information as she knew and was frustrated to learn he would have to wait until the doctor came to examine Sky to find out any more.

"We think she might be pregnant, well we hope she is." He added. "Will all of this have harmed our baby?"

"I can tell you she is." The nurse said softly. "Her sister, Mrs. Yannisos warned us before we took her into theatre so we did a few tests. We will do some more later when your wife is feeling up to it. I must tell you though she will be in and out of consciousness for a few days yet. The doctors are going to keep her sedated in order to let her rest but we won't know for sure if the baby is OK for a few weeks yet. It is very early in the pregnancy and we will need to do some scans." Nicos nodded as he listened. "Mrs. Yannisos and Mr. Maxwell left you a message. They will be back after breakfast. They returned to the Hilton for the night."

"Thank you." Nicos said quietly not wanting to disturb Sky. His stomach had other ideas though; just the mention of breakfast and it gave a loud rumble. It had been almost 24 hours now since he had eaten, no wonder he fainted last night.

"I will fetch you some food." The nurse smiled. "It sounds as if you could do with something." She gave an attractive giggle as her eyes gave the come on signal. It was not everyday she was in the company of someone quite so handsome and so rich as Nicos Mandros, now was her

226

chance. His wife a cripple and now possibly blind surely he would want something a little more exciting?

Nicos knew under other circumstances he would have made a play for the very fetching girl. In a crisp white uniform which strained over her ample breasts, shiny dark hair held up in a chignon, shapely legs that looked endless, and a tight wide belt exaggerating her slim waist she looked very tempting indeed. He watched as she moved to the other side of the bed, her hips swaying slightly. Yes he could have played with her quite easily, but that was all in the past.

Sky and his family were now his only concern.

"That would be wonderful thanks." He replied and turned his attention to Sky who muttered something in her sleep. "When will the doctor be here?"

"Soon. Very soon." The nurse replied a little sharply as she realised her chance had gone, but never mind perhaps she would try the other one. At least Mr. Maxwell was single as well as being very rich, he must be rolling in it, all of this family were.

Nicos watched as she tended to the sleeping Sky and read the charts at the foot of the bed.

"Right food for you." She said putting the board back which a clink. "I won't be long." With that she left the room and a very amused Nicos. He could see what she had been trying to do and it made him smile.

At least she had achieved something, made him smile.

The strong very sweet coffee and pastries dipped in honey that were brought to him tasted like nothing on earth. He could feel his body react to sustenance and thought of old Tomas. What was it he used to say, "Sugar in your blood. That's what you need." He was right, Nicos could actually feel it doing him good. Now all he needed was a good wash and shave followed by a couple of cigarettes, then he would feel human.

Scouting about in the bathroom adjoining Sky's room he found all he needed to refresh himself. Carefully he showered not wanting to wake her with any noise, but also not wanting to dislodge any of the stitches in his face. It had surprised him to see just how badly he had been cut. A long line of black wove its way down his bruised face. Gently he touched the skin tracing the mark that Paulo's gun had left, it was tender and sore, the shave would have to wait. As he dried his body he heard another tap at the door.

227

"Nicos it's only me." Paris peered around the open door. "I've got you some clean clothes." She whispered. "Can I come in?"

"Of course. I'm in the bathroom won't be a tick." He tied a towel around his waist and padded barefoot back into the room. "Hey. Thanks for these, I really needed something." He kissed her cheek and took the clean clothes from her arms.

"We had to break your case I'm afraid but I thought you would be feeling a bit grubby and wouldn't mind." She smiled at him and put her hand to his face. "That looks nasty."

"I'll live." He replied and went to get dressed. "The doctor should be here soon, do you want to wait and see what he has to say?" He called from the bathroom.

"Please. I'll just go and tell Gabriel, he is waiting in reception."

"Ask him to keep a look out for the girls for me would you. Storm and Gina, and perhaps even Eleni should be here soon."

"Ok will do." Paris went off in search of Gabriel.

Poor boy, what an introduction to the family he had had, but bless him, he had taken everything in his stride, and apart from the stitches in his head wound he had in fact found it all quite exciting. Like something out of a film, he had said to Paris when they were discussing the day's events.

When Paris returned Nicos was dressed and sat once again at Sky's side.

"She keeps muttering in her sleep but I can't understand any of it." He said bemused.

"That will be the drugs." Paris replied. "They say you talk all sorts of rubbish when you have an anesthetic."

They sat each side of the bed for a few moments listening to Sky but not understanding.

"I think we should talk." Nicos said eventually. "Andros said it was all my fault for seducing you that night. I'm so sorry." He went on to tell Paris everything that had been said the day before. He told her about the pictures of Andros and Giovanna, the ones of her and Matthew, in fact everything. "He said he divorced you years ago."

"So Gabriel told me. I have been in touch with my solicitor and he said that is rubbish. Evidently Andros forged my signature on the documents and they are not legal, but he was right about Matthew and me. I love him Nic, in fact nothing would have pleased me more than to divorce Andros but he always said. 'Over my dead body,' well now unfortunately that has come true." Paris looked down at her hands. "It was such a mistake, me marrying him, I knew it as soon as he started talking about his work and him living over here. All he really wanted from life was money." A tear slid down her face. "So it's just as much my fault really. One, I should not have let you seduce me and two; I should never have married him. Don't blame yourself Nic." She paused for a while to compose herself.

"He said he did love you before our night, and for a while after, but he just couldn't get it out of his mind." Nicos said quietly.

"I still loved him you know. Even after that awful night when he was so nasty to me. I realised he needed to do something, but to rape me, well, how could I ever forget him doing that?" Paris looked over at Nicos surprised face. "I assumed you knew."

"I had an idea he had been a bit rough and vaguely remember young Eleni saying something strange, in fact he told me himself that he had been ungentlemanly, but rape, that is a very strong word Paris."

"I remember it as if it was yesterday but that is all in the past now and so is poor Andros." Paris took a deep breath and sat up straight patting her knees. "Let us look to the future now Nicos, and helping Sky all we can."

"I couldn't agree more." He replied smiling. "What strange lives we have all had, but as you say that is all in the past. I wish we had some champagne to make a toast to the future but that can wait until I get Sky home."

"Truce then?" She said very softly. "We will never be bosom buddies again Nicos, but let's have a truce for her sake."

"Truce." He replied. "And thanks Paris."

They both nodded and looked down at the sleeping woman still mumbling away in her dreams.

For now their argument would be put to one side. Once Sky had recovered, well who knew what would happen then.

• CHAPTER •
21

The following few weeks seemed to be a constant stream of funerals and memorial services. Nicos felt exhausted mentally and physically. Each new day brought visits to solicitors, churches or the police.

He was helping Paris all he could on the legal side, making sure he attended all of the masses said for those who had died, including Andros; it gave him a strange feeling of comfort. Had it all been his fault? No one would ever know, least of all Nicos.

Plus he was still talking to the police who wanted to go over the details time and time again, it was all so frustrating.

Added to that was his daily ritual at Sky's bedside, Nicos was one very tired man and it was beginning to show. His hair was now much grayer, his skin much paler than usual, and his weight had dropped considerably.

"You are making yourself ill papa." Gina said softly. "You must rest or you will be in hospital too." She had come to visit the still sedated Sky.

Complications had set in and further operations had been necessary.

Each operation brought days of sedation where Nicos could only sit, watch and pray that she would recover.

Her right eye had been removed but the doctors had put in a fierce fight and her left eye was starting to mend. At least she would still be able to see, her biggest fear of being permanently in the dark would not now be realised. For that Nicos was grateful, but at present she seemed to have reached a plateau regarding a full recovery and it worried him deeply.

The baby was showing in her now very thin frame and as Gina looked down she giggled as it kicked.

"Look papa the baby she is moving." Gina gently laid her hands on Sky's stomach. "I can feel her here give me your hand." Nicos let his daughter place his hand on the moving flesh.

"What makes you say it is a girl Gina?" He said with a smile not really caring if it was or not, the only thing that worried Nicos was that the baby had not suffered because of the treatment Sky had received.

"I can feel it here." Gina put her hand over her heart. "Just here. A little girl, trust me I know." It was at times like this she reminded him so much of her mother.

Poor Giovanna betrayed by her brother, sold like a slave just so he could indulge his evil fantasies. Andros was as much to blame though, bailing Paulo out and providing the money for drugs, God how he must have hated Nicos to ruin so many lives, but as Paris had said he was now in the past.

A movement from the bed brought Nicos out of his thoughts.

"Jack is that you?" Sky croaked. "Is there any water I am so dry?" Her voice sounded as if she had a really bad cold.

"I'll fetch you some." Gina replied quickly and went over to the fridge where a stash of fresh water was kept.

"Gina its lovely to hear your voice. How are you darling? I'm so sorry about Allesandro." Sky immediately reverted to her roll of mother and even though she was so very poorly her concerns were now for Gina.

"Thank you Sky. I am OK but it was all such a shock. Not only did I lose Allesandro, but uncle Paulo and uncle Yanni."

"Who?" Sky was puzzled.

Uncle Yanni, or so Gina had called the man, was in fact Andros. It was the name he had used when dealing with Paulo and Giovanna Nicos explained.

Gina continued. "I think Storm felt it more than me I feel she loved Allesandro deeper than she let on, but now I look to the future and I think so does she. In fact we have become very good friends."

Gina fixed a straw into the water bottle and brought it over for Nicos to help Sky drink.

"Only a little at a time now." She sounded like one of the nurses. "Not too quickly you will upset the bambina."

"Yes boss." Sky giggled. It was the first time for weeks she had giggled and the happy sound brought a stinging mist to Nicos's eyes.

"Oh look the bambina, she is moving again." Gina's voice had now taken on her excited Italian accent. "Quick Sky feel your tummy."

Sky put her hands down and felt as the child inside her moved slightly. Thank you, she said a little prayer, thank you so much.

"I must go now Sunni and Emily want to come in to see you. Chao papa, chao Sky see you next week." She kissed her father and then his wife. "Look after that bambina for me."

Sky giggled again. It was pretty obvious that she would get plenty of help when the baby eventually arrived, Gina was as excited as they were, as in fact were all of her family.

Storm had at first been horrified to think she was getting a brother or sister and had attacked her father verbally, but with Gina and Emily's obvious excitement she had eventually begun to feel the thrill of a baby in the family.

Everything had been such a life changing string of events for Storm that she had needed these last few weeks to settle down.

At first she had blamed her father and the confrontation that he had expected upon his return from Kalymnos had erupted over this instead.

Storm flew at him, her eyes flashing fire, just like the day she had been born, screaming like a banshee and calling Nicos everything from a pig to a dog. He let her take all of her frustrations and hurt out on him as she pummeled his chest with her fists and slapped his face. He needed it as much as she did. Father and daughter, so much alike in their fears for Sky's life they fought between themselves, only to collapse in a heap crying in each others arms.

They cried for Sky, they cried for Allesandro and unexpectedly they cried for Andros, and deep down they were crying for themselves too.

Sunni had taken a different approach to what had happened. It was in his stars to be calm and collected. In fact at one point he sympathized with Andros saying how awful it must have been for him to feel like he did for so many years. He even felt sad that this man who he had known for so long had been that mentally unstable he was driven to act in such a way.

None of the others quite understood Sunni's way of thinking, but none of them argued with him. He had always been this way, being like Sky in that respect, always seeing both sides of every argument, in fact his words came as no surprise to anyone.

As Nicos was helping Sky with her drink Sunni and Emily came through the door.

"Hi mama. Its good to see you are awake for a change." He teased before kissing his mother's cheek. The bandages were now just over Sky's eyes allowing her mouth and cheeks to receive the customary meeting kisses, something she really looked forward to. "Papa." Sunni patted his fathers back.

"Something smells nice." Sky said her voice now not quite as croaky.

"Emily has brought you some flowers mama."

Since Sky could only see blackness her sense of smell had heightened considerably.

"Well they smell as if they look wonderful my darlings. Thank you very much."

"And some of your favorite nougat." Sunni added handing over a box of the sweets.

"Oh yum!" Sky quickly delved in, almost knocking the lot on the floor as her hands stumbled about feeling for the pieces of soft nougat. She popped a piece in her mouth. "Umm delicious. Now come and tell me all about the wedding plans."

233

On the odd occasion Sky had been awake she had told Nicos to make sure the wedding still went ahead. She knew she would be unable to attend the London ceremony but said she would be more than happy to be there just for the Greek service.

"They are going very well thank you Sky." Emily now joined in the chat. "Everything is just about ready. It's such a shame you won't be there but I will make sure we get lots of photographs."

Coming from one of the world's best photographic families there was no doubt they would be superb. Sky had insisted Nicos attend their son's wedding and take his cameras with him.

"I can't be there but your pictures will show me everything I need to see." She had said when at first Nicos protested. "You must go Jack, for me. No one else takes pictures like you do. Please." She had put on a childish whine. "Pretty please."

Sky knew she would feel broken hearted on that day but she also knew she was in no fit state to travel. The wedding was only a few weeks away, and she had one more operation yet to go. In fact the only thing she wanted at the moment was to get that over with and get home.

In her mind she dreamt of being on her sun terrace, feeling the warm rays on her body and listening to her birds in the garden.

Her garden, the smell of Emily's flowers had brought a picture of it into her mind. The tubs of pretty geraniums dotted around, red, white and orange, cherry blossom trees with beautiful pink and white marshmallow flowers in spring, the mass of primroses flowering a paint box of colours. Huge clumps of wild red poppies and even taller bright yellow sunflowers, and of course her many bird feeders hanging from the trees and shrubs that gave the garden greenery. Here and there pretty marble statues peeked out from between the plants, one holding a large birdbath high over her head. Her lovely garden, her haven, and the place she felt safe and content.

But the smell, what was it?

In her minds eye Sky scanned the garden, what could it be? She thought to herself as an imaginary film ran through her head and stopping at the large fountain by the terrace.

" Lilies, lovely lilies." She suddenly said out loud.

"Pardon?" Nicos jumped slightly as she spoke.

234

"Emily's flowers are lilies, I can smell my garden. I know they are lilies."

"They are as well. Fancy you noticing their smell amongst all of these." Emily looked around the room.

On almost every flat surface stood a vase of beautiful flowers, roses, and all sorts, but hers were the only lilies.

"Pure white lilies just like the ones by the fountain at home, but I didn't think they smelt that strong." She bent to sniff a bloom. "Nice but very delicate."

"To me they smell marvelous and I am even more determined now to get out of this place. I want to go home like yesterday Jack." Sky sounded as if she was about to cry.

"I'm sorry if they have upset you, shall I take them out." Emily was concerned her gift had set Sky back a bit.

"Don't you dare take them anywhere! I can lay here and think of home. Put them right next to the bed so I can get a good sniff." Sky almost ordered the young girl to do as she wished. "In fact give them to me." She reached out into space and felt the flowers being placed into her arms. Sky brought them as close to her face as she could and took a deep breath.

"Wonderful. Oh look the baby likes them too." The child inside her began to kick furiously. "As Paris has said we must now all look to the future and this is my future." She gently stroked her extended stomach. "Our future starts here Jack. I feel so much more positive after smelling these, I don't know why, but they have awakened something. I'm tired but raring to go home."

Her voice did indeed sound stronger and the smile on her lips gave Nicos more hope than he had felt for a long time.

"We'll leave you to rest then mama. See you next week." Both Sunni and Emily kissed Sky then Nicos before leaving. "Bye, bye." they chorused before closing the door behind them.

"Bye darlings. Safe journey home. Phone when you get there." Sky was all motherly again. "And thank you."

"Right sleep for you my girl." Nicos said taking the lilies from her arms. "Don't worry I shall put them close." He added as he felt her reluctance in letting them go. "Just on your cabinet right next to the bed."

"Jack do you think I could have something to eat. I'm starving." It was the first time she had asked for food, in fact Nicos had noticed how after only one piece of nougat she had clumsily replaced the lid.

"Tell me and I'll get anything you fancy."

"Well then, your body first, then a big juicy steak." She giggled.

Sky was definitely on the mend.

Unfortunately all she was allowed for her first meal was thin soup followed by fresh salmon sandwiches but to her they were marvelous. To taste food again after all of these weeks was a wonderful experience.

During her days of unconsciousness she had been fed nutrients through a tube and this snack was the first thing to pass her lips, apart from the nougat, for a long time. Glad now her request for a steak had been turned down she nibbled slowly on the fresh bread with its fabulous filling but only managed to down one sandwich before her stomach told her it had had enough.

"I hope it stays like this Jack. Just think after one sarnie I'm full I could be thin for the first time in my life. Well no second. Remember how skinny I was after that bout of sunstroke. I didn't think it was possible to loose so much weight so quickly and that was only after a few days." She paused and turned towards the sound of Nicos breathing. "How long have I been in here Jack?" She asked seriously.

"Um? Ten weeks my love." He replied realising he too had almost lost track of time.

"I'm just a bag of bones then?" She let her hands run over her protruding ribs.

"Not quite that bad, but you will certainly need some filling out when we get home."

"I've got to for her sake." She stroked her stomach again.

"That's you and Gina saying it's a girl. How do you know?" Nicos was baffled.

"Woman's intuition. You watch next time Storm comes I bet she says it's a girl too." Sky yawned and slid down between the sheets. "Sorry Jack I'm bushed." She was fast asleep before Nicos could clear away her tray of food. He sat in silence and finished what was left of her snack.

236

Over the next few days Sky really began to perk up. Her sense of humor returned and Nicos loved to hear her giggle at her own comments. Her face, what he could see of it, began to take on a bloom that he had not seen for some time and her ribs no longer looked as if they would split through her skin. Now she was allowed to go into the bathroom to wash instead of the very embarrassing bed baths that she had been enduring.

To sit on the toilet again brought a sigh of contentment and a stream of naughty comments that had them both laughing for quite a while.

Unfortunately the thought of one more operation whilst she was now feeling so well had a devastating effect on her.

Her sparkle left and a depression set in.

"Just look at me Jack. I'm a wreck." She cried the night before her visit to theatre. "One gammy leg and now only one eye. What if it goes wrong?" Tears flooded down her cheeks. "It will be torture to go into darkness forever, I'm not having it, I don't want to be messed about like a piece of meat. Please Jack help me. I don't want the operation."

Nicos held her and tried to talk, but for every encouraging comment he made she had a downbeat answer.

In the end he took her by the shoulders and looking straight into her bandaged face told her not to be such a baby, she was in good hands, let the doctors do what they knew best.

"For God's sake Sky grow up!"

Luckily the sharp words Nicos said had the desired effect and by next morning Sky was once again joking on her way down to theatre.

The doctors had told them that it would be a three-hour operation but afterwards they hoped that she would be able to see almost as well as before.

Nicos kissed her as she was trolleyed from the room, then took the chance to rest for a while. His body ached and his mind still sifted through the events of that awful afternoon, but he slept like a baby once alone, now he too could hardly wait to get home.

The three hours flew as Nicos slept, and it felt as if he had only just closed his eyes when Sky was being wheeled back into the room. He was amazed to see she was awake and speaking to the nurses.

"They only needed a local anesthetic Jack. Good or what?" Sky said excitedly.

"That's brilliant! How do you feel now?" He helped her back into her high bed.

"And how long before we know about your eye?"

"Well the bandages should come off in a day or so, that reminds me I shall need some sunglasses." Sky replied. "I suppose I'd better start designing eye patches too." She giggled. "I'm not having a stuffy old black one. I think I shall make them to match my outfits. When is Emily coming back?"

Nicos was so relieved to hear her being so positive it was like a weight lifting from his shoulders.

"They are calling in before going over to London next week. Why don't you phone her and tell her what you want. I'm sure she will be more than pleased to help."

Emily had completely taken over Sky's shoe business in her absence. She now dealt with all of the orders and invoices, and had on occasions designed some of her own sandals with handbags to match, something that Sky had not thought to include before.

"I think I will. She has a real talent for the unusual and I bet she comes up with some good ideas."

Sky really looked happy. Her whole outlook seemed to have changed.

Normally she would have returned from an operation still unconscious, not bubbling like today. Nicos left out a long sigh, Sky reached out towards him.

"Thank you for being here Jack. I don't know what I would do without you." Nicos lifted her hand to his lips and kissed her fingers.

"And I don't know what I would do with out you my darling. Thank God you are on the mend at last."

The next few days saw a real improvement in Sky who seemed to be constantly on the telephone. She chatted to Emily about the eye patches, and about the wedding. On many occasions Nicos heard her laughing as she spoke to Storm and Athena, but her longest conversations were always with Eleni.

Both arriving on Skiathos at about the same time, marrying within weeks of each other, and giving birth days apart, had meant their friendship and trust in each other was as strong as steel. They often

238

had afternoons together when at home on the island. Both loved to talk girlie stuff and quite often could be found sitting at the little table by the bar at the taverna on the beach. The taverna run not only by Marco and Tomas these days, as Eleni talked Sky realised Gabriel too was now deeply involved.

"He has what he calls theme nights. They are very popular." Eleni told Sky. "The twins love it as it gives them more time to mix with the customers if they are not cooking, and Gabriel loves to show off his skills. Last week he did a Thai Night and boy did that go down well."

Even though Eleni had lived on the island for many years occasionally her American accent surfaced as she spoke. Sky giggled as she listened to her friend knowing her own English accent was never far away, especially when she was excited or angry. "You should see the way Marco eyeballs Gina." Eleni continued. " I think we may have a match there."

The twins had never really had time for long-term girls, in fact the only female to really have any effect on them was Storm and that had been right from day one.

Nicos sat listening, quite bemused the way Sky and Eleni were obviously discussing Gina's future with Marco plus a million other topics, all in one telephone call. It must be a woman thing, he thought. Men say what they have to then put the phone down. These two were talking about everything under the sun. He could not help laughing when within a split second of putting down the phone Sky moaned that she had forgotten to ask Eleni something.

"Well phone her back then." He said with a huge smile on his face.

"No I'll wait until tomorrow then she can tell me all about tonight's theme night. Evidently Gabriel is doing Italian, Marco has asked for it. Eleni says he has booked a table for himself and Gina. Sounds like a proper date to me." Sky clapped her hands excitedly then turned to where she thought Nicos was sitting. "You don't mind do you?"

"Of course not. I want her to be happy. That poor girl has had so much to cope with recently, I just want her to be happy." He replied looking at the bandaged eyes of his wife. "I felt sick when I saw those photographs of her with Andros and then when she called him uncle Yanni I didn't know what to do. If he hadn't already been dead I think I would have killed him with my bare hands." His voice sounded angry and sad if that was possible.

239

"It's all gone now Jack." Sky reached out into space. Feeling his hand on hers she closed her fingers tightly around it. "All in the past." She could feel the vibration as he nodded his head.

That night Sky could not sleep. Her bandages were coming off for the first time early in the morning. Would she be able to see, or would her world just be darkness from now on? Her mind would not rest and her constant tossing and turning kept Nicos awake as well, by the time the doctor came they both felt exhausted.

As the door opened and the nurse walked through, both of them let out a huge sigh. This was it, the big day. After so many weeks of waiting the next few minutes would be the ones that counted.

The doctor greeted them with a smile, obviously confident in his recent handywork.

"Kalimera Sky, Nicos. How are you today?" He spoke in a soothing voice. "Now let me see." He sat gently on the side of Sky's bed and turned her head towards him. "Do you have the sunglasses Nicos?"

"I certainly do doctor." Nicos handed over a fabulous black and gold case which held made to measure Dior glasses. They had the slimmest of gold frames with large dark lenses; they looked and were the best money could buy.

"Right then Sky. I'm going to take the bandage off in a minute and don't panic if you can't see anything clearly. It will take a few minutes for your eye to work and everything may be slightly fuzzy for a few days yet. You must wear the glasses until I tell you they may be removed. OK."

Sky nodded not daring to speak. She felt like a child at Christmas, full of wonder and hope.

As the doctor began to slowly unravel the bandages he noticed she was shaking and taking very shallow breaths. The doctor laughed slightly. "Now stop worrying we are nearly there and breathe properly or you will faint. Come on deep breath. In and out, in and out, that's better."

Sky could feel her head become cooler as more of the covering came off. She felt lighter and wanted to shake her hair free.

"No shaking just yet. Let me finish." The doctor was reading her mind. "There it's all off. Now let me look." Very gently he wiped her eye with a cool solution and lifted her eyelids apart.

Panic set in. All Sky could make out was a very bright light and it hurt.

"I can't see!" She cried. "Jack I can't see. It's all white and hurts. I'm blind."

"No you are not." The doctor said softly. "Give your eye time. Now blink very gently and try again."

Sky did as she was told, this time to her amazement she could make out fuzzy shapes. She blinked once more, now a very cloudy Nicos came into view. The tears poured from her eye and down her cheek. "Jack I can see you." She held her hand out towards him. "Look I know where you are."

They laughed and cried together, hugging each other, oblivious to the others still in the room.

"Right now for your glasses Sky." The doctor gently placed them on her face and immediately Sky felt the pain of the bright light disappear.

"Oh that's heaven. I shall never take these off again." She laughed.

"I think you will, but not just yet. Be a good girl and wait until I say." The doctor patted her hands.

"Can I go home now?" She asked impatiently.

"In a couple of days as long as everything goes well. If you do as you are told then I don't see why not. The only thing is you must not fly. The pressure on the plane would do you no good at all, so it will have to be by boat."

"I'll swim if I have to." Sky giggled. "Just get me home Jack." They hugged once more and Nicos kissed her gently.

"Leave it with me." He whispered.

After the nurse and doctor had left Sky sat back and looked around at the wonderful array of flowers that brightened up her room. She tried to read the tiny cards placed by the vases, but this proved to be beyond her.

"Let me." Nicos said seeing that she was struggling. "These are from Paris, these Eleni and Vanni, next Marco and Tomas, Storm's and of course the lily's from Sunni and Emily."

There were bouquets from friends and even some from customers of her shoe business. All had cards with little messages on and lots of kisses;

Nicos read them out to her. "You see how much you are loved Sky, all of them love you, but none as much as me." His voice was soft and gentle.

"So you love me eh? So where are your flowers?" She prodded him in the chest.

"I have something much better than flowers for you my love, just wait and see." He replied with a smile. He stood by the wardrobe and examined its contents. "Now rest. Tomorrow I shall arrange for your dresser from Dior to visit, none of these clothes will fit, and you will need something nice to travel home in. You rest and think about what you want. I'm going to sort out ferry tickets for us." He kissed her head. "Now just behave, I shouldn't be too long."

"You bet I'll behave. I want to go home Jack and I shall be as good as gold never fear." She waved as he left the room.

Sky lay back and began to think of home, nearly there she said out loud, nearly home. She drifted off to sleep thinking about sitting once again on the terrace and looking out over her garden and the beautiful beaches below.

242

• CHAPTER •
22

Sky sat in a huge bamboo chair on the deck of the most wonderful yacht, looking every inch a film star.

She wore her new, pure silk, pale gold trousers and tunic and lovely gold sandals. On her head she had the huge hat Nicos had brought her and of course she wore the very glamorous sunglasses. In her hand she held a beautiful crystal glass filled with champagne and as she lifted it to her lips the sun glistened on the wonderful diamond bracelet Nicos had presented her with that morning. He had said his gift would be better than flowers and it certainly was. Now not only did she look like a film star, she felt like one too.

It would be a long time before she was really well again, she knew that, but just to be sitting here in the fresh air made her feel so much better.

At first though, as fresh air hit her lungs she had become quite queasy. After so many weeks in the hospital room, it smelt wonderful but for a second or two her body reacted a little strangely, it was almost as if she were drunk.

243

Looking around the deck she noticed Nicos talking to the captain and gave him a little wave.

"Thank goodness for Eleni." Nicos said sitting in the chair next to hers. "She's also letting Sunni and Emily have this for a few weeks as a wedding present. They are going around the islands for their honeymoon."

Eleni had only recently bought this new yacht; it certainly was something special and easily the largest private vessel in Piraeus harbour.

Her old one was used to give the underprivileged children of New York short holidays; it was one of Richard's ideas some years ago. Now the charity could keep it.

A few days ago "The Eleni" had arrived here in Athens for her to inspect before making its way to London where the newly weds would board for their trip. Cheekily Nicos had asked if he could use it to bring Sky home. Eleni was more than pleased to help and had arranged for flowers and champagne, along with a superb light meal to be waiting for them.

"She can't wait to see you." Nicos said sipping at his glass. "In fact everyone wants you home, home where you belong." They chinked glasses in a toast. "To The Eagles Nest."

The soft humming of the yachts engines and the gentle rolling of the waves soon had them dozing in their huge chairs.

"It's a pity we aren't on it for longer." Sky said with a twinkle in her eye, not that Nicos could see it for the dark glasses, but he heard a naughty suggestion in her voice.

"Well then let's make the most of it whilst we are." He nudged her over in her chair and joined her. There had been more than enough room for one, but with two they were nicely squashed together.

"That's better." Sky breathed as Nicos kissed her long and hard. "So nice."

They wrapped their arms around each other and snogged. There was no other word for it, they snogged like teenagers, eventually coming up for air and giggling. The baby moved inside Sky's tummy and gave her the most wonderful tickling sensation. "I think she is jealous. She wants her daddy to kiss her too." Nicos bent his head and gently lifting

244

Sky's tunic kissed the little round lump. "A spring time baby, what more could I ask for."

As the yacht slowly made its way over the gentle sea the sun began to lower in the sky and the late summer warmth of the day eased slightly.

Gulls flew high above them, dipping and floating on the gentle breeze, and occasionally a brightly coloured flying fish jumped from out of the water.

They sat in silence looking at the wonderful scene.

Skiathos was now a large dark shadow in the distance, lit from behind by a huge orange ball.

"It looks as if it's on fire." Sky breathed softly. "What a sunset. It's so beautiful."

A sudden call from the bridge made them both jump slightly.

"What is wrong?" Nicos called to the Captain who replied with words lost on the breeze but they followed his pointing finger with their eyes. "Sky just look. They have come to greet you."

A large shoal of dolphins could just be made out in the distance. Jumping and splashing in the waves like a bunch of children.

"Help me to the front Jack." Sky started to struggle to get out of the chair. "I want to stand at the front." Nicos bent and lifted her from the seat. He carried her towards the very front of the yacht and set her down her gently against the railings.

"Oh! Just look." Sky's face lit up as the dolphins came closer. "Oh and another." She could not turn her head fast enough to keep up with the wonderful fish that were jumping close by. "There's some here too." She pointed towards the clear water below them where the lovely creatures could be seen just below the surface. "I hope we don't run over any." She added rather concerned, as they seemed to be so close.

"Don't worry they will move." Nicos laughed.

The dolphins continued to jump and splash almost leading the boat towards the island that now had the most amazing deep red sky behind its craggy hills.

"What a homecoming. I can't believe it." Sky was so excited she clapped her hands to release the feelings that were trapped inside. "So wonderful."

The sun dipped suddenly leaving them in darkness for a moment before the yachts soft deck lights flickered into life.

"They have all gone." Sky searched what she could still see of the water. "What a shame."

"They don't jump after sunset my love but they will be back tomorrow never fear."

Nicos carried her back to the chair where a waiter busied himself clearing away the food and glasses.

"Coffee madam?" He asked in a very soft American accent. "Liqueur?"

"Yes please. I think that would be lovely. Just a small cognac for me, what about you Jack, Metaxa?" Nicos nodded his reply.

Once again they squashed into the one chair sipping the strong coffee and delicious liqueurs as the yacht slowly inched its way into Skiathos harbor.

Sky could see Storm, Sunni, Gabriel and Paris standing on the old stonewall waving frantically as they sailed nearer. Then she made out Eleni, Vanni, Tomas and Marco, Gina stood at his side, Emily at hers.

In fact before long a huge crowd were waving and cheering. Music could be heard and soon a chain of dancers were stomping their way along the harbor road.

"Just look at that lot." She laughed, her arms waving like a windmill in a hurricane as she tried to return everyone's greeting.

"They have all missed you." Nicos said kissing her once again. "Now stop jumping about remember what the doctor said, be careful." He knew he might as well be talking to a brick wall, but at least he had tried.

Sky continued to wave but did slightly slow her arm movements.

As soon as the walkway was let down on to the harbor Sky and Nicos were in their children's arms, kissing and hugging as if they had not been together for ages.

"Mama it is so good to have you home." Storm's eyes flickered a beautiful deep amber. "I have missed you so much." Now they filled with tears.

The locals insisted that both Sky and Nicos stay for drinks, and before long Nicos was pulled from his chair to go and join the dancers.

Sky sat and watched slowly sipping lemonade. The cognac would be the last alcohol to pass her lips until the baby was born, it had been delicious but that was it, no more.

Storm had not left her side, and now as they watched Nicos dance mother and daughter sat holding hands.

"There was a time when I thought I would never see the island again." Sky said very softly stroking the back of Storm's young hand. "It was touch and go if they could save either of my eyes, but at least I can see with one. I can honestly say one is better than none."

She managed a weak smile but the thought of never witnessing Nicos dance, or see the harbor lit up at night, or the million and one other things she had taken for granted before, brought a lump to her throat.

"Darling I can see your papa is enjoying himself too much to be dragged home, but would you mind taking me. I feel so tired all of a sudden and would love just to crawl into my own bed."

Sky thought about her large soft bed, what a nice change that would be, just to lie there and look out over the hills and into the black velvet sky towards the moon. "Would you mind?"

"No mama of course not. Let me just tell papa and Sunni and we can be off. My car is just round the corner. Wait here and I'll fetch it." Storm was off like a shot, anything to help her precious mother.

Sky had not been the only one in her fears of never seeing Skiathos again, Storm too had wondered, but not because of her eyesight, purely whether she would live or not. Many nights had seen the young girl tossing and turning, or kneeling at her bedside praying that Sky would come home. Her wish had been granted and now she wanted to do anything to make her mother happy.

Nicos strained hard to hear what Storm was shouting into his ear, the loud bouzouki music making it difficult to understand anything. Suddenly it dawned on him and he ran over to where Sky sat.

"Do you feel poorly my love?" He asked panting from the exertion of the dancing.

"No Jack, just very tired. You stay though; Storm has said she will take me home. Don't be upset though if I am asleep when you get in."

247

Sky knew there was a good chance Nicos would be here in the harbor until dawn. Once the local people started dancing and drinking the party could well go on until the sun rose.

"Look after your mama." He instructed Storm who took offence at his words. As if she wouldn't. Her eyes flashed a spark of fire. "Sorry love, of course you will." Nicos had seen that look many times before and knew immediately he needed to apologise.

If Storm ever lost the ability to speak, her eyes could do the job quite adequately, he thought. One flash and you could almost see what she was thinking. No wonder she got through so many men, if they didn't read the signs, then their time was more than probably up.

Storm fetched her car and helped Nicos load the luggage into the boot.

"Don't stay out all night papa," she warned. "And don't get too drunk."

Nicos smiled, she was speaking to him like his mother used to, it was strange, his wayward outspoken daughter had suddenly grown up into a sensible woman.

As they drove, slowly for Storm, along the coast road Sky let herself relax. She took a few deep breaths of the fragrant, familiar air and said a little prayer of thanks in her mind.

"I'm sorry to drag you away from the party Storm but it was all getting a little too much for me. What a day it has been I feel exhausted."

She told of her day's adventures from leaving the hospital room right up to seeing the dolphins greet her on the way home, she yawned as she spoke.

"It's OK honest I'd had enough anyway, and as for the dolphins, well I'm so glad they came. I love them myself, but then show me a Greek who doesn't." She replied smiling at her mother in the darkness.

For once Storm brought her car to a sedate stop and not the usual gravel flirting halt. She jumped out and held the door open for Sky, then gently helped her into the villa.

Alexi and Athena, who had been watching and waiting, walked slowly from their home as Storm was unloading the car.

248

"Is Sky OK?" Athena asked, her old voice wavering slightly. "Do you think we could go and welcome her home? Just for a minute, we won't stay long." She too could read Storm's eyes and noticed the warning.

"Of course grandma but only for a while. She needs to rest but please go in." Storm nodded towards the door.

The old couple shuffled along and tapped softly at the door before walking through.

"It's only us Sky. We just wanted to say welcome home." Athena used much of her sparse energy in running across the room and pulling Sky into her arms. "Oh I have missed you so much." Now she was crying.

"And I you." Sky could feel the lump in her throat once again. "I hope the children have looked after you both?"

One of Sky's house rules was that the children should see their grandparents every day, when they were at home that was, and if abroad they were to telephone.

"Very well, and young Gina can never do enough for us." Athena smiled up into Sky's face. "We had better go or Storm will be after us," she giggled. "We are under orders not to stay too long. Sleep well darling and we will see you tomorrow." Athena kissed her daughter in law's cheek, Alexi followed suit.

It struck Sky how thin and frail they both looked and she noticed how Alexi's hands shook as he held her close. They were coming to the end of their lives but inside her a tiny being was not far from beginning hers. Life goes on, she thought to herself and gently stroked the bulge in her tummy, and life goes on no matter what.

Storm helped her mother undress and gently made sure she was comfortable in the lovely large bed.

"Night cap mama?" She asked softly. "We can have a nice warm drink together and watch the stars." She knew that was one of her mother's favourite things. To lie in bed and look at the wonderful vista.

"That would be lovely darling. You are looking after me so well, thank you." Sky smiled up at her daughter, the girl who had so many different characters. One minute she could be soft and gentle, the next a ball of fiery anger. She could look so young, and then seconds later a sophisticated glamorous lady. No one knew which she would be, but her eyes always gave the game away regarding her temperament.

249

The one person who really did know Storm though was young Tomas. From the day they were born the twins had looked towards her for guidance, Tomas more so than Marco as they grew, and even now he still did.

Storm trotted off to the kitchen and Sky could hear her banging about in the cupboards. They may be amongst the richest families in the world, but Sky had made sure her children could look after themselves, the noise from the kitchen made her realise that during her weeks away they had probably been waited on hand and foot.

"There you are." Storm handed Sky a large china mug of hot chocolate topped with cream. "Delish" She sipped her own and licked her lips.

"Here, sit by me darling." Sky patted the empty side of the bed. "Let's watch the stars together. It reminds me of when you and Sunni were young. Remember?" Storm nodded.

Many nights she and her brother had shared Sky's bed where they lay for hours watching the velvet sky, listening to their mother tell stories about the God's and the fairies. The God's were the planets, the fairies the stars. Search the sky as much as she could Storm never got to see a planet.

They lay together sipping their drinks and watching in silence. Occasionally an aeroplane, with its lights flashing and jet stream glowing would move gracefully across the still darkness.

"This is wonderful mama." Storm reached over and kissed her mother's cheek. "It makes me feel so sleepy watching nothing. Wonderful." She slowly settled down on the bed until she was lying flat out, her eyelids so heavy now, and her breathing rhythmic.

Sky recognised the signs and pulled the sheet over her now fast asleep daughter. Just like when she was a child Sky thought and smiled down at the stunning face.

As babies it was always Sunni who fell asleep first, but as they grew it was Storm who had never got to the end of one of her stories, always sleeping just like this, way before her brother who always wanted to know what was going to happen before he too would lie down and rest.

Would Achilles catch up with Apollo in a swimming race? He might, but it didn't really matter as long as he had tried.

Would Zeus confiscate their football because they hadn't eaten all of their supper? He might.

And would Hera be angry if they told lies. Yes she would!

Sky had learned well from Nicos and turned the stories of the Gods into lessons for her children.

Nicos would have to stay in Storm's room tonight, that was if he came home at all, she thought to herself, and knowing her husband as she did she doubted very much if he would be seen for many hours yet.

Sky pushed the remote control panel to close the blinds then inched her way slowly down the bed. In her sleep Storm rolled over and laid her arm protectively over her mothers tummy. The baby inside gave a little flutter; it was as if she knew her sister was there.

Sunni and Emily could see that the villa was in darkness as they pulled up in the car.

"Mama looked so tired down at the harbor." Sunni said quietly closing the car door. "I bet she is fast asleep now." He put his finger to his lips as if to tell Emily to be silent. "I'll just have a quick look in her room and then it's bed for us too."

They entered the villa and tiptoed towards Sky's room, the door was slightly open and they could hear the soft sound of someone sleeping. Sunni turned to Emily and smiled.

"Told you," he whispered. Peering round the door he felt a sharp pang of jealousy when he saw Storm curled up in bed with their mother. How many years since he had done that? But he smiled anyway; trust Storm to make doubly sure Sky was all right.

"Sunni is that you?" Sky's voice was a soft whisper in the still night air.

"Just checking you are OK." He replied as quietly as he could.

"Well come and join us then. I'm sure Emily won't mind just for tonight." Sky gently nudged Storm over a little further in the bed. "There's plenty of room."

He didn't need asking twice. Turning to Emily his eyes asked for him.

"Go on." She kissed him then putting her hands on his shoulders turned him around and gently pushed him further into the room. "I'll see you in the morning." She gave a little wave as he went towards his mother's bathroom.

"Be with you in a minute mama." He called.

"This is lovely." Sky sighed. "All my children together, but I'm sorry no story tonight."

Sunni smiled and settled down beside his mother.

"Never mind you will have to tell me one tomorrow. Night night mama." He kissed her cheek just as Storm had done and within seconds he too was fast asleep.

Sky lay awake for a short while thinking how lucky she was before the tiring events of the day inevitably took their toll and she too drifted off into a deep sleep.

The following morning Gina shuffled into the kitchen and was amazed to see Emily laying a tray with three cups and assortment of biscuits. She yawned and stretched then shook her hair free.

"Not eating for two are we?"She pointed to the tray.

"No follow me." Emily whispered.

Gina did just that and seeing Emily nod towards Sky's bedroom door opened it slowly. She wanted to burst out laughing when she made out the sleeping bodies in the dim light.

"A mama with her bambino's." She giggled.

Sky was first to rouse.

"Morning all. Oh thanks Emily, just what the doctor ordered a lovely cup of tea." Gently she shook the shoulders of her sleeping children. "Sunni, Storm we have visitors." They came out of their slumbers slowly, yawning and stretching just as Gina had done moments ago. For a second or two neither of them seemed to know just quite where they were.

"That was the best nights kip I have had for ages." Storm smiled, still managing to look stunning after her sleep.

"And me." Sunni added.

"When did you get in then?" Storm asked sharply.

"When you were well in the land of nod. Typical. Supposed to be looking after mama and what do you do, fall asleep." He pushed her roughly on the arm.

"Now children, children, no fighting." This was turning out to be more like when they were young than Sky at first realised.

252

Every morning, when they were allowed to stay all night, you could lay bets on the fact that they would wake up arguing. Not that they ever meant it though, two closer children you would have a job to find.

"Now why don't you fetch your tea girls and we can all get in together." Sky spoke to Gina and Emily, who looked slightly out of place standing when everyone else was in a semi lying position.

That was how Nicos found his wife. Surrounded by the children, as she still called them, all in bed drinking tea eating biscuits and laughing.

"I hope you won't leave any crumbs." He said before anyone had noticed his arrival. They all turned and greeted him.

"Kalimera papa." Storm said her face one huge smile. "You will have to get your own drink this morning. We are all looking after mama."

Nicos went to the kitchen and filled a large mug with steaming hot coffee, he had never liked Sky's English tea especially after a long night on the wine.

He stood with both hands holding the hot mug and stared out of the window. He watched as the birds flitted from tree to tree, and the bees slowly waking to another day of pollen collecting. His heart thumped in his chest. The sight that had just met him was one of such happiness and love. His children all together with his wife. He felt the hot tears stream down his face, not from the joy of the sight, but from the guilt that burned in his loins.

Nicos the serial womaniser had certainly lived up to his old reputation. Back on the island for such a short time, already he had made love behind Sky's back, and he had enjoyed every second.

The thought of Olivia's young supple body, the smell of her soft skin and the way she had taken control, made him smile for a second.

What a good idea of Sunni's to let her have the rooms above the Gallery. So not only did she work in the shop, she slept there too, not that they had done much sleeping. Yes, he thought, Olivia would certainly get another visit.

"Jack what's keeping you?" Sky called bringing him back down to earth with a crash. "Come and join us."

Nicos sighed and wiped his eyes, slowly walking into the bedroom he pasted a grin on to his face, but in his mind he was back in the little flat over the Gallery.

Some things would never change, and some people would definitely never change.

• CHAPTER •
23

The day of the wedding saw Sky sitting alone in her lounge.

On the table at the side of her was a small oblong parcel with written instructions that it should not be opened until 10am. She watched as the hands of the clock slowly made their way around to the appointed time and stared at the box. Not that she was very interested in its contents, she wanted to be with them all in London so what good this was going to do she had no idea.

It reminded her of a jewellery box, one that contained a necklace or bracelet.

What intrigued her though was the look on Sunni's face when he gave it to her. His eyes sparkled and his face was lit with a huge grin. Behind him stood Emily and Storm, their expressions mirroring his. So what was it?

She had promised him that she would wait, so wait she would, but nothing her son had bought could make up for missing this very special day.

Sky felt very sad and very lonely.

At last the clock struck 10. Thank God for that, she sighed to herself and picking up the parcel began to unwrap it carefully. For a moment she hadn't got a clue, it looked just like an ordinary television remote control. Feeling disappointed she read Sunni's hand written instructions, aimed the control at the giant plasma screen on the wall and pushed the button that was covered with a red sticker.

Sky gasped as the screen sprang into action. Within seconds the plain blackness changed.

There before her was Sunni waving.

"Hi mama. Welcome to my wedding day." His voice boomed out from speakers hidden in the lounge. "Sis is working the camera at the moment but you can see her in a sec." He walked towards the lens, his chest covering the entire screen as he neared. Then came a good shot of a carpet before Storm came into view.

"Hi mama. Like my outfit." Storm did a twirl. The manly Armani suit made her look amazing and so sexy the way it fitted every curve of her body. "You can talk you know, we will be able to hear you."

"I don't think I can darlings, I'm well, just gob smacked." Sky was stunned for a moment. "Thank you so much."

She listened as Sunni instructed his sister to hold the camera again.

"Now mama we have asked Tomas and Marco to work this during the service so you will be able to see and hear everything, but for now we will have to switch off whilst we finish getting ready and get to the church. Give us about 15 minutes then push the button again. See you in a short while." He blew a kiss and Sky could see Storm's elegant fingers waving in front of the lens.

As the screen went black again she looked quickly over to the clock.

10am Greek time, that meant it was noon in London, or was it 11, Sky felt totally confused.

Hearing a noise behind her she turned to see Maria entering the room carrying a tray with a mixture of delicious things to eat and beautiful champagne flutes. Placing it on the table she returned to the

256

kitchen to fetch two silver wine coolers that Sky could see already had the champagne bottles inside.

A knock at the door heralded the arrival of Alexi and Athena.

"Kalimera Sky." Athena greeted her with the usual kisses, Alexi followed suit. "Have you seen them yet?" Athena asked excitedly.

"Well yes." Sky was stunned yet again. "You knew about this?"

"Sunni told us just before they left for London. He said we must not say anything to you. Is it a good picture?" Alexi looked at the completely blank screen.

"It's wonderful. They are switching on again in a short while." Sky was still in shock and her voice wavered with emotion.

Maria poured the champagne and handed round the glasses.

"Maria you must join us too. After all you have spent almost as much of Sunni's life with him as I have." Sky held the old woman's wrinkled hand and saw a smile form on her lips.

"Thank you I would love to." She replied, her voice almost as shaky as Sky's.

Alexi poured Maria a drink and topped everyone else up.

"To Sunni and Emily." He raised his glass and the other's followed in his toast.

Sky looked at the clock and pressed the precious red button once again. Immediately the television sprang to life.

"Hello all." It was Marco on the screen. "Now we will do our best, but Sunni only asked us the other day so we have not had much practice. He and Storm are already here, they are in with the vicar at the moment sorting something out but we will try to show you everyone as they arrive."

"That's great." Sky said noticing how Alexi looked at her in surprise. "Yes we can talk back to them as well, and no, don't ask me how it works."

Marco laughed at her words.

"Right then all set. Let's get cracking." He saluted and began his commentary of those entering the church.

There were friends of Sunni's from all different parts of the world. Some famous models, some rock stars and even a few film stars.

Sky spotted Paris on the arm of Matthew and noticed how relaxed and happy she appeared to be. In her outfit of a rich deep red and cream she looked superb. Marco aimed the camera towards her and those watching at home heard him instruct her to wave. The smile that lit her face as she did pleased Sky so much it almost hurt, her lovely sister, happy again at last.

The camera then focused on Emily's family and friends and Sky could see they were all a little in awe of those in the pews on the other side of the church. She saw how her young friends nudged each other as another famous face was recognized. This was a day they would not forget in a hurry.

The camera changed hands and Tomas appeared. He talked as Marco showed the marvelous stained glass windows and the pretty alter where in a short while Sky's son would stand to take Emily as his wife. Sky could feel the prickle of tears in her eye.

Doreen was then shown leaving the comfort of the huge black Rolls Royce car that had brought her and the bridesmaids to the church. It looked beautiful with its thick white ribbons and posies on each handle.

Athena spotted Gina first and got quite animated.

"Oh look how beautiful she is." She exclaimed as they watched Doreen help to straighten her long rose pink dress. In her dark hair she wore a little ring of silk rose buds, their colour matching her dress, and in her hands she held a pretty little arrangement of the real thing. "Oh just look Alexi, she looks wonderful." Athena was emotional and her tears had already started to fall.

Tomas now behind the camera again turned to the other bridesmaid, Sarah, a lifelong friend of Emily who was dressed exactly the same, although with her pale skin the rose pink did not have quite the same effect.

Marco came into view and it was obvious from the look in his eyes, and the fact that his mouth was open, he had also spotted Gina.

"And just look at the goldfish." Tomas said softly into the camera making them all laugh. "Anyone would think he had never seen a bridesmaid before." He added with a naughty giggle.

He may have seen thousands, Sky thought to herself, but none that had got that reaction before.

The camera swung round again, this time it concentrated on Sunni and Storm.

"My babies!" Sky cried. "Just look at my babies."

Her hand went to her tummy where the unborn child had suddenly begun to move with little flutters. "You know she does that every time I mention Storm or she hears her voice," she giggled. "I think she is your favourite already," she added looking down at her bulge.

"Not just hers." Alexi said as he watched the screen. "I think Tomas likes her too." The camera spent much more time on the amazing looking girl than on her brother.

Sky realised she was breathing very quickly as the pair went into the front pew, and not wanting to faint did as the doctor in Athens had told her. Breathe in then out, slowly, in then out. Almost immediately her head began to clear.

She could see Nicos standing behind with Eleni and Vanni, and watched as his hand patted his son's shoulder reassuringly.

The bridal march echoed around the wonderful old building and Tomas now pointed the lens down the aisle towards a very proud George leading his daughter towards her husband to be, half way down he stopped and allowed Luke to walk the rest of the way with his granddaughter.

Suddenly the door flew open making Sky jump, a breathless Gabriel bounced into the room.

"Have I missed it?" He said slumping into one of the huge armchairs. "May I?" He nodded towards the champagne bucket.

"Of course help yourself, and no you have not missed it. Emily is just walking down the aisle." Sky laughed at her brother.

He had not attended the wedding today, even though he had been for a suit fitting, instead he insisted that the taverna should stay open and he would do the honours. He also wanted to be near Sky. To have only just found his sisters and so nearly to have lost Sky he had this over whelming need to protect her.

"I put a sign up on the bar saying I wouldn't be long, mind you there aren't many down there today. I think they all expected the taverna to be closed." His breathing was almost back to normal. "I like the look of that bridesmaid, isn't she pretty?" His eyes shone as he noticed Sarah

259

walking at the side of Gina. Not another one, Sky thought and raised her eyes to the ceiling.

The music boomed out of the speakers as Emily and her grandfather walked slowly down towards where Sunni and Storm now stood. They had left the safety of their pew and were standing side by side in front of the vicar. Sunni turned and smiled as his eyes took in the wonderful sight of Emily.

Her dress, designed by the Emmanuel's, was out of this world. It was of the most stunning white silk, off the shoulder and pulled tight into her waist. The bodice had hundreds of tiny pearls sown in the shapes of flowers, their center a single tiny diamond. The skirt was so full it swished against the pews as she walked and her train, which Gina and Sarah were having a little difficulty in controlling, was of the finest silk web that money could buy.

She wore a delicate tiara in her hair, which had been preened and curled in a way that showed her lovely glowing face off at its best.

Her long, but not overly large bouquet was of similar rose buds to that of Gina and Sarah's flowers.

She was the bride of his dreams and everyone could see the pride in his eyes as she neared.

Luke nodded to Sunni and took one step to the side.

The service began.

For some unknown reason all of those that were sitting in Sky's lounge leaned forward as the vicar began to speak. Not that his deep and dramatic voice was unclear, it just made them feel closer.

The tears that had threatened to fall trickled down Sky's cheek as she listened to her son speak his vows.

When prompted Storm stepped forward and placed the gold rings on the cushion the vicar held forward. My babies, how grown up you both look, she thought.

It all seemed to be over so quickly, far too quickly for Athena and Sky.

"I hope you are recording this." Athena said as Sunni and Emily emerged from the back of the church having just signed the register. "I shall want to see it again."

"I don't know." Sky replied panicking. "I hope Sunni sorted that bit out for us, I'm sure he will have done. After all they will want to watch it themselves." Sky had not thought of that and for a moment she was worried. What if she should have done something pushed another button or pressed a knob.

"Don't worry. Tomas is recording everything." Gabriel reassured them. "It will be on the disc in his camera so stop panicking." He patted Sky's knee.

"Oh look how pretty." Athena was watching as the wedding guests threw thousands of flower petals into the air, and within seconds Sunni and Emily were covered, they looked into each other's eyes and laughed, it was a very touching moment.

Marco now had the camera and he scanned the scene talking as he went.

He stood behind Nicos as he took the wedding photographs in order that Sky could see exactly what was being shot, but they all noticed how time and time again he focused on Gina.

"Told you." Alexi said smugly. "He has his eye on that young lady."

After the photographs had been taken the wedding party set off in numerous cars to the Savoy where the reception was taking place. Athena gasped as the wonderful buildings of London passed and the hotel came into view.

"Well done Marco," she called. "That was lovely to see a bit of London."

"That's OK." Came the reply.

He treated them to the sights of the reception room where Sunni and Emily greeted their guests. He walked around the tables showing the place settings and beautiful flower decorations in the center of each.

"What a surprise he is sat next to Gina." Alexi was getting smugger by the minute.

"Yes but Tomas is next to Storm. Just think about that one." Gabriel said with a wink "Like two peas in a pod they are. No one takes any notice because they have always been together, but to someone like me, an outsider, I spotted it as soon as I laid eyes on them. Made for each other they are."

Sky looked at him with a frown and thought about his words. True, they were always together, usually larking about or talking and laughing, heads so close they touched, but then they had always been like that. Time will tell, she thought, and went back to watching the guests arrive.

The screen went black.

"What's happened?" Sky looked frightened and puzzled. She didn't want to miss one moment of her son's wedding day.

"Sorry about that." Marco's voice came through again as did the picture "The battery ran out, just changed it, now where was I?"

Sky let out a sigh of relief and relaxed her tense body.

As the speeches began Maria refilled the glasses ready for the toast. George was first to his feet, then came Storm.

She told amusing stories of their childhood, bringing both Tomas and Marco into her tales. Then she spoke of their work together, praising her brother for making her such a success; lastly she talked about her own feelings for her brother and the girl who was now his wife. It was very emotional, both Sky and Athena let the tears flow freely.

"I shall never understand why women have to cry at weddings." Alexi said with a sigh. "It's supposed to be a happy day and look at you two."

"I am happy." Sky was not far from sobbing. "It's all so wonderful." She blew her nose loudly. "You men just don't think like we do."

Sunni was last to stand and make his speech. Short and to the point. He never was one to be in the limelight quite happy to leave Storm as center of attention whilst he hid behind his camera. Sky noticed how Emily patted his hand in a comforting gesture. She already knows him so well; she thought and smiled at the screen.

The meal was served and soon the dancing began. So far it had been so English, so traditional, but now after a few drinks they all began to relax and soon the Greek dancers took to the floor. Sunni, Marco, Tomas, Storm, Nicos and Gina tripped and stamped their way across the floor. Everyone clapped loudly at the finish. It set the tone for the rest of the afternoon.

"Do you mind if we go now?" Marco was dying to dance with Gina and he could see Tomas was already sweeping Storm across the floor.

"Of course not darling. Thank you so much it has been wonderful. You go and enjoy the rest of the day and we will see you all tomorrow. Just let me say bye to Sunni and Storm if you would though."

Marco took the camera over and tapped Tomas's shoulder. He told Storm he was finishing the filming.

"Bye mama see you tomorrow. What a lovely day it had been." She blew a couple of kisses.

Next came Sunni. Jacket now off, top shirt button undone, and tie slightly askew, his arm draped over Emily's shoulder. He looked so happy, they both did.

"Bye mama, gramps. See you after our honeymoon." He said to the camera. "Love you all." He kissed his hand and blew towards the screen.

"Yes see you soon." Emily added. "And thank you for everything."

After the screen had gone black they all sat in silence for some time, remembering in their minds the lovely sights they had just witnessed.

"It was nice to see Olivia there." Alexi said as he refilled everyone's glasses. "She has worked for us a long time now."

Sky had not noticed the young Gallery worker there, but then there had been so much to look at.

Nor had Athena who sat quietly, her mind sending a prayer to The Blessed Virgin Mary.

Please no, she thought, I beg you no.

• CHAPTER •
24

Storm ran into her mother's arms, talking as if her life depended upon it. She hardly managed to draw breath as she told of the wedding and all the excitement.

As she finished Gina began, her eyes sparkling as she recalled the events of the day.

Nicos on the other hand was quiet.

"Something wrong Jack?" Sky asked frowning.

"Not a thing love, it's just I can't get a word in edgeways with these two. Anyway did you enjoy the web cam?" He kissed her cheeks, a little chastely, and then held her in his arms, his eyes searching the garden for inspiration. "Our son a married man, who would have thought it eh?" Sky reached up and kissed him back.

"Making you feel old is it?" She asked with a giggle, trying to lighten his obvious down beat mood. "And yes the web cam was brilliant thanks. Me and your mama cried nearly all the way through."

264

All Nicos could think about was the time he had spent with Olivia. This young woman had got under his skin in a big way, even to the point where he felt confused by his feelings. Their night of passion in London was one he would not forget in a hurry. She certainly was a live wire. Nothing seemed to be out of the question when it came to sex. The only problem was now his back sported a tangle of scratch marks that Sky would see the moment he took his shirt off.

"The doctor in Athens called." Sky said softly. "He wants me to go over for a check up I don't want to go alone but I'm worried about Alexi. He is looking so old and tired just recently I don't think we should leave him on his own. Would you mind if I took Paris with me instead of you?" Nicos tried hard but the sigh of relief that left his lips was long and loud. "Surely its not that bad Jack, you only have to look after him for a couple of days whilst I go for some tests. Don't be so selfish." Sky was annoyed, why was it always the women who had to look after the elderly, it's not as if Nicos had spent that much time with his father anyway over the last twenty years. Surely a couple of days were not too much to ask.

"Sorry love. It's just you know I hate being apart from you." He lied convincingly. Now his back would have at least a short time to heal slightly, and it also gave him time to think of a good excuse before Sky returned. "But you go with Paris, Gina can stay and help me. That's when she's not down at the beach with Marco, and Storm will be here so don't worry. Sorry if it sounded selfish but I love you, I want to be with you." He nuzzled her neck.

"Oh yuck papa." Storm pulled a face. "Leave mama alone for two minutes will you." Deep down she was thrilled to see her parents so happy, but thought it only proper as their daughter, to tease them anyway.

"Right I'll give Paris a call." Sky picked up her mobile and phoned her sister. They chatted for a while about this and that before Sky remembered the reason for her call. Paris happily agreed, she had to go anyway to see the solicitors who were dealing with the Will Andros had left, a couple of days with her sister, and a little time to shop would help her get through the ordeal.

Was Andros sane when he had made the Will, that was the big question now being argued and although Paris didn't want any of his money, out of loyalty to the man she had once loved she was trying to unravel the mess he had left. After all she was his widow.

Meanwhile his billions were just growing by the day.

It looked as if Eleni, whose money he looked after anyway, and Vanni his one time business partner, were in for an absolute fortune.

The lovely Athens mansion and the rest of his belongings; well who knew what would happen to them?

"Right that's fixed then. We'll go tomorrow on the early flight and be back before you know it."

"Why don't you stay with Paris tonight darling. It will save you some time in the morning." Nicos was clutching at straws, anything to stop Sky seeing his shredded back. "Tell you what, why don't we all go for a meal in town then I can drop you off at hers after."

It sounded like the sensible thing to do as the early flight to Athens left at 6am.

"Brill papa." Storm piped up. "The only thing is me and Gina are off to the beach tonight. Gabriel is doing a Mexican night, the twins have asked us to go and we will be stopping at Eleni's."

"OK you two go to the beach, me and mama will go into town. Then after our meal I'll come home. Easy as that." Nicos smiled widely, that was even better. He could have his meal, drop Sky off and then visit Olivia. Everything he could ask for in one night. It wasn't that he didn't love Sky, he just loved sex more, and with Olivia that was mind bending.

He couldn't wait.

A couple of hours later Sky kissed the girls before they left for the beach.

"Just look at them Jack, so happy and glamorous. It's nice they get on so well at one time I feared Storm would reject Gina, but she seems to have taken her under her wing especially when Emily is not around." Nicos just nodded.

They stood and waved as their daughters sped off in Storm's black sports car, listening as it roared down the hillside, the thump thump of the stereo audible over the familiar clack of the crickets.

"I wish she would drive a little slower and turn that blasted music down." Sky said almost to herself.

"She's a young headstrong girl love, you should know by now how she drives and how loud she likes that awful racket she calls music." Nicos laughed a little too long and loud, he felt so excited.

Two down, one to go. How on earth was he going to get through the meal tonight, he had to stop thinking about later.

As Sky packed her bag for the trip Nicos showered, the hot water made him wince as it hit the raw spots on his back, but at least with Sky busy he was able to dress without her seeing anything.

"Have you cut yourself Jack?" Sky held up a blood stained towel.

"Yes when I was shaving." He stroked his stubble free chin. "It's stopped now."

"Looks like someone was murdered." Sky laughed and threw the towel into the washing basket. "Should come out though. Will you ask Maria to put some bleach on it for me? That should clean it up a treat."

"OK will do. Now are you ready?" Nicos was pacing the bedroom.

"Yep. How's that." Sky stood before him in the nicest dress he had seen for a long time. Pale pink layers of silk and chiffon that fell from a heart shaped neckline. Emily had obviously been working hard and Sky's eye patch matched her lovely dress. "Got to give the baby room to move these days." She stroked her bulge.

"You look lovely." Nicos meant it; with her hair falling over her shoulders and the pretty dress on she really did look nice. "Come on gorgeous." He held his arm out for her to hold. "Let's go eat before I eat you."

Olivia was for the moment just a memory.

In the end Nicos enjoyed the night out with Sky. They sat in the taverna where they had first met all those years ago, and even at the same table. Their meal was delicious and their chatter interesting. Nicos spoke of the wedding, giving as many answers to Sky's continuous questions as he could, or dared, while she spoke of what they had seen on the screen.

"Who looked after the Gallery Jack?" Sky asked. "Your papa said he saw Olivia there. I must say I was a little surprised that she had gone, but then I suppose she has worked for Alexi and Sunni for a few years now."

"The new Saturday girl kept things running smoothly whilst we were away, but don't forget Olivia works for me as well now, so she is almost part of the family." Nicos smiled but inside he felt sick. What else had

Sky seen during the day? He prayed Marco and Tomas had concentrated their filming on the newly weds.

They finished their meal with coffee and chocolates before slowly walking back to the car.

"Now just look after yourself over in Athens and if Paris wants to shop let her. Don't go wearing yourself out trailing about in the heat." Nicos was concerned, he knew only too well once Paris hit the shops she could be there for hours.

"I'll be OK Jack. Stop whittering."

Nicos drove carefully up the winding road that led to Paris's hillside villa. It had the enviable position of being over the town, yet far enough away to be secluded. The views from her terrace were as stunning as those from The Eagles Nest; on clear days the islands of Skopelos and Alonysos could bee seen in the distance plus just below the busy and very colourful town harbor.

Paris and Matthew were relaxing in the cool of the evening taking in just these sights when Nicos and Sky arrived.

"Fancy a drink?" Paris asked when Nicos had taken Sky's things to the guest room.

"No thanks Paris. Must get off. Mama and papa are on their own at the moment. The girls have gone to the beach and with the other two away, well its up to me." He gave Sky a hug and kiss before he left, issuing more orders for her not to do too much whilst she was in the capital.

"Anyone would think we are going away for weeks," Sky laughed. "Now off you go and just behave yourself."

Nicos drove quickly away. Her words ringing in his ears, did she suspect something, no she couldn't, could she. Guilt was playing with his mind. Don't be silly man, he said to himself, just go and enjoy yourself. He felt a deep pang of unease.

He parked the car in a dark, narrow cobbled street at the back of the Gallery and using his own key opened the door that led to the flat. Once this had been the staircase to the stock room, now it was the stairway to heaven. He started to hum the song, puzzling over who had sung it originally, but who cared, certainly not him at this moment.

Olivia opened the door the second he knocked. Dressed in a skintight black rubber cat suit, impossibly high stiletto shoes and a whip dangling in one hand, a huge grin lit her face, she took his breath away.

In fact she did just that time and time again, as the warm black night turned into dawn.

Narrow rays of sunlight illuminated her young slim naked body as Nicos awoke; he switched on his phone, which immediately sprang into action. He could see from the dial it was Sky.

"Hi babe." He replied yawning. "Flight OK."

"Jack for God's sake where are you." Sky sounded almost hysterical. "I've had countless calls from Athena, she found Alexi dead in bed this morning. She has been trying to get hold of you. I said you were at home but she say's no one is there."

"Calm down love. It's my fault I stayed at a friends." Nicos was trying to think quickly. What a mess, why did his papa have to go and die this morning selfish old sod. He quickly felt guilty for thinking such things.

"Jack you promised to look after them. They are your parents now get over to help your mama. I'm coming home as soon as I've seen the doctor, should be back by this evening. Then you can tell me the truth you lying bastard. I don't know who she is and I don't want to, but never lie to me Jack." She clicked her phone off before he could reply.

Now the proverbial would hit the fan big style. Nicos began to cry, for his father, or himself or for Sky, he had no idea, but cry he did. What a mess. His father dead no doubt his mother in a right state, and now his wife with a bag on. What a pig of a morning and that was putting it mildly.

The short journey home was one of the worst in his life. So many thoughts running amok in his brain it was a wonder he arrived in one piece.

Athena ran from her villa as soon as she heard Nicos's car drive up to his home.

"Where the hell have you been Nicos? I've been trying for hours to get in touch. Papa is dead, come and look son, your papa is dead."

Her eyes looked wild with grief, her actions were jerky and uncoordinated. Nicos swept her into his arms, more to protect her from herself than anything. He had to calm her down, and quickly, or she too would not see the day out.

Hand in hand they walked to the villa and into the bedroom where Nicos could see immediately his father had been dead for some time. He held Alexi's cold stiff hand to his cheek and wept. His father gone, gone forever.

Suddenly Nicos hated the man he was. Ever since he could remember sex had ruled his life, and now he had missed the last moments a son would have with his father, just to be with a woman.

But then Olivia was no ordinary woman.

Whilst he waited with Athena for the doctor to come and examine Alexi he phoned Eleni.

"Can you ask the girls to come home Eleni. Papa has died in his sleep and I need them to help with mama." His voice wavered with emotion. "I need them to help me too. Would you ask one of the twins or Gabriel to drive, I don't want Storm behind the wheel when she is upset, her driving is erratic at the best of times."

Next he phoned Olivia.

"Please close the shop today." He said his whole body now shaking as he told her nothing she didn't already know, but as Athena was sitting at his side he had to pretend the news was new to her. "I'll come over later." He said before clicking off the phone. "Anyone else you want me to phone mama?" Athena slowly shook her head and Nicos noticed how tiny she suddenly looked. It was if she had shrunk in just those few hours.

"Oh my lovely, what a shock." Maria burst into the room and hugged Athena, her bulk almost covering the whole of the distraught woman's shaking body. The two women hugged and cried for the man they had loved and respected for years. "He was such a nice man, always a gentleman." Maria cried. "Such a lovely man to work for."

The two old women held each other and continued to wail.

Nicos needed some air, he felt as if the room was closing in on him, but knew he could not leave them alone. He sighed with relief as Storm's car screeched to a stop outside, obviously she had driven herself.

"Grandma!" Gina and Storm shouted together as they ran into the now rather crowded room. They hugged and kissed the old woman before standing at the side of Alexi. Both kissed the old man's cheeks and hands.

Nicos was never more proud of his daughters than at that moment. They could be rowdy, they could stretch his patience, but standing there together mourning their grandfather, they looked and acted perfectly.

Storm had managed to get her grandmother to shower and change into her mourning clothes while Gina helped Maria provide cakes and drinks for the countless people who soon began to file into the villa. It seemed as if the entire population of the island wanted to pay their respects.

Once Eleni and Vanni arrived things seemed to calm down slightly, as immediately she took control of the proceedings.

The twins and Gabriel came loaded with a breakfast buffet, which they quickly laid out, on the terrace of Sky's home. Coffee, beer and wine were available from the kitchen and it looked as if the whole thing was in danger of eruption into a huge party.

Matthew came over giving Nicos someone to talk to; the wailing of the women was now getting on his nerves.

"I can't believe there is so much to do." Nicos sighed as he walked with Matthew to the very full terrace in order to get another glass of wine. "I don't know where to start. I wish Sky was here, she is always so organized, or Emily." He clapped his hand over his mouth. "God I forgot Sunni and Emily. How do I tell him? So close to that wonderful happy wedding day, now this." Nicos shook his head in disbelief.

"Let me speak to him." Matthew was strong and calm.

"No it's my job. Thanks anyway for offering. I'll just go into the office and do it from there." Nicos slowly shuffled over to Sky's office and sat behind her desk. He reached slowly for the telephone, knocking the computer mouse as he stretched; her screen came to life with a picture he had taken of her by the church on Kalymnos. Nicos sat and stared at her face hidden partly by the huge hat and gaining strength from the image before him, he prayed that yet again she would forgive him.

He relayed the bad news to his shocked son before wearily returning to the others on the terrace.

He felt so old, so tired, and yes so sad.

"When's Sunni getting here?" Storm asked as he appeared.

"They will be sailing into Skiathos in a couple of days. I told him no rush as the funeral is not until Friday."

"But I need him with me." Storm's shoulder slumped, she began to sob.

"Come here. Will I do for now?" Tomas wrapped his arms around the crying girl. "You will have to do with me until he gets here." He kissed the top of her head trying to comfort her, his hand rubbing her back. "Do you want me to stay for a while?" Storm nodded and returned his comforting hug. She felt safe and warm against the bulk of his chest.

Had her mother had been right all along? "There is someone special out there for you." Sky had once said. "It's just a matter of finding him, or him finding you." Storm knew at that moment who that special man was. She stood on tiptoe and kissed his cheek. Tomas smiled, he had known Storm was the only one for him since they were children. Now he realised she knew that too. At least something good had come out of Alexi dying.

The next few days flew past as preparations for the funeral got underway. Sky and Paris did most of the organizing, as Nicos seemed only able to mope around with a long sad face.

Meal times were the only chance Sky had to talk to her husband, although she found it difficult to say anything.

"They let me come home for the funeral but the doctor wants me back next week. He has a few more tests to do, but don't worry Jack I'll go with Paris." Her voice was cold and sharp. "Have you decided if you are going to tell me the truth yet?"

"I did my love. You go and ask Dimitri at the taverna. I stayed with him that night. I know I shouldn't have but I stopped for another drink on the way home and one thing led to another, you know how it is, and I ended up having too much to drive."

Nicos knew Dimitri would cover for him. They had been friends for years, and besides that a hefty hand out of Euro had already sealed the deal.

It had also cost him a great deal of money to pay off Olivia, who sensing a fortune had threatened to spill the beans.

"Ever heard of a taxi Jack." She almost spat the words out.

272

"Of course but I wasn't thinking straight was I." He was trying to use all of his sexual skills to win Sky round but his eyes looked huge and misty, his body defeated.

"Well trust me I will ask him and until I get an answer you can stop at your mother's."

This was going to be hard Nicos thought, but I suppose I deserve it.

The morning of the funeral saw frenzied action at the two villas. Sky's was being used for the wake afterwards and the twins along with Gabriel were working flat out in order to make sure enough food and drink would be available.

Athena's was once again full of people viewing Alexi. He had been embalmed and now looked like a waxwork figure as he lay in the silk lined coffin wearing his best suit. Storm and the others were in no hurry to see him like this, but for their grandmother's sake filed past swinging their rosaries and saying their prayers.

The air was thick with the smell of incense from the numerous candles around the room, and everyone was pleased to get back out into the fresh air, although no one actually admitted it.

Huge wreaths of flowers arrived, and not just from the islanders.

Alexi and his photographs were known the world over and many of his fans had sent not just flowers, but cards expressing their loss, thanking him for the wonderful images he had produced.

Nicos was proud as he read time and again how the strangers who had taken time to send these things described his father as a lovely man.

With the service over and his mother once again in the arms of her friends Nicos felt the strangeness of an anticlimax. Not that he had expected Alexi to rise out of his coffin or anything, but he felt as if he needed something to mark the day.

The wake, as at all good funerals, went on for hours and ended up with the smashing of plates and a long line of dancers whooping into the night air. The constant stream of wine had turned the sad day into one where many would be nursing hangovers for some time to come.

After the last of the guests had left Nicos paced the terrace. He glanced at the mess left on the buffet table and shrugged that could wait until tomorrow. Maria and the other staff had long since gone and Nicos felt he was in no state to tackle it himself. He felt tired and fraught; his muscles ached from holding his body upright for so long, yet his mind would not shut down.

If he could have fought with someone he would and boy it would have been so good to get rid of this pent up frustration that was eating into his mind.

Was it from the death of his father, or from the fact he had yet again cheated on Sky. Perhaps it came from knowing he had bribed both Dimitri and Olivia to keep quiet. But wherever it originated he needed to get rid of this tension, and quickly.

He saw Sky's bedroom light go off, no joy there then. Sadly he noticed the villa was now in total darkness, he had never felt so alone in his life.

Sitting on the terrace looking out over towards Eleni beach he heard a noise behind. It was Athena.

"Mama can you not sleep either?" He asked quietly.

"No son but it doesn't matter soon I shall sleep for ever." She replied flatly.

"Don't talk like that, not today of all days."

"But it is true son. I have no wish to live now. My body aches, my bones ache, everything hurts, and I am ready to go now I have buried your father. I have waited years to do that and I must say it gave me as much pleasure as I had hoped it would."

Nicos sat up straight at his mother's harsh words.

"You don't mean that mama surely." His face crumpled into a frown.

"Oh but I do. That man murdered the love of my life and I swore then I would out live him. I promised myself he would go first and I would see him in on his grave."

"Mama you are rambling, please stop." Nicos was worried, should he call the doctor, had Athena's mind gone?

"I have a story to tell you son and then see if I am rambling or not, and don't worry I'm not mad. I can see in your eyes you think I have gone insane."

274

Nicos was stunned, he felt sick. This was his mother speaking but he felt as if he was in the company of a complete stranger.

"Let me fetch Sky." He was getting desperate.

"No son this is for your ears and no one else's, but first fetch me some wine. I think there is some over there." She pointed to the messy buffet table.

Nicos searched amongst the empty glasses and plates returning to where his mother sat with a half empty bottle and two clean glasses, the only two he could find. He poured their drinks and waited to hear what his mother was going to say.

"Do you remember that night at Eleni beach when your father and Tomas spoke about Marco?" She began. Nicos nodded, how could he forget, that was the night that led to his affair with young Eleni.

"Well they went on about how Marco was coming back to find his long lost love and the son he never knew he had. In other words Andros and his precious mother. Rubbish!" She said sharply. "That was just an excuse. Really he was coming back for me." Athena smiled in a strange manner; her teeth glowed white in the dim lights of the terrace. "You see we were lovers. I met him at the exhibition in New York the first night we opened, and we just fell in love the moment we set eyes upon each other. I tried to stay faithful to your father but it was impossible, I knew this man was the one for me." Athena looked towards the dark sky as if in a trance.

"The exhibition lasted for two glorious weeks and we saw each other every spare moment we had.

Young Eleni thought her father was mad coming to see the photographs as much as he did, but she was also pleased that at last he was getting out of the house. You see after his wife was killed he had seemed content to stay at home most of the time, but now all of a sudden he was going out for meals, coming to the gallery, but unbeknown to her, he was seeing me.

He actually brought a couple of the photographs, just to make his visits look a little more authentic. We planned our future together laying naked in a huge bed."

"Mama please I don't want to hear." Nicos put his hands over his ears.

275

"Oh but you will hear." She hissed. "Now where was I? Oh yes lying there with Marco in my arms we dreamed of our life together. But first I had to come back for you and so I did. You are my son and I felt it was my duty, but looking back I should never have bothered.

A short while later Marco phoned to say he was coming to fetch us, but when he spoke to Tomas he told him he was coming to see Eleni and Andros. It was the only way he could come back to the island without raising any suspicions.

I was so excited, so happy I could hardly control myself and told Alexi I was leaving. I know I should have waited but I was so full of happiness I could not keep it to myself any longer." Athena paused. "As you know Marco never set foot on the island. His plane crashed into the sea between Athens and here. I know it was your father's doing, they said it was a mechanical failure, but I know better. It was your father's doing." She stared at Nicos with hatred in her eyes. "I know it was him but I could never prove it." She sat quietly for a moment. "I left Alexi shortly afterwards; I couldn't bare to even look at him, and went to stay with my parents in Athens. You were always out with your friends or some woman, and I suspect hardly missed me. I was gone most of that year."

"But why tell me all of this now?" Nicos was puzzled and more than a little disgusted with his mother. How could she have been unfaithful to Alexi?

"Because I have watched the video of the wedding again my son."

"What the hell has that got to do with anything?" He was feeling angry as well as confused now. Today of all days, his father only put into his grave hours ago and now this.

"I saw the way Olivia looked at you and that glint in your eye when you spotted her, that is why I am telling you. You have a lovely wife in Sky. The mother of your children and soon to give you another, or had you forgotten?" She looked towards him again. "Leave Olivia alone Nic. She is not for you do you hear me?"

"But what has that got to do with anything mama. Are you sure you are all right. I think I will phone the doctor after all." Nicos was totally puzzled.

"You will do no such thing, just sit and listen. During that year away I gave birth to a little girl. Mine and Marco's daughter, such a pretty little baby, so beautiful and so content." Tears fell down the old woman's face.

"But I had to leave her. My father insisted that I return to Alexi, and he was more than happy to welcome me back. He promised to forgive me if I returned, he also threatened that if I did not then I would never see you again. I had no choice, with my father on his side and the thought of never seeing you again, well what could I do but return.

I made the best of things, and yes I will admit I was happy enough with your father, but I could never ever forget what he had done.

The baby was brought up by the Minerva family on the island of Skopelos as one of their own, and being so close it enabled me to see her regularly; thankfully we managed to create a bond between us. She was never told I was her natural mother, but just a friend of the family. When she reached the age of 18 I went over and offered her a job in the Gallery. I taught her everything I know and now she is as competent as me at dealing with all of the things you and your father never had time for."

Athena sat back and sipped at her wine, watching as Nicos spilled the contents of his stomach on the nearest bush.

"I see I am too late." She hissed at him. "You have already taken your own sister to bed. Are you listening Nicos, your own sister." Her voice was loud in the still of the dark night. "You have not only betrayed Sky yet again, but now you have committed a horrible crime. I wish you were dead as well as your murdering father."

"Stop it mama for God's sake stop it." Nicos was crying with hurt and rage. "It is your fault, all this is your fault. If you hadn't had that disgusting affair."

"Disgusting eh? So it's OK for you to have affairs, but not me, is that right, and what about all the women Alexi had, that's different too is it?" She was mocking him now and he knew it. "But mine was no ordinary affair, Marco was the man of my dreams not just some piece I picked up for a bit of fun. You are just like the rest Nic. It's OK for you but not for me that's how you think isn't it?"

"That's not the point. How was I to know she was my sister?" He sounded like a spoiled child.

"Sister or not you shouldn't have gone to bed with her. You have been back on the island; back with your wife and family for such a short time and here you are at it again. Ever since you were a teenager you have been at it like a rampant bull." Athena was angry at his attitude. "But now you know and so it must stop. Never go near her again do you hear me, or I will personally see to it you end up in the same place as your father."

"But what explanation can I give. Sorry my mother says I can't see you again." His voice sounded like it did when he was a boy.

"You don't have to give one do you. She knows you are married so why worry about anything. Just stay away son."

"But I must see her one last time." Suddenly he was desperate. What she had done to him was unlike anything he had experienced before. They were consenting adults, he couldn't see the problem.

Nicos was trying to make it right in his own mind, and just like a child being told not to do something all of a sudden he felt as if he had to see her again and again and again. Sod this cranky old woman, for all he knew she was making the whole thing up just to spite him, that was it, she was making it all up.

"But you can't stop me, or have you forgotten she works for us, or are you going to sack her just because she is my lover."

"You can see her every day if you like, but only at the Gallery. If I ever hear that you have been near her again in any other way I will kill you." With that Athena rose and shuffled over to her home.

Nicos sat in silence twirling the wine glass between his fingers, his mind in chaos.

In the shadows Storm stood rooted to the spot, she had heard everything. Having left her room to enjoy one last cigarette in the cool night air she had heard every last word.

It wasn't the fact that Olivia had turned out to be Athena's daughter, but the fact that yet again he had strayed. What had her mother done to deserve this? She was kind, loving and so gentle, yet time and again he abused her trust.

A red mist descended.

• CHAPTER •
25

"What the hell is going on down there?" Matthew said pointing towards the harbor. He and Paris were enjoying breakfast together, before along with Sunni and Storm he was flying off to London. Another advertising photo shoot, and it was to be Storm's last. She had decided to finish her modeling career and settle down, much to everyone's surprise.

Storm and Tomas, who would have thought it, everyone except themselves.

"Haven't got a clue babe, but I'd better go and see." Paris's journalistic nose had begun to twitch; she lifted her large sunglasses to take a closer look. It must be something worth writing about; after all it wasn't everyday you saw so many blue flashing lights in Skiathos, and all in one place too.

"I'll come with you." Matthew said picking up his briefcase. "I've got to meet the others at the airport soon anyway."

"OK fancy a lift on the bike?" Paris asked laughing. Just lately she had taken to riding a Harley Davidson machine. Much nicer than being

279

cooped up in a stuffy old car, and quicker in the narrow streets of the town. Sky had put it down to middle age madness, but Paris had insisted it was nothing of the sort. "Practical." She called it.

"OK but just go steady." Matthew kissed her uplifted cheek. "Let's be off then."

Paris started the engine, which purred menacingly as they drove down the windy road towards town.

The police had sealed off nearly all of the roads and by the time she had managed to get anywhere near it was time for Matthew to be at the airport.

"Drop me off at the gates." He shouted over the noise of the engine. Paris nodded and headed off towards the tiny airport. They hugged and kissed as they parted.

"Back in a couple of days. Just be careful on that thing." Matthew waved as he walked away then began to trot as he saw Sunni and Storm standing at the terminal entrance.

"Any ideas what's going on?" He asked panting slightly.

"Not a clue." Storm replied and waved as Paris sped off. "But I bet she finds out pretty soon."

They all laughed, knowing Paris as they did and her knack of finding out everything. It was a gift that had made her into one of the best journalists England had produced. Not that she did much for the newspapers these days, now she concentrated more on her books, but Storm knew her aunt would have all the answers well before they were in the air.

"That's our flight being called." Sunni said tilting his head to one side in order to hear better. "Come on off we go. London is calling."

Once Storm had announced her retirement from the modeling scene they had been inundated with requests from all over the world. Everyone wanted to have her in this last photo shoot but the one she had chosen came from a little known firm in England. They made the most superb sunglasses; in fact the best Storm had ever seen, quirky and stylish. Not that the UK was known for its sunny weather and that seemed to intrigue her even more. Their letter along with a sample pair, which she hardly ever took off, appealed to Storm. She had had enough of the

280

large international firms and surprised everyone when she chose this small company.

As for the owners, they could hardly believe their luck. This would get them on the map no doubt about that, international fame was calling. With the beautiful Storm Mandros modeling their goods they couldn't fail.

The young secretary, whose idea it had been to write and ask, was immediately given a huge bonus. K & T were on the way up and everyone was filled with excitement.

Paris sat in the taverna listening to the conversations around her. Everyone was talking about the young girl whose body had been found by some fishermen early that morning. No one seemed to know really what had happened, as no one had witnessed anything, but it seemed she might have been murdered.

One raised voice took Paris a little by surprise.

"But I did see him I told you." The lone voice was followed by howls of laughter.

Paris concentrated on listening to what he had to say. Slowly she took her eyes from the blank notepad on her knee and tapping the pen on her teeth took a quick look around. She spotted a group of young English men sitting not far away. Some were already drinking Amstel, others large cups of coffee, all were tucking into a good breakfast of eggs and bacon.

"Look John who the hell is going to believe you. Just think about it for a minute mate. Last night we went on the Greek night yeah." The others nodded. "And what did we do? Get plastered." They all cheered and agreed it had been a brilliant night out. "So what do you do? Come down to the harbour in the early hours trying to walk the booze off and what do you see? Come on mate tell us again." They started to mock the one who was obviously John.

"Well as I was walking along I felt sick so I sat on the wall just over there." He pointed to a flat part in the rickety stonewall partly hidden by a large hibiscus bush. "I heard this noise as if someone was dragging something and watched this tall thin bloke chuck something big into the sea. Then he ran off. That's it really."

"What did he look like? Tell us again."

281

Paris's ears only heard the men's voices now. The noise from the busy harbor no longer registering in her mind.

"A panther. He looked like a panther. All dressed in black, he even had a balaclava on, but it was his eyes, they were huge and so glaring, almost like fire. Just like a big cats and he ran just like a panther I'm telling you."

John knew he looked foolish, but he also knew what he had seen. The others once again burst out laughing.

"Look mate who the hell is going to believe you and anyway how do you know it was a man? Just because he was tall and thin doesn't mean it was a man, could have been a slim woman, thought about that then? Plus the fact you were well over the limit, know what I mean, two E's in the old body and a line of the white stuff. If I were you I'd stay quiet. Start telling the cops that story and before you know it they'll have you locked up or something. You've heard tales about what these Greek jails are like. What's the saying, the murderer is always the last person to see the victim alive. Well think about it and stay quiet." The others all nodded again. "We go home tomorrow so don't bother, I wouldn't. Anyone agree." They all cheered.

Paris doodled away at nothing absorbed in her own thoughts; inwardly she was digesting what the young man had said.

Thank goodness his friends had persuaded him to keep quiet.

Deep in thought she jumped slightly as two policemen came to sit at the next table. They nodded to her before sitting down and Paris noticed the group of young men finished their drinks and leave quickly. The policemen laughed.

"I bet they think we are after them for something." One said to the other. "At least it is good to see they are still wary of our authority not like in England." They both laughed again.

Paris sadly knew this was true. Young men like that had no respect for the police back home, but here where guns were carried as part of the uniform their attitude changed considerably. Perhaps she should write an article on it one day.

She beckoned for another coffee and sat waiting for the policemen to start talking again. She knew they would, after all how often did a murder happen on this lovely quiet island. She didn't have to wait long.

"Sounds to me as if it was one of her clients." The first one said. "They recon she had that much sex stuff in that flat there was enough to start a shop." They both giggled. "Fancy old Nicos not knowing what was going on. I bet he feels as sick as a parrot, you know what he is like for getting his leg over, well used to be. There it was going on right under his own roof." This time they laughed loudly. "She had pots of money too and God knows how much coke stashed away. Must have been at it for ages."

"Must have been good at it too." The other one said sipping at his thick black coffee. "But still, she didn't deserve to be thrown into the water no matter what she was up to."

"Perhaps it was Nicos, maybe he found out what she was doing and did her in?"

"Not a chance. He hasn't been right in the head since his mother died. Remember it was the night of old Alexi's funeral. Strange how she went though, drowned in the bath they recon. Storm found Nicos struggling to get her out but it was too late. Now tell me who has a bath at that time of night. Sounds like she went a bit loopy after the old man died." He paused to think. "Must have been such a shock it's affected his mind. I've seen him about though; he still goes to the Gallery every day but just to work in the shop, he looks all thin and haggard, he wouldn't have the energy for that young piece. No it wasn't him, couldn't have been."

So Nicos was not a suspect Paris thought to herself and settled down to listen again.

"No it was definitely one of her clients. Just think about it. The bed looks like a tip, she must have been giving someone a right seeing to. I bet it was a bloke who caught her stealing his wallet or something. Just flipped, mind you I would too if some scummy tart tried to knick my money. They say she has been strangled with one of her own chains so perhaps it was a sex game gone wrong. It happens you know. Mind you what a way to go." He had an excited ring to his voice.

"It won't be news for long I suppose. Whoever did it will be miles away by now, first plane out of here if he's got any sense. Things will soon settle down just wait and see."

Their conversation now focused on the skimpily clad holidaymakers who had come to look at the grisly scene.

It was a good job the young girls who passed by could not understand what the two men were saying, or their own wives hear them for that matter, it was very crude.

Paris sighed and looked down at her scribbling pad.

Back at her stared the face of a cat with large beautifully shaped eyes, remarkably like her own, or was it Storm's that glared at her; maybe it was Gabriel's?

Underneath were the words. Nicos, Athena, BATH?

The local newspaper had a field day. They trashed any semblance of respectability Olivia had. She was made out to be this perverted drug crazed hooker who enjoyed a string of men, locals and tourists, in fact whoever she could get her claws into.

The money and drugs haul that had been found in the flat was greatly exaggerated, but still in amounts to be believable, and where they got photographs of men going in the back door from was a mystery to all who saw them.

A few days after the publication Nicos's partly decomposed body was found amongst the bushes high above Eleni beach.

A single gunshot wound to the head.

No gun was found, his camera was also missing.

• CHAPTER •
26

Sky concentrated on her new baby.

The news of Nicos's death had sent her into a very early labour and being born prematurely the child needed all the love and attention Sky could provide.

She got it, not only from her mother, but also from all of those around her.

She was the apple of everyone's eye, especially Storm's. In fact Sky almost named her apple, but after much thought decided upon Lilly. It reminded her of that time in hospital when she felt so low, and Emily's flowers had given her the will to recover.

She now hoped this child would help her recover from the death of Nicos. It was a very heavy burden for the little child to carry.

Lilly, it suited the tiny girl down to the ground. Pale golden hair, pretty amber eyes and skin so fair it was almost white, Lilly was the image of her mother, especially when she wore her large brimmed straw sunhat.

285

Not only did Sky now have Lilly to think about, but the pending double wedding of Storm and Gina to the twins. The service was to incorporate the postponed blessing of Sunni and Emily; it was a day to look forward to.

Life was continuing, things were happening, the sun still shone, and the birds still sang.

All of these things were helping her mind to heal, but Sky wondered if her heart ever would.

ABOUT THE AUTHOR

Born in Stamford, Elizabeth now lives with husband Peter in the pretty market town of Uttoxeter.

They both enjoy travelling and love to visit mainland Greece or one of the many beautiful surrounding islands.

Having recently retired she is now able to spend more of her time writing and enjoying a number of various hobbies.

Set on the lovely islands of Skiathos and Kalymnos "Sky" is Elizabeth's second novel and follows the fortunes of certain characters readers first met in the popular "Eleni Beach".

Printed in the United Kingdom
by Lightning Source UK Ltd.
120710UK00001B/30